EYES OF TITAN

A FANTASY ADVENTURE

PAUL MOUCHET

PAUL MOUCHET PUBLISHING

CONTENTS

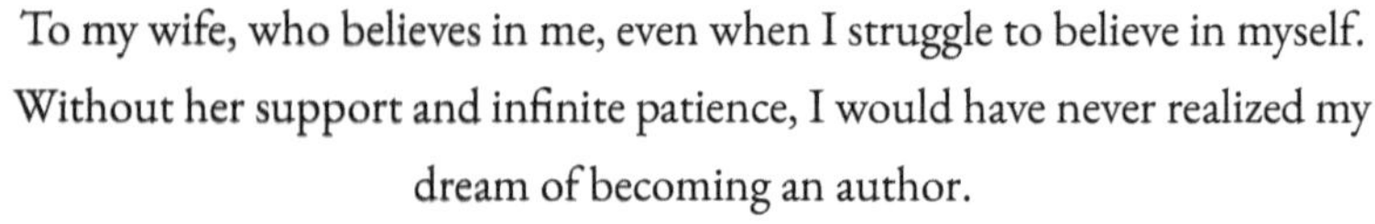

To my wife, who believes in me, even when I struggle to believe in myself.
Without her support and infinite patience, I would have never realized my
dream of becoming an author.
And, to my big sister Louise, thank you for helping me bring my stories to life.

Chapter One

To Silverhawk

It was late afternoon when the group set out from Aarall to the city of Silverhawk. The sky was clear and bright, and the road heading north had few travelers on it. Mount Toka, the tallest peak in the kingdom of Arnnor, was well behind them. Far to the east, another mountain range loomed, standing in stark contrast to the vast expanse of grassland and low rolling hills through which they were traveling.

When Kit had last visited Silverhawk, she had warned Nicks, and the other Auctioneers at the Crimson Ale, that she would return with the new moon, and that she expected a new batch of well-treated slaves and her share of the gold. Kit had never thought she'd end up in control of a slaver operation, but life was full of twists. She had, for a moment, considered that this was yet another challenge that Titan had placed before her, to strengthen her, to help her on the path to freeing her god. If it was, then she was going to make sure that she passed the test by solidifying her hold on the operation.

After an hour of hard running, Lin's horse was beginning to flag. Indie's long black hair was snapping behind him as he brought his black stallion up close to Angel, Kit's enchanted roan. He had a look of concern on his face. He stole a quick look over his shoulder, watching the woman riding her exhausted mare.

"We're already behind schedule," Indie said, trying to keep his voice low. "We're going to have trouble getting to Silverhawk before the new moon if Lin can't keep up."

"We need to have her with us," Kit said, shaking her head. "But you're right. We only have three days to get to the city, and at this rate, we're not going to make it on time."

Lump, the golden retriever wolfdog, and Runt, the oversized dire wolf puppy, both barked excitedly as they raced on ahead. The boys, as they were affectionately referred to, were always up for a romp through the countryside.

"You know I can hear you, right?" Lin called from her position far to the rear. "If we can make a detour, I can see about putting a speed charm on my horse." Kit spoke to her mare, Angel, through their bond, asking her to slow enough for Lin to catch up. As much as the Fate Tyr got on her nerves, Kit would need to thank him for the gift of being able to communicate with her horse.

"She'll never be as fast as your horses," Lin continued, "but if we can get some pony hair, I can put a couple of enchantments on her. It should be enough for us to get to the city on time."

"Pony hair?" Kit asked, turning in her saddle to face the woman. "We need to find some wild ponies, then?" Lin nodded.

Indie scrubbed the back of his neck as he considered Lin's suggestion. "Ponies are everywhere around here. We'll likely cross a herd on our way, without even taking a detour."

"Frost thistle would be better," Lin suggested, hoping that Indie might know how to find it. The young Nomad was an excellent tracker, and he knew the land well. "But a pegasus feather would be best."

"Frost thistle is pretty rare, and we won't find it along the road," Indie said. "There is only one known location of pegasi in Aarall, and that would take us well off course. Even if we got there, finding a loose feather is highly unlikely."

"Where are the pegasi?" Kit asked, her mind racing to try to figure out a way to get to Silverhawk before the night of the new moon. "Runt and I could search while you three continue to the city. He's got an amazing nose and can likely find anything I ask him to."

Indie pointed to a snow-topped mountain range far off to the east. "They live near the top of that mountain. They come down to the valley to feed. But

Runt won't be able to help you. He won't have any idea what scent to search for. Besides, he would only slow Angel down."

Kit planted her forehead into her hands, swearing under her breath. She was trying to find a solution to the problem, one that didn't involve leaving Lin behind, but everyone seemed to have a reason why her suggestions wouldn't work. She pulled out her map, trying to gage the distance to the mountains.

"It looks like it will take me four or five hours to get there. If you four continue on towards Silverhawk, I'll meet up with you in the morning. I just need to know where to find you."

"You can't go on your own." Indie's face was etched with worry. "Pegasi aren't the only things that live in those mountains. There are also fire drakes, and they hunt pegasi. I'm guessing they'd be willing to munch down a pretty little girl and her horse."

"She won't be alone," Fury intoned, "and I might enjoy some time with my cousins." The battle hammer that hung at Kit's back was infused with a part of the soul of the sky dragon: Fury. At some point in his past, this Dragon Lord's essence had been pulled from his body and separated into five parts. Kit had received one of those parts in the form of a dragon-bone cane; yet another gift from the Fate named Tyr. When Fury merged the cane with her battle hammer, he created a fully sentient and overly opinionated weapon.

"And I'd love a chance to really run," Angel said to Kit through their bond. *"I haven't found out how fast I can actually go yet. I was holding back when we raced around Lake Titan with Char and the boys."*

"It's settled then," Kit declared, leaving no room for objection. "Just show me where to meet you after I get the feathers." Indie groaned at Kit's pronouncement, but Lin appeared to be ecstatic. Apparently, the idea of getting her hands on that particular reagent was more than she would have ever dreamed possible.

Indie surveyed the map, gaging how far he thought Lin could travel and how long it would take Kit to meet up with them. "Here," he said, marking the place on Kit's map.

"If you get there before me, leave the boys there and you two continue on." Kit remained totally focused on the map as she formulated her plan. "If

I'm delayed, I'll meet the boys, and they can track you. We'll have no trouble catching up. If I get there first, I'll wait for you. And one more thing; where might I find frost thistle, just in case?"

"It grows at the base of the mountain," Lump offered, right after switching into human form. His ability to switch at will between wolfdog and human was yet another gift from Tyr. Kit had never really considered how much the Fate had done for her – and yet she didn't trust him one bit. Nope, not in the slightest. When Lump noticed the odd look Kit was giving him, he beamed brightly at her, his big brown eyes sparkling all the while.

"The lands around the base of the mountain, particularly in the foothills, are home to a variety of flora, including frost thistle," Lump continued. The entire group stared at the golden, shaggy-haired young man. It was hard to tell if they were astonished at his knowledge, or if they simply couldn't explain how a golden retriever might know that. "*Flora and Fauna of Orth* was one of the books I read in the library," he said with a smile and a small shrug. "The abundance of frost thistle and larkspur is why the pegasi are there, and the pegasi are why the fire drakes are there. There is also a small tribe of Hill Giants in the foothills. They're there because of the fire drakes."

Indie whistled, "You're one smart puppy!" His comment made Lump smile from ear to ear. It was at that very moment that Kit saw his unmistakable resemblance to his natural wolfdog form.

"What are we waiting for, Kit?" Angel asked, pawing at the ground. *"I'm dying to run! We've got about three hours of daylight left. I can probably get us there before sundown."* Kit agreed and she let Angel know through their bond.

"I expect we've got about three hours before sundown," Kit said, parroting Angel's remarks. "I can probably get there before dark. If it goes smoothly, I expect I'll beat you all to the rendezvous point." Before anybody had a chance to object, Kit wheeled her horse around and headed off to the mountains at a slow gallop.

"Just let me know when I can run full out," Angel said eagerly. Even through the bond, Kit could feel her excitement. She smiled, patting her horse on the neck.

"Right now, I'm just the rider. You know where we're going and you're the best judge of how fast you can run. I'm ready when you are." No sooner did the words leave Kit's mouth, than the small roan burst forward like a bolt leaving a crossbow. The power of her takeoff forced Kit to grab hold of her saddle before falling over backwards.

Angel slowly increased her speed, trying to find her comfortable limit. The power of her hooves hitting the ground sent sparks flying. As her speed increased further, Kit's hair was streaming behind her, snapping about like a flag in a hurricane; the wind in her face forced Kit to squint. The sparks from Angel's hooves were quickly becoming more pronounced; brighter and brighter until her hooves were ablaze.

"Your hooves are flaming!" Kit screamed. In their wake, tiny fires were beginning to spread, burning up the leaves and grasses. Kit called to her horse again, urging her to slow down.

Angel immediately broke from her gallop into an easy canter. Her chest was heaving badly, making wheezing noises with each breath. *That was incredible!* she cried out through the bond. *I could have gone faster; I just know it!*

Kit's pulse was beating just as fast as her horse's. *If you'd run any harder, your heart would have exploded! Look at the trail of fires you left behind. You're amazing!* She ran her hand down Angel's neck, patting it as she did. "And you're barely even sweating."

I think the wind was drying me off, Angel replied. *Can I run some more? I'll keep a better pace, I promise.*

"Like I said," Kit laughed, *"I'm only here for the ride. You do you."* And with that, Angel broke into a gallop, racing along until her hooves were once again sparking as they struck the ground. At some point, Angel found a comfortable rhythm. The horse settled in, her strides becoming easy and regular. Kit looked across the verdant fields to their destination. The mountain range that had once appeared to be so far away was starting to come into focus.

As they approached the outskirts of the mountain foothills, Kit asked Angel to slow down so that she could take time to inspect their surroundings. "Apparently, there is important flora for us to look for, feathers to find, and enemies to be wary of."

"I can't help much with finding the flora or feathers, but my eyes are good, and my hearing is excellent. You look for your prizes and I'll watch for enemies." Angel's words made Kit smile, happy to hear that her horse wasn't just a mount to get her around, but an actual partner, willing to help her achieve her goals.

Chapter Two

Frost Thistle

"If you'd like," Fury offered, "I can fly above, scouting for both flora and fauna."

"Do you know what we're looking for?" Kit asked. Apparently, the question was insulting, or something, because Fury refused to answer. "What? My question offends you?" The hammer continued to ignore her. "Oh, great and wondrous Fury, please accept my apologies for daring to question your infinite competence!"

"Your obsequious response is not required," Fury intoned, "but I appreciate it. I may be but a shadow of my true self, but I am still magnificent beyond reckoning." And with that, Fury floated up into the air to improve his vantage point.

Kit watched for a few minutes as Fury floated about, heading upcountry into the foothills of the mountains. *"C'mon Angel, let's keep looking for ourselves. Watching him isn't helping us find any flora or pegasi."* With no further instructions, Angel started trotting up a bit higher into the foothills, making sure to maintain an escape route if they were set upon by Hill Giants or any others who might wish to harm them – or eat them.

Kit stared up into the mountain's rocky crags high above. The foothills which rose up as a gentle slope were generally smooth and grassy, except for large boulders which appeared to have been strewn randomly about. A chill air rolled down from the snow-capped height, carrying with it the fresh smell of a winter storm. The sensation took her back to her time on Mount Uha, where Kit had taken her Rite of Abandonment.

The sun was starting to set behind the mountain range, casting long shadows across the ground. Kit urged Angel to pick up her pace, hoping that she would spot something, anything, before the light became too dim to see by. Their path took them higher up into the foothills. With the setting sun and the higher altitude, the temperature was dropping at a noticeable rate.

"Angel, do you see where the ground glitters up ahead?" Kit asked as she strained to see.

"It's very pretty," Angel replied, adjusting her direction towards the phenomenon. *"Any idea what it is?"*

"I'm hoping it's frost thistle," Kit sighed. *"I've never seen it before, but we studied it at the Temple. I should be able to recognize it when we're up close. One of its properties, which is how it got its name, is that it glistens in the sun, like frost on a leaf."* As they approached, Kit became more and more certain that they had found a large patch of the rare plant. When they got near, Kit slipped down from her saddle to give the flora a closer inspection.

"Light green in color, flourish of silver at the top, small sharp spines along the stem and leaves," Kit recited the description of the plant she'd learned while studying botany at the Temple. That was Brother Rime's class. She chuckled lightly, hoping that he was rotting in the City Watch dungeons at this point. She shook her head, bringing herself back to the here and now.

"It seems to fit all the criteria," Kit said, smiling up at Angel, practically dancing with excitement. "There's enough here to make dozens of speed enchantments." As she pulled out her dagger to uproot the first plant, Angel interrupted her.

"We're not alone," Angel whispered through their bond. As Kit spun around, looking for whoever may be nearby, she reached for her battle hammer, only to find that her sheath was empty. After cursing for a few moments, she lowered herself into a crouch, drawing her dagger, holding it at the ready.

"I don't see anything," Kit whispered. "Where's the threat?"

"Don't look, listen. I didn't say there was a threat; I said we're not alone." Even though Angel was speaking to Kit through their bond, her thoughts continued to come through as a whisper.

"Who's there?" Kit hissed. "Show yourself." Trying to look as intimidating as possible, she held her dagger out before herself, letting it sway slowly from left to right. "We're only here to harvest some plants, and then we'll be on our way."

"You bear the mark of Spritekind," said a deep, masculine voice, perhaps a dozen paces from where Kit stood. Her head snapped around, but there was no one there. "How did you come by that mark?"

"I helped a friend," she replied, while continuing to scan the area, looking for whoever was talking to her. "In return for my kindness, he bestowed this gift upon me."

"What kindness did you perform?" asked the voice, now coming from behind her.

"I don't like having conversations with someone I can't see," Kit said as she spun about, attempting to follow the source of the voice. "I rescued some people from slavers in Silverhawk. His wife was among the prisoners."

"Whoever it is you're talking with is standing right beside me. He smells wonderful!" Angel sounded practically giddy in Kit's head. *"He smells of horse, but not horse. Do you think he's a...?"*

"I don't know much about your kind," Kit said in Angel's direction, "but I'm guessing you possess strong magic. Invisibility spells are not easy to perform." Kit bowed solemnly. "If you would be so kind as to show yourself, it would make this conversation more enjoyable."

With a hint of laughter, the voice replied. "I am not invisible because I fear you, young girl. The drakes are in the air and the Hill Giants have left their caves. I am here to eat, not to be eaten." There was a momentary pause. "The plants you wish to harvest are my food. They are of little use to humans, so why do you want them?"

Sensing that the mystery man was of no threat, Kit put her dagger away. "It's a long story, one that I don't have time to share, but I need the plants for speed enchantments; for my friend's horse."

"Is your friend a Sprite?" asked the voice, now closer to Kit than it had been previously. His warm, moist breath puffed across her face. It smelled like honey and clover.

Kit shook her head, as she reached out with her palm towards the voice. "No, she is a Nomad, like me. We need to get to Silverhawk before the new moon, and her horse is not as fast as Angel here. Without the enchantments, we'll miss our opportunity to free more slaves." Her hand touched warm, silky-soft skin, covered in what felt like long, delicate hairs. "Are you a pegasus?"

"You are not as you seem," said the voice, as he pulled away from Kit's touch. "But, if my kin trust you, then so do I. I am a pegasus, one of many that inhabit this area."

"You're kin to the Sprites?" Kit couldn't hide the surprise in her voice, even if she tried.

"Not like you might think," the pegasus responded. "We are born of the same magic, allowing us to share a bond that runs deeply through our kind. So, in a sense, we are related."

A boulder half the size of Kit crashed on the ground only a few paces from where she was standing. A series of harsh, guttural screams followed. To any-body else it would have sounded like a war-cry of some kind, but thanks to the book of languages Kit read in the library, she understood what the creature was saying. "Urig's breakfast!"

Kit spun around, turning in the direction of the voice. A heavily muscled, somewhat misshapen creature, standing nearly ten feet tall, was barrelling down the side of the hill. Considering his size, the creature moved extremely well, practically dancing between trees, large rocks, and fallen debris.

"Hill Giant!" the pegasus screamed as he took flight. A rush of wind from his mighty wings raised a cloud of dust and blew Kit's hair about, making it difficult to see. She again reached for her battle hammer, realizing, once again, her sheath was empty. Her jaw dropped open when she saw Angel racing up the hill towards the giant.

"Angel, no!" she screeched, terrified the marauding creature would crush her friend. In seconds, Angel was galloping so fast that she looked like a blur racing towards their attacker. By the time Angel reached the Hill Giant, Kit could no longer see her, save for the trail of sparks and fires she had left in her wake. The giant swiped wildly at the ground, trying to catch the horse with his massive hands.

"I'm here and I've brought help!" cried Fury, as the hammer sailed through the air toward Kit, alight in blue flame. Just before Kit was able to grasp the hammer, three fire drakes began flaming at the giant, swooping and diving in a coordinated attack. "Finish him!" Fury roared while he continued to light up the area with his own blue flames. As Kit grabbed the haft of the hammer, those same blue flames enveloped her hand, running up her arm, filling Kit with unexpected power.

I'm coming! Angel cried out in Kit's mind. *We'll take him while he's distracted.* When the horse moved in beside her, Kit leapt to her back and grabbed a tight hold on the saddle. As Angel lurched forward, Kit dug her heels into the horse's sides, trying desperately not to fall. The horse's movements were powerful and erratic as she closed the distance on the giant. In moments, Kit's body fell into sync with her horse, and they began moving as a single unit. Just as Kit closed into striking range, the drakes ceased their flame attacks, preventing them from accidentally setting the young priest ablaze.

While the giant swatted at the drakes who were still buzzing about his head, Kit took a sideways arcing swing, bringing her hammer down on the giant's knee. There was an immediate flash of light and blue flame, along with a horrible crunching noise as the bones in the giant's leg snapped like kindling. He bellowed in agony, clutching his leg and tumbling down the side of the hill. Before he had a chance to come to a halt, the fire drakes were already falling on him, flaming him, tearing at him with their terrible claws and teeth.

"My kin are safe because of you," Fury declared, his voice victorious. "Gather what you need and let's get going."

"But I found no feathers, only frost thistle." Kit's breathing was still erratic as she tried to calm herself.

"Let's get them and get going." Fury sounded more agitated than normal. "If we stay up here in the foothills, our next encounter might not go so well.

The drakes only helped because you were fighting their enemy. The impudent children wouldn't listen to me when I asked for their help in locating some feathers."

Sensing Kit's agreement with Fury's plan, Angel took her back to where they had found the frost thistle. Not wasting any time, Kit dismounted and promptly dug up four plants, carefully wrapping them in a cloth before stowing them in her saddlebags. While climbing into her saddle, something skittered across the ground, catching Kit's eye. She quickly raced towards the movement and squealed with joy at the sight of a beautiful pearl-white feather. "He must have dropped this when he flew away."

"I never left," declared the pegasus, sounding like he was directly behind her. "I wanted to see how you'd handle the situation, and I haven't eaten yet." Kit again felt his warm breath on her face. "You only took what you needed, and no more. It's a small act, but it was not lost on me. There is a second feather, a few paces from the thistle patch. May it hasten you to your destination."

"Thank you," Kit said as she picked up the second feather from the ground. She took the two feathers and carefully wrapped them in another cloth. "I am happy that we met. I hope that someday I'll get to see you." There was no response to Kit's last comment, so she headed back to Angel. She quickly added the feathers to the plants stowed in her saddlebags and mounted up. "Do you think you can run in the dark?" she asked as Angel began her descent down the hillside.

"Running doesn't tire me, at least not like it used to. With your hammer's light, I should be able to maintain a steady speed with little risk of tripping. I will rest when we make camp with our friends."

Unable to hide her wide smile, Kit called on Fury to light the way. In a moment, the hammer's light burst forth, illuminating everything within twenty paces. "Let's ride!" Kit exclaimed, gripping her saddle in preparation for Angel's burst of speed.

Chapter Three

WOLF SOLDIERS

Danny, with his cousin Breayn at his side, followed Ulip and Ryn as they made their way through the heavy underbrush. Ulip, the uncharacteristically aggressive Gigas, was at the lead, choosing their path as they sought their quarry. While the majority of the forests in northern Berrathia were pine trees, they were currently working their way through a forest of oak and yew. The leaves had come out early this season, and the canopy provided a good deal of shade from the mid-morning sun. The smell of earth and mushrooms was pleasant enough, but it was a poor substitute for the heady scent of pine. The songs of sparrows and jays helped to cover any noise they were making as they moved wordlessly through the trees.

They were hunting the Split Crows, Berrat slavers who had a chokehold on northern Berrathia. After the Crow had taken control of Taseko, they quickly became the most ruthless, savage group of the seven houses in the Auctioneers. Shortly after they took ownership of the city, House Nobilis declared its own city, Ravenlord, as the new capital of Berrathia. With the unanimous support of the other five houses, House Nobilis stripped the title of Capital City away from the Split Crows.

The group had decided the best way to fight the Crow was to have House Nobilis fight the battle for them. Everyone knew there was bad blood between the two houses, so it seemed like starting a war between them would be easy enough. If two of the houses went to war, it was likely the other houses would join in. If it was done properly, the slavers would tear themselves apart.

"For a big man, he sure does move silently," Danny said, drawing a look of ire from Breayn.

"Quiet," she hissed. "We're nearing the Split Crows camp."

They were about three hours north of their own camp. Ryn, Breayn's mate, had insisted they hunt as far away from home as they could. He wanted to make sure their actions didn't bring the Crow down on their base. What had started off as a quasi-military group had turned into a village of families trying to escape from the slavers. The sound of clashing steel brought the group to an immediate halt.

"I'll take a look," Ryn said, just before his Berrat form melted away, replaced by a peregrine falcon. This was just one of several animals Ryn had merged with. Danny had also seen him take on the forms of a great white bear and a great hawk. With a couple of quick beats of his wings, the bird cleared the trees and took off to where the skirmish was taking place.

"How many animals has he bound with?" Danny asked, his voice barely a whisper. Breayn's head snapped around to him, giving him a death glare. "What? They're busy fighting. They won't hear me whispering."

"Who's to say there aren't more around? Shut it," Breayn growled at him. Danny's face flushed somewhat as his red-headed cousin berated him yet again. Her gray eyes looked like a storm ready to break. He was just about to retort when two fair-skinned men dressed in wolf hides came crashing through the brush, heading towards the battle. A look of *I told you so* immediately crossed Breayn's face.

Moments later, Ryn returned, switching back to his Berrat form when he was still a few feet in the air. He landed gracefully, a profound look of satisfaction on his face.

"What's up ahead?" Breayn asked him, keeping her voice to a hoarse whisper.

"The morons are doing us a favor," he grinned. "It's a group of humans fighting a group of Crows. Fewer humans and fewer Crows. Looks like a win - win for us."

"Why do you want the humans to die?" Danny asked, his voice much louder than necessary. "Shouldn't we be helping them? We need the Crow uniforms and they're helping us kill them."

"The only good human is a dead human, as far as I'm concerned," Ryn replied, crossing his arms. "We can finish off whoever wins."

"You're the moron," Danny said, rushing past Ulip. "If they're fighting Crows, then they're our allies. Simple as that." He had his bow nocked before he slipped into the trees, using large, heavily leafed bushes for cover. Ulip looked back over his shoulder and shrugged.

"Hunting is hunting. Let's finish off the Crows and then we can decide what to do with the humans. I'm not leaving without killing at least one Crow."

Breayn cocked an eyebrow at her mate, waiting for him to follow the others. He shook his head slowly. The woman growled and took off after Ulip. Shortly after she had disappeared into the brush, Ryn drew his own bow and followed.

***

There were at least ten Crows fighting against a handful of humans, who were all dressed in wolf skins. One of the men was wearing a white wolf hide, the great beast's head fashioned into a helm. The man in white was wielding a pair of long, thin-bladed swords. He was defending against five Crow who were all attacking with spear and shield. There had likely been eight at one point, based on the three dead Crow near his feet. The man danced between his enemies, parrying their attacks while he waited for an opening. The other four humans, all dressed in gray wolf pelts, were wielding similar looking weapons, but they didn't have the same grace as the man in white.

When it looked like one of the humans was about to be overrun by a pair of Berrat, Danny drew back his bow and fired. Despite there being a good number of trees, his arrow found its mark, skewering a Crow just below his ear. The Berrat, dressed in a black-feathered cape, froze for a moment before collapsing face first to the ground. The second Crow lost concentration for a moment when his ally fell. The human darted in, sliding his narrow blade into the Berrat's chest. He took a quick look over his shoulder to see from where the shot had come, but Danny had already moved behind cover as he nocked another arrow.

Mayhem ensued as Ulip came crashing out through the trees, coming to the aid of the man in white. While the Crow tried to split their attention between the human and the rampaging Gigas, Danny loosed another arrow, dropping yet another Crow.

Breayn blew past Danny so quickly that he might have missed her. She cut the legs out from beneath the first Crow she passed before throwing herself into the group, who was now engaged with Ulip. The humans continued to fight the Crow, but the unexpected arrival of allies had surprised them. Their fighting became less coordinated, seemingly confused as to who was a friend and who was foe. When Danny's arrow dropped another Crow, two of the black-feathered Berrat decided to turn tail. One yelped out in terror as a great white bear broke through the trees and removed his head with the swipe of a paw. The second ran headlong into the trees, directly toward Danny. Using his bow like a quarterstaff, he struck the fleeing Berrat across the throat. The Crow's feet lifted out from underneath him, sending him crashing down to the ground on his back. Danny plunged his dagger into the Crow's throat, instantly sending him to the Great Cycle.

By the time Danny raised his head, the Crows were all dead, but the fight was not over. Two of the wolf-clad humans were circling Ryn in his white bear form, while the other three were teaming up against Breayn and Ulip. "We're on the same side," Danny screamed, stepping out from his place of hiding. He had an arrow knocked and drawn.

The great white bear bellowed out a challenge, peeling his lips back from his oversized fangs. He huffed several times, lifting his front feet from the ground and crashing them down. Slobber flew from his maw as he flung his head from side to side. Sensing the great bear was about to attack, Danny changed his aim, pointing his arrow at the bear's head.

"Ryn, stop," Danny screamed, pulling his bow string a bit further back. The great bear stood on his hind legs, making himself even taller than Ulip. He bellowed out another roar, this time at the heavens above.

"You aim that weapon at me again," Ryn said as he switched back into Berrat form, "and I will end you." Danny lowered the tip of his arrow, but kept the bow drawn. He wondered if he would have actually shot his cousin's mate had he attacked the humans.

"Thank you," the man dressed in white said, breaking the tension between Danny and Ryn. "We didn't think there was anyone left willing to fight the Split Crows."

"What are you doing in Berrathia?" Ryn asked, growling out like he was still in bear form. "The only humans in Berrathia are slavers. Which house are you from?" Two of the humans dressed in gray wolf pelts readied their weapons, preparing to strike.

"Lower your weapons," the man in white ground out. "We don't fight our allies."

"Just because we have a common enemy does not mean we are allies," Ryn growled. His hands were mid change, his fingers were long, wicked claws.

"Ryn!" Breayn screamed out. "Enough!" The woman's eyes looked like a winter storm, ready to unleash its fury upon the world. While the mated Berrat stared each other down, Ulip scowled at his enormous blade.

"I only got to kill one," the Gigas said, sounding heart broken. He swung his blade sharply, sending what little blood that still covered it onto the moss-covered ground.

"But the one you killed was the leader, and you sliced his head in two," the man in white said. "An impressive kill if I've ever seen one." The man's comment seemed to have appeased Ulip. His frown lessened somewhat as he rolled his massive shoulders.

"I am Ulip of the Fire Drake Clan."

"I am Aput. I have no clan. I have no family save for these four men." Pointing to each of them in turn, Aput introduced his group. "This is Pana, our healer. This is Pilip and his brother Ahanu. And this is Calian, my... brother." At the introduction, Calian turned away and began inspecting the dead Crow.

"How old is Calian?" Danny asked. "He doesn't even look old enough to grow a beard."

Aput glared at him. "His age is not of your concern. He is a fine warrior, and his skills will probably surpass my own before the season ends."

"You never answered Ryn's question," Breayn said. The look of a storm brewing behind her eyes hadn't passed. "What are you doing in Berrathia?"

"This is where we live," Aput offered. The man tossed his wolf-head helm back, revealing an uncharacteristically bald head. "We were born in Berrathia, but we have never been welcomed here. My people moved here from Lycos, hoping to learn more of the Berrat and their shapeshifting ways."

"Lycos?" Ulip said. The kingdom of Lycos was just south of Berrathia. "You're werewolves then?" Aput ignored the question.

"Our village was attacked by the Auctioneers when I was a boy. The Berrat who lived in our community were taken as slaves and the Lycosians were killed outright. My mother spirited us away during the attack. To the best of my knowledge, we were the only humans to survive."

"Where is your mother now?" Breayn asked. The storm in her eyes had receded, returning them to their normal smoky gray color.

"She passed to the Great Cycle a few summers later, when I was only twelve. A Split Crows hunting band was nearly upon us. She led them away so that we might escape." Aput spoke of his mother with pride and honor. Whatever sadness he felt at her loss had long since been burned away by the hatred he was now carrying for the slavers.

"If you survived in the wilds as children," Ulip said, inclining his head slightly, "then you were well raised. Human children are weak and frail, but you survived anyway." What sounded like a thinly veiled insult was, in fact, a huge compliment, something Ulip didn't offer very often.

"Aput is a strong leader," Ahanu said. "He taught us his mother's ways." Aput glared at him, shaking his head very slowly. Ulip caught the interaction, making him smile lightly. The look on the giant's face could have easily been mistaken for a snarl.

"Does that include wearing wolf hides?" Danny asked. He was watching Aput's younger brother closely. He was staying clear of the group, busying himself with the bodies of the Crows. He seemed to be searching for something.

"They allow us to get dangerously close to Crow camps," Aput stated. "If the Crow happen to see us, they believe us to be wolves and they leave us alone."

"The Crow won't attack wolves?" Ryn sounded skeptical.

"They believe all wolves are under the command of the great wolf, Shade," Calian said, finally looking up from the corpse he was inspecting. Danny cocked an eyebrow. Calian couldn't have seen more than twelve or thirteen summers. His skin was smooth, and his eyes were big and brown, like the eyes of a young deer. When the boy noticed Danny staring at him, he quickly busied himself with the dead body in front of him.

"We have heard them speak of the dire wolf, Shade," Aput continued, moving between Danny and his younger brother. "In our wolf skins, we were able to keep within hearing range while they gathered around their cookfire. We learned much about them and we use what we learned against them."

"Makes no sense," Ulip said, crossing his arms over his bare, near-black chest. His muscles rippled beneath his skin as his eyes narrowed. "Why would the Crow care about a great wolf?"

"Because they are allied with the ice god, Ymir, and Ymir commands the great wolf."

"Holy Helja," Breayn said. "The slavers are working with a god?"

"Only the Split Crows," Calian said, stepping over the dead body. "We believe it's how they have risen in power so quickly." Even though the boy was wearing a wolf skin, it didn't hide the girl's curves. She was no boy. Danny laughed to himself as she neared.

"So, Aput, how long has your sister been your brother?" He raised his eyebrows at Calian, daring her to deny the obvious. The ring of steel being drawn from scabbards told Danny that his assumption was correct. Before anybody had a chance to attack him from behind, he burst into flame and launched himself into the air.

Chapter Four

Ulip's Fall

The world turned red when the phoenix's flames engulfed Danny. It was an aspect of his firebird form that he particularly enjoyed. What he hadn't noticed before was the color of the people around him while he was aflame. They were all bright yellow, except for Ryn who was showing up as orange. The dead bodies of the fallen Crow were almost invisible, as they blended in with the forest floor. As he circled, the humans who had just drawn their swords were looking up, their mouths agape, their swords now on the ground beside them.

Danny circled one more time before landing near the center of the group, switching to his Berrat form when he was just a few feet from the ground. He landed off balance, crashing hard onto the soft earth. He tried to tumble and pop back up to his feet, but instead, skidded across the loam on his back. He laid there for a moment before hopping up.

"You're the phoenix?" Calian asked, her voice a mixture of awe and skepticism. "The one foretold in the prophecies." Danny tousled his flame red hair and gave the girl a grin and a shrug.

"It's a possibility," Ryn said with a sneer, "but it's unlikely."

"You really don't like me, do you," Danny said. "Even my phoenix can see you, as you truly are."

"I don't know what that means," Ryn said, his sneer turning to a snarl, "but no, I don't like you. If you are the one foretold in the prophecies, then I will need you, we all will, but I will *never* like you."

"Challenge accepted," Danny said with a grin, pressing his fists to his hips and pushing out his chest. His antics elicited a giggle from Calian.

"If you have finished talking," Ulip interrupted, "we have uniforms to collect and a war to start." Ryn's and Breayn's heads snapped over at the Gigas. Ryn closed his eyes and slapped his forehead. Breayn's eyes turned into swirling gray storms yet again. Even though Ulip occasionally seemed a bit dim, their reactions were not lost on him.

"I know an ally when I meet one," the big man said. "Danny is our ally and so are these men." His eyes darted to Calian, and a look of confusion crossed his face. "Are you a man or not? I don't like guessing games."

"Calian is my sister," Aput said. "It's just safer if nobody knows that." Danny chuckled and sidled up to the woman.

"They'd have to be blind to not see your feminine beauty," he cooed at her, a cocky half-grin pulling at the corner of his mouth. With a remarkably swift hand, she punched him in the throat. Danny's hands went to his neck while his eyes bulged from his head. He labored to draw a breath, but he still managed to hold the woman's gaze. His grin was not quite so cocky anymore.

"Why do you need Crow uniforms?" Calian asked. She directed the question to Ulip, stepping away from Danny as she did. Ulip, Ryn, and Breayn all seemed to be trying to hold back their laughter while Danny continued to struggle to draw a breath.

"We plan on attacking Ravenlord," Ulip said, standing a bit straighter as he did. "We will disguise ourselves as Crow, making them think they are the ones behind it." The humans laughed at the statement.

"You," Aput said, "plan to disguise yourself as a Berrat?"

"He'll be our pet," Danny said, barely managing to get the words out. His fingers were busy, massaging his throat, trying to ease the discomfort. Ulip's face turned purple at Danny's comment. His heavy brow practically covered his beady black eyes as he bared his teeth.

"Our *pretend* pet," Danny quickly corrected, taking several quick steps away from the Gigas who looked like he was about to burst into a full rage. "What else would explain a Gigas fighting alongside a group of Berrat slavers."

"And you wonder why I can't stand this fool," Ryn said under his breath. Ulip grunted his agreement.

"It's unlikely that they'd believe it, even if they saw it," Aput commented. "There is no way that any Gigas would side with slavers."

"Do you really think that any of them are going to be thinking that, when they see him come thundering across the ground carrying that sword of his?" Danny asked, giving Ulip his best grin. "Especially if he comes flying in on a fire drake."

"A fire drake?" Aput asked, his eyebrows raised.

"Our plan was for Ulip to seek out the fire drakes his clan lived with. He believes he can find one willing to bear him into battle."

"I don't think it will matter much anyway," Breayn said, rolling her eyes. "He won't leave any standing to tell the tale." Ulip smiled at the comment, but it stilled looked like he was snarling.

"How can we help?" Aput asked. "We are too tall to pretend to be Berrat."

A new idea popped into Danny's head; something that might indirectly help Kit, or at least the village she grew up in. Danny had learned that Lilloet, the major city just north of her village, had been taken over by Lord Byssus. He headed the one house that was possibly even more cruel and ruthless than the Split Crows.

"Can you do the same thing we're doing, except in Lilloet? It would get the Crows fighting on two fronts. I suspect they wouldn't last long."

"Lord Byssus is crazy enough that it wouldn't take much to bring him to war," Breayn said. "But we'd need to make the Crows think he's attacking them. Since most of his army is made up of humans, you folks could pretend to be from his house."

Aput and Calian exchanged a look. Their rapidly changing facial expressions almost made it look like they were having a conversation between themselves. It appeared as though Calian was pleading with her brother while Aput was scowling and shaking his head. It didn't take long before everyone noticed their ongoing, non-verbal debate.

"It's annoying, isn't it," Ahanu said, pulling his wolf-head helm back, revealing his bald, heavily tattooed pate. "They have conversations in their heads, excluding everyone else around them."

"You can barely carry on a conversation as it is," Pana offered, pursing his lips to hide his grin. His comment drew a snarl from Ahanu, who shook his head and walked away. Pilip followed his older brother. His expression suggested he was planning to have a bit more fun at Ahanu's expense.

"You can't attack Ravenlord," Aput said, shaking his head at his cohorts' antics. "The bulk of King Faol's army is there. They are far too strong right now."

"The vampire king is in Ravenlord?" Ryn asked. "Why? Why would he leave Faol? We've always been told that he never leaves his castle."

"King Faol is not in Ravenlord, but much of his army is," Calian replied. She pulled back her wolf-helm as well, revealing her bald, tattooed head. Unlike the swirling shapes of Danny's traditional tribal tattoos, the markings that covered her skin looked more like runes. "He is making a play against us, to wipe us out completely. If we're gone, Faol will take the entire Berrathian kingdom." Danny's eyebrows shot up as he puckered his lips.

"You five? You're going to stop the vampire king's army? And people say I've got a big ego." Even Ryn laughed at Danny's comment.

"Not just us, you idiot," Calian growled. "Mortem Lupus, our clan."

"Aput said you had no clan, just the five of you," Danny commented, bothered by the inconsistencies of their story.

"I would not speak of our alliances, not unless I knew you were our friends," Aput replied. Danny couldn't make out the man's expression, except that he looked annoyed.

"You're dog soldiers?" Ulip asked. He was slowly nodding his head in approval. "A mighty clan indeed." Aput's eyes turned bright green as he peeled his lips back into a snarl, exposing some rather formidable canines.

"We are not dogs, you oversized dullard. We are wolves." Aput's declaration made Ulip laugh.

"Dogs, wolves, what's the difference? You all sniff butts to greet each other." Ulip feigned a sniffing action while he scrunched his face in disgust. While Aput's face continued to contort in rage, the rest of the group, including the other dog soldiers, roared with laughter.

"If I didn't think this one might be the phoenix, I'd rip you all apart." Aput's chest was heaving badly as he struggled to get a hold of his rage. "We are not dogs," he added one last time. Calian blew out her cheeks and rolled her eyes.

"So, you are actually werewolves then?" Ryn asked as soon as he got his laughter under control. "You are bound to the phases of the moon. You are bound to the god Medeina."

"We prefer the term lycanthrope," Aput said. "Those of us afflicted with the disease take on different traits, depending on our parents."

"It's a disease?" Ryn said, taking a step away from them. "Can I catch it from you?" The Berrat's reaction made Calian grin.

"If you were to be bitten, but not killed, there is a small chance the affliction could be spread, but it's very rare."

"Creating a conflict between House Byssus and the Split Crows is our best plan," Aput said, putting an end to the werewolf conversation. "We have already heard rumors that Lord Byssus' soldiers have been having skirmishes with the Split Crows along the borderlands between Wantage and Lilloet. Apparently, Lord Byssus was never happy being forced out of Wantage by the Crow."

"If they're already skirmishing, what good will it do us if we kill off a few ourselves? It will just be more of the same." Danny ran his fingers through his hair. Planning wasn't his strong suit, and he really knew nothing about the Berrathian cities. Breayn smiled, like she had an idea.

"We need to make it hurt. Hit Lord Byssus where he will have no choice but to retaliate."

"We steal his daughter," Calian said, finishing Breayn's statement.

"Nothing is more important than family," Ulip said, his brow in deep creases. "I, too, would go to war to save my family; to restore my clan." Danny got the feeling there was something more, much more, to the big guy's statement, but now was not the time to delve into that story.

"Prisoners are problematic," Ryn said. "Why don't we just kill her? Won't that have the same effect?"

"Do you know that she deserves death?" Aput asked. "I have heard no tale that she is an active member of the Auctioneers. Or do you feel that the sins of the father are carried by his children?"

"Are we not at war?" Ryn said, taking a menacing step towards Aput. "There are casualties in war. Sometimes good people die. Do you think the Split Crows or House Byssus would afford us the same courtesy? Do you think they cared when they murdered women and children, or sold them off to be blood slaves to the vampire king?"

"Be careful of the path you choose," Calian said, "or you will become that which you despise." The comment struck a nerve with Ulip. A look of confusion and concern crossed his face. His head dropped low before he turned and walked away. He slowly began to undress the fallen Crow, relieving them of their black-feathered uniforms. Ryn watched carefully as the giant went about his business. He moved closer to the Gigas, offering him what advice he could.

"Sometimes we have to go against our nature for the salvation of those around us. Sometimes we have to do horrible things to keep the innocent safe. Our enemy puts no restrictions on their actions. If we have a soft heart, we will have no chance."

Aput opened his hands to the heavens and tilted back his head. "And they will cleanse the lands with ice and fire. From the ashes, a sword will rise. From the wilds, a child will seek the passive, a mighty roar unleash. From the heavens, a star will fall, to lay waste to the wicked and break the circle."

"How is it that you know our prophecies?" Breayn asked. Danny, too, was more than a bit surprised at the man's ability to recite the prophecy from the cave.

"They are not your prophecies," Aput said. "We Lycosians have sought out *the three* since the gods, Pele and Medeina, went silent, supposedly killed by Titan or his petulant children, Ollin and Bael."

"Three will try. Eight shall die. Three will go. Two shall grow. One will lose. One will choose. This is the prophecy of the three," Danny said. "What's the point? None of it makes any sense."

"The point, my fiery friend, is that our enemies and their lack of concern for the lives around them, are bringing about the end of days. The signs are there if you take the time to look. The phoenix, the primordial fire elemental, has been absent from our lands for thousands of years, only to return now. Why do you think that is? Why has he chosen you as his host?" Danny's face went blank at Aput's words. He had never considered himself a host. He had assumed that he had somehow absorbed the spirit of the firebird, which allowed him to take on its form. He also wondered why, if Breayn hosted Boreas, the North Wind, why did it tax her, when hosting the phoenix caused him no pain at all?

Ulip dumped the Crows' feathered cloaks in a heap on the ground. For the first time since Danny's arrival, the man looked small, defeated.

"I cannot help take a girl from her home," he said. He looked like he was carrying the weight of the world on his shoulders. "I can no longer lead this group. I must return home and try to gather what is left of my clan. I must pay for my crimes." Danny was about to object, but he couldn't get past the beaten look on the big man's face.

"You have committed no crimes," Breayn said, dashing to the Gigas' side in the blink of an eye. "By your own laws, you are permitted to protect your people, to protect yourself. Our actions, all of them, have been to protect the people of the north; my family, your family, all families."

"I started off killing to avenge my clan, but now, I kill because I enjoy it." Ulip looked lost, like his entire world had just fallen in upon him. He pulled his sword from its sheath and dropped it to the ground. "I will fight no more. I must atone for my sins."

Ulip disappeared as he moved into the forest. The group stood in silence, looking down at the man's massive sword that he'd left on the ground.

"I didn't mean to," Calian started, her eyes seeking out Breayn. "I…"

"It's been a long time coming, I think," Breayn replied. "I have never heard of a Gigas with such a lust for violence before, even those who have been wronged find a way to turn the other cheek."

"We can't just let him leave," Ryn said, wringing his hands together. "The entire group looks up to him."

"Because he's nearly twice as tall as all of you," Danny said. It was a weak attempt at humor, trying to lighten the mood. Based on the way Breayn and Ryn were glaring at him, they didn't appreciate the comment.

"Where will he go?" Aput asked, moving next to his sister.

"Home, most likely," Ryn said, staring down at the Gigas' massive sword laying lifeless on the ground. "Back to where his clan once lived."

Aput shook his head.

"What will he do when he gets there? How will returning home heal him?"

"It won't," Breayn said. "But he won't know that until he witnesses it for himself."

"You can't just let him walk away," Danny said, picking up the massive blade Ulip had left behind. He was surprised at how light it was, well, how relatively light it was. Based on its size, the fact that it was nearly as long as he was tall, he didn't think he'd even be able to lift it. "I thought you were his friends."

In moments, Danny disappeared into the trees, following Ulip's path through the forest.

⁂

"Ulip, hold on," Danny called out as he tried to follow Ulip's path into the forest. Danny ran aimlessly through the trees, hoping to stumble upon the man, but he was having no luck at all. The Gigas, even in his downcast state, moved silently through the forest, leaving nary a trace that he was ever there.

"Ulip, please," he called out again. "I won't try to stop you, I just – I just want to know – I want you to tell me who I am. Your ancestors passed down information. You said they were just stories, but you know they're not. They're real. You don't have to fight, but you need to share your wisdom with us."

There was a thunderous crack, like the breaking of a tree trunk. The trees parted from behind Danny as the grim-faced Gigas came shuffling out. His shoulders were slumped forward, his chin to his chest. He raised his head, but his heavy brow still managed to hide his sullen eyes.

"Nobody has ever called me wise."

"Everyone looks up to you," Danny said, that small infectious grin spreading across his face, "and not just because you tower over them." He waited a moment or two to see if he could get a response, but the Gigas' face was like stone.

"The people you have helped, those you have saved, they all respect you and follow you. When you speak, they listen. Not out of fear, but because they know you are there for them. When their world was crashing down upon them, you stood tall and protected them. Now they feel safe because they know you're standing watch and while you do, they feel no harm will come to them."

Ulip's brow raised enough that his black eyes came into view. "I took pleasure in killing. I broke our laws."

"We do what we must in order to cope," Danny said, tossing the giant's blade at his feet. "You found a way to deal with killing when, from the time you were very young, you were taught it was wrong to take a life. We all find ways to live with our decisions. If we don't, we can't survive."

"My tribe would not help. We would not fight against the slavers. We would not help the Berrat, our neighbors, in their plight."

"Peace is better than war," Danny said, "but sometimes there must be war if there is to be peace."

"You are wiser than you act," Ulip said, the slightest hint of a smile appearing at the corner of his mouth, and then disappearing just as quickly. "I will protect my new clan, but I will not seek out the enemy any longer." He reached down and picked up his massive blade. Having it in his hand seemed to make him whole again. He stuffed it into its scabbard and started heading off.

"Wait," Danny said, his head swiveling about. "I don't know how to get back to Breayn and the others." His comment elicited a groan and possibly an eye-roll. It was hard to tell under the man's heavy brow. Ulip pointed to the Berrat's left.

"They are less than one hundred paces in that direction. You've been running in circles while trying to find me." Danny's face burned at the comment, but his grin quickly covered it up.

"You see, we're lost without you."

"Breayn was right," Ulip said, shaking his head. "You are an imbecile."

Chapter Five

PLAN TO KIDNAP

Danny followed Ulip's directions, returning him to where the others were waiting. They all looked expectantly to him as he stepped out from between two large oaks, their trunks nearly three paces across.

"Well?" Breayn asked. Her body looked stiff while she chewed on her lower lip. "Were you able to find him?"

"He found me," Danny said with a shrug. "I have no idea how such a big man can remain hidden the way he does."

"And?" Ryn asked, tapping his foot on the soft, loamy ground.

"He's heading back to camp. He said he'd protect the others, but he will not seek out conflict." Ryn's mouth flopped open. He seemed shocked that Danny was able to turn the big guy around.

"How's about we talk about how we're going to snatch the Lord's daughter," Aput interrupted. "And we're going to need to dispose of these Crow bodies. We can't just strip them and leave them here. It will raise too many questions."

"I'll set them on fire, just before we leave," Danny said. "There will be nothing left but ash by the time I'm finished."

"It will take us several days to get to Lilloet, even if we are in wolf form," Calian said. "We should get moving before the Crows send a scout here to check up on this group."

"We can get there in a few hours," Breayn said. "We should be able to carry this out with just the three of us. Besides, the more we are, the easier it would be for us to be caught."

"And how exactly do you plan on getting inside a human city where all Berrat are slaves?" Aput asked. "I doubt there are any free Berrat within the city."

"Has anybody been to Lilloet? Do we even know what it looks like?" Danny was quickly coming to the realization that they had no clue what they were walking into. He was thinking he'd rescue some beautiful damsel from within a tall tower. He'd fly in, sweep her off her feet, and then fly away. Of course, there was the flaming ball of death problem to work out as well.

Everyone stood and stared at one another. Here they were, eight willing heroes with absolutely no sense of how to proceed.

Ryn shook his head. "It's a Berrat city. It will be very much like Taseko, designed in a circular pattern with the most important buildings at the center. There is no doubt that Lord Byssus and his personal guard will be living in the core of the city and the slave lord will take control of the community building for his home."

"Ryn's right," Breayn said. "Lilloet is an old city. It will be in the traditional Berrat design. We can fly in, find the lord's daughter, and leave after dark. We'll need to leave some dead bodies outside the city's walls, so they know the Crow had been there. If we kill enough of Byssus' soldiers, they may even think that The Claw was directly involved." She bowed her head, shaking it slowly. "It's too bad that Ulip won't be with us. The trail of death he leaves behind would certainly look like the work of The Claw."

"Who or what is *The Claw*?" Danny asked. He had a vague recollection of the name, but that was far as his memory went. His question drew groans from most of the group.

"The Claw," Calian said, speaking slowly as though Danny was a child, "is one of the three ruling members of the Split Crows." She paused for a moment, waiting to see if Danny was paying attention. "He's their warrior. He leads their army, but he is a destructive force all on his own. The Beak is their mouth-peace. She is the face of the Split Crows. She appears to be their leader, sitting on the throne at Taseko."

"Appears?" Danny asked.

"Appears," Calian replied. "She's a figurehead. The true leader of the faction is The Wing, the assassin. He runs the organization from the shadows."

"I see," Danny said, nodding knowingly. He rubbed the stubble on his chin and turned to Ryn. "How many dead Crow can you carry along with Breayn?"

"Two, at most," he replied. "I can fly very fast as a great hawk, but the bird cannot bear much additional weight."

"If I fly myself, I can likely carry four or five," Breayn said. "We can't just leave a couple of corpses for Byssus' men to find. It needs to look like it was a significant operation."

"Absolutely not!" Ryn said through gritted teeth. "It's too long a time to try to keep him under control. Even now I can feel you struggling to hold him. Those are his words coming from your mouth."

"Whose words?" Calian asked. "What are you talking about?"

"Nothing!" Breayn, Ryn, and Danny said in nearly perfect unison.

"Two Crows will be enough," Danny said. "Fewer dead bodies will make it look more like a precision attack, like it was this Wing person having led it."

Beads of sweat were apparent along Breayn's brow line. Ryn's assessment that she was in constant battle with Boreas, the North Wind, was now obvious. When the elemental saw a chance to escape his host, the woman who hosted his spirit, he pushed hard to make it happen.

"How am I going to get close enough without being seen?" Danny asked. It would likely be dark by the time they arrived at Lilloet, and his firebird form would stand out like a beacon against the night sky.

"Can you not change into something less conspicuous?" Ryn asked, blinking rapidly. "Surely, if you can change into a phoenix, you've picked up a few animal spirits along the way."

"I can change into a vole," Danny said, more than a bit sheepishly. "I claimed his spirit by accident. I don't even really know how it happened. Nobody ever taught me how to spirit bind with an animal." The revelation didn't go over too well with either Ryn or Breayn. Meanwhile the wolf soldiers looked on, not having much of a clue about anything the Berrat were discussing.

"We will find you a small bird to bind with," Breayn said. Her voice was soft and comforting. Ryn got a wicked look in his eyes.

"Pick something tasty for my falcon spirit," he said with a laugh. "I haven't let him hunt in many moons."

"You can try," Danny said with an equally wicked grin. "I hope he likes his food spicey." The two immediately locked into a stare down, each one practically begging the other to throw a punch.

"And what exactly do you expect us to do?" Calian asked. "Wait here until you return?"

"You are free to return to whatever business you were doing before we saved you," Breayn said, tilting her head to the side, pursing her lips. It was Calian's turn to lock in, as she glared at Breayn.

"Enough, all of you," Aput growled out. "We will head for Cormorant, as we had planned. The ships will set sail soon. We need to do what we can to prevent the shipment of silvered weapons from making it to Ravenlord. If they make it into the hands of King Faol's army, we're as good as done, anyway."

"Even with our allies in Cormorant, we won't be able to stop the ships from leaving port," Calian said. "We need to find another way. The moon will be dark in three days, and the Mortem Lupus will be next to useless in a fight until Medeina, once again, shows her face in the night sky." Aput glared at his younger sister.

"So, it's true then," Ryn said. "With no moon, you dog soldiers can't shift." Aput continued glaring at his sister.

"Do you still doubt that they are our allies?" Calian asked, returning her brother's glare. The two continued to lock onto each other's gaze. Their eyes, which were dark brown, flashed of jade green. A low rumble in Aput's throat put an end to the standoff.

"It sounds like we've got a bunch of shifters who can't shift," Breayn said. Danny's face heated badly at the comment. "I can probably help Danny learn how to meld with an animal spirit, but I'm afraid I can't do anything to help with your... situation."

Calian and Aput stared at the woman for several seconds, considering her words. Ryn cleared his throat.

"Okay, since we have that settled, can we get going? We're going to be out of daylight soon and Danny is going to light up the night sky if he flies in his phoenix form." Ryn slipped on one of the Crow costumes. The black-feathered cloak had a good amount of blood on it, but it was otherwise in decent condition. He picked out a reasonably clean cloak from the pile of uniforms and handed it to Breayn.

Danny helped himself to one of the black feathered cloaks. As he slipped it over his shoulders, a bright tinkle caught his attention. He rummaged through the cloak's pockets and pulled out two vials.

"Can anybody tell what type of potions these are?" He held up the two vials. One contained a dark red liquid, and the other was pale yellow.

Pana, the dog soldier's healer, took a look at the two ampoules, giving the yellow bottle a critical eye. He pulled the cork and gave it a sniff. "Well, the red vial contains a healing potion. Based on the color, I'd say it's quite powerful. The yellow potion is, unless I'm mistaken, a potion of fire resistance. I believe it is also a very high-quality potion."

"Why would they want a potion of fire resistance," Calian asked, stepping closer to get a better look at the vials.

"Because of our phoenix friend," Ryn said as he went through the pockets of his robe. He frowned when his search came up empty. "I'm guessing they've seen too many of their ranks burned to a crisp."

Danny snatched the bottles back from Pana and stowed them in his cloak.

"That reminds me, why doesn't my gear burn up when I shift into my firebird form?" he asked. "The first time I changed into a phoenix, my clothing burned away."

"He's like a child," Ryn said as he started rummaging through the pile of Crow uniforms. "Are we going to have to teach him everything?"

"He grew up in a Nomad city," Breayn said, coming to her cousin's defense. "He can't be expected to know our ways."

"What do you mean, he grew up in a Nomad city?" Aput asked. "Which one?"

"Aarall," Danny replied. "I grew up at the Temple of the Fist."

"You're a priest of Titan?" Calian asked. For whatever reason, all the dog soldiers took a keen interest in this bit of news. Danny shrugged in reply.

"I grew up in the Temple, but I never became a priest." Danny scrubbed the back of his neck. His birthmark felt itchy again. He wished he had never learned of its existence because it had been bothering him ever since.

"You're the son of Paylor and Dyanna," Aput said, his brow furrowed. He turned his attention to Calian. After a few moments she nodded, and a wicked grin spread across her face as she turned her gaze on Breayn.

"And that would make you his cousin," she said. "It looks like our fortunes have changed. We will live like royalty, and we can finally rid ourselves of these accursed lands." As she finished her words, Pilip and Ahanu changed into their wolf form, if one could call it that. They remained on two feet. Their heads transformed into those of wolves. They appeared to stop mid-shift, stopping in a half wolf, half human form. Danny had never seen a werewolf before, but the wolf heads seemed huge, their teeth longer and their jaws stronger.

He had an arrow nocked and drawn before anybody could say a word. In a heartbeat, he loosed the missile, targeting the bald-headed Aput. The human had not shifted like the others. As the arrow flew towards him, he tilted his head to the side, allowing it to pass harmlessly into the forest behind him.

As Ryn changed into his great white bear form, Breayn streaked across the clearing and grasped Aput by the throat in less than a heartbeat. She lifted him from the ground and slammed him hard onto his back.

"Enough," Calian screamed out. "He's not The Wing."

Breayn had already lifted Aput from the ground and slammed him down a second time before Calian finished getting the words out. Danny loosed another arrow, aimed at one of the dog soldiers, grazing the side of his gray furred face. The man was incredibly fast, avoiding the arrow that should have struck him between his dark-green eyes.

"Stop, everyone," Calian screamed out again. "We're on the same side."

"You have a funny way of showing it," Danny said, as he trained an arrow at the woman's chest.

"You look an awful lot like The Wing," Calian said. "I needed to know you weren't him, pretending to be someone else. Dannith has not been seen in over ten cycles. When you said you were him, we thought you were setting a trap for us."

An uneasy calm came over the group. The dog soldiers changed back into their human form. Breayn maintained her hold on Aput's throat. Ryn didn't change out of his bear form. He walked slowly towards the two dog soldiers, a fierce rumble still coming from deep within his chest. With each step he took, his six-inch claws dug deeply into the forest floor's soft loam. Danny maintained his aim on Calian's chest.

"We're on your side," she repeated. "We have the same goals. We're going to bring an end to the Split Crows and the Auctioneers."

"You've met The Wing?" Breayn asked, loosening her grip on Aput's throat enough to allow him to breathe. Her eyes were swirling masses of dark gray. Beads of sweat had gathered along her hairline, dripping slowly from her temples.

"We've not met him, but we've seen him," Aput replied. "We watched as he and his Crow soldiers butchered everyone in a village while they searched for Danny."

"Why do they want me so badly?" Danny asked, lowering the tip of his arrow, slowly releasing the tension on his bow. "How could they know that I melded with a phoenix?"

"They don't know that," Calian said, slowly lowering her hands. She gave Danny a questioning look, waiting to see if he was going to raise his bow again. When he finally released all the tension on the bowstring she continued. "At least, it's unlikely that they know that. They are searching for you because your family has the purest Berrabbithi blood of any Berrat ever seen. Against all odds, you and your cousin may be the key to King Faol's plans."

"And what are these plans?" Breayn asked, directing the question to Aput. "What does our heritage have to do with the vampire king?"

"He has trouble finding people who can accept the change when they're turned. The newly sired vampires usually lose their minds because of the blood-lust. He's hoping that with your blood, they will get more of the new vampires to accept the transformation." Aput gently put his hand on Breayn's wrist and pulled her hand away from his throat. The storm in her eyes subsided, and she helped the man to his feet.

"We Lycosians have been trying to bring Berrat blood into our tribes for hundreds of years, to help us control our change. It has rarely been successful. Those of us who can control the change do so through magic." Aput rubbed his bald head, referring to the tattooed patterns on his scalp. "The magic in our markings, it's unpredictable. It usually has no effect, but when it works, we have complete control of our wolf half."

"Our father was a Berrat shifter," Calian chimed in, "but not all the Berrat who have joined with us are able to shift. Those who could, seemed to have the highest likelihood of producing offspring who could control their animal side." Danny's face scrunched up like he was trying to solve an unsolvable puzzle. Breayn left Aput to move closer to her cousin.

"Do you remember what I told you, that the Berrat are losing their ability to spirit bind? There are very few left who can do it with anything other than the smallest of animals." She raised her eyebrows to Danny, waiting for his response. He gave her the slightest hint of a nod.

"The Lycosians mate with Berrat, hoping to pass the shapeshifting gene on to their children, so that they can control the wolf within them. If their Berrat mate cannot shift, it's unlikely that their children will benefit from the union."

"Do all Lycosians have a wolf spirit, or the disease, or whatever it is within them?" Danny asked. He suddenly wished this was a topic he had read about in the library.

"No," Aput answered. "Only a small percentage of us are born to the wolf. A much smaller percentage, like Calian and myself, are born to the dire wolf."

"This is all very interesting," Ryn said after he returned to his Berrat form. "But we are almost out of daylight, and we need to leave."

"What will you do?" Danny asked. Calian and Aput stared at each other for a few moments.

"We have met our objective. If you will allow us, we'd like to join with your group," Aput replied. "If not, we'll head east to Cormorant."

"You cannot fly, and we cannot carry you," Ryn said. His eyes were wide as he stared at Breayn, practically pleading to get going.

"We wish to join your group," Calian replied. "We will follow Ulip back to your camp, if you'll let us." Danny scoffed at the comment.

"Follow Ulip," he said with a grin. "You might as well try to follow the wind. He's impossible to track." The comment made the dog soldiers laugh.

"We can pick up his scent easily," Aput said. "We could likely pick it up two days from now if we wanted to."

Ryn's eyes went wide, and his lips pressed together in a slight grimace. His gaze shifted to Breayn and then back to Aput. The man put his hands on his hips and blew out his cheeks. "If we were your enemies, would we have told you that?"

"I trust them," Danny said. It was perhaps the only time he hadn't made a wisecrack. He felt the urgency of the moment and he did not sense any misdirection in Aput's voice.

"Fine," Breayn said. "Follow him if you can, but we will not tell you the way." She turned to Ryn and gave him a nod. He immediately switched into his great hawk form.

"What about my gear?" Danny asked, looking to his cousin. "You never explained why my clothes were turned to ash the first time I changed."

Breayn glided over to him and pressed her lips to his ear. "When we shift, we picture everything we have as being a part of us, and the spirit lets it happen. The first time you shifted, I expect you didn't tell the phoenix to protect your clothing. Since then, I'm guessing she's been looking after it for you. Maybe she doesn't want to see you naked, ever again."

"The phoenix is a girl?" Danny suddenly felt ashamed, but he didn't know why.

"Yes, she is," Breayn said with a grin. "I'm surprised you didn't discover that on your own." She gave him a wink. There was a slight puff of wind and Breayn was suddenly sitting atop the great hawk's back. How she could traverse the distance in a moment was something he'd have to ask her about.

"You go ahead," Danny said, giving Breayn a brisk nod. "I've got to light up these dead Crow and I'll come join you as soon as they're ash." Ryn immediately flapped his great brown wings and lifted off, raising a thick cloud of dust and debris in the process.

As the great hawk disappeared over the canopy of leaves, Danny hopped onto the stacked bodies of the dead Crows. He gave Calian a wink and set himself ablaze. He pumped more and more of his flame into the corpses until there was nothing left but a black stain on the ground. He switched back into Berrat form and walked over to Aput.

"If you do manage to find Ulip," Danny said scrubbing the back of his neck, "tell him for me that I'm glad I got to meet him, and that I'm a better person for it."

"When I find him, I'll pass that on. And," Aput said, his face grave, "if you get to Cormorant before the shipment of silvered weapons leaves port, set the vessel ablaze. It cannot reach its destination. If it does..."

"If it does, we will continue the fight," Calian said, hooking her arm around her brother's elbow. "I hope we get to meet again, Danny Fox-Dancing. I enjoyed fighting with you."

Danny's green eyes sparkled at the comment. A moment later, he was aflame and flying up into the evening sky.

Chapter Six

Enchantments of Speed

Kit could smell the cookfire long before she arrived at her cohorts' camp, nestled in a small copse of evergreens. "Please tell me there's more food," she exclaimed as she dismounted, grinning from ear to ear.

"I wasn't sure how long you'd be, so I only cooked enough for us to eat right away." Indie pouted as his gaze shifted from Lin, to Lump, and finally to Runt.

"I'm so hungry, I'll eat it raw. What have you got?" Kit had already started to drool at the thought of some fresh meat.

"I killed a boar, but there isn't much left, I'm afraid. Runt has a voracious appetite." The dire wolf smiled at Indie's words, his tongue lolling out the side of his mouth.

"You ate my dinner?" Kit said in an accusing, yet playful tone. "You couldn't save some for me?" Runt's mouth slammed shut; a worried look crossed his face. "I guess a growing pup needs his food. Do you think you can help catch me some dinner?"

"No need," Indie said as he pulled out a spit with a large haunch of freshly cooked meat on it. When Kit saw the food, she wiped her mouth with the back of her hand. Indie pulled out a large hunting knife and spun it in his fingers, presenting the handle to the young priest.

Kit eagerly took both the knife and the spit. She stared intently at the roasted meat, its still-red juices pouring down the side. Not wanting to waste any time, other than to say a quick prayer of thanks to Titan, she quickly carved a strip off the roast and shoved the food into her mouth. She was certainly not concerned about how she might look while she ravaged the roast, its juices dripping down her chin and hands. As Indie and Lin watched, in a mix of horror and amusement, Kit simply shrugged as she pushed strip after strip of meat into her mouth.

With the last few bites of the haunch in her hand, Kit caught sight of Runt and Lump; both were drooling hard enough to leave a puddle on the ground in front of them. "This is mine," Kit managed to mumble out with her mouth stuffed with food. "You had yours." Her admonishment did nothing to dissuade the boys as they shuffled a bit closer, hoping that she might share some of her dinner with them. "Fine," she finally said, giving in to their begging. She cut the remaining roast in two nearly equal portions, tossing the larger piece to Runt. "Sorry, pal," she said to Lump. "He's a lot bigger, and he's a growing puppy." Lump seemed like he couldn't care less if he got less than Runt. He quickly tore apart his chunk of meat, swallowing down each piece in rapid succession. When he finished devouring his treat, he looked up, waiting for more. Runt hadn't bothered tearing the meat up and had wolfed it down whole.

Lin was staring at Kit, waiting impatiently for her to finish stuffing her face. She started to groan as Kit slowly, methodically, started licking the juices from her fingers, her hands, and her wrists. "Well?" she finally asked when she simply couldn't wait any longer. Kit responded with a blank face, unsure of what her friend was asking her. Lynn's look turned to pure exasperation.

"Did you find any of the reagents I asked for?"

"Oh, right!" Kit exclaimed, startled by the realization that she hadn't said much more than *I'm hungry* since rejoining her friends. "One moment." She picked herself up off the ground and half-heartedly wiped the dirt from her posterior. She furrowed her brow when she couldn't see Angel nearby.

"Char took her to find some sweetgrass while you were... eating," Indie chuckled. "They're not far from here." As Kit began heading out of the thicket, both Char and Angel came trotting through the trees.

"I should have told you to take the saddle bags before I left." Even through Angel's mental connection, she sounded breathless.

"I'm guessing that your leaving with Char had something more to it than just sweetgrass," Kit giggled as she unlatched the belly-straps of her horse's saddle. There was no reply from Angel other than her whither shuddering. *"Have a nice night and try to get some sleep. Okay?"* she added, patting her roan on the neck. *"We've got a long, hard ride ahead of us tomorrow."* Angel giggled again at Kit's choice of words before she and Char trotted back out through the trees.

After Kit found a suitable place to leave the saddle, she pulled her treasures out of the saddlebags. She walked over to Lin and presented her with a cloth-wrapped package. As Lin pulled back the wrapping, her eyes went wide, and a broad smile spread across her face. "You found frost thistle," she declared as she inspected the plants. "There's more than enough here to put several enchantments on Whistler."

"Whistler?" Kit asked, never having heard the name before.

"My horse," Lin said, her face still beaming with joy as she continued to examine the plants. "By the time we got here, she was huffing and puffing so hard, she was making a high-pitched whistling noise. Nobody ever told me her real name, and I couldn't keep calling her *horse.*"

"It's a nice name," Kit replied. "I'm sure she likes it." Inwardly, Kit thought it was a terrible name, but she didn't want to ruin the mood. She was hoping that Angel would be able to get the horse's real name before *Whistler* stuck permanently. "I also have this for you," Kit said as she presented a second bundle to Lin. "It's not frost thistle, but hopefully you can use it."

Lin had a hopeful look on her face as she accepted the package. The shape of the parcel made Lin think it contained a dagger of some sort, but it was much too light for that. When she pulled back the cloth, her hands started to shake badly. Tears of joy sprang from her eyes and rolled down her cheeks.

"You found two pegasus feathers? They are pegasus feathers, right?" Lin was practically vibrating. She was so excited with what Kit had given her that her words came out shrill. "I can't believe you found them. They're incredibly rare."

"I got to touch one," Kit said, remembering her encounter.

"You brought them here, how could you not have touched one?" Lin raised an eyebrow and gave Kit a look that suggested she was more than a bit dim.

"Not the feathers," Kit said rolling her eyes. "A pegasus. He was invisible, but he came so close to me I could touch him."

"No way," Indie exclaimed. "They won't let anybody touch them!"

"That's not entirely true," Lump interrupted after changing into human form. Kit couldn't help but laugh when she looked at him. He always had the same mussed hair and sad puppy-dog eyes. "The pegasi that are indigenous to this area are more social than their brethren from other regions. They have an innate ability to sense the heart of a creature, and if it poses no threat to them, they're more willing to engage with said creature." When Lump saw everyone's dumbfounded look, he smiled and shrugged. "I learned a lot in the library."

After Lump shifted back into his dog form, Kit regaled the group about her adventures, telling them how amazing Angel was, and how instrumental Fury had been in the success of their mission. Fury, of course, did not miss the opportunity to congratulate himself on his heroic deeds and how, indeed, he was the force that had turned the tide during the battle with the Hill Giant. He floated about, taking time to speak individually to each member of the party, allowing them to bask in his grandeur.

It was only after Fury stopped talking about how wonderful he was that Kit finally got a chance to get a word in. "Fury, why was it that you were so angry with the fire drakes?" Apparently, the question struck a nerve, a big nerve, which caused Fury to flame uncontrollably.

"They had no idea who I was!" He sounded incredulous, as though what he was saying couldn't be possible. "They didn't know my name. They had never heard of me, or even Ouroboros." There was another small gout of blue flame as he snorted in derision. "The Dragon Lords have been forgotten."

"Who's Ouroboros?" Indie asked, in part because he wanted to know but also because he was enjoying Fury's overreaction to the drakes not knowing who he was.

Fury stopped immediately, spun around, and fell lifelessly to the ground with a resounding *thud*.

"Fury, don't be so dramatic." Kit gave him a small nudge with her foot. When he didn't react, she picked up the hammer and stared at the dragon-head pommel. "Who cares if they don't know who the Dragon Lords were?" When Fury still didn't respond, she gave the hammer a shake, like she was trying to rouse him from a deep sleep. When she still got no reaction from him, she rolled her eyes and decided to just ignore the moody dragon.

Completely disregarding Kit's conversation with Fury, Lin looked up from the reagents Kit had just given her. "Pegasus feathers can be used for a lot more than just speed enchantments," she declared, trying to catch her friends' attention. She had a pained look on her face. She was obviously hoping that someone would ask for more details. When neither did, she practically whimpered, imploring them to question her further. With no response forthcoming, she huffed in frustration. "Fine, since you're not going to ask me what they can be used for, I'm just going to tell you."

Neither Indie nor Kit reacted in any way. Kit gave Fury another small shake, wondering why the self-centered, will-never-shut-up dragon was still silent. Indie seemed to be staring dreamily into the fire, running his fingers through Runt's fur. A smile finally tugged at the corner of Indie's mouth when Lin started making strangling noises. "Please, Lin. Tell us what else they're good for – before you burst."

"They can be used for flight enchantments!" she mumbled, like a petulant child whose parents refused to acknowledge her presence. When she saw a look of shock on the faces of both Indie and Kit, she smiled broadly, and began rambling about the enchantment possibilities; how to perform them, what they could do, and last but not least, how she lacked the necessary skill to execute the spells.

"You can use them to make a speed enchantment, but you lack the skill to make a flight enchantment?" Even though Kit had received some training at the Temple on how to do enchantments, it wasn't something that had ever held her interest.

"Flight spells, especially the good ones which require quality reagents, are hard to learn and even harder to cast. If you fail casting the enchantment, the spell fails, and the reagent is wasted." Lin was still staring at the feather, running her fingers along its edges. "I can use some of the frost thistle to enchant Whistler and she'll be fast enough to keep up for now, or I could use a feather and make her even faster than Angel." Lin started shaking her head, like she was having a discussion with herself, denouncing the thought before she finished saying it. "But doing that would be a waste, I think."

"Do you have enough frost thistle to add an enchantment to Char as well?" Indie's question made Kit laugh to herself. She remembered back to when Indie used to joke about how much faster his great stallion was than her small roan, but now the tables had turned. The more she thought about it, the more his request surprised her. It wasn't Indie's style to be concerned about whether Kit's horse was faster than his. Most likely, the request came from Char himself; hoping to sooth his male ego, the one Angel shattered when she bested him in the race around Lake Titan.

"There is enough frost thistle for up to eight speed enchantments," Lin replied, her fingers still running up and down the pegasus feather. "I suggest I put three on Whistler, one on Char and one on each of the boys. We can save the last plant; in case we need it later." Lin's suggestion brought a huge smile to Indie's face. When Kit cocked an eyebrow at him, the smile instantly waned.

"How long does it take to put the enchantments on the animals?" Kit asked through a yawn. It was only at that very moment that she realized just how tired she was.

"I can do three right now on Whistler, and the other three in the morning," Lin replied, finally wrapping up the pegasus feathers. "I'll need some sleep before enchanting Char and the boys. These sorts of enchantments are exhausting." Not waiting for Kit's approval, Lin hopped up from her spot and headed off to where the horses were.

"Do you know what we're going to do when we get to Silverhawk?" Indie asked as he moved to sit beside Kit. Her body tensed when he wrapped his arm around her, but a moment later, she found herself sinking into his embrace. He brushed a strand of hair away from her face, slowly moving his lips until they were just a few inches from her neck. His amorous advances came to a halt when Kit began to snore softly.

Fish, River, Jump

The sun was barely up when Kit awakened. The cool air and the dampness of the morning dew made her shiver. After yawning away the last of her sleepiness, she poked her head out from her blankets to find Indie busily working over a small campfire. "Good morning," he called out to her before returning to his chores.

"That smells good," Kit said as she continued to watch him. Even while performing mundane tasks, there was a simple grace to his movements, and a joy on his face that warmed Kit's heart. "I thought we were out of boar."

"Venison," he replied as he held up an enormous steak at the end of his knife. "Complements of the boys." Kit's face perked up at the sight of the food. As she looked around the campsite, she gave Indie a questioning look. "Lin's with the horses, finishing up her enchantments. The boys are, somewhere, likely finishing off the remains of the stag they caught."

Kit slipped out from beneath her blanket and padded over to the young man. The ground was wet and cold beneath her bare feet, but she enjoyed the connection it gave her to the land. "So, we're alone then?" she asked as she bent to give Indie a slow, gentle kiss on the cheek. Indie moaned at the softness of her lips as they pressed against his flesh. As she continued her kisses, he turned into her, taking Kit into a tight embrace.

"Aww," Lin said, following up her *comment* with kissy noises, making both Kit and Indie jump out of their skins. "Sorry, didn't mean to break up your moment." That might have been what she said, but the mischievous expression on her face told a completely different story.

"Are you sure you're sorry?" Kit asked as Indie busied himself with breakfast again, the redness in her face slowly draining away. "How did the enchantments go?" She was clearly changing the subject, and it wasn't lost on Lin, who gave her a coy smile.

"Enchantments are all done. We'll be able to make excellent time now, without overtaxing the animals." Lin strolled past Kit, placing her hands on Indie's broad shoulders. "So, when's breakfast going to be ready – lover boy?"

Indie shrugged his shoulders, pushing Lin away in the process. It wasn't clear if he was embarrassed by Lin's unexpected arrival or if he was annoyed. "It's ready now," he said, carving off a large piece of meat and placing it on a tin plate, handing it to Lin. "Don't choke on it."

"No need to be testy," Lin said, playfully grinning at him. She gave Kit a sideways look, waggling her eyebrows as she did. "This boy's too tense."

Ignoring Lin's last comment, Kit accepted a plate full of venison from Indie. The meat was perfect, lightly charred on the outside and bloody on the inside. The sight of the ruby-red juices and its wonderful aroma made Kit's mouth water uncontrollably. Not even bothering to cut it, she picked up the meat and ripped a chunk off with her teeth. Its hot, delectable juices poured down her chin as she did. She gave Indie a grunt of approval before finding a comfortable spot near the fire to finish her meal.

"You know," Lin said, as she sat much too close to Kit. "I was thinking about the enchantments on Angel and how incredibly fast she is." Kit gave Lin a questioning look as she ripped another bite of meat from her steak. "It doesn't add up."

"Why?" Kit mumbled, trying to keep her food from leaving her mouth as she asked the question.

"Enchantments, even the most powerful ones, only increase the speed of the animal by a percentage of their normal, natural speed. A fast animal benefits more from an enchantment than a slow animal does." Lin raised her eyebrows, waiting to see if Kit was following. When Kit finally nodded at her, she continued. "Angel's enchantments are very good, but she's much, much faster than she should be." Kit frowned and shrugged, obviously not knowing where Lin was going with this. "I think it's *you* that makes her that fast."

The last comment made Kit chuckle, causing bits of juice to escape from her lips. She took another bite from her steak and gave it a good chew before swallowing it down. "I'm not much of a rider. I can't see how that's possible."

"Me neither," Lin said as she cut a strip of meat off her own steak, eating it much more carefully than her friend. "It's the only thing that makes sense to me though."

As the two girls contemplated the implications of Lin's comments, Runt and Lump took a seat next to them. Before Kit could even acknowledge their arrival, they both had long gobs of drool hanging from their mouths. Lin cut a slice from her steak and tossed it to Lump, who swallowed it whole. A sudden look of distress crossed Runt's face. He moved in closer to Kit, his eyes pleading for a morsel, the fur on his chest soaked from his slobber. Kit rolled her eyes and tossed him the last of her steak, not that there was much left. As she stood up, the boys converged on Lin, eyeing the substantial piece of meat still on her plate.

"Someday, we'll get some alone time," Kit said as she took a seat beside Indie. He was carefully eating his breakfast, occasionally glaring at Lin, huffing at her. "Let it go," Kit suggested while she stared at the remainder of his steak. When he offered it to her, she batted her eyes – and took a big bite from it. "You're the best," she declared, spraying bits of juice in the process.

Once everyone had had their fill, it only took the group a few minutes to break camp. "It's shorter if we head cross-country," Indie suggested, but it's likely faster if we head back to the road.

Kit walked over to Angel and gave her a pat on the neck. "The horses want to run. Let's just head north, shorter means faster, as far as I'm concerned."

"And we know the path across the rift," Lin added. "We don't need to head to where the bridges are."

Indie gave Kit a questioning look. "We came this way the last time we went to Silverhawk." It seemed to have been enough in the way of an explanation. Indie simply shrugged. In a few minutes, the group was on its way.

As they raced across the countryside, Kit tried to explain to Indie about the natural bridge that the Sprite, Feigh, had shown them. She had a lot of difficulty conveying the message, especially because of how fast the horses were running. Even though Indie seemed doubtful, he wasn't objecting to the plan.

As the group continued to cover ground at an incredible pace, Kit's heart soared; the exhilaration of the wind in her face bringing her deep joy. Judging by the looks on the faces of her cohorts, they all felt the same way. Lin, in particular, appeared to be reveling in her horse's newfound speed.

They ran for many hours before coming to the trout-filled river Kit had crossed on her first trip to Silverhawk. The river was fairly wide, but very shallow – easily traversable by the horses. However, it was clear that Indie and Char had other plans. "We're going to try to jump it!" he yelled out as Char surged forward in a burst of speed. Kit looked over at Lin, who promptly smiled before urging her own horse into a faster gallop. Kit didn't need to ask Angel if she wanted to try to make the jump. Seeing the horses speed off towards the river, the boys joined in, racing to keep up with Char.

When the group took off for the wide stream, they were perhaps a hundred paces from it. Despite the short distance, and the other horses' head start, Angel had no difficulty passing them. Just as they reached the edge of the river, Kit whispered to Angel through their bond, *"Fly!"* At that very moment, the small roan pushed off the ground, causing Kit's stomach to lurch at the sudden change in direction. She marveled, watching the horizon dip in the distance, as the pair *flew* over the river. The sensation was exhilarating, but more importantly, at that very moment, it felt *natural.* When Angel's hooves touched down, she came to a skidding halt, spinning around at the same time so they could watch the others as they attempted the same feat.

Char cleared the river with room to spare, with Lump landing only a few feet from him. Runt landed squarely in the middle of the river, while Lin's horse came crashing down hard on the soft ground of the riverbank, causing both horse and rider to tumble out of control. Fear that Lin, or Whistler, was severely injured drove Kit's heart up into her throat. Without Kit even asking, Angel rushed forward, bringing Kit to the side of Lin in the blink of an eye. The young priest hopped down from her horse to find Lin face down in the mud. Without thinking about it, she pulled Lin over by the shoulder, revealing a wide-eyed, smiling woman, her teeth filled with grass and bits of muck.

"We almost did it!" Lin whooped out, pumping her fist in the air. "That was incredible!"

"Whistler is uninjured," Angel declared to Kit through the bond. *"Her reaction is not unlike Lin's. She told me she'd have made the jump if she hadn't doubted herself."* Kit gave Angel a mental smile as she dragged Lin up off the ground by her forearm; a wince of pain crossing Lin's face as she did.

"You're hurt!" Kit exclaimed as she checked Lin over.

"You should probably examine me," Lin suggested, giving her rescuer a demure smile. Kit gave her a solid punch in the shoulder, causing Lin to actually squeal in pain. "That hurt," she screamed, pouting all the while.

"We should take a break, have some food, and give the animals a breather," Indie suggested as he and Char stared down at Lin. She frowned back at him, gingerly rubbing her shoulder. "Are you too hurt to continue?" he asked with genuine concern.

"Aw, you do care," Lin teased with a coy grin – causing Indie to snort and ride off towards the river. "I'm fine to continue on, by the way," she called out to him. Kit was about to walk away as well when Lin took her by the wrist. "He's a good man, Sister Kit. You're lucky to have someone who loves you as much as he does." Kit's face turned scarlet at the use of the word *love,* and she pulled away from Lin's grasp.

While Kit and Indie were busy gathering kindling, Lin held out her bow to them asking, "Who's hungry?" Before either of them had a chance to respond, Lin launched three arrows into the water in rapid succession, each one finding its mark, pinning three large trout to the bottom of the riverbed. "You two start a fire, I'll prep the fish."

Indie had already set a sizeable number of dried branches ablaze when Kit moved in beside him. "Did you see how far Lump jumped?" she asked, fanning the flames with her hands, coughing when the wind shifted, blowing the fire's smoke into her face.

Indie nodded as he poked at the fire, trying to coax the flames to grow higher. "I also saw how far Runt jumped. He barely made it halfway across." Indie chuckled as he replayed the memory in his head. "He looked pretty happy though, when he landed in the middle of the river."

"I swear, that young wolf can find joy in everything," Kit said, smiling broadly when she saw Lin coming to join them with three large trout ready for the fire.

Chapter Eight

The Rift and the Kappa

"We're well ahead of schedule," Kit offered, licking the last of the trout from her fingers. She looked over to Lin, acknowledging her part in getting the group here so quickly. "It took us about eight hours to walk from here to the rift," Kit continued, doing some mental math. "On horseback, we can likely be there in under two hours."

"How far from the rift to Silverhawk?" Indie asked. He'd never been this far north before, at least not since his family had moved to Arnnor when he was a young boy, and that journey had been by ship.

"Once we cross the rift, maybe thirty minutes?" Lin asked, looking to Kit for affirmation. "Why don't we spend the night here then," she suggested. "A good night's sleep will do us all some good. We've been running hard for most of the day."

Kit shook her head. "No, I think we need to press on. We should make it to Silverhawk by nightfall. I think I like the idea of arriving at the Crimson Ale early. They're expecting me to return tomorrow." Kit paused a moment, waiting for an objection. "Besides, if we deal with them tonight, we can take a room in the city and head to Cormorant first thing in the morning."

"Cormorant?" Indie asked. He had a strange, almost excited look plastered across his face. Kit didn't understand his reaction, but if he was anxious to go there, he likely had a good reason.

"When we were in Silverhawk last time, I met some Berrat at the marketplace. They told me that the black ships, the slaver ships, left Cormorant on the new moon. The man who took Treedale may not have left yet. The idea of him getting away with what he did – well, it gnaws at me."

"What are we waiting for then?" Lin asked before she started making her way to Whistler.

"Why are you so excited about going to Cormorant?" Kit asked Indie, once Lin was out of earshot.

"Vampires," he replied with a grin. "The captain told us of them during our training. He said there is a nest there. King Faol assigns them to the port city to inspect the slave shipments that come in from across Berrathia."

"Captain Harding, my father, knows about the slavery operations in Berrathia and yet does nothing about them?"

"The City Watch have no business in Berrathia." Indie's face was firm. "There are more troubles in Aarall than he can deal with, let alone send guards into another kingdom."

"He could have told me," Kit pouted. "He must have known we'd be heading that way, eventually."

"There's no way he could have known," Indie insisted. "But he anticipated that you'd cross paths with them at some point, especially with Pental involved in all of this."

Kit just shook her head and picked herself up off the ground. "Let's get going." Indie sighed, pressing his lips into a tight line. Most of the time he understood Kit, her motivations and why she did what she did, but her moodiness was completely confusing to him.

Again, it didn't take the group long to break camp, and in minutes they were racing across the countryside once more. Every so often, Kit surveyed the landscape as it went racing past her. This part of the kingdom was completely unpopulated, its majestic beauty unspoiled. They were traveling across sprawling grasslands, but there were forests, hills, and mountains in practically every direction. Deep within herself, perhaps down to her very soul, she felt like this was *home*. Her mind wandered, remembering the words the spirit of the black dire wolf, Runt's father, had spoken to her. *My thanks are forever with you, as will I be. My strength is your strength; my heart is your heart.* This was his domain, his home. Perhaps that's what she was feeling right now, the wolf's spirit longing for rest.

"We're here!" Lin yelled out, reining in Whistler, slowing her to a trot. The rest of the group followed suit, slowing to a walk until they were at the edge of the rift.

"That's a long way down," Indie said with a small whistle as he peered over the edge.

"A long, painful trip to the bottom if you're not careful," Lin replied, rubbing her recently broken leg. It wasn't hurting, but the memory of the injury was still strong in her mind.

"How deep is the river?" Indie asked, scanning the rift in both directions. "Can the horses walk across it?"

"I have no idea how deep it is but walking across isn't an option. It's full of Kappa, huge turtle-like creatures that will rip us apart if we get too close to them." Kit frowned and pointed to the far side of the river. "There's one there. We're going to have to find Feigh's bridge."

Lin started moving east along the edge of the rift. "I think it's this way," she offered, staring over the edge. The group picked up its pace, moving at a slow canter. "There!" Lin said, pointing again to the far side of the river, at a large rock protruding from the cliff face. "There's Feigh's home."

"Titan's snowballs," Kit swore. "The bridge is hidden again. It's going to be hard enough to cross if it's visible, but it's going to be impossible if we can't see it." She hopped down from Angel and walked along the cliff's edge. Without notice, she slipped over the side, heading down to where the bridge should have been.

She managed to control her descent well enough that she was able to make it to her intended destination in just a few minutes. Even though it was invisible, she figured she should be able to feel it if she touched it. Sure enough, she caught a root or a branch from the fallen tree with her foot. As she reached out to steady herself, her hand grasped onto a piece of wood. Immediately, the tree-bridge materialized. Kit then noticed that the mark Feigh had given her was glowing faintly.

"Found it," she cried out.

As Kit examined the bridge, she scowled at it. As quickly as she had come down, Kit started clambering her way back up the cliff face, sending small rocks and other debris tumbling as she did. By the time she got to the top, she was filthy, and her hands had multiple small cuts on them. Both Indie and Lin were watching her closely as she crested the cliff face, looks of concern on their faces.

"There's no way the horses can cross that," Indie finally said, shaking his head.

Lump shifted into his human shape. "Unless I'm in this form, I don't think I can cross it either. There are too many branches to move safely along the trunk."

Kit took a deep breath, trying to control her disappointment. "And if you can't cross it, neither can Runt." She looked at the distance to the far side of the bank. "Is there any hope that you could jump the rift?" Lump didn't even think about it. He started shaking his head adamantly.

"The horses can jump it," Angel said to Kit. *"Whistler is scared, but if we can raise her confidence, she can do it."*

"If anybody fails to make the jump, it will mean certain death. It's not like jumping the river." Kit bit on her lower lip as she considered the potential outcome of failing.

"It's our only option." There was a finality to Angel's statement.

"Lin," Kit said, swallowing hard. "Do you think you and Whistler can jump the rift?" The question made Lin's face blanch. "I'm confident that Angel and I can make the jump..."

"Char knows he can make it as well," Indie interrupted. "He thinks Whistler can, too, if she has enough confidence in herself. With the enchantments Lin put on her, she can easily get up enough speed to clear the distance."

"What about the boys?" Lin asked.

Kit looked to Lump. "You easily jumped the river. Do you think Runt can make it, too?"

Lump looked to Runt who was tentatively looking over the edge of the cliff. "Runt can make the jump. He's bigger and faster than I am, but he's too frightened to try. He panicked just trying to jump the shallow river."

"Maybe you can help him not be afraid?" Lin suggested as she, too, watched Runt near the cliff's edge.

Lump shook his head.

"What's the use of us getting across if they can't?" Lin asked. Kit got the feeling that Lin really wasn't up to this, and if the boys couldn't get across, it was a good excuse for her to not even think about it.

"They'll get across," Kit said with absolute certainty. "But it's up to you if you're willing to try to make the jump."

Lin's lower lip was quivering badly. "If it will prove my devotion to you, we'll try."

"Oh, Lin. Don't speak like that. You don't need to prove anything to me." Kit gave Lin her absolute best smile. "I know your heart, and it's pure gold – even if you chose some strange paths in life." She gave the woman a deep hug. "Do you trust me?" she asked, whispering into her ear. "If you have faith in yourself and in Whistler, you can do this. Indie and I will ride right beside you the whole way. We'll make the jump together."

Lin tried to give Kit a reassuring smile, but it came out looking uncomfortable, like she was having intestinal issues. The tears that welled up in her eyes, desperately seeking to pour down her cheeks, were not helping to convince Kit of her confidence.

"Char and I have spoken with Whistler. She's confident enough in herself. She just needs Lin to be sure they'll make the jump." Kit nodded to Angel, understanding what to do.

Kit took Lin's face in her hands, intently holding her gaze. "You just need to have faith," she whispered to her. "Faith in yourself. Faith in Titan. Faith that I will never let you down." Kit's eyes flashed golden when she said the last sentence.

"C'mon Whistler," Lin said as she immediately hopped up on her horse's back. Setting her jaw with determination, she rode away from the rift at a slow gallop.

"Is she leaving?" Indie asked, as he moved in beside Kit. "What did you say to her?"

Indie's jaw dropped open as he watched Lin spin her horse around, running at a full gallop towards the rift. "Sweet Titan!" he cried out, pushing Kit out of the way of the oncoming horse. Her hooves were beating the ground so hard it sounded like thunder.

A moment later, Lin and Whistler leapt into the air. There was a strange calm as the sound of thundering hoofbeats came to a sudden halt. Both Kit and Indie stared, stunned, as the horse and rider sailed through the air over the deep, forbidding canyon. Whistler's hooves broke the silence as they touched down on the far side of the rift, with a dozen paces to spare. Lin pulled hard on the reins, causing her horse to skid to a halt. "It's easy!" she screamed out from the far side. A moment later, she vomited up her dinner.

"Our turn," Indie said, giving Kit a sideways glance. "Try not to throw up on me afterwards though."

Kit couldn't help but laugh. "I just need a moment to talk to Lump and Runt, and then we can make the jump." Indie gave her a questioning look, which she ignored and headed over to Runt, with Lump right behind her.

"Lump, I want you to cross the bridge. After I get Angel across, I'm going to help Runt get across." Kit raised her eyebrows, waiting for some sort of acknowledgement from Lump. "Do you understand?"

Lump shrugged. "I know what you're saying, but how is Runt going to cross?"

"Let me worry about that," Kit said, taking his hand in hers. "I want you two to head down the embankment and wait by the bridge. If any of those beasts start heading your way, don't wait, run!" Runt whined in response. He didn't like this plan, but he would follow it if that's what Kit asked of him. "Go now," she said, giving both boys a warm smile. "I'll be with you shortly."

Lump shifted back into dog form before he and Runt headed off down the side of the cliff. "Our turn," Kit called to Indie who was already ready to go. Kit hopped up on Angel's back.

"Time to fly," she said to Kit as they moved away from the rift, giving the mounts enough room to get to top speed.

Following Lin's example, the pair of horses thundered towards the canyon. The moment Angel's hooves left the ground, Kit felt her stomach lurch once again from the sudden change in direction. The feeling quickly passed and was immediately replaced by a feeling of pure joy and utter freedom. Other than the wind whistling in her ears, the world fell into a blissful silence. Every bit of stress melted away as they glided across the great rift. Sadly, the sensation came to an abrupt halt when the two horses landed safely on the far side of the canyon.

Not even bothering to savor the moment, Kit slid off Angel's back and ran towards where the stairway down to the river should be. Just as with the bridge, as soon as she came into contact with it, it suddenly materialized. When she got to the bottom of the stairs, she raced towards the bridge, to the waiting pups. Runt was snarling, his teeth bared, and his hackles raised. Kit looked further down the embankment to spot two Kappa at the river's edge, looking up at the boys.

Kit picked up a large stone from the ground, throwing it with all her might at the river monsters. The stone missed the mark by a good distance, but it got the attention of the creatures. "Lump, get going across the bridge. Runt, wait for my signal."

Lump quickly shifted to human form. "I'm crossing with Runt!" he yelled out. "I'm not leaving him alone."

"He won't be alone," Kit yelled back. "Get across the bridge." Lump shifted back into dog form and took his place beside Runt. "*Bad dog,*" Kit muttered.

The two Kappa that were on the far riverbank were now in the water, heading towards Kit. She took a quick breath before racing down the bank, bringing herself precariously close to the river's edge.

"Titan, hear me," she called out under her breath. A moment later, a pale-blue shroud enveloped her hands. "Freeze!" she screamed, releasing a spray of frost at the water. On contact, ice formed at the river's edge, quickly spreading out towards the middle. One of the Kappa swam under the sheet of ice, while the other tried to clamber up on top of it.

As Kit continued pushing more and more ice towards the river, Runt started doing the same thing, freezing the river from his side. Streams of ice pellets were spewing out from his maw in a focused narrow cone. Lin and Indie cursed as their arrows bounced harmlessly off the Kappa's thick bony shell as it clambered up onto the forming ice bridge. As soon as the creature pulled its mass onto the ice, it barrelled towards Kit with amazing speed considering its bulk. Kit quickly pulled her hammer from its sheath and began racing across the ice towards the Kappa. The blue flames she experienced last time she wielded Fury were not there, leaving the hammer feeling dead in her hands. There was no time to contemplate it though, as she leapt through the air to engage the monster. In a full, two-handed overhead swing, she brought the hammer down onto the shell of the creature with a thunderous crack, releasing a blinding burst of light on contact. The creature screamed out in agony from the attack, trying to spin around at its attacker who was now behind it. Using its enormous claws, it dug into the ice, quickly bringing its bulk to bear, snapping menacingly at the girl.

The bites were coming fast and furious with Kit doing everything she could to avoid the onslaught. Just when it seemed that she was done for, Runt flew past her, catching the Kappa's head in his massive jaws. As he pulled the monster away from Kit, she took the opportunity to strike its shell multiple times with her hammer. Each swing created a series of cracks across the Kappa's back.

Despite the amount of damage Kit was inflicting on the creature, it tossed Runt about like a rag doll, trying to get him to release his grip on its head. Lump practically upended Kit as he went racing past, lunging at the creature's throat. The two canines continued their death grip on the Kappa while Kit kept beating away at it until it finally slowed. It was near death, or it was simply giving up the fight.

Kit called off the two boys, ordering them to race for the riverbank. At the same time, they both released the monster and rushed across the ice towards the river's edge. Just as they were about to make good their escape, the ice near the edge exploded upward, followed by the hulking body of the second Kappa. Unable to stop on the slick surface, both Lump and Runt crashed into the underbody of the creature, falling into the dark river water.

"I come!" Angel said through their bond just as she came crashing down onto the back of the Kappa, driving it into the water. Terror flowed through

Kit, watching as her horse and her two canine companions thrashed about in the river, fighting against a creature that was at home in the dark, turbid waters. It was at that very moment that something inside, something deep inside Kit's mind, snapped. Wrath, unbridled, sprung forth from her soul, driving her forward in a berserker rage. With inhuman speed, she raced across the ice, launching herself at the creature, bringing her hammer down on it with every ounce of her being. On her hammer's impact, there was a dazzling flash of golden light.

⁂

"Kit?" Somebody was calling to her, seemingly through the mists of time. "Kit, wake up." Whoever it was sounded familiar, but it wasn't enough to pull her from the fog clouding her mind.

"Kit. Come back to us," someone else said, familiar, yet faceless. Kit continued to float along in an endless void, disconnected from the tethers of her world. It was cold, but she wasn't alone.

"It's time to return to your friends," said a third voice, this one much closer, much softer, much warmer, and definitely feminine. The coldness immediately vanished.

"Who are you?" Kit asked, searching for whomever it was speaking to her.

"Return to your friends," she said again. "We will meet very soon."

Kit's eyelids fluttered open, revealing Indie and Lin hovering over her, Indie's fingers gently caressing her brow. She bolted upright. "Where are the boys? Where's Angel?"

"We're all safe," Angel said through the bond. *"Thanks to you."*

"They're all fine," Indie said, his face suddenly full of concern. "Your eyes!"

"What about them?" Kit said with a coy smile, batting her lashes at him.

"They're pure gold," Lin said with a low whistle.

"What do you mean?" Kit picked herself up off the ground, searching the area for Angel and the boys. It was only then that she realized that she was no longer inside the canyon.

"They're spectacular," Indie said, lifting Kit's chin so he could look at her directly. "I didn't think it was possible for you to be even more beautiful."

Kit's heart raced at the intimacy of the moment, her face flushing as she returned the intense stare that Indie was giving her.

"You two can make kissy faces all you like after we deal with things in Silverhawk." Lin practically pushed herself between them. "It's going to be dark soon."

Chapter Nine

LILLOET

The world was once again cast in shades of red as Danny soared up into the evening sky. Being airborne gave him a feeling of exhilaration like nothing else in his life. He thought it unfortunate that he couldn't hear the rush of the wind over the crackling of his own flames, but he didn't mind. He especially enjoyed climbing rapidly, and then just stop flapping. When he did, for that brief moment of weightlessness, there were no troubles to be faced, there was no sadness from being away from his friends; everything in his world was right as rain.

Right as rain. That's a funny saying. I wonder what happens to my flames in the rain.

That was about as much as he could think about just before he started plummeting earthward. The feeling of acceleration was almost as good as the weightlessness, but there were no more than two hours of sunlight left, so if he was going to make it to Lilloet without looking like a fireball in the sky, he was going to have to hurry. It took him no time to catch up to Ryn and Breayn, who had left for Lilloet well ahead of him. While in phoenix form, he was unable to communicate, and he needed to let Ryn and Breayn know that he was going to fly ahead. It was the only way he was going to make it on time.

Unsure of how to pass on the information, he flew alongside the hawk, occasionally bursting forward, trying to convey his desire to go faster. Breayn was yelling something at him, but between the wind and his flames roaring in his ears, he couldn't make out a word. It was at that moment that he made the decision. It was likely an idiotic move, but he couldn't see any other option.

With a couple of beats of his flaming wings, he climbed above Ryn. He quickly banked so that he was over top of him before rolling over onto his back. A moment later, Danny took on his Berrat form and started free-falling, hurdling down towards his cohorts.

"I'm going to fly ahead," he screamed out, spreading his arms, hoping that somehow, doing so might slow his descent.

The only reaction he could make out was Breayn's bulging eyes. He wasn't sure if they had heard his message, and he was about to fall below them. He yelled out again, hoping beyond reason that they might hear his words over the sound of the rushing wind.

As soon as Danny passed by, Ryn rolled and went into a dive, matching Danny's speed until they were only a few feet apart. It appeared Ryn was going to try to catch him. His claws were extended, ready to clasp his falling body.

"I'm okay," Danny yelled again. "I'm going to fly ahead! Dark!" As soon as the message became clear, Ryn pulled back his feet and banked hard away from the falling Berrat. Danny stole a look down. The ground was coming up at a horrific rate. If he wasn't going to be able to make the change in time, he was going to slam hard into the ground. He wondered for a brief moment if he would be reborn in his phoenix form, like the first time he had fallen to his death. He had the strangest feeling. He almost felt a desire to find out.

He was barely more than a hundred feet above the ground when his body erupted into flames. He didn't recall choosing to change forms. It must have been the phoenix's desire to not be crushed by the impact. In moments, the young Berrat was in firebird form and swooping out of his perilous freefall. When he started to bank upwards, the flames were barely kissing the rocky ground below. Tiny fires ignited beneath him as he soared back into the heavens. He tilted his wings in salute to his cohorts before beating them heavily, gaining speed by the second. Within a minute, he was at top speed, resembling a comet streaking across the evening sky.

The sky ignited with brilliant oranges and reds as the sun started to dip over the horizon. Trying his best to remain unseen, the phoenix dipped low, flying just above the trees when necessary, diving between the great evergreens when possible. The city of Lilloet was coming into view when the last of the sun dipped out of sight, plunging the sky into deep purples. There was no way he could continue flying without being seen.

The phoenix dipped his head and started his descent towards the forest floor. A clearing had appeared that was broad enough for him to land without igniting the trees on fire. Just before touching down, Danny reduced his speed and transformed back to his Berrat form, landing gracefully on the ground. His vision was still in shades of red and his skin still tingled after the transformation was complete. It would take a few minutes before he fully felt like himself again.

He was left wondering how Ryn and Breayn were going to find him. The only plan he had was that he would fly on ahead. He was several miles from Lilloet's outskirts, so he decided to move closer. By the time the others would arrive, the sun would have fully set and there would be little chance of seeing him if he stayed in the forest.

Despite how far north he was, only a few miles from the North Sea, the trees here were still healthy and numerous. The thickly needled branches of the Berrathian Pine, one of the few trees that grew this far north, provided excellent cover as he continued to head further towards Lilloet. The trees' needles covered most of the ground, cushioning his footfalls, making his movement nearly silent.

He burst out from between two thick pines, stumbling upon two families of Berrat foraging for food. They all paused and stared. Danny raised his hands in peace, but they took it as an attack.

"Run," the oldest of the Berrats said as he drew his dagger. The others ranged in age from about five to perhaps fifteen. The older children gathered up the younger ones and disappeared into the forest. The oldest, a man of perhaps twenty-five cycles waited until his cohorts were gone.

"I mean you no harm," Danny said, taking a step back. "I'm here to fight against your oppressors. I have no quarrel with you."

The man strode towards Danny, reversing his grip on his dagger in preparation to strike. Danny moved away from the man and quickly unslung his bow from his shoulder. Before his attacker could take another step, he had already nocked and drawn an arrow.

"I mean you no harm. Leave now. Be with your family and may Gaia protect you." The knife wielding Berrat took a look to the trees where the younger ones had vanished.

"May she bless you and your family," the man said before he darted off into the forest. Danny blew out a deep breath and returned his arrow to its quiver and shouldered his hunting bow. After making a quick check that the Berrat he had just met were not circling back, he continued heading towards the city, running hard, staying close to the trees to remain hidden in the shadows. When the first of the outer-ring huts came into view, he skidded to a halt. If he were to enter the city, he would surely be spotted, and in his Crow costume, that likely wouldn't go well. He didn't know if there were any free Berrats within the city and he was confident that Lord Byssus' men would know a Crow uniform if they saw one. He had no way of knowing how the soldiers would react if they met.

He had also considered switching into his vole form. He hadn't done it since he was a child, but he felt confident he could still make the change. The hoot of an owl gave him pause. There was a good distance of open ground he'd have to run across, and if there were any predators about, they'd spot him for sure. Deciding he had little other choice, he wrapped his cloak tightly about himself and started trotting towards the nearest hut.

Once he had cleared the treeline, the pine covered ground gave way to tall grasses and low bushes. He did his best to move stealthily through the reedy brown grass as he went from bush to bush. More often than not, the path forced him to move away from the huts as he tried to maintain cover. The progress was painfully slow, and he wasn't sure how stealthy he was actually being. He took a quick look up at the sky to find the moon was barely more than a sliver and light clouds obscured the stars. He took a deep breath and blew it out slowly. Ignoring the bushes, he started heading directly towards the nearest hut, doing his best to stay low and letting the blue-black feathers of his cloak provide him the cover he needed.

Danny's heart sunk as a pair of human soldiers came out from the outer ring of huts. They were dressed in leather and chainmail, with dark surcoats, possibly red. They said something unintelligible to one another before splitting up and heading out in opposite directions. After just a few steps, one of the two guards stopped and turned back to the other.

"Nobody is going to escape," he called out. "They will not risk the lives of the other Berrat. Let's get back inside, where it's warm."

"And if Byssus finds out we've skipped out on patrol duty, what do you think he'll do to us?" the second one responded. "The next group will be here to relieve us before you know it, and we can get back to staying warm."

"I'll see you soon then," the first of the guards said as he turned and resumed his patrol. Danny watched as the pair moved off. When they were a good thirty paces away, he dashed to the building, pressing his back against the mud and branch wall. He moved around the small hut, staying low, keeping his body in the shadows. He made his way to the side of the building, easing himself between the adjacent huts. There were several feet of space between the two shelters, and he continued to keep tight to their walls. When he was in a position to move across the path on his way to the city's center, he heard the first of two voices. He dropped down to his belly and crawled the rest of the way until the people behind the voices came into view.

"The night will be growing colder," the Nomad man said, his voice soft and his eyebrows raised. "Don't you think you'd be more comfortable sharing a bed with me tonight."

"Just because my mate is on patrol doesn't mean he won't be back soon," the Nomad woman replied, moving a bit closer, staring up into the eyes of the other. There was a look of hopeful anticipation in the man's face as he stepped nearer, eliminating any space between the couple. "If he found you with me, he'd gut you and use your skin to make another war drum." A wry smile crossed her lips. "If you're willing to take that chance..."

Without another word, the man spun on his heel and made his way toward the inner ring. The woman laughed and headed into her hut, the same building that Danny was hiding behind. Using the sound of the man's movement for cover, Danny slipped out from between the buildings and followed in his footsteps.

The further Danny traveled towards the city center, the more and more people he was seeing. Most everyone looked to be Berrat, just going about their daily existence. If he hadn't known better, he would have never guessed this to be an enslaved city.

"Oy," a voice called from behind where Danny was standing. He had become so engrossed in watching the people, he had stopped being concerned about staying hidden. "You, what are you doing skulking in the shadows?" A million different things raced through Danny's head, ranging from turning to fight, to bolting into the gathered Berrat, hoping to disappear among the people.

"Who's asking?" Danny said, turning slowly toward the voice. Of all the things he had considered doing, this wasn't one of them. Standing behind him was a Nomad man, dressed in chainmail and a red surcoat, carrying a spear and a buckler. A thick iron helm covered most of his face, making it impossible to get a read on what he looked like. Even from within the shadows that hid his face, Danny could see that his eyes were wide. The man stammered for several seconds, looking to his left and right, like he was searching for an exit.

"My apologies," he stammered, "I... I,"

Danny had no idea why this man was so frightened, but he wasn't going to let this opportunity go to waste.

"I, I, I... what?" he said as he took a step towards the guard. The Nomad took a step away, maintaining his distance. Danny stepped forward again, cocking his head to the side. His hand moved to the dagger at his hip and the man stumbled as he tried to retreat further. He scrabbled about for a moment before dashing off between the huts, disappearing into the darkness. For several seconds Danny could hear the man running. He had no idea why he had reacted that way, but now he needed to see if the gathered Berrat would act similarly. Without saying a word, he moved out from between the huts toward the gathered people.

It wasn't until he was practically standing among them that the first of the Berrat reacted. Her eyes went wide as dinner plates before she threw herself to the ground, bowing deeply to the red-headed man dressed in a Crow uniform. Within seconds, the entire group followed her lead. None looked up. None said a word. A smile tugged at the corner of Danny's mouth as he walked calmly through the group before he disappeared into the shadows between the next row of huts. Whoever they thought he was, they were terrified of him.

"You are the spitting image of The Wing." That's what Calian had said when they'd met the dog soldiers. Could it be true? Could he look so much like him that he could pass for the man?

Row upon row of huts passed by as Danny continued his way toward the city center. This would be the place where Lord Byssus' family would be. He didn't press his luck showing himself to the people. Instead, he kept to the shadows but moved confidently whenever he was in the open. He put on an air of somebody who belonged. It wasn't long until he saw the glow of a massive fire. It seemed as though the city held to the custom of a nightly bonfire where the citizens of the Berrat city would gather. He wondered if there would be a village elder telling stories to those assembled. He didn't remember much of his time in Berrathia as a youth, but Kit had shared many such tales with him.

He didn't know how long it took him to make it to the city's center but when he came to the last of the buildings, a great open courtyard came into view. At its center was a lavish building made of white stone, reflecting the yellows and oranges of the bonfire. There were no elders telling tales. There were no Berrat gathered here at all. There were only Nomads, seated at long trestle tables being served a lavish feast. Berrat women and children moved about, carrying trays of food and large decanters of drink. As a barely dressed Berrat woman was filling a Nomad man's goblet, he decided it was a good time to grope her. His action surprised the woman, and she knocked over his cup spilling the drink all over his food and his lap. With a swipe of his arm, he struck the woman in the face, sending her sprawling across the ground.

Two Nomad guards quickly dragged the battered woman away while two other serving girls came to appease the cruel man. A fire burned from within

Danny's chest, and he longed to release the phoenix and bring justice upon the horrible person. His gaze turned back to the woman being dragged off. The guards took her past the white stone building and into the darkness.

There were at least twenty guards standing in front of the bright stone house, which stood in stark contrast to the rest of the city's mud and stick structures. This had to be the home of Lord Byssus. The only outstanding question now was whether or not the lord's daughter was inside or if she was with those who were being waited upon. His eyes scanned the tables, looking for someone who might be around the right age. There were many women present, but most of them appeared to be too old. Those who were young enough, were totally engaged with whomever they were seated next to. If only he had an idea of what the woman looked like, he might be able to locate her.

On a whim, Danny decided to follow the guards who had carted off the serving girl.

Chapter Ten

Tiny Beginnings

Less concerned for his own safety, and anxious that the serving girl was going to be executed for her actions, Danny threw caution to the wind and sprinted between the huts, doing his best to keep the woman and the guards dragging her away, within view. Even though the bonfire lit up the area like it was daytime, it also cast deep shadows where the Crow-cloaked Berrat could hide and disappear from view.

The two guards dragging the woman were both male, and they were dressed in the same armor and red surcoat as the guard Danny had encountered earlier. They took the woman into a smaller than average hut. When they pulled back the hide that covered the entrance, a bright light spilled out from within. They were inside for barely a minute when the two guards emerged.

"Stand watch," one of them said as he turned to go back inside.

"You stand watch," the other replied, grabbing him roughly by the shoulder. "I get first go this time."

"You can have first go when you outrank me," the first one said, shoving the other back. His hand went to the short sword at his hip. He cocked an eyebrow, practically daring the other to object. His look of superiority vanished when Danny's arrow struck him in the throat. As his hand went to where the fletching was protruding from his neck, a questioning look went to his cohort who stood dumbfounded before him. He was just about to raise an alarm when an arrow struck him in the throat as well. One after the other, the two guards dropped to their knees and fell over onto their faces.

Danny burst from his place of hiding, another arrow nocked and ready to be released. He rushed past the two fallen guards and stepped into the hut. The building was empty, save for the Berrat woman, who was kneeling in the middle of the room, next to a circular fire pit. The dirt floor stained her bare knees, and her split mouth was bleeding badly. She had a look of resignation on her face, as though her fate had been sealed.

"Be at peace, little sister," Danny said as he slung his bow over his shoulder and stepped back out past the animal hide door. A moment later he dragged the first of the two guards into the room. He brought him off to the side, while the Berrat woman stared silently, carefully watching his every move. He slipped back out the door and returned with the second guard. He dragged him across the hut and piled him on top of the first. The squelching noise caused by pulling his arrows from their necks made him grimace.

"Get me something to cover them with," Danny said to the woman. "I'll make sure no one saw what I did." Without waiting for a response, he crept back out the door, into the night.

Outside of the shadows being cast by the bonfire and the sounds of voices from the dinner tables, there was no sign of anybody in the area. After a couple of quick checks, Danny backed through the hide door into the hut. When he entered, the Berrat woman was still sitting back on her heels, next to the firepit in the middle of the room. She looked up at him and started to untie the laces that held her shift closed. Large tears spilled down her cheeks.

"Don't do that," Danny said, his voice harsh. "I'm here to help you, not to… do that." The woman stopped and stared up at the red-headed Berrat dressed in a Crow uniform. She went back to pulling the laces from her shift.

"Please, stop," Danny said. This time his voice was soft and compassionate. "I am here to help. Please, you must believe me."

"You are Split Crows. You are not here to help anyone but yourself."

"No," Danny said, staring down at his feathered cloak. "This is just a disguise. I'm here for Lord Byssus' daughter."

"She will not take a Berrat as a mate, no matter who you are." The woman sneered and looked at Danny from head to toe. "No matter how handsome you *think* you are."

"Please," Danny said again, his head swiveling back to the entrance. "I just have some questions and then you are free to go." The woman laughed at his comment.

"Free to go? And where exactly do you think I can go? Perhaps I can just walk out of the city and into the forests, to live my life as I wish?"

"If my plan works, that is exactly what I hope for you." Danny glared at the woman. She held his gaze, returning it in kind. "I just need to know what Lord Byssus' daughter looks like. I need to find her."

The woman regarded Danny for several long seconds before she finally replied. "Lady Kandyce is within their stone hut. She has not emerged in many days. An illness has taken her."

"What does she look like?" Danny asked, breathing a bit easier now that the woman was talking. "Where will I find her?"

"She is young with long black hair and dark brown eyes. She looks like every other Nomad woman who has befouled our city."

"Please, I know you're angry, but if I don't have a good description of her, I won't know that I've found the correct person." The woman stared at Danny; her mouth clamped shut. "Can you tell me where in the house she might be?"

"She will be above, in the room at the top." She waited for a moment, perhaps trying to gauge Danny's response. "Her room is at the top of the stairs to the right. Lord Byssus' room is to the left."

"There are only two rooms on the second floor?" Danny asked. The woman didn't seem to understand what he meant by *the second floor,* but she eventually nodded. Berrat buildings were built close to the ground. There were no such things as stairs or second floors in a hut.

"Will you be okay?" Danny asked as he started moving towards the hut's exit. The woman's eyes went to the two dead soldiers. Of course, she wouldn't be okay. There would be no way for her to explain these two men. Danny lowered his head and considered the situation. He slipped off his feathered cloak and grabbed the first of the men by his feet and dragged him to the central fire pit. There was a large opening in the hut above the fire to let the smoke escape. He tossed the man upon the burning logs and went back to fetch the second one.

The Berrat woman held her nose at the smell of burning flesh. She quickly moved to a wall, coughing badly as smoke began to fill the room.

"The fire is not hot enough to burn flesh and armor," she said from behind her hands. Danny ignored her protestations and dragged the second man to the fire pit. He tossed him atop his cohort and started coughing as the amount of smoke doubled.

"Shield your eyes," Danny said. "It's going to get bright." He groaned when the woman refused to follow his instructions. He decided to disregard her actions before placing his hands onto the back of the now smoldering guards. A second later, dancing red flames covered Danny's entire body. He pushed his fire toward the guards, the heat growing more and more intense. As his fire grew, Danny lost control of himself and morphed into his phoenix form. There was no way to hide what was happening, so he took advantage of his shape and moved on top of the soldiers, pushing more and more of his heat at them until they turned to ash and molten metal. When the task was complete, he hopped out of the fire and returned to his Berrat self.

The woman was on her hands and knees, her forehead pressed to the earthen floor. Her body was trembling uncontrollably.

"Will you be okay now?" Danny asked. He had no idea what to say at this point. The woman was nodding furiously, but her forehead never left the ground.

"I told you, I'm here to help. You have no need to fear me." The woman gave no reaction to his comment, so Danny donned the Crow cloak and slipped back out into the night.

⁂

As soon as the hut's hide flap closed behind him, Danny took a deep breath of the crisp night air. He looked up into the starry sky, wondering how he was going to meet up with Ryn and Breayn. Again, he scolded himself for not having had a plan on how they'd meet up after he flew ahead. The only thing he knew was that they were all expecting Lady Kandyce to be at the city center. In retrospect, the one garish stone building in a city filled with grass and mud huts should have been enough of a clue as to where to find a noble human in a Berrat city.

The shadows cast by the bonfire continued to provide him excellent cover as he worked his way towards the entrance of the white stone building. Guards here were numerous, but the majority of them seemed more interested in the revelries than doing their duty. Perhaps they just assumed that nobody would be crazy enough to try to enter into the heart of the city of the most sadistic slaver in all of Berrathia.

They didn't expect me.

Danny laughed to himself. He was crazy. He had to be. Nobody in their right mind would be trying to kidnap this man's daughter right out from under his nose. He started to wonder about the woman's illness. What was wrong with her that her father was keeping her within the house for so long. What if her illness was contagious? What if she was already on her deathbed? Could he steal a woman who was already preparing to rejoin the Great Cycle?

He continued skulking in the shadows until he pressed himself up against the back of the white stone house. The stonework was shoddy and uneven. After spending many cycles within the walls of the Temple, its construction beyond reproach, he found himself strangely critical of the quality of this home's craftsmanship. The task of building the home likely fell on the Berrat, and unless they had spent time living amongst humans, they'd have had no experience, or interest, in crafting stone buildings.

A light spilled out from several windows on the second floor. Danny had no way of knowing if that was Lady Kandyce's room or not, but since there were only two rooms, he had at least a fifty-fifty chance that it was where he needed to be. He reached up to grab hold of the edge of a stone, thinking that he could perhaps scale the wall. The construction was so uneven that he thought there was a chance to avoid having to enter through the house's front door. As he gripped the first ledge, the mortar crumbled in his fingers, and he immediately lost his grip.

He stared back up at the windows and blew out a long, slow breath.

The front door, it is.

The way to the side of the house was dark, but the bonfire lit up the entire path along the side wall. The only way he was going to make it to the front was if there was a diversion of some sort, or if every person within view was blind. Danny hung his head down and moved back behind the house and crouched in the shadows.

"I don't care what his rank is, I'm not doing that," said a decidedly female voice. The sound of two people approaching forced Danny to retreat into a darker alleyway.

"But he's also really cute," said a second female. "Who knows, maybe you'll enjoy it." The two women burst out in laughter as they continued past the house and Danny's not-so-good hiding spot. They were both dressed in chainmail, but neither wore a helm. They had long black hair that shone in the night, catching the light of the bonfire. They both had tall tankards in their hands and their steps were unsteady.

The Berrat held his breath as they walked past, just inches away from him. His hand sat on the hilt of his dagger as he waited and listened. The two women paused, barely a couple of paces away. They had stopped talking. He was sure they had spotted him. He dared not move. His lungs were starting to burn from holding his breath. He was going to need to breathe, and soon, or he was going to pass out.

"You know, my hut's not too far away," one of them said, her voice suggestive.

"And I'm not that drunk," replied the other. "Maybe we can both find somebody to warm our bed tonight. Nobody has *warmed me* in nearly a moon." The two women burst into laughter again and they continued along. He slowly let out his breath and quickly sucked in some fresh air. He watched for several more seconds as the women retreated between the rows of huts. Danny looked up again at the windows above.

If only I could fly without being seen.

He couldn't fly but another idea came to him. He furrowed his brow and concentrated. He tried to will it into happening, but he could not. He tried just allowing it to happen, but that brought about no success either. He thought back to how he had changed into his phoenix form. He didn't have to force it, he just thought about it, and he *became* the phoenix. Suddenly, everything became very bright and exceptionally large. His heart was racing out of control. He looked down at his hands. They were now paws, tiny little claw-tipped paws. He had changed into his vole form. His night vision had improved dramatically, and his sense of smell had become so strong that he could almost taste the footprints of the women who had just walked past. It had been many cycles since he had taken the vole form. He had completely forgotten how amazing it was to be the tiny rodent.

Chapter Eleven

KANDYCE

Danny, the rodent, looked up to the second-floor windows. Warm yellow light poured out, lighting the way to his destination. He tentatively took hold of the wall with his front paw, testing his grip. His tiny claws easily found purchase on the rough white stone. Pushing off with his back feet, he grabbed hold with his free paw, barely an inch above where he was. He hung there, frozen, barely off the ground. The claws of his back feet were able to get a secure grip, allowing him to reach up with his first paw, taking him barely another inch closer to his destination. He paused and looked up at the light. If he didn't hurry, it would be sunrise by the time he reached the window.

His ability to grip onto the stone was far better than he could have hoped for. With each step he took, scaling the side of the wall, his confidence grew. After barely more than a dozen steps, his pace picked up until he was scampering up the side of the wall at nearly full speed. At no point did he fear he'd fall. He found himself taking something of a zigzag pattern up the steep climb. He just instinctively seemed to know the best path. He had no trouble letting the vole spirit within take charge. after all, what did Danny know about climbing. His last great climb ended with him plummeting to his death, an experience he did not want to endure a second time. Before he realized it, he was sitting on the window's ledge, peering into the room. His beady black eyes immediately adjusted to the brightness within.

A Nomad woman, dressed in a pale-yellow nightgown, was seated on an ornate bench at a black and gold dressing table with a wide mirror. The table and bench shared a similar design. They were both beautifully crafted and were completely out of place with anything else that might have been found in the Berrat city. She was brushing her long black hair with an unsteady hand. She seemed to struggle to hold its tortoiseshell lacquered handle as it passed over her wavy black locks. Danny adjusted his position on the window's sill to get a better view of the girl's reflection. He couldn't be certain, but this had to be Lady Kandyce.

The woman's face was sallow and almost gray. Her big brown eyes had no life in them. She seemed to be staring vacantly at her own reflection as she tried her best to smooth out her mane that reflected the roaring fire within the hearth. Her hand trembled badly as she tried to put her brush down on the table, spilling it onto the rough wooden floor. She sighed deeply as she stared at her wayward brush. She swung her legs around on the bench and tried to pick it up, but she couldn't seem to muster enough strength. Her arm was shaking badly as she reached out. When it appeared hopeless, she waved her hand dismissively at the brush and groaned. She looked to be on the verge of tears.

"I'll get that for you, dear," said a middle-aged westerner who had just entered her chambers. He was overweight, with long blonde hair that had been heavily oiled and tied off in a ponytail. He was perhaps in his late forties or early fifties. Danny had trouble guessing people's ages. Anyone over twenty-five cycles looked old to him, especially humans. The man held a tray with what looked to be a large bowl of broth and a mug. The vole's nose twitched. Even though the man wreaked of lavender and musk, something in the food smelled off. He recognized that odor, it warned him of danger. It was the scent of hemlock, the scent of poison.

The man placed the tray on the girl's dressing table. She looked at the contents of the bowl and mug and shook her head. "I'm not hungry, father. I think I'd just like to go to bed." She had the saddest eyes Danny had ever seen. She seemed to be pleading with her father, begging him to not feed her the food.

Her father. This is Lord Byssus.

"Nonsense, child. You need your strength." He made a grand motion towards the tray, the long pillowy sleeves of his red silk robe waving about as he did. He stroked his daughter's hair as he pushed the tray closer to her.

Why would he poison his daughter? What is to be gained by such an action?

"I will, Father. I promise I'll eat it later. I just want to rest my head for a little while. Brushing my hair... drained what little strength I had."

The man stepped past her and picked the brush up from the floor. He blew on it, like it had somehow been soiled for touching the wood. He gently ran its bristles over the girl's hair. With each stroke of the brush, the jewels of the many rings on his fingers caught the light from the fire's dancing flames. "We have servants who can do this for you. You should save your strength."

"You mean slaves," she retorted. "Servants are paid, and they can leave at their leisure. Nobody here is allowed to leave, including me."

"Oh, child. Why would you want to leave? Where would you go, especially in your condition? You know how sickly you've been." The smallest hint of a spark lit in her eyes. It didn't last long, but it was there.

"Can I have some privacy, please," she said, doing her best to wiggle away from her father's touch. "I just want to rest for a short while and then I'll eat my broth and drink my tea." The man's cheek twitched at her words. The slightest hint of a sneer appeared at the corner of his mouth.

"As you wish, child. I'll come back in a while to check in on you. Rest well."

The girl rose from the bench on shaky legs. It was perhaps ten paces from where she sat to the edge of her bed. She shuffled her feet, her arms outstretched before her. Her father stood and watched as she made her way. He did not offer to assist. She practically collapsed onto the mattress when she reached the bed, landing in an awkward position. She fumbled about for several moments until she finally righted herself. She kicked off her moccasins and, with the help of her hands, pulled her limbs onto the bed. Her nightgown lifted slightly in the process, exposing her deathly thin legs.

Lord Byssus huffed slightly as the girl pulled up her covers. Without another word, he left the room. Lady Kandyce whimpered quietly and closed her eyes.

"Your father is poisoning you," Danny said. He had shifted back into his Berrat form. He was sitting on the window ledge with his feet hanging into the room. The girl gave a small shriek at the sound of his voice. When she looked up at him her face turned sour.

"Are you here to finish me off?" she asked. It seemed she recognized Danny. It also looked like she despised him.

"Why would you say that?"

"Because you Crows are murderous bastards and you're the worst of the lot." Danny raised an eyebrow at the comment. He had been mistaken for The Wing yet again. He looked down at his black feather cloak and sighed. He gave the woman his best grin and ran his fingers through his red hair. She stared blank-faced back at him. Her chest was rising and falling with each rapid, shallow breath she took. Even though she was putting on a good front, his presence was causing her a great deal of stress.

"Who exactly do you think I am?" Danny asked as he hopped down from the windowsill. He walked casually across the room to where her soup and tea sat. Without his vole senses he could no longer detect the poison. He sniffed at the soup. It actually smelled pretty good.

"There is only one red-headed Berrat in the Split Crows. Are you denying that you're him?"

"And who is this devilish man you speak of. What is his name?" Kandyce propped herself up in the bed and glared at him. The corner of her mouth looked like it wanted to curl into a sneer, but she managed to keep it in check.

"I don't know your name, but I know that you're The Wing – or whatever it is your crazy followers call you." The girl's jaw was now set hard, and her eyes narrowed. "If you're here to kill me, then get it over with."

"And why would you think that? Why would I kill you?"

"Because my father is taking too long. His poison isn't working fast enough."

"You know that your father is poisoning you?" This encounter wasn't unfolding anything like how Danny had expected it to. The truth was, he really didn't have much of a plan at all. He'd been winging it ever since he got to Lilloet.

"Are you surprised that I figured it out? Is that why you've come to finish off what he started?"

"I am not who you think I am," Danny said. "My name is Danny Fox-Dancing, and truth is, I had come to kidnap you. To use you against your father." His comment made the woman laugh. "I am here to put an end to the slave trade and to liberate my people."

"I hope you have an army, or a dragon, to support you," Kandyce said, her voice filled with cynicism, "because kidnapping me will gain you nothing."

"But why is your father poisoning you? Why are you letting him? If you know the food is tainted, why do you eat it?"

"I don't, at least not after the first time he gave it to me." The woman's big brown eyes were on the verge of tears, while the growing tension in her jaw stood in stark contrast. "I have been feigning my illness, with a simple glamor."

"A what?"

"A bit of simple magic, that I inherited from my mother. I can, with some effort, make myself to look however I'd like. I can be beautiful, or I can be sickly." She ran her fingers through her long black hair. "Lately, I've been making myself look ill so that my father would believe I've been consuming the poison he's been feeding me."

The idea that her father was poisoning her made Danny's stomach churn. He had no idea what it meant to be a father but torturing your child with diluted poison was cruel beyond reasoning.

"Why?" Danny shook his head, still unable to wrap his mind around the situation. "Why would he want to kill you?" The tears in the woman's eyes finally broke free and tumbled down her cheeks.

"For the same reason that he killed my mother. She spoke against him, publicly. She said that she did not approve of the way he treated the people here in Lilloet. She said that she would not allow him to ruin the city the same way he ruined Wantage. She didn't want to be exiled once again because of my father's cruelty. Before the moon went dark, he publicly murdered her." The color seemed to return to the woman's skin. Whether it was her anger that had wiped away the sallowness of her face, or that she had stopped putting magic into her glamor, she suddenly no longer appeared ill. "The soldiers rebelled against him. If it wasn't for his personal guard and the support of the Crow, he'd have been publicly lynched, just like my mother."

The door to Kandyce's room creaked open, pushing Danny's heart up into his throat. His back was to the door. The look on the girl's face told him that her father had just entered the room.

"Lord Wing," Lord Byssus said. His voice trembled as the words came out. "I wasn't expecting you."

"Why is this girl still alive?" Danny asked, keeping his back to the man. "We cannot have her causing a rebellion like her mother."

"I, um, am working on it," Lord Byssus replied. Kandyce's eyes immediately filled with tears. She already knew he was poisoning her, but somehow, hearing the words from his own lips cut her deeply.

"I'll... I'll do it right now." The sound of steel being drawn from a sheath made Danny wince. It sounded like the man had drawn a dirk. There was no way he could draw his bow in time. He slowly let his hand slip beneath his cloak to pull his dagger. Kandyce's eyes flicked between the two men.

"You would draw your dagger at my back?" Danny growled. "Perhaps it is me you're trying to kill?" Lord Byssus' weapon clattered on the floor. A look of revulsion crossed Kandyce's face.

"You are nothing more than a sniveling coward," she said. "I can't believe you found the courage to kill mother. I can't imagine how you ever managed to climb to a position of power."

Danny pushed his dagger back into its sheath. His heart rate returned to normal. His back was still to the lord.

"Status report," Danny growled out.

"Lord Wing?" Byssus' voice came out as a high-pitched squeak. The floorboards creaked as he shifted his weight from foot to foot. "A status of what? I don't know what you're asking me." Danny dropped his head low and growled again.

"If you don't know how to provide a status report, perhaps I should replace you with someone who does."

"No," Lord Byssus sputtered. "No need for that. Status report. I can do that." There was an awkward silence as the man tried to gather his thoughts. Danny cleared his throat and the man practically jumped.

"My soldiers are primed and ready to head out. I will have them seaside, ready for boarding the ships when the sun rises." Danny furrowed his brow. Where would they be sending the soldiers? It wasn't a question he could ask. If the Wing was expecting soldiers to be loaded on ships, it had to be for an invasion of some kind.

"How many soldiers will you have at the ready?" Danny asked. It seemed like a reasonable question. If The Wing was sending him ships, knowing the number of soldiers was critical information.

"I will have four thousand soldiers as agreed upon, Lord Wing."

"And are these soldiers all loyal? Do you trust them all?" Danny asked. "How many will you be leaving behind to maintain the peace here?"

"My soldiers are all loyal to me," Lord Byssus stated. Even though Danny had his back to the man, he could tell from his voice that Lord Byssus was puffing out his chest. "I will maintain a garrison of five hundred soldiers here. More than enough to put down any rabble that dares to stand against me."

"Your men are not loyal to you, father. They fear what Lord Wing here will do to them if they act against you. Without the backing of the Split Crows, you are nothing." The woman's voice was full of venom. But Danny got the impression that the comment was as much for his benefit as it was for her to spurn her father.

"Quiet your mouth, girl. You are as empty-headed as your mother. I will never understand why the soldiers loved that woman the way they did. She was weak, like you. She would have coddled the entire lot, like they were her children. Soldiers are weapons to be wielded. Nothing more."

"Mother did not *coddle* the soldiers. But she would not force them to perform the heinous acts you demanded of them. If you could have your way, you'd turn them all into butchers. Using the lives of women and children to force your soldiers to fight for you is not loyalty. You're a sick, twisted, coward. You will never be anything more." The woman's comments made Danny laugh.

"You can't even garner the support of your child? How can you expect to have the love of your soldiers?"

"I do not need their love," Lord Byssus spat out. "I only need them to follow my orders. How I get them to do that is irrelevant. When I put their feet to the fire, they move, or they burn." Whatever fear the man held of The Wing disappeared, his true nature bubbling to the surface. Danny's hands ignited in flame.

"An interesting choice of words," he replied. He turned around to face Lord Byssus for the first time. Danny's eyes, too, were now aflame, turning their once hazel-green color to a fiery red. "I wonder how you will behave when I put *your* feet to the fire." The lord didn't even flinch when Danny turned towards him.

"Do you expect your little parlor trick to scare me?" Lord Byssus' hands turned blue, like they were made of ice. A wicked grin crossed his lips. He brought his hands together and a swirling ball of blue frost formed between his fingers. He threw his hands forward, releasing the ball like it was shot from a catapult. The impact of the blast sent Danny across the room, his back landing hard against the wall. The impact was bad, but the pain from where he'd been struck felt like he was on fire – except fire didn't hurt him. This pain was agonizing. The flames in his eyes were the first to go out, followed shortly by the flames on his hands.

Another blast from Lord Byssus crashed into Danny's left shoulder, slamming him into the wall a second time. Numbness spread across his arm, all the way down to his fingertips. His skin was turning a pale shade of blue. He could feel it slowly spreading down from his shoulder towards his hand. Lord Byssus' eyes were wide with a crazed look of glee.

"A minor mage pretending to be the great Lord Wing. I do like your pretty wig though. Maybe I'll keep it for myself. I've always thought I would look good with red hair." He strode over to Danny to look down upon the fallen Berrat. He had a maniacal look on his face. He looked like he was in ecstasy as he gloated over the injured man. He reached down and grabbed Danny by the hair and gave it a solid tug. When the Berrat screamed out, it made the man laugh even harder.

"You're an actual red headed Berrat. Lord Wing will reward me greatly when I deliver you to him. To think, he's been combing the entire kingdom looking for red-heads and I catch one sneaking into my home." He was practically dancing on the spot. "I cannot believe my good fortune. Perhaps when the Crows take Ravenlord, they will appoint me as Lord Protector."

The pain in Danny's chest and arm was excruciating, as his skin continued turning a pasty, pale blue. He tried summoning the phoenix, but it was nowhere to be found. It would not heed his calls.

"Guards!" Kandyce called out. "Guards, to me!" she called out again. Moments later, six Nomad men dressed in chainmail and blood-red surcoats came bursting through the doors. They were carrying spears and light, round shields. There was a look of apprehension on their faces as they saw their lord standing over the red-headed Berrat dressed in a Crow's feathered cloak.

"Take my father into custody. He has attacked Lord Wing and he must pay for his crime."

"Fools," Lord Byssus bellowed out, "this is not The Wing. He's an imposter." The man's eyes went wide like he suddenly had an idea. "He conspired with my daughter to kill me. Take them both into custody. We'll have a double hanging in the morning." The guards stood motionless, torn between who to believe.

"My father has been trying to poison me. Ever since he murdered my mother, he's wanted me dead." Kandyce pointed to the bowl of soup and the cup of tea. The captain of the guards, Garret Bowwind, gave her a dubious look. "Try it if you don't believe me."

The man looked at the food and then back at Kandyce. Lord Byssus' face was getting redder by the moment. In the few seconds, while the guards considered their stories, the lord lost his mind.

"I said, take them into custody," he bellowed out again. He was stamping his feet and pumping his fists by his side. When Captain Bowwind continued to waver on what to do next, the lord's hands once again became encased in ice. Holding his hands out in front of himself, he advanced on his own men.

"Burn!" Danny ground out. He could feel the phoenix deep beneath the surface, struggling to free itself. It was as though the man's cold attack had created a disconnect between Danny and the phoenix spirit within him.

"Burn!" he said again. He could not call on the flames, but he could feel the warmth of the fire spirit within himself. Its heat was radiating outward, coursing through his body. The pain of his frozen limb dissipated, replaced with warmth that filled his soul. His hand's normal color was slowly returning. He clenched and unclenched his fist several times before looking up at Lord Byssus. He was still bearing down on his own men. They had leveled their weapons at their lord, trying to do what they could to keep him at a distance. This act of self defense enraged Lord Byssus even further. He grasped hold of the tip of the spear closest to him. An evil grin spread across his face as frost poured out of him, running up the shaft of the weapon until it reached the guard's hand. He yelped and released the weapon when the frost contacted his skin. He stared wide-eyed at his now frozen hand. The frost continued spreading up his arm and across his neck and head. In mere seconds, the man was a block of solid ice. A weak gasp escaped his mouth before he fell forward onto his face, smashing into hundreds of tiny ice shards.

"How many of you must I kill before you take this man into custody?"

Captain Bowwind's eyes moved to Lady Kandyce. He looked to be pleading with her. She nodded her head slightly. She didn't want to see any more of the guards killed.

"Your weapons, all of them," Captain Bowwind said, holding out his hand. Danny reluctantly handed him his bow and quiver, which the man slung over his shoulder.

"All your weapons," the captain said. "Don't make me have to search your body." Danny groaned and pulled his dagger from its sheath and handed it over. The captain turned his attention to Kandyce, who returned his look with one of outrage.

"And where exactly do you think I might have a weapon? And if you lay a finger on me, I'll scratch your eyes out."

"Take him," the captain said, motioning towards Danny. The other guards immediately fell on the Berrat and dragged him out the door. The captain inclined his head slightly to Kandyce. He held his hand out towards the exit, beckoning her to lead the way.

Chapter Twelve

The Crimson Ale

The sun was low in the western sky when the group made it to the outskirts of Silverhawk. Its bright white walls glistened in the late-day sun while the single, blue-topped spire reflected the oranges and reds of the day's dying light. The platforms that lined the spire formed the city's rookery of great-hawks and griffons. A few of the hawk-riders were circling the city, their long red banners flapping behind them. They were likely on their final patrol before darkness swallowed up the city streets. Kit found herself staring longingly up at the riders straddling their feathered mounts.

Most of the merchants who sold their wares in the garishly colored tents outside the city gates had closed up and left for the day. All that remained were a few stragglers, plus those who had more permanent structures. The city gates still remained open, but there was a larger contingent of guards present, seemingly more alert than those Kit had encountered the first time she had come to the city.

"State your business," one of the City Watch bellowed at the group, slamming the haft of his long spear onto the ground.

"We seek food and shelter for the night," Indie called back, turning Char towards the guard. The explanation was apparently enough for the Watch, moving out of the way to let the group pass. One of the guards commented on how handsome the dogs were.

"The tavern is this way," Kit said as she headed off towards the Crimson Ale. "Don't forget, they're expecting me to be in charge."

"Yes, Mistress," Indie replied, lowering his head in respect. "By your command."

"And don't forget it," Kit added with just a hint of a smile.

It was only a few minutes from the front gate to the tavern where the Auctioneers were located. Hopefully, there would be no members of the Scarlet Tide present. It had been a long day and getting into a fight with vampires, or even vampire wannabes, was not a part of Kit's plans. All she wanted to do was make sure that the slavers had treated their captives well, and that they clearly understood that Kit was in charge.

"I guess we're here," Indie said, staring up at a sign hanging off the building to their right. The thick wooden placard was shaped like a shield with a beer-mug carved into it. The mug's contents were painted red with a bright pink foam on top. Below the mug were the words, "Crimson Ale."

"Let me know if anything is going on outside," Kit said to Angel through their bond.

"As you wish, Mistress!" the little roan whinnied in response, making Kit laugh to herself.

The group dismounted from their horses outside the tavern, tying them up to the available hitching posts. Suddenly, Lin gasped and dragged Kit close enough to whisper to her. "We don't have the tattoos anymore. What are we going to do?"

Kit got a concerned look on her face as her hand instinctively reached to where the tattoo had been. "Don't worry about it. I'll talk my way past it if it comes up." Without so much as another word, Kit pushed open the door to the tavern. Runt and Lump scrambled around Kit's legs, trying to get in before her.

Torches burned on the walls and a large fire blazed in the hearth, chasing away the evening's gathering darkness, casting the tavern in a warm, guttering glow. The aroma of stale beer and urine assaulted Kit's senses, making her cringe internally. Old sturdy tables filled the left side of the tavern. A number of surly looking people looked up briefly as Kit entered before quickly busying themselves to avoid making eye contact with her. The long wooden bar that took up the right side of the tavern had several more people seated at stools. Like the others, they quickly turned away as the group entered. When Kit caught sight of the bartender, she bellowed at him.

"Carver, where's Nicks?"

The bartender's face went bone white. "Mistress, you're early."

"You didn't answer my question," Kit threatened, her eyes flashing golden.

The balding bartender, with a heavily stained apron that struggled to hide his ample belly, stared at her for a moment, blinking rapidly. "She's on a raid and won't be back for a while. She left me in charge while she's gone."

"Show me the prisoners you have so far," Kit said as she started striding towards the back of the tavern, to where the cell was. Patrons began scrambling to get out of her way while Carver raced out from behind the bar. Kit groaned to herself when she remembered that she was too short to see through the small window near the top of the door. She stared intently at a nearby chair before her eyes fell to Lin.

"Here, Mistress," Lin said as she quickly dragged a chair to the front of the door. Indie and the boys took up a defensive position as many of the patrons started to gain interest, gathering around them with a look of expectation on their faces.

With no acknowledgement to Lin, Kit climbed up on the chair and peered inside the cell. "Four?" she screamed out. "In all this time, you only managed to secure four prisoners?" As Kit asked the question, she could hear the sound of steel ringing as Lin drew her swords.

"The... the masters came and took who we had." Sweat was already pooling on Carver's brow, his head swiveling about like he was searching for an escape route.

"They were not theirs to take!" Kit snarled at the petrified barkeep. "They were mine to deliver and receive my dues," she practically screamed.

"G-g-get the purse from behind the till," Carver called to a man sitting on a stool near the entrance. He was nursing a tankard of ale, all the while using the sleeves of his tunic to polish the bar's badly marred wood. "They paid handsomely," Carver said, turning back to Kit. "They were extra pleased that the prisoners were in good condition."

"When did they come?" Kit asked as a man scurried over to hand her the purse. She took a quick peek, finding a good number of gold dragons inside.

"Late last night," Carver replied, mopping the sweat from his brow with a rag from his waistband.

"They've left for Cormorant already?" Kit asked, tossing the purse to Indie. When she saw Carver nodding furiously, she moved in a bit closer to him. "Why's Nicks on a raid then, if the prisoners have been paid for and shipped to the docks?" Carver stared blankly at Kit, mopping more sweat from his face. "Was she planning on hiding last night's sale?" Before Carver could even reply, Kit pressed with more questions. "And what of these four? Where did they come from?"

"Drunks," the bartender replied, as several more beads of sweat dripped down the side of his forehead. "They came in and drank their fill but couldn't pay."

"Idiot," Kit growled. "Release them. Now! If they're from the city, people will be looking for them. We don't need the Watch breathing down our necks." When a look of confusion crossed Carver's face, she scowled heavily at him. "What?"

"We own the Watch." Carver wiped his brow again, cringing slightly, fearing that he was about to take a beating.

Kit quickly remembered Lin's comment when they were here the first time; how she believed the Silverhawk Watch were in on the operation.

"Yes, she knows that," Lin interjected, running her hand across her face. "Think! Even if we've bought and paid for them, they still need to appear to be doing their job. All we need is some do-gooder that's not on the payroll showing up, asking questions, shining a lantern where we want to keep things in the shadows."

"Yes, Mistress." Carver pushed the chair away and pulled the key from around his neck. When he opened the door, the people inside cowered in the corner of the small cell. Unlike the last time that Kit was here, when the cell reeked of moldy straw and feces, the room was somewhat clean and the odor was, at least, bearable.

Kit pulled Carver out of the way and stepped inside. "Leave," she said, in a low threatening tone. "Come back again and your life is forfeit. Speak of this to anyone, and your life is forfeit, along with the lives of everyone you've ever cared about." She turned back toward the door, stopping just before she exited. "Consider your freedom a courtesy. Remember my face. Remember my name – Kit Standing Bear – and remember that it's because of me that you're still drawing breath." When she looked at the prisoners, they were all nodding. One was weeping openly. "I suggest you leave now and don't look back."

Kit motioned to a table in the back corner of the tavern. There were already several patrons there, likely all members of the Auctioneers. "I want that table. Clear everyone out." Both Lin and Indie gave Kit a wicked grin before they started making their way over. Long before they arrived, however, everyone within three tables had already scrambled to get out of their way.

"What's available from the kitchen?" Kit asked Carver, her tone substantially friendlier than it had been.

"Whatever you desire, Mistress," he replied with an obsequious bow.

Kit struck him firmly with the back of her hand, busting open his lower lip in the process. "That's not what I asked you, now is it?"

"We have boar and beef, Mistress." Carver lifted his head to Kit while managing to keep his eyes lowered. Blood trickled down from his split, quivering lip. "We also have roasted brown beans, and onion soup – but I wouldn't recommend the soup. We also have freshly baked breads."

"That's more like it," Kit said giving the bartender a small grin. "Bring it all to my table. Except the soup. But keep the soup hot – extremely hot. I might have use of it when Nicks shows up."

Kit had barely taken a seat with her cohorts when two scantily clad women came over with trays heaped with food. One woman had long yellow hair, the color of wheat in the fall. The other woman had chin-length, mousy brown hair. Kit's mouth almost instantly started watering, even though the meats all looked charred to the point of being inedible. "Are you cold?" she asked the servers after they put the trays on the table.

"Mistress?" one of them asked, wringing her hands, wilting under Kit's scrutiny. "Cold, Mistress?"

"You're barely wearing any clothing," Lin chimed in. "Mistress Kit asked you if you were cold." Both girls immediately started shaking their heads. Lin gave them a warm, yet disarming smile. "Just so you know, she really does not like being lied to."

"Yes, Mistress. We're always cold." The serving girl briskly rubbed the goosebumps that covered her arms to make her point.

"From now on," Kit said with enough volume that everyone in the tavern could hear her. "From now on, you will wear whatever you choose to wear, covering up whatever you choose to cover up." The two women stared at each other; their expression full of terror.

"You have nothing to fear," Kit said with genuine warmth. "Have you eaten today?"

"No mistress," one of them responded, looking down at the copious amount of food at their table. "We eat when the tavern closes."

"At what hour does it close?" Indie asked.

"Never," replied the yellow-haired woman, a hint of a scowl crossing her face as she turned her attention to Carver.

"Then sit and join us," Kit said, motioning to two chairs at one of the empty tables beside them. As the girls went to sit at the table, Kit interrupted. "Not over there. Join us at my table. Bring those chairs with you. There is enough room for us all." When the women stopped and stared, Lin jumped from her place and brought one of the chairs and set it down next to her own. When she motioned to it, the brown-haired server reluctantly took a seat. The other server shrugged and dragged her own chair, taking a place opposite Kit.

"What are your names?" Kit asked as she cut a large chunk of meat from the boar roast. She sliced off a thick piece and jammed it into her mouth. She quickly carved off two large chunks and tossed them to the boys who had taken up residence beneath the table. "Please, help yourselves," she said with a juicy grin. Even though the meat looked horribly overcooked, it was remarkably tasty.

"My name is Sellina, and my friend's name is Jayne," the yellow-haired girl said as she took a small loaf of bread. She was holding it expectantly, waiting for permission to eat. Seeing her nervousness, Lin quickly grabbed a plate from one of the trays and started heaping it with various foods. Indie gave her a smile and did the same thing. A moment later, both of the serving girls had large plates of food in front of them.

"You," Kit started to say before swallowing the overly large piece of meat she had been masticating in her mouth. "You two were here when I was playing cards with Gaoler. Is that not correct?" Both of the girls nodded lightly, their eyes searching each other out.

"Yes," Sellina answered, taking a small nibble off the hank of beef on her plate. "We are much happier having you as our owner, if you don't mind me saying." Kit's eyes darkened at the comment.

"I do not own you. Nobody owns you. I will be sure you are properly paid for your services here. If you want to seek work elsewhere, you are free to do so."

"We have no place else to go," Jayne said. "If it's all the same to you, we'd like to stay."

"Good," Kit muffled out as she stuffed yet another hunk of meat into her mouth.

Changing of the Guard

The group ate their fill, emptying every platter on the table. Sellina and Jayne both looked like they were about to fall into a food coma. "You're much nicer than Gaoler was," Jayne said as she finished her tankard of ale. "I haven't eaten this much food... well, ever."

"If you treat her with respect, she will return it tenfold," Lin slowly whispered back to her, letting her lips linger close to her ear. "She can be your best friend, or your worst nightmare."

"I know good people when I see them," Sellina replied, with a slight slur. "You can trust good people, especially ones with beautiful, golden eyes like yours." Sellina rocked slightly in her chair, using the table to steady herself. "Just like that other lady, with the golden eyes. Everyone is terrified of her, but she's always been nice to us."

"What other lady?" Kit asked.

"She comes here, from time to time," Jayne said, as she continued to stare at Lin. "They're afraid of her. They all are. But she's always kind to us."

Kit suddenly remembered the woman who spoke in her defense during her card game with Gaoler. "Where's she from? Why does she come here?"

"I don't know," Sellina said, her eyes becoming less and less focused by the second. "She just comes, eats some food, watches, and leaves." Sellina gave Kit a crooked smile. "She don't talk much."

Kit's heart started racing, her mind spinning. She had never seen anybody with gold eyes like hers. It couldn't be a coincidence. The tavern door crashed open, interrupting Kit's musings. People in manacles came tripping in through the doorway, pushed by some unseen force. Two of them were children, wailing at the top of their lungs.

"With the four we've got, this lot makes twelve," bellowed someone from behind the crowd of prisoners. "Open the cell and pour us a round!" There were loud cheers from the rest of the tavern's patrons. "This ought to be enough to make our new *mistress* happy." Thugs started shepherding the prisoners to the cell until Kit blocked their way. "What's the hold up, get these sheep into their pen before I start slaughtering them."

Kit pushed her way through the mass of bodies until she was standing face to face with Nicks. "Is that any way to treat *my guests*?"

"Mistress Kit." Nicks gave Kit a slight bow. "I wasn't expecting you until tomorrow."

"Clearly," Kit growled, stepping closer to Nicks. "Report!"

"It's been slow. We only had four prisoners, so I rounded up some more," Nicks began seeking out the other members of her raiding party. Every time she looked at them, they lowered their gaze, seemingly afraid to make eye contact. "Now there are twelve. A nice number to bring to the masters, don't you think?"

"You've only managed twelve since I left?" Kit rested her hand on the head of her battle hammer, her fingers drumming along the side of its ornate mithril head.

"Like I said, it's been slow." Nicks gave Carver a motion, like she was requesting a round of drinks. He was slowly, almost imperceptibly shaking his head, clearly trying to warn her, but Nicks was too frightened or too dim to catch on. Carver poured a mug of ale and slid it over to the woman, clearing his throat as he did. Again, completely missing the cue, Nicks took a long pull from her draft. "Where's your mark?"

"Excuse me?" Kit said, now pulling her hammer from its sheath.

"Have your lies made you deaf? The masters don't know you. When I spoke to them, they said they'd never heard of you before." Obviously feeling like she had the backing of her entire crew, Nicks gave those around her a smug smirk. Again, none of her supposed cohorts met her gaze. A moment later, they parted as Runt moved in beside Kit. When Nicks saw him, the blood drained immediately from her face. "W-w-wolf!" she stammered, just before her eyes glazed over. She coughed suddenly, spraying small droplets of blood from her mouth, before dropping face first to the ground. Behind where she had been standing was Sellina, a bloodied dagger in her fist.

"She won't lay a hand on any of us ever again," the yellow-haired woman said with a dangerously innocent smile.

"You are more than you seem," Kit said as she wiped the blood spatter from her cheek.

"No, Mistress, I'm nobody. But today, you made me feel like somebody worthy – even if I'm just a bar wench." Sellina slid her bloodied dagger into a hip-holster high on her thigh.

"Carver, who was second in command?" Kit asked as she used her toe to nudge Nicks, checking to see if she had passed to the Great Cycle.

"I guess I am," he replied nervously. "I used to answer to Nicks, but now..."

"You answer to me and only me – not even the masters." Kit's eyes flashed at him as she spoke.

"Yes, Mistress," he replied, bowing slightly.

"My name is Kit, and that is how you will refer to me. Am I clear?"

"Yes, Mistress Kit." Carver, along with a good number of the other patrons, replied back in unison.

Kit growled under her breath, deciding not to bother pursuing the matter any further. "Sellina and Jayne are your seconds. Understood? They're going to run the tavern and you're going to run the operation. Spread the word to the members. If anybody objects... follow Sellina's example. Now, who has the keys to our *guests'* manacles?" Sellina knelt beside Nicks' body and slipped off the keychain that hung from her neck. She gave Kit a smile as she tossed it to her.

"I want fresh bedding and hot meals for all the guests." It was only at that moment Kit noticed that the two crying children were silent. As she moved back through the group of prisoners, she saw why. Both Indie and Lump were entertaining them. Lump was letting one of them rub her face in his fur, while the other, a small boy of maybe six cycles, was twirling Indie's long braids.

"Where are your parents?" Kit asked the older boy. His face immediately screwed up, like he was about to start bawling again.

"They were either killed or left behind," a Berrat woman sneered, disgust spreading across her face. "What do you care? You're just going to sell us off, anyway."

"Not this time," Kit whispered back to her. "Not while I'm around."

She worked her way through the group of eight prisoners, unlocking the manacles on each of them – starting with the children. She spoke softly to each person, offering them whatever comfort she could. Only after Jayne had delivered fresh bedding and blankets did Kit guide them into the cell. "Make sure they have everything they need," she told Carver. "Being kept in a cage is bad enough; we don't need to make it any worse for them." One of the captives spat at Kit, hitting her squarely on the side of the head. With no sign of anger, she turned to the group in the cell. "We'll be leaving at first light. Sleep if you can, it's going to be a long day." And with that, she closed the door to the cell and Carver locked it. "I want the best food you have brought to them. Understood?"

Kit called Sellina and Jayne over to her. "Where can we get a place to sleep for the night? Someplace quiet."

"The *Sleeping Dragon*," Jayne replied, almost immediately. Sellina nodded in agreement. "It's a bit of a walk to get there, but the rooms are clean, and the owners are *friends*. We can show you the way if you'd like."

"Thank you," Kit said, inclining her head to the woman as she did. "We'll leave after I finish up my business here."

Kit walked to the front of the tavern and stood up on a chair. Before she had a chance to call for attention, Indie's voice thundered through the room. "Listen up, all of you!" The entire tavern went instantly silent. Indie gave Kit a playful grin.

"Thank you, everyone!" Kit began, with honest confidence. "This day, you chose to stand behind me, despite the rumors you may have heard. I am leaving Carver in charge of the operation, and Sellina and Jayne in charge of the tavern. You will obey them, without question. If they fail me, I will hold them responsible – not you. If you fail them, then you'll need to make peace with your god, whoever it may be." The group cheered at Kit's words, some even whistled. She certainly wasn't expecting that sort of reaction.

Kit hopped down from the chair and walked over to Carver. "I want our guests fed and ready to travel at first light. I want a wagon large enough to bear them comfortably, provisions for the journey, and a team of four horses to pull it. I mean to have them at Cormorant before sundown tomorrow. Understood?"

"Yes, Mistress Kit. All will be ready for you." Carver gave her a small, nervous smile. "I won't disappoint you."

SHADOWS OF THE PAST

Captain Bowwind inclined his head to Kandyce. His face was hard as stone, but his eyes had an unexpected softness to them. He and his men had led them away from Lord Byssus' manor to a hut not far from the city's center. Unlike the other huts that used hides for entry-flaps, this building had an iron-bound wooden door. It was attached to a thick frame made from heavy timbers.

"I'm sorry, Lady Kandyce," he said as he held open the thick door to the jail-hut. The woman glared at the soldier as she entered the building. Danny didn't even look at the man. He simply moved passed him, doing his best to calm his mind. He was actively trying to plan an escape and his thoughts were a jumble of rapidly changing ideas. He blew out a breath as he stepped inside.

The interior of the building was round, with a small fire burning in the central hearth, its smoke exiting out a chimney in the conical roof. The walls, rather than being made of mud and twigs, were covered in stone. The roof was not thatched like those of the other huts but, instead, was constructed with heavy, exposed timbers.

"I suppose this is nicer than being stuffed into a dungeon cell," Danny remarked. Captain Bowwind huffed at the comment. He ordered his soldiers to stay on guard outside before he closed the door with an ominous bang.

"We have no need of dungeons," he replied, pushing Danny towards the hearth. "Anybody we take into custody is typically executed within days. We have no need for long-term accommodations. This hut serves that purpose well." He waited for a few moments, perhaps gauging Danny's reaction. "Besides, Lord Byssus plans on hanging you at first light. He wants to make a public display of Lady Kandyce's treason. I'm guessing he hopes it will gain him favor with the people, proving to them that his execution of her mother, Lady Krystyne, was both warranted and necessary."

Danny looked around at the windowless room with its heavy door and stone walls. Escaping from the building would be a challenge unless the prisoners could fly. A hint of a grin pulled at the corner of his mouth, which the captain picked up on.

"Something amuses you?" The captain stepped closer, putting his significant height advantage to good use.

"We won't ever see the hangman's noose or the executioner's ax," Danny said staring defiantly up at the much taller, much broader man. He tried calling upon the phoenix, but it still wouldn't answer. He could feel it, but ever since Lord Byssus' cold attack, it refused to be summoned.

"I'm very sorry," the guard retorted, with a thin-lipped grin of his own, "but you will. Nobody escapes Lord Byssus' judgment. Ever." Danny curled his hands into fists.

"Perhaps you'd like to try to carry out that judgment right now?"

"It would give me great pleasure to grind that arrogant little face of yours under my boot but if I were to deny Lord Byssus his spectacle, it would be me swinging from the gallows in your place." The heat of the phoenix rose in Danny's chest. It was just below the surface now but still beyond his calling.

"Coward!" Danny took a step back and raised his fists, encouraging the captain to engage. His heart was racing. He could feel sweat building inside his fists.

C'mon phoenix, where are you?

Captain Bowwind drew his sword and moved into a ready stance.

"Garret, stop! Both of you, stop!" Kandyce moved between them, her eyes focused on the captain. "He's an ally. He's here to help." The captain moved to brush her aside, but she held firm. "Titan's peace upon you," she said with a chastising tone. The look of fury in the man's face drained away, instantly replaced with a look of contrition.

"And upon you, my lady."

"You are worshipers of Titan?" Danny's eyebrows shot up. "I wouldn't have expected..."

"Because my stepfather is a slaver?" she asked, rounding on him. "Perhaps you think I should be a follower of the spider god, Arachnielle? Or maybe I should worship the demon lord, Gorgaraeth?"

"We are not all evil," Garret said as he shoved his sword back into its scabbard. "Most of us are just trying to survive. You witnessed for yourself Lord Byssus' cruelty. He can kill my men at his leisure, without ramifications or remorse." Danny straightened his back.

"When I trained at the Temple of the Fist in Aarall, we were taught to stand against injustice in all forms, regardless of the consequences."

"You are a priest of Titan?" Kandyce asked. "You're a long way from home, priest." Judging by the look on her face, she didn't believe him for a second.

"I never said I was a priest," Danny protested, cocking an eyebrow. "I said I trained at the Temple. I never went beyond being an acolyte."

"Can you perform Titan's magic?" Garret asked, "Can you prove what you say?" Danny shrugged at the question. He had no desire to prove anything to anyone, especially a slaver guard. Seeing his reaction, Garret shook his head and dragged a chair over to the door. He took a seat and crossed his arms over his chest.

Truth was, after leaving the Temple, Danny didn't know if he would still have access to Titan's graces. He had abandoned him for his own personal reasons. He turned his back to the others and stared into the fire. The flames seemed to call to him, almost daring him to enter the hearth and be cleansed by them.

"Why are you here?" Kandyce asked. "Why did you come to my room? Why would you put yourself in this predicament?" Danny chuckled at the questions. Why indeed? He had come to kidnap the girl and instead, he found himself trying to help her.

"Leverage," he said. "You were to be leverage against your father to force him to attack the Split Crows."

It was Garret's turn to laugh. The thought was absurd. Lord Byssus only cared about one person, and that was himself. The guard's laughter wasn't lost on Kandyce. A deep frown said it all.

"Do you know Kit Standing Bear?" asked a voice from the far side of the room, beyond the hearth. Everybody, save Garret, jumped at the voice. An ancient-looking Berrat, huddled in the corner, stared at Danny, his bright blue eyes evaluating him, measuring him.

"She's my best friend," Danny replied. "How do you know her?"

"She grew up in my village," the old Berrat said. "She left for Aarall about five cycles ago. I would like to know how she faired."

"She is well. She just celebrated her sixteenth cycle. The girl is a force beyond reckoning." Danny's words made the old Berrat smile. He stood up from his place in the shadows. His face was deeply wrinkled, his eyes sunken. He ran his fingers over his long gray braid. He had a grin on his face that said he was not surprised by the news.

Garret regarded the conversation in which the two Berrat were engaged. He shared a glance with Kandyce. Her eyes widened slightly, and she nodded, almost imperceptibly.

"Do you believe he speaks the truth, Sky Eyes?" Garret asked. "Do you believe he spent time at the Temple?" The old Berrat pursed his lips as he stared at Danny.

"I believe him," Sky Eyes said. "If he is friends with Kit, then I would believe his heart to be true."

"We should have killed Byssus when we had the chance," Garret said, his eyes hardening. "This Crow upset our plans. I couldn't be sure what side he was on."

"I am no Crow," Danny said defiantly. "I am Danny Fox-Dancing, and I am here to end the slaver's reign of terror."

"You? You are Dannith Fox-Dancing, son of Paylor and Dyanna?" Sky Eyes asked as he glided across the room to stand in front of the young Berrat. Despite the man's advanced age, he moved with the unparalleled grace of a mountain lion. Danny held up his hand to keep the old Berrat at bay.

"I suppose you want to see my mark, to prove I am me."

"I have no reason to doubt you," Sky Eyes replied. "What you are saying is worse than a death sentence if heard by the wrong ears. Nobody would willingly say they are you." Danny blinked at the old man, his face blank. "You are perhaps the most sought-after person in all of Berrathia, and those who seek you would do you harm. Has it happened yet?" Danny took a step away from Sky Eyes, catching his heel on the ground, practically falling over backwards.

"Has what happened?" Danny's gaze moved to Kandyce and Garret. They were both looking at him with wide eyes and slack jaws. "What?" he asked, almost yelling out the word.

"Are you The Phoenix?" Kandyce asked. "Has the prophecy come to pass?"

"How could you know that?" Danny was now backing away from all three of them. "Who are you people?" The question made Sky Eyes smile.

"We are who we said we are. I am Sky Eyes, and this is Lady Kandyce and Captain Garret Bowwind. Your coming was foretold by a seer, Kit's mother, some fifteen cycles ago. The woman's visions were typically vague, except in your case. She foretold how you would be chosen by The Phoenix, the primordial elemental of fire. She spoke of how your family would suffer to protect you. How they would give their lives so you could live on and fulfill your destiny."

"You're The Phoenix?" Kandyce clutched her hand to her chest. She blinked at Danny a few times before snapping her head around to face the captain. "Garret, return his weapons to him." The captain gave her a questioning look, earning him a scowl. With obvious reluctance, he pulled the Berrat's bow and quiver from his shoulder and handed them to him.

"My dagger too, if you would be so kind," Danny said, holding out his free hand. The captain pulled the blade from his belt and gave it to him. Once he had his weapons stowed away, Danny turned back to Sky Eyes.

"Do you know where my parents are? I was told they haven't been seen since they took me to the Temple of the Fist?" The words connecting him to some destiny, foretold by his best friend's mother, immediately fell from his mind.

"I cannot say for certain," Sky Eyes said, placing his hand on the young man's shoulder, "but I do not believe they are alive."

"Why? Why would you say that? If you don't know where they are, how can you say they have passed to the Great Cycle?" Danny's voice was breaking as tears stung at his eyes. He wiped his nose with the back of his hand. He could feel the fire of the phoenix roaring up within himself.

The old Berrat's eyes showed a profound sadness. He squeezed Danny's shoulder and tilted his head slightly to the side. "I don't believe they'd have survived the blooding process. King Faol wants their power. He believes he can create stronger soldiers if they feed on Berrabbithi blood."

"King Faol hopes that his new vampires will be more capable of surviving the turning," Kandyce added. "The Berrabbithi were unparalleled in their ability to transform themselves. They seem to be able to join with any race and create viable offspring."

"Your parents," Sky Eyes added, "were the closest thing to pure Berrabbithi known. The likelihood that you would be born a true Berrabbithi…"

"And that's why they want me? To drain me of my blood?" Danny dropped to a knee. He didn't fully understand the meaning of what the old Berrat was saying. But he did understand that if it was his parents' blood that was important, they would likely have drained them dry. He dropped down to both knees and sat back on his heels. He was having trouble breathing. The world was crushing in on him. The idea that his parents had been tortured to death wrapped around his heart, squeezing it until it seemed like it would burst.

"Is that why King Faol wants Berrat blood slaves? He's hoping to capture enough Berrat that he'll stumble upon a Berrabbithi?" Danny asked, his chin resting heavily on his chest.

"In part," Sky Eyes said. "Our blood, at least those of us who still carry the Berrabbithi traits, is strong. But there are very few such Berrat left. Our bloodline has been so diluted that hardly any of those remaining can shape change at all. We are losing our ability to spirit bind with the animals of the north. In a few generations, I expect there will be none."

"If my parents are still alive, where would they be?" Danny asked as he rubbed at his chest with a shaky hand. The tightness that had clamped onto his heart refused to loosen. He swallowed hard, waiting for a response.

"In the kingdom of Faol," Kandyce replied. "All Berrat who show any ability are sent to Cormorant and then they are shipped directly to Faol."

"What about The Wing?" Danny asked. "If he has red hair, is it not possible that he, too, is Berrabbithi?"

"He is," Kandyce said, shaking her head and rolling her eyes. "He's being kept for stud purposes. They're trying to see if he can produce Berrabbithi offspring."

"But I thought he was some sort of assassin. The way I heard it, he is one of the most feared men in all of Berrathia."

"Oh, he is," Garret chimed in. He rose from his place by the door and moved closer to the hearth. "Because of his shifting abilities, he can get almost anywhere. Rumor is, he can shift into a frost drake. In that form, he could travel across Berrathia in less than a day."

"And where is he now?" Danny asked. Both Kandyce and Garret shrugged at the same time.

"It's not like we've ever met him," Kandyce said, rolling her eyes. "I only know what I know about him because my father never expected me to live. I think sometimes he would just blather on about his meetings with The Wing because he desperately wanted to brag about having met him. The Wing just shows up when he wants something of my father."

"Sometimes he shows up long enough to murder three or four of my soldiers, just to prove he can," Garret said. The firelight made his already stern face look downright sinister. "He wants to prove to us and to Lord Byssus that none are safe unless they are loyal to the Split Crows."

"Fear is a powerful weapon," Sky Eyes chimed in, "and The Wing wields it like a master." The old Berrat clasped his hands behind his back and walked over to the room's central fire. He stared deeply into the flames for several moments. "But it can also lead to an uprising. When people feel they have nothing to lose, they can become very dangerous. If they feel they have something to gain, the effect is twofold."

"Has anybody other than your father ever met The Wing?" Danny asked. "If you believed me to be him, then maybe everyone else would as well."

"To what end?" Garret asked. No sooner had the words left his mouth, the door to the hut burst open, sending Garret's chair tumbling across the floor. A tall, lanky guard dressed in a blood-red surcoat rushed through the door with several more guards at his heels.

"Captain Bowwind," he said, "we have a problem with the..." The guard's face turned white, and he dropped to the floor and took a knee. The other guards all had a similar response. "Forgive me, Lord Wing, I didn't know..."

"Report the disturbance," Danny said, moving quickly to stand before the guard. "You'd better have a good reason for this intrusion." The red-headed Berrat looked over to Kandyce and gave her a small wink.

"We found two Berrat sneaking amongst the huts," the guard replied, his eyes never looking up from the floor. "We gave chase, but they evaded us." Danny's heart began to race. It had to have been Breayn and Ryn. They must have come into the city to carry out the mission when they couldn't find him.

"What did they look like?" Danny asked. "Were they dressed as warriors or as hunters?"

"My Lord?" the soldier barely got the words out. When Danny growled at him, he continued. "They were dressed in Split Crows uniforms, like yourself. When we tried to greet them, they ran." The guard paused for several moments. "One of them had fire-red hair, like yours."

Chapter Fifteen

THE SLEEPING DRAGON

There was only the slightest sliver of a moon that peered out through the clouds that blew across the night sky. The air was a bit warmer than expected this far north, for this time of year. Regardless, both of the serving girls were shivering badly within seconds of stepping out of The Crimson Ale. Lin wrapped her arm around Jayne, rubbing her bare skin to help warm her up.

"Thank you," Jayne said as she pulled away from Lin's advances. "I appreciate it, but I'll be okay."

"Lin, why don't you get these ladies some blankets from our saddlebags," Kit said, holding back a laugh.

"Is there lodging for our horses at the Sleeping Dragon?" Indie asked.

"Like the inn, the stables are tired, but they are clean. Your animals will be well cared for." Sellina tried to stifle a yawn, failing miserably.

"We can make our way on our own," Kit said with a small frown. "You two must be exhausted."

"We'd prefer to show you the way," Jayne replied, glaring at Sellina, as though urging her to agree.

"Yes, if it pleases you, Mistress Kit," Sellina continued where Jayne had left off. "If you will indulge us, we need to speak with you, in private."

Kit willingly agreed to the women's request. They all quickly mounted up, Sellina joining Indie on his horse and Jayne on Lin's. As Lin gave her a hand up, Jayne gave her a look, a practiced look from working in a tavern with handsy customers, to keep her paws to herself.

The group moved to the side of the road when a procession of soldiers, dressed in brightly colored surcoats of yellow and blue, came marching down the street towards them. The guards surrounded a brilliant white carriage, trimmed in gold and silver, as it clattered along the cobblestone street. The carriage's driver, a tall thin man with a short-cropped beard tipped his plumed hat as they rode past. Curtains within the carriage were quickly drawn closed, hiding its occupants from prying eyes.

There were few citizens moving about, except for those who spilled out from brightly lit taverns and the night workers who would beckon to them, offering shelter and a warmed bed. Small groups of City Watch guards were on patrol, but for the most part, they seemed more interested in chatting up the night workers than they were in keeping the peace.

Lanterns, suspended from tall, iron posts, lit the streets in irregular intervals. Where their light was absent, the shadows of those who lived in the darkness would slip in and out of view along the way. With wary eyes they traveled to the inn in silence, speaking nary a word to one another.

A collective sigh escaped the group when they arrived at *The Sleeping Dragon*. It was a tall, narrow building, constructed of stone and wood. The warm yellow light of the building's common room welcomed the weary travelers. A few patrons stood outside, chatting quietly amongst themselves. With a courteous nod, they welcomed the group before returning to their private conversations. Indie offered to get the horses settled in the stables, while Kit and the other women arranged for rooms for the night.

⟐

Sellina had secured a large single room for the group to stay in. It had four feather beds, a dining table, and a deep, stone hearth surrounded by an enormous mantle that was carved to look like the open maw of a dragon. Kit gave her dragon hammer a shake, thinking that if Fury would decide to grace her with his presence, he might enjoy the homage to his kind.

Shortly after Indie finished lighting a fire, Kit turned to Jayne and Sellina. "What is it that you want to talk about?" The boys started tussling for position on one of the four beds in the room, drawing Kit's attention away from the task at hand. When they finally settled down, she raised her eyebrows to the women, encouraging them to speak.

Jayne and Sellina shared a look, both urging the other to speak up. Finally, Jayne cleared her throat and began. "When you first came to the Ale, we weren't sure who you were – but today, we're almost entirely certain."

"And just who is it that you think I am?" Kit asked, crossing her arms, leaning against the plaster wall nearest the door.

Jayne swallowed hard. "You are Sister Kit Standing Bear, Priest of Titan, and daughter of Aurora Windsong, leader of Aurora's Guard." Kit's face went slack at the declaration. "Aurora was here, the last time you were at the Ale. Your eyes are identical to hers. You must be her daughter."

Kit's pulse began beating so fast that she feared she was going to black out. If what they were saying was true, then she had actually *met* her mother. Even though she could feel her blood thumping in her ears, Kit tried to maintain a modicum of self control. "Why would you think I am a priest of Titan?"

"Because we are members of Aurora's Guard, and we have been watching you for most of your life," Sellina interjected. "Well, not us personally, but your foster mother, Riva, has. Jayne and I, we've been posted in Silverhawk for the past three cycles."

"You're taking a big risk, sharing this with us," Indie said, moving to stand beside Kit. The women's words had visibly shaken her. He guided her over to the bed currently occupied by the boys, knowing that she would be comforted by just being close to them.

"I don't think so," Sellina said, her heart aching for the young priest. "We've watched how Kit handles herself with the others, how she deals with the prisoners, and how she cares for the people around her."

"If we're wrong, then all is lost anyway," Jayne finished, plopping herself down next to Lin, who had been quietly soaking in the details of the conversation.

Kit slowly came to grips with what the women were saying. "Why?" she asked. "I'm not someone to hang your hopes on. I'm one girl, pledged to free Titan from his prison – trying to help the victims of these slavers along the way."

"I'm not sure if that's false modesty or not," Sellina said, "but if it isn't, you need to take a good, hard look at yourself in a mirror. You are not just one *girl*."

Completely ignoring what Sellina was saying, Kit finally asked what had been on her mind this whole time. "My mother's name is Aurora?"

"It is," Sellina said, taking a seat beside the young priest. It suddenly dawned on Kit that this woman was considerably older than she thought. "She's an incredible woman, strong and fierce, but full of compassion. Much like you, I believe."

"But why hasn't she sought me out?" Kit started to tear up, but she didn't care.

Sellina pushed an unwilling Lump aside, shimmying closer until she was sitting shoulder to shoulder with Kit. "I can't say for sure," she said, brushing a tear from Kit's cheek. "She's rarely in the same place for more than a moon, and she's warring against some very dangerous people." At that moment, Sellina was fighting back her own emotions. "Leaving your children behind to fight a war that is impossible to win, well, it's the hardest thing a mother can ever do."

Kit could feel the intense surge of Sellina's misery crashing against her like waves upon a rocky shore. "How many children have you left behind to follow my mother's quest? Your heart is breaking for them."

"Three. They are my life and my soul, and I left them behind to follow your mother and her cause."

"And what is my mother's cause?"

"To destroy King Faol and put an end to the vampire scourge." And with that, Sellina stood and motioned to Jayne. "What are your plans for the prisoners?"

"I will leave with them at first light and give them their freedom once we are clear of Silverhawk."

"Be sure that you are well beyond the walls of the city before you do," Jayne jumped in. "The hawk riders will be watching. Trust none but the white riders.

Not all the other riders are under the Tide's control, but too many of them are – and while they're in the air, you cannot tell friend from foe. No enemy has infiltrated the whites, the healers; not yet anyway."

And with that, the two women bade the group good night and took their leave.

A Plan Hatched

The smells of coffee, eggs, and cheese tugged at Kit's nose until they coaxed her eyes to open. After rubbing the sleep from them, she saw Indie handing something to a middle-aged woman dressed in a white shift and a dark-colored apron. There was a pair of lanterns sputtering on the room's table, illuminating what appeared to be two large trays of assorted foods.

"Thank you," Indie whispered as the woman exited the room. When he turned back, he found Kit propped up on her elbows. Her long black hair with its thick red stripe was a mass of tangles and knots. "Good morning, beautiful" he offered, with a small smile on his face. "Sleep well?"

Kit nodded and fell back, letting her pillow envelope her head. She could hear him tiptoeing across the room towards her. She closed her eyes tightly and let her thoughts drift away.

"First light will be here before we know it," he said, his mouth so near that Kit could feel the warmth of his breath on her cheek.

Her bed jounced from his weight and his warm breath suddenly turned to wet, slobbery licks across her neck. A cold wet nose started trying to push its way past Kit's pillow. When she pushed the fur-covered muzzle away, the happy-go-lucky Lump looked down at her, his big brown eyes reflecting the dancing lights of the lanterns. As always, his huge puppy-dog smile covered his face, while his tongue lolled lazily out of his mouth.

"Good morning, Lump," she said with a sleepy smile. "Do you need to go outside?" Both Lump and Runt scrambled for the door, causing Kit to groan.

"Alright, I'm coming." Kit quickly pulled on her boots and wrapped a blanket around her shoulders.

As soon as she opened the door to the street, the boys bolted out and disappeared down an alley. Kit leaned against the hotel's front porch railing, letting the morning's chill air wash over her, pushing away the last of her sleepiness. Their enthusiastic yips and barks announced the boys' imminent return, so she headed to the door, holding it open for them as they rushed past her.

It seems I'm not the only one who wants their breakfast. She chuckled to herself and headed for the stairway up to their third-floor room.

When Kit stepped in through the door, she found her friends already eating, their plates nearly empty. Indie tossed two large, meat-covered bones to the boys who possessively took their treats to a corner, away from the others. Indie motioned to a large plate of eggs and cheese sitting next to him.

"What's the plan?" Lin asked, as she wiped the corners of her mouth. "Finish breakfast, head to the Crimson Ale, pack up the prisoners, and then what?"

As Kit finished scraping the last of the eggs onto her plate, she admitted that she had no clue what would happen after that. Her plans hadn't gotten much further than what Lin had just outlined. Without saying much in response, Kit began working her way through the pile of food she had served herself.

As she pushed the last of her breakfast into her mouth, Kit finally shrugged. "We let them take the wagon and go home, I guess. We'll look for Treedale and Mukale when we get to Cormorant."

"They're not expecting us until tomorrow," Indie said as he pulled on his obsidian armor. "We moved our schedule up a day, remember? Nobody knows we're coming."

Kit gave her friends a wide smile. "We'll figure it out."

⌘

When the group headed outside, they found their horses saddled and ready for travel. Angel whinnied a good morning to her rider, with Char and Whistler following suit. The sky had turned a deep purple, heralding the sun before it broke over the eastern horizon. There was already a good number of people on the streets, heading towards wherever it was their life was taking them. Shopkeepers across the way were unfurling their blue and white awnings while others set up their wares on the sidewalk, hoping to make some early morning sales.

By the time they made it to the tavern, there was a large wagon out front hitched to a team of four draft horses. The *guests* were all on board, each one of them looking downcast.

"Have you all been properly fed, and your needs taken care of?" Kit asked, looking over the people to ensure they were all healthy and whole. Several looked like they were ready to spit at her. She couldn't tell them she was trying to free them, even though their fear and loathing of her cut Kit to the core.

When none of them answered, Jayne stepped in. Rather than the skimpy attire she had worn the previous night, the woman had dressed herself in loose leather breaches and a snappy, white linen tunic that hung down to her hips.

"They were all offered a good meal, but only some of them accepted it; at least the children ate, though." She dropped her voice low enough that nobody, save Kit, could hear her words. "There are enough supplies loaded to last three days. They may need to take a longer than necessary route to get home." When Kit acknowledged her understanding, Jayne pulled a parchment out from a pocket and handed it to Kit.

"Take this to the harbourmaster in Cormorant. His name is Rayan Staul, but everyone calls him, Captain. He is not an ally, but he is also not a slaver. He's just a man working to survive in these trying times."

Kit tucked the parchment into her armor without looking at it. "What's in the note?"

"You're going to need to pay Staul off," she said with a bit of a grin. "It's a letter of property ownership, a plot of land with a small house on it. It's good land. He and his family can live there, safe and free."

"What will I receive in return for this payment?"

"Information, mostly. But more importantly, he has the keys to the storehouses at the docks. All of them." When Jayne saw the dumb look on Kit's face, she couldn't help but chuckle. "For such a renowned warrior, you don't know much about the world around you." When Kit growled at her, Jayne stopped chuckling. "No need to take offense, it's a simple truth." When Kit's demeanor didn't change, the woman continued. "The storehouses are where all cargo is stored when it arrives at the docks, or when it *leaves* the docks."

"Oh, of course." Kit's face suddenly heated, feeling somewhat foolish for having required an explanation. "What happens after we pay this guy for his information? If he leaves, who'll take his place? Inserting someone who is our ally seems like a good plan."

Jayne raised her eyebrows in surprise. "I'm sorry that I underestimated you. You catch on quickly." Kit shrugged in response. "Aurora has a man there, Ailman Juuls. He is Lord Karter's chief advisor."

"That's a lot of names," Kit said, rubbing the back of her neck. "Any chance..."

"That I could write this down for you?" Jayne interrupted, holding out another parchment to Kit. "It's got the names of everyone we have there. It might be best that you keep this safe, on your body, at all times." Jayne took a small satchel from her shoulder and handed it to Kit. "And, just in case, here are a few healing potions, plus a couple of complacency potions, just in case your guests decide to struggle. But hopefully it won't come to that."

"It won't," Kit said, looking at the sullen faces of those riding on the wagon. She tucked the parchment inside her boot and threw the satchel over her shoulder. "One last thing," she added, inclining her head, "Thank you. Thank you for everything you and Sellina are doing."

No sooner had the conversation ended than Carver joined the pair. "Everyone's ready to go, Mistress. Any instructions for me before you leave?"

"Yes," Kit said, as an idea suddenly struck her. "No more raids until you hear back from me."

"Mistress?"

"How many people are there in this operation?" Kit asked, her mind racing as she continued trying to formulate her make-shift plan.

Carver paused for a moment as he tried to figure out the answer to Kit's question. "There used to be two members of the Tide, but you killed both Gaoler and Nicks. So, now it's just us Auctioneers left." Carver screwed up his face as he started counting off on his fingers. "By my count, there are about sixty, maybe seventy Auctioneers posted here. Plus, we've got a little more than a dozen inside the Watch who work for us."

"Can we trust them?" Kit asked.

"Those who know you," he said with a bit of a chortle, "they're terrified of you. Those who are in the Watch, well, they go where the gold is."

"Good," Kit said returning Carver's laugh. "Fear and greed are easy to feed. Do we have enough money in the treasury to pay the Watch double what we're paying them now?"

"We'll make sure we do," Jayne answered. "What are you intending?"

"I want the hawk-riders to locate every group operating in the Silverhawk area. When they locate them, I want my people to liberate them of their catch, and anything else of value with them. Those who want to live can join with me; the rest – kill them."

"The Tide's not going to like this," Carver said, clearly nervous about trying to implement Kit's plan.

"The Tide wants blood slaves. How they get them, or from whom they get them, is irrelevant." Jayne started shaking her head as Kit told Carver her plan. "Do you have a problem with this, Jayne?"

"No, Mistress," she responded with absolute certainty. "It's a bold plan, but if it works, you'll have control of the region before the moon is new again."

"Exactly!" Kit said, her tone suddenly dangerous and foreboding. "The prisoners are to be treated with as much care and respect as possible. Treat their captors with ruthlessness. They will get one chance to join us or die. Understood?"

"Yes, Mistress," Carver replied. "But where will we keep them, our *guests*? Our cell can only hold a small number. If we take everyone else's catch, we will probably have in excess of a hundred of them, not to mention housing the additional *members*."

"Use the tavern if you have to. Just figure it out." Kit barked the instructions at Carver, making him wince slightly. "Any other questions for me? The sun's up and I need to get this group to market."

"No, Mistress," Carver and Jayne replied in unison.

"If I'm not back before the next new moon, ship our guests to Cormorant. You will treat them with kindness and respect, regardless of how they act towards you. I'll clear everything with the harbourmaster before they are delivered." Kit didn't wait for a response before joining Indie and Lin, and the wagonload of guests. Indie was in the driver's seat of the wagon, with Char standing untethered at the rear. Seeing that everyone was ready to move out, Kit mounted up and began leading the troop towards the main gate.

THE RESISTANCE

The group was barely clear of Silverhawk when Kit spied five hawk-riders, four with red banners and one with a green banner, leaving the rookery, heading out in all directions. It looked like Carver wasted no time in getting the word out to locate the raiders working in Silverhawk. As the green rider flew over Kit, she tipped her wings in salute, allowing Kit to breathe a sigh of relief. The riders weren't following her, and they were acknowledging their loyalty.

After about an hour on the road to Cormorant, Kit called everyone to a halt. Several of the prisoners cowered in the corner of the wagon, pulling the young ones to themselves, shielding them from whatever evil was about to fall upon them. Angel brought Kit next to the cart, allowing her to speak with the prisoners more easily. "I can't tell you how sorry I am for what's happened to you and your families," Kit started. Whatever it was that the prisoners were expecting, this wasn't it.

"You say you're sorry, but you're taking us to be sold as blood slaves," one of the prisoners said, each word filled with loathing. The outspoken person was a Nomad man, maybe in his late thirties. His face looked soft and kind, but his words and mannerisms presented the complete opposite.

"I'm not taking you to Cormorant," Kit replied. She would have loved to have been able to say something meaningful, or inspiring, but right now, the terrified faces of the prisoners had left her completely dumbfounded. Unfortunately, her choice of words had not produced the desired effect. The adults holding the children clutched them even more tightly, as they tried to use their own bodies as shields. Others scrambled to the farthest corner of the wagon in an effort to put distance between themselves and Kit.

"Sweet Titan, no!" Kit was practically screeching. "I'm not going to hurt you. I'm letting you go home. You're all free." She quickly repeated the words, this time using a traditional form of Berrat, one that they would likely understand, if even only in part.

The terror quickly turned to confusion. "Why?" asked the same outspoken man. Where the others cowered, he had moved closer to Kit, putting himself between her and the other prisoners, jutting out his chin in defiance. "Why would a slaver release her merchandise?"

"What is your name?" Kit asked, trying to be as non-threatening as she could.

"I am Kallik," he replied warily, questioning the necessity of his captor knowing his name.

Kit did her best to give him a warm smile. "Kallik, my name is Sister Kit Standing Bear, and I am a priest of Titan." While her declaration seemed to mean something to Kallik, it did nothing to assuage the fears of the Berrat prisoners. "You have no reason to trust me, but I'm going to ask you to do that for me right now." When nobody responded, other than to look questioningly at Kit, she pressed on. "I mean to bring an end to slavery in the north."

Kallik scoffed. "You're taking us to be sold, and yet you claim to be ending slavery."

"We're not taking you to be sold," Indie interrupted. "We're setting you free. You will all be able to return home."

"To our homes that have been destroyed by your raiders?" one of the Berrat woman yelled as she stroked the hair of the tiny girl she was holding. "What of the people who were killed during the raid? What of our homes and businesses that were torched?"

The woman's pleas made Kit's heart ache. "I'm sorry. I cannot undo the past. I can only try to prevent it from happening again."

"And just how will you do that?" Kallik practically spat the question at Kit.

"One operation at a time," Kit said with a bit of a shrug. "I don't exactly know yet how I'll do that, but that's what I'm going to do. It's only been a few days since I took control of the Silverhawk operation. They will not be raiding any more and they've been ordered to seek out and destroy any other slavers operating in Silverhawk."

"I'll ask you again," Kallik said, not bothering to hide his suspicion. "Why?"

"Because people are meant to be free." It was the only answer Kit could come up with. "What the slavers are doing is abhorrent. Those who purchase these people, well, what they do might even be worse. Each and every one of them needs to be brought to justice; swift, lethal justice."

It was unclear what it was, exactly, that Kit said to change his mind, but Kallik's demeanor towards Kit changed. "How can we help?"

Kit sighed deeply. She couldn't have asked for a better question, not in a dozen lifetimes. "I wish I had an answer for you. I'm still not sure how I am going to go about bringing down the slavers. Right now, I'm striking them in obvious places, but I'm going to need to do more. A friend once told me that destroying the slavers will be like killing a hydra – and that I need to know which head is the critical one."

"Your friend is wise," Kallik said. "The difficulty is, like a hydra, killing one head will only spawn two more. To defeat them, you must kill the hydra from within, making it tear itself apart."

"And how are we to do that?" Indie asked, folding his arms across his chest.

Kallik smiled at him, perhaps like a father might smile at a son who does not understand his teachings. "It might be easier than you think. The slave houses of Berrathia hate one another. They all want what the other has, and right now, many of them have their hearts focused on taking hold of the Berrathian capital of Ravenlord."

Kit was perplexed. This man seemed to know a lot about the slavers, and she knew that every word he spoke rang of truth. "How do you know this?"

"There is a resistance spreading across the lands. We are not strong, yet, but we are willing to do what is needed to protect our families, our neighbors, and our community." Kallik stared hard at Kit, trying to assess her reaction. Sharing this information with her was obviously dangerous, but something told him that it was a necessary risk.

"I wish I had known that before we left Silverhawk," Kit remarked to nobody in particular. "I have friends there who could have helped coordinate matters."

"We can send Lump and Runt back to Silverhawk," Lin suggested. "Lump can speak with Jayne and Sellina; tell them about the resistance. They'll know what to do."

Kit got a worried look on her face. Lin had just shared dangerous information; information that could get the two women killed. "Does the resistance have a name?" Kit asked, pressing her face close to Kallik's. "If you want to help, speak true."

"Your friend shares too much information, too willingly," Kallik responded, shaking his head. "But I'm guessing that if you're unhappy with what I say, we won't ever be leaving this wagon." When he saw Kit's flat expression, he continued on. "We don't have a name, not really, but the women you named, they both belong to Aurora's Guard, and we are their eyes in Silverhawk and northern Berrathia."

"Neither Jayne nor Sellina revealed that you are who you say you are." Nothing this man was saying was a lie, but his story wasn't adding up. If he was working with Aurora's Guard, shouldn't these women have known him?

"We work from the shadows, feeding information to a single person, who then shares that information up the chain. That way, if the Auctioneers or the Scarlet Tide captures any one of us, there is little risk of us giving out information on any of the others. Every one of these people I'm with could be in the resistance, and I wouldn't know it." As Kallik finished that sentence, the other prisoners all started shaking their heads, obviously afraid that if they admitted they were in the resistance, their lives could be forfeited.

Kit's head was beginning to swim again. This was more information than she could cope with. She knew nothing of espionage, secrets, or anything else of that sort. She was a warrior, a justice dealer, a blunt tool designed to handle problems directly in front of her. She quickly looked to Indie and Lin for some advice.

"How many spies report to you, and who do you report to?" Lin demanded. "How many are in the resistance? Are you able to mount a physical strike, to attack slavers in order to free any prisoners they have taken, or better yet, attack them before they have a chance to carry out a raid?"

Kit blinked a few times at her friend. There was so much more to her than Kit would ever realize. She turned to Kallik, nodding at him, prodding him to answer.

Kallik frowned slightly, shaking his head. "There are very few of us who are warriors, so attacking anybody isn't much of an option for us. We have no coordinated combat strength. We are farmers, smiths, bakers, and the like. Some of us are trackers, hunters, and scouts, but whatever our background, we are the watchers, the purveyors of information. Few, very few, have ever spent any time training for combat. Those of us who stand and fight, die."

"What of my first question?" Lin pressed. "What are your numbers? Who reports to you? Who do you report to?"

"You're asking a lot," Kallik replied. He folded his arms across his chest and pursed his lips. "I will tell you everything, but I will tell you nothing. If you don't like what I have to say, well, you're going to do what you're going to do."

"Tell us what you are comfortable with," Kit said, trying her best to give him a sense of reassurance that his life was in no danger.

Kallik nodded and took a deep breath, allowing himself a moment to gather his thoughts. "There are seven who report to me, but I don't *know* them. I meet each one on a different day, in a different location. They share information with me, and I report it to somebody else. The person I report to, reports directly to Jayne."

"How can you possibly know that your contact reports to Jayne?" Lin asked, putting her hands onto the handles of her swords.

"I could say that I discovered it accidentally, but that would be a lie." Kallik looked for Kit's reaction to his comment, but her blank stare revealed nothing. "I put my life on the line every day. In doing so, I put my family's lives at risk. I needed to be sure that I was working for the right people."

"Spying on your cohorts? You put a lot of people at risk," Lin said, easing her grip on her blades.

"I will do whatever I can to bring an end to the incarceration of my people," Kallik replied, "but I will always put my family first."

"You said your people cover Silverhawk and northern Berrathia," Kit said, ignoring what Lin felt was an indiscretion.

"Our organization as a whole, does," Kallik corrected. "My people are from Silverhawk, mostly. Only one of my contacts ever goes to Cormorant."

Kit sighed heavily. "Okay, tell me what you can of Cormorant." Everything that Kallik was telling her about their spy ring was interesting, but she needed to get to Cormorant before nightfall, and this conversation was burning up time. "We need to leave if we're going to stop the black ships from setting sail tonight."

"Cormorant's slave operations are run by House Hanse. I don't know much about them, except that the younger nobles are open to ways of getting out of the slave trade. Since Taseko fell as the seat of the Berrathian government, the northern slave trade has become violent, much more violent than it used to be." Kallik stared hard at Kit, waiting for her reaction. Her expression remained flat, so he pressed on. "I'm afraid I can't tell you much more. My connections are to the east of Silverhawk, but there are others in our collective who work in the area. I don't know who they are, but I might be able to get word out, allowing them to find you while you're there."

"Can you see these people safely home?" Indie asked. Like Kit, he wanted to bring this conversation to a close so they could get moving. "Take the wagon and the provisions. There are three days worth of supplies here. Hopefully it's enough."

A look of hope spread quickly amongst the prisoners as they suddenly realized that their ordeal was coming to an end. "I can and I will," Kallik replied with a sincere bow. "And thank you for what you are doing. Even if you can't see us, know that you are not alone."

Kit pulled out the purse of gold dragons that she had received from Carver, the blood-slave money. After weighing it in her hand for a few seconds, she tossed it to Kallik. "Use this gold as you see fit. Give it to the villages that these people came from or use it to strengthen your network. Use it to help the community. Don't make me regret trusting you."

Kallik's eyes went wide when he looked inside. "These are gold dragons," he said. "There is a small fortune in here."

Indie quickly hopped down from the driver's seat, leaving the reins for Kallik to take over. "Don't disappoint the lady," he whispered as Kallik climbed past him onto the front seat of the wagon.

Chapter Eighteen

The Turning Tide

The sun had not yet risen, but the eastern sky was lightening, turning from deep purple to a brilliant orange. While the approaching dawn pushed the darkness from the sky, a light breeze from the north brought with it a mild chill.

Playing up his part as Lord Wing, Danny immediately took charge of the search for Breayn and Ryn, sending the captain's soldiers out with explicit orders to return the pair unharmed. He had made it perfectly clear that he would mete out any punishment the two Crow imposters would receive and if anyone took that pleasure from him, they would feel his full wrath.

There were so many soldiers coming and going, the group had moved out of the jail-hut to better manage the ongoing barrage of reports coming in from the search parties. Nobody dared ask why Lady Kandyce was not being held inside the jail.

Danny had just sent a small group of the red-cloaked soldiers to search the outer limits of the city when a self-important looking lieutenant, dressed in a gold surcoat with black trim, approached. The red-cloak soldiers gave the lieutenant a wide berth. The man wore an open-faced helm with a ridiculous gold plume. He had six similarly dressed soldiers behind him, but without the showy head covering.

"Who's this peacock?" Danny asked Garret, not too surreptitiously.

"Lieutenant Regnor Barclay," the captain replied with a groan, his expression taut. "He's the commander of Lord Byssus' personal guard."

"What's he doing here?" Danny asked through clenched teeth. Garret snapped to attention and motioned for his men to surround Kandyce.

"We're about to find out," he replied.

"The Crow imposters are not within the city's center, Lord Wing," the lieutenant reported. "I have searched the area around Lord Byssus' home, and I've tripled the guard to ensure they cannot get within one hundred paces of him. For his own protection, Lord Byssus has moved to his secret chambers. He said you are to meet him there." Danny swallowed hard and glanced over at Garret. The captain's face was stoic. Danny turned to Kandyce and raised an eyebrow. She shook her head slightly.

"Fine," Danny said, motioning with his hand, "lead the way." The lieutenant's hand moved to his sword while the other six guards spread out behind him. They each wielded a small round shield and a steel-tipped spear. A look of hopeful anticipation crossed their faces as they pointed their weapons at the Berrat's chest.

"No, Lord Wing. I was instructed to let *you* lead *me* to Lord Byssus' location. He said that if you are who you say you are, you would know the way." Danny's mouth parted slightly, and his eyes went vacant. He again looked to Garret and Kandyce hoping for some assistance. When Garret pulled his longsword, and the dozen red-cloaked soldiers behind him did the same, Danny turned back to the stern-faced lieutenant.

"Are you willing to die for your lord?" he asked. His chest was a blast furnace, his flames begging to be set free.

"I am not the one who will be dying," the tall, slim lieutenant replied with a smug chuckle. A dozen or so more gold cloaked soldiers moved in behind Danny and his cohorts. "You and Lady Kandyce will be hung before the people break their fast." His gaze fell on Garret. "And it seems Captain Bowwind will be swinging from the gallows by your side."

"You didn't answer my question," Danny said as his vision continued to redden. "Are you willing to die for your slaver lord?"

"No," the lieutenant responded, pursing his lips. "I would not die for him, but neither will I give him a reason to send me to the gallows."

"Then lead me to where he is hidden, and you will live to see another sunrise." Danny looked off to the east where the sky was beginning to lighten.

The lieutenant paused for a moment, as though considering his options. His eyes went to his soldiers, finding only looks of deadly intent. "I'm sorry," he said, "but I will not give my lord a reason to execute me or my men." He quickly motioned with his chin to the spear-wielding gold-cloaked soldiers. "Take them."

The phoenix inside Danny didn't give the soldiers a chance to react. He burst into flames and screeched out a war cry. In a heartbeat, the firebird was airborne and circling above the group of soldiers. Even in the dim morning light he could see the looks of astonishment on their faces. He unleashed another war cry as he swooped down at the lieutenant, sending him and the other gold-cloaks sprawling onto the ground. As he rose back up into the purple sky, he saw Breayn and a white bear making their way towards him.

"Side with us and you will not fight alone," Danny said as he landed awk-wardly before Kandyce and Garret, transforming into his Berrat form as he did. "Berrathia is uniting, and the slavers will fall. It's up to you to decide which side of history you wish to be on."

The lieutenant was still prone when Breayn and Ryn came bursting between the huts. The bear roared out as he barrelled towards the group. Breayn had her bow nocked and ready to fire. The soldiers turned their spears away from Danny and lowered them toward the oncoming threat.

"Hold," Danny cried out. "Nobody needs to die." The white bear slowed and Breayn lowered her bow, pointing her arrow to the ground at her feet. Several dozen more red-cloaked soldiers came wending through the huts, their weapons drawn and ready. A group of the captain's archers also appeared and immediately loosed their arrows at Ryn. Before they could find their mark, a gust of frosty wind blasted out from Breayn, sending the arrows skyward, knocking many of the newly arrived soldiers onto their backs.

"Lower your weapons," Kandyce screamed out. "Our salvation is at hand. The Phoenix has risen, and the evil shall perish." The gathered soldiers were nearly one hundred strong as the woman called out. They may have heard her words, but their eyes were locked on Breayn. Her long red hair was swirling about her head and her eyes looked to be a storm brewing in the north. Ryn, now in Berrat form, was rushing to her side as a tempest swirled about her, raising dirt and debris.

"No," he screamed out as he fought through the whirlwind. "You cannot take her!" The wind lifted the Berrat off his feet, tossing him into the air like a dried leaf in a windstorm. He quickly shifted into falcon form and dove headlong into what was now a sizable, growing tornado. As his body penetrated the outer winds, he flapped furiously, trying desperately to make it to the eye, to his mate, Breayn.

"Go," Sky Eyes screamed at Danny over the deafening sound of the raging winds. "Boreas holds no domain over The Phoenix." The young Berrat had no idea where the elder had come from, but he wasted no time shifting into his phoenix form. While the soldiers ran in search of protection from the beating winds, Danny screeched as he rose into the now lightening sky. From within the churning mass of dust and debris, the limp, lifeless body of Ryn swirled about. In his firebird form there was no way he could help Breayn's mate. All he could do was trust the old man and try to breach the wall of wind. Throwing himself into a full dive, he increased his speed until everything was a bright red blur. As soon as his body struck the whirlwind, Boreas screamed out in rage and the winds immediately ceased. Breayn collapsed in a heap at what was the epicenter of the storm. Danny quickly switched back to Berrat form and dropped down at her side. Her hair was wet and plastered to her deathly pale face.

Ryn's body slammed to the ground with a sickening whump a dozen paces away. Danny left his cousin where she lay and sprinted to her fallen mate. His body was twisted in an unnatural position, his arms and legs bent into obtuse angles.

Pressing his ear to the fallen Berrat's chest he listened for the sound of his beating heart. He could hear nothing over the sounds of the commotion that was raging on around him. Soldiers and citizens alike were clambering about, trying to catch a glimpse of the phoenix or to simply witness the mayhem that had transpired. Danny placed his hand next to Ryn's mouth, hoping to feel his breath. He may have been breathing but if he was, his breaths were so shallow he couldn't say for certain.

The tiny bottles hidden within the lining of his cloak clinked as he leaned away from Ryn. Danny fished out the two potions and examined them briefly. One was a pale yellow, and the other was a deep red. According to Pana, the dog-soldiers' healer, the red vial contained a powerful healing tincture, and the yellow liquid was a potion of fire resistance. He had never been much of a healer and had very little knowledge of potions in general, despite them being a part of the Temple's required curriculum for its acolytes. But he had faith that Pana had given him accurate information. He didn't believe Ryn had long to live if he didn't receive immediate help. Danny put the vial of yellow liquid on the ground beside him and pulled the cork from the healing potion. He tried lifting Ryn's head enough to pour the potion into his mouth.

"Don't move him," Sky Eyes said as he knelt beside Danny. "Give him just a few drops, wait a few moments, and then tip his head up."

Danny did what the elder suggested and slowly began trickling the potion over his lips. After several drops had been administered, he raised Ryn's head and poured more of the swirling red liquid into his mouth. As he continued, Sky Eyes repositioned Ryn's arms and legs, putting them into more natural positions.

"He's not getting better," Danny said. Small drips of the potion were escaping from the corners of Ryn's mouth. "He's not swallowing the potion."

"Hold his mouth closed and pinch his nose," Sky Eyes said as he moved to the other side of the wounded Berrat. "It should force him to swallow, even if he's unconscious." Again, Danny followed the elder's instructions. He clamped Ryn's mouth closed and pinched his nostrils shut. He waited for a reaction, but none came. He lifted his eyes to the old Berrat, wordlessly begging for some reassurance he was doing the right thing. The seconds ticked by without any reaction or response.

"Was he too far gone?" Danny asked. "Was he beyond the help of a potion?"

"Ryn!" Breayn screamed as she fell beside her mate. "What happened to him? Why are you holding his mouth closed?" As Danny released his hold on the man's chin, his jaw flopped open, and the healing potion leaked out from the corner of his mouth.

"I tried to heal him," Danny said, but he had already passed to the Great Cycle. Breayn was searching his body for wounds but there was no visible damage to him, except for a deep bruise across his neck.

"He tried to rescue you, child," Sky Eyes said, reaching out to comfort the woman.

"I didn't need to be rescued," Breayn screamed out. "Heal him. Bring him back." Her eyes had become a swirling gray, like a storm was about to be unleashed once again.

"He's gone," Danny said, shaking his head. "The healing potion didn't work."

"He's not gone. Not fully." Breayn screamed as winds once again began to swirl around her. "The Phoenix can bring him back."

"I don't know how," Danny screamed, trying to be heard over the growing winds. Sky Eyes snatched up the vial of yellow liquid and quickly poured it over Ryn's face, neck, and chest.

"Do as she says," the elder screamed out, his voice barely penetrating the tempest swirling around them. His long gray ponytail was flapping about his head. He moved away from Ryn, shielding his eyes from the swirling dirt. Danny placed his hands across Ryn's chest and called upon the phoenix. The firebird erupted, engulfing Danny and Ryn in its orange-red flames. Ryn's eyes snapped wide open for barely a moment before they slammed shut and his face became contorted with agony. He swallowed hard before screaming out. The phoenix immediately receded, leaving Danny hovering over Ryn, his hands still pressed to the man's chest. His body was covered in severe burns in every location except where Sky Eyes had poured the yellow potion.

"Ryn," Breayn called, falling across the body of her mate. The winds quickly diminished as she took Ryn's face in her hands. "Come back to me, my love," she whispered. The burns on Ryn's body were slowly dissipating, being replaced with fresh skin. The healing potion was finally taking effect. The man's eyes snapped open, and his face became racked with terror. He sat bolt upright and began patting himself down, like he was still aflame. It took several moments before he regained control of himself. He gazed upon his mate, wide-eyed, before wrapping his arms around her, pulling her body close to his.

"I thought I was going to lose you to him," Ryn whispered in Breayn's ear, squeezing her more tightly. "I thought Boreas had finally won."

"I will never leave you, you fool," Breayn whispered back. "I am yours for eternity." The pair's embrace tightened. The sudden outpouring of intimate emotions made Danny uncomfortable.

"I like your new look," he said with a grin, patting the top of Ryn's head. "I'm sure your hair will grow back, eventually."

Chapter Nineteen

The Dawn of Rebellion

The rising sun broke over the horizon, lighting the sky in glorious reds, oranges, and yellows. The remnants of the night sky vanished with the sun's arrival. The four Berrat who were still huddled close together turned towards the morning light.

"Arise, Pele," Sky Eyes called out. His sonorous voice was rich and loud.

"Arise, Pele," the others repeated. A moment later, dozens of Berrat slaves stepped closer, repeating the morning mantra. Lady Kandyce, along with many of the soldiers who were still present, raised their face to the east and, in the same fashion, welcomed the sun god.

"On this morn, you will be freed of your bonds," Kandyce said to those gathered. "Slave and soldier alike, you will be free."

"With The Phoenix as our vanguard," the lieutenant stated, taking a knee, "the cycle will be broken." The gathered soldiers all took a knee, following their lieutenant. Garret immediately followed suit, bowing deeply to Danny. Looking as though somebody had just punched him in the stomach, Ryn, too, bowed deeply.

<hr>

The group had taken the conversation inside the reenforced jail-hut. It wasn't a particularly large building, and it felt rather confining with the number of people present. While they tried to have a conversation, there was a growing crowd of Berrat gathering outside. The raised voices of soldiers could be heard, warning them to stay back.

"We need to deal with my father," Kandyce said, staring blankly into the fire blazing in the middle of the hut. "As long as he draws breath, he will continue to poison the well."

"You would have us execute your father?" Breayn asked.

"The man stopped being my father the day he executed my mother, not that he was ever a father to me. He married my mother to gain her station when we lived in Wantage. She held a seat of power, and their union elevated his status considerably. I had already seen six summers when they met. He kept me around as 'his charming accessory,' as he called me."

"Well, the gallows are already set up," Garret stated. There was a bit too much enthusiasm in his voice. He quickly rubbed the back of his neck when everyone's eyes turned to him. "Just saying," he said, trying to cover up how badly he wanted to see the lord dangle from the end of a rope.

"We just need to find him," Kandyce said. "I have no idea where he would have hidden himself away."

The captain turned to the lieutenant, who had been quiet during their impromptu meeting. He raised his eyebrows, waiting for him to say where the lord was safely ensconced.

"Well, Lieutenant Barclay?" he asked. "As the head of his personal guard, you would be one of the few who knows the whereabouts of this secret location."

"I don't know where he is," the man stammered. "We left him in his room. How he gets out and where he goes is unknown to me. He only said that if this man was actually Lord Wing, then he'd know where he'd be." Danny considered the words for a moment.

"You left him in his room, and he never exited?" When the lieutenant nodded, Danny smiled. "If that's the last place he was, then I can follow him." The lieutenant furrowed his brows, drawing them tightly together.

"But the door is locked and likely barred on the inside," the man said, shaking his head. "It would take a battering ram to get through that door. The ferrous-wood it's made of is at least a foot thick." The idea that anything wooden could keep Danny at bay made him chuckle.

"Is this the right course of action?" Kandyce asked, directing her question to Sky Eyes. Like the lieutenant, the old Berrat had been sitting quietly in the shadows; watching and listening.

"Only Gaia knows," he said with a shrug. "What little knowledge I have of these events has nearly drawn to its completion."

"What do you mean, oh Wise One," Breayn said, lowering her head slightly as she addressed the elder.

"Please," Sky Eyes said, waving his hand, "don't call me that. You may call me by my name, even if it is nice to hear somebody hold on to the old ways." The old Berrat's eyes sparkled in the firelight. He had a calming presence about him. "But, to answer your question, somebody dear to me shared her visions of the future. She told me much of what was to transpire here in the last moon."

"Is that why you sought me out?" Kandyce asked. "Because you knew what would happen?"

"Yes, to a degree," Sky Eyes said. "Riva's visions were often vivid but muddled. She told me this is where I needed to be on the sixteenth anniversary of her daughter's birth."

"Titan's snowballs," Danny exclaimed. "You're *that* Sky Eyes? Kit's village elder? And the Riva you speak of is her mother?"

"I am, and she is," Sky Eyes said with a broad grin. "I would have expected you to put that together when I introduced myself, but I'm happy to see that you were able to eventually figure it out." Danny's face flushed hard, turning the color of his flame-red hair. Both Ryn and Breayn looked like they were going to explode with laughter.

"If you're all finished," Kandyce said, crossing her arms over her chest, "perhaps we can get to the matter at hand." Danny was clearly relieved that the uncomfortable conversation was being waylaid, allowing him to put on a better face.

"I'll go check out his room. Maybe I'll be able to figure out where he's holed up," Danny offered, perhaps with a bit more puffery than he had intended. His ego was still bruised, and he was looking for a way to heal it – quickly.

"You won't get in," Lieutenant Barclay said. "The door is impenetrable." The soldier's comment made Danny grin.

"Why don't we go visit the lord's chambers then, so you can watch me do the impossible?" Danny said, his lips pursing slightly while his eyes widened. He loved a challenge, especially one he knew he could complete – and would make him look good in the process.

"I don't think it's a good idea that we march through the streets as a group," Garret offered. "Even if Lady Kandyce now has the support of most of the soldiers, it's unlikely that she has the support of *all* of them." His jaw tightened as his eyes shifted to the lieutenant. With a defiant look, Barclay took a step towards the captain.

"Why don't you both escort me to the lord's quarters then," Danny said, running his fingers through his long red mane. "Surely, even those who stand with Byssus would not openly attack men such as yourselves." The feigned awe Danny put into his words was not lost on either soldier, or on Ryn.

"Just go and get it over with," Ryn said. "Return with what information you can gather."

⸎

"Phoenix," several people uttered and bowed as Danny emerged from the hut. If this had once been a secure location for Kandyce to meet with people, it was no longer. The red-haired Berrat crossed his arms over his chest in the Temple's traditional way.

"Titan's peace upon you," he said, drawing strange looks from those close enough to hear. He had forgotten his place. In the true north, the Berrat were all worshippers of the old gods, Gaia, Pele, and Medeina. The fact that many of the humans who lived here also worshipped them was not too surprising. "May Gaia watch over you and keep you safe," he quickly added.

The trio continued through the city until they reached the lord's manor, such as it was. There was a large contingent of perhaps thirty gold-cloaked guards standing outside the building's front. They were dressed in heavy, gray-enameled armor with weapons at the ready.

"Is this a problem?" Danny quietly asked Garret.

"These are Lord Byssus' personal guard. They were all hand-picked by him," Barclay replied.

"Do we need to bring more soldiers?" Danny wasn't sure how much damage they could do to him in his phoenix form, but he wasn't exactly ready to put that to the test. Not yet, at least.

"There is no need for more soldiers," the lieutenant said. He strode directly towards the group. As he approached, the guards closed ranks, barring him from going any further.

"You will stand down," the lieutenant ordered.

"We don't take orders from you. Not anymore," the guard nearest him responded. Based on his tone, he was begging the lieutenant to defy him. "We were told to let nobody enter, save Lord Wing. Are you him, Lieutenant Barclay?" The lieutenant eyed the lot of them. Some averted their gaze while the rest intently stared back.

"Well, Corporal," the lieutenant said, stepping in close to the lord's personal guard, "I can kill you, here and now, for not letting me pass, or we can let Lord Byssus publicly execute you and your family for your insubordination. Either way, choose your next words very carefully." The corporal stood nearly a head taller than the lieutenant. He held his weapon at the ready while the lieutenant stood before him, empty-handed. The guard had nearly thirty of his comrades at his back. He stood confidently, glaring at his lieutenant until Danny stepped closer, shaking out his long red mane as he did. The corporal's face lost its edge, but he did his best to maintain his surly demeanor. As Danny continued to stare at him, the guard shifted his weight uneasily from foot to foot, crumbling under the Crow-cloaked Berrat's scrutiny. He visibly had difficulty swallowing.

"Captain," Danny said as the tiniest of flames licked from the corner of his eye. "Gather your soldiers and take these fools into custody. I don't have time for this nonsense." The captain spun on his heel and left. As he did, the guard's undaunted expression faltered.

"You two may pass," the corporal said, taking a step to the side and lowering his weapon. There was an extended moment of indecision amongst the other guards, but they too eventually relented and cleared a path to the lord's manor. Neither Danny nor the lieutenant gave the guards a second look as they strode past them towards the door. While the phoenix burned just beneath Danny's skin, he felt somewhat invincible.

The building's shoddy workmanship was as bad on the inside as it was on the exterior. Either the Berrat who built the lord's home were incompetent or they simply chose to perform their task with substandard artistry. Several times Danny tripped when his toe caught on one of the many uneven stone slabs that made up the floor. Regardless of why everything was so poorly made, he smiled internally knowing that this lord was not living in a lifestyle that he had been accustomed to. It seemed that Danny had lingered too long, drawing the lieutenant's ire.

"Move," the man said as he led the way up the staircase. Danny followed a few steps behind while he continued to take in his surroundings. There were three doors leading off from the main entrance and all of them were closed. He had no way of knowing what was behind the doors, but he feared there were more of the lord's personal guards lying in wait.

When they reached the top of the stairs, there was a small landing with two thick wooden doors on either side. A small window facing the east allowed the morning sun to light the space with its warm rays. He wondered if this was the Berrat builders' way of giving a nod to Pele, letting him into the manor at morning's first light.

"The door will be barred from the inside," the lieutenant said in a condescending tone. "Would you like me to knock?" The man had a strange look on his face, one that Danny couldn't read.

"No need," he replied as he spied the bottom of the door. There was at least a two-inch gap between the floor and the door. In a heartbeat, the air around Danny shimmered just before he melted into his vole form. He took a quick peek over his shoulder to see the raised boot of the lieutenant. Not wanting to discover if his intention was fair or foul, he scampered under the door and into the lord's room.

Chapter Twenty

Cormorant

The sun was already making its descent when Kit and her friends rode up on the outskirts of Cormorant. Unlike the stunning, brilliant beauty of Silverhawk, this city was squat and dingy. The dark clouds to the north, along with a biting wind, did nothing to brighten the visage. Formidable walls surrounded the outer city. They were gray and stained with dirty white streaks, drained of any beauty as the sea's salty air slowly ate away at them. Kit's heart started to beat faster as they continued their approach. She still had no real plan for what they were going to do once they got there. All she had were just a lot of half-baked ideas.

"State your purpose," a well armed and armored guard bellowed out. Like the other guards, she was dressed in matt-black gear, carrying a ten-foot spear.

When Kit was slow to react, Indie responded to the guard, projecting as much confidence as he could muster. "We are here to secure passage to Ravenlord."

"Passenger vessels leave at first light," the guard replied. "Go to the Rusty Anchor, near the harbor. You should be able to secure passage there."

Kit moved closer to the helpful guard, so she wouldn't have to shout at her. "Where can I find the harbourmaster?"

The question seemed to surprise the guard. "Port Authority offices are just north of the main harbor. You'll find him there - but he'll be of no help in securing passage."

Kit gave the guard a thin-lipped smile. "My business with the captain is... personal." The statement seemed to satisfy the woman. She immediately stepped away, rejoining the other guards stationed to the side of the gate entrance.

Considering the city was in Berrathia, Kit was surprised that she didn't see a single Berrat. There was a significant human presence, mostly Western and Eastern humans, as well as ebony skinned Southerners. What was quickly obvious was that there were two distinct classes of people in this city – the extraordinarily rich and everybody else. Whether it was out of respect, or out of fear, the poor gave the rich a wide berth as they flaunted their wealth, wearing their fine clothes, and riding in their fancy carriages. On the rare occasion they happened to take notice of *the common folk*, they looked at them with disgust and derision. More often than not, they appeared to consider them a nuisance or an eyesore.

There was no signage to direct the group towards the harbor, but they had no difficulty finding their way. The briny smell of the sea, comingling with the stench of rotting fish, quickly guided them to their destination. As they got closer to the harbor, the cobbled roads ended, the horses then kicking up mud and gravel with each step they took. Boardwalks lined both sides of the streets. The wood had turned gray, and like the city's walls, it was heavily stained by the salty sea air. The railings that would serve to protect pedestrians from stepping onto the street were all but gone. Those that remained were rotted beyond repair.

Even though there were shops selling general goods and food, blacksmiths, tanners, and the like, the vast majority of the establishments were taverns and inns. Even though it was only early evening, every establishment had a large number of patrons inside, while flesh peddlers were turning an even better business outside. Men and women of all ages, barely dressed despite the cold, called out to the group as they passed by.

Just as the expansive harbor came into view, so did a thirty-foot tall, land-locked, rust and barnacle encrusted anchor. Despite it leaning at a precarious angle, people walked under it without concern. There was a single wooden shingle dangling from it with the words, "Rusty Anchor." Kit was thinking that this particular inn was in a better state of repair than most, when three men came tumbling out the door, throwing punches and cussing at one another. As one of the men drew a dagger, the other two quickly jumped on him and ripped him apart with their bare hands. When they stood, they were both covered in the man's blood, with a good amount of it around their mouths. Without a word, they simply walked back into the inn, leaving the remains of the man on the muddy street.

"Are they vampires?" Lin asked as a shiver ran up her spine.

"No," Indie and Kit replied at the same time.

"How can you tell?" Lin asked, directing her question to Kit.

"I just know," she replied, shaking her head. "When I met Pental, well, he felt different."

"They didn't move like vampires," Indie continued. "Perhaps they're hoping to be turned, but they were just maniacs who like to chew on people."

"This city is sick," Kit growled out. Runt and Lump, who had been following a few paces back from the group, took up positions on either side of her, surveying the area around them. "Just stay close, boys," she told them. "Don't do anything unless I say so."

When the group cleared the tavern district, the entire harbor opened up before them. Kit inhaled the briny sea air, letting it wash over her, rejuvenating her. She marveled at the shear size of it, spreading out before her in all directions. There were more docks than Kit could count. Even though the water sparkled like diamonds in the setting sun, everything there looked tired and dilapidated. There were dozens of large merchant ships, several enormous barges, and what looked like hundreds of fishing vessels. Kit's blood started to boil when she spied, on the far side of the harbor, seven black ships that rivaled the size of the largest merchant vessels in the port. Even at this distance, she could see sailors moving on and off the ships like ants in a pantry.

"Bring me closer," Kit said to Angel through their bond. *"But not too fast."* Angel immediately moved into a slow canter, with the rest of the group keeping pace. As they traveled across the harbor, Kit took note of the large, wooden buildings across from the docks; dozens of them. She could only assume that

these were warehouses, the storerooms for whatever cargo was being passed in or out of the city. Her stomach started to churn when she thought of how these same warehouses may be storing people.

The group rode in silence until they got closer to where the black ships were moored. Slaves, trudging off two of the ships, shuffled along in silence, their heads down, their hands tied together. Each slave was linked to the one walking in front of them. Most of the slaves were dwarves and some other blue-skinned race that Kit had never seen or heard of before. They were about the same size as the dwarves, but that's where their similarities ended.

"Why are they bringing dwarves and hobgoblins into the city?" Lin whispered to Kit.

"Hobgoblins? Is that who those other people are?" Kit had never heard of such a race before. They were not a part of the Temple's curriculum. Unlike the stern-faced dwarves, the hobgoblins looked excited to be there; their eyes wild, strange grins plastered on their faces.

"They're subterranean magical creatures," Lin replied, making a disgusted face. "They're in league with the dwarves, digging up minerals and gems and whatever other valuables they may find beneath the surface. Those pointy eared, blue-skinned freaks creep me out." Kit raised a questioning eyebrow at her friend. Lin smiled and shrugged in response. "I read a lot and they're some of the best enchanters on all of Orth, even better than the elves and dwarves."

A scuffle broke out between the slaves and their captors, cutting the conversation short. Without warning, two dwarves managed to overpower one of their captors, relieving him of his weapon. In a flash they used the small sword to cut their bonds just as three more slavers fell on them. With deadly skill the two dwarves quickly dispatched them, passing out the slavers' weapons to other dwarves. They were about to free some more of their brethren when a putrid smell blew past Kit. Seconds later, two tall, pale-skinned men had the escaped dwarves by their throats, dangling them in the air, grinning as their captives' feet kicked feebly about. The first of the pale-skinned men pulled back his hand, exposing long clawed fingers. He smiled grimly and plunged it into the belly of the dwarf, causing him to scream out in agony. The second, in a similar fashion, plunged his hand into his captive's chest, pulling out the dwarf's still beating heart. With a cruel sneer, he gorged on the organ, sucking it dry like it was juice-filled fruit.

"Those are vampires," Indie whispered. The boys were now growling, low and menacingly as they took up defensive positions to the left and right of the group.

The two vampires tossed their respective dwarves onto the docks and watched for a brief time while the procession of slaves once again started marching forward. The few dwarves who held liberated weapons, immediately dropped them to the ground, taking a terrified step away from them.

"You're not as stupid as you look," one of the vampires sneered. "If we didn't need you..." he let the words hang there as he kicked the weapons off the dock. When it appeared that the slaves were no longer resisting, the two vampires left as quickly as they had come.

The procession of slaves and their captors completely ignored the mutilated dwarves, their lifeblood pouring out of them, dripping between the rotting deck-boards into the salty sea below. Once the docks had been cleared, Kit dismounted and ran to the fallen men. There was no helping the dwarf who'd had his heart ripped out, but the other dwarf, the one who had taken the stomach wound, was still alive, groaning.

When Kit bent over the dwarf, he turned his head to face her. "Are ya here to finish me off?" he asked. "If so, be quick about it, would you?"

"Shield me," Kit said to Indie and Lin. As soon as they moved around her, Kit placed her hand on the wound. "Titan, hear me," she called out, like she had so many times before. Again, before she could begin the prayer to her god, Kit's hands took on the familiar golden aura. As the glow spread out across the dwarf's abdomen, Kit grimaced and buckled over from the pain that ripped through her own belly. Many seconds later the pain passed, and with it, so did the golden aura. When the dwarf tried to sit up, she pressed him back down on the dock. "Everyone thinks you're dead," she hissed at him. "If you stand, they'll just come and collect you."

The dwarf grabbed Kit by the wrist, struggling to free himself from under Kit's hand until her eyes flashed golden.

"Who are you?" he asked as he released his grip on her. "Why did you heal me?"

"I am a friend," Kit said with a small smile. "That's all you need to know."

"Kit, people are coming," Indie whispered. "They've got a small wagon with them."

"Can you swim?" Kit asked. Even though he shook his head, Kit stood up and kicked the dwarf over the edge of the dock, the sea water instantly swallowing him. When the men with the wagon started to shout, Kit kicked the dead dwarf into the water as well. "They had nothing of value on them," she said to the men with the wagon, interrupting their protestations. "Who wants to cart their smelly-ass bodies around when the sea will take care of it for us?"

"Who are you?" one of the men asked as he reached for a wicked-looking blade at his hip.

"If you have to ask, then you don't need to know," Lin replied with a sneer. Her ability to easily slide into this bad-ass persona threw Kit for a loop. She seemed too comfortable pretending to be a villain. When the men didn't leave quickly enough, Lin stepped toward them. "Perhaps you'd like to join your smelly friends?" she offered, motioning to the water. Suddenly, there were a series of huge splashes under the dock.

The three men with the cart blanched and shook their heads. They all took a step away from the edge. "Not with the Makara, we don't." Kit didn't know what Makara were, but whatever they might be, nobody was willing to risk swimming with them. Without another word the three men left, moving back towards the shore with Kit and company close behind.

"Move it!" Lin yelled at them. "Speed up, or step aside." When the three men practically broke into a sprint, Lin looked back over her shoulder and grinned.

"What's a Makara?" Kit asked, cautiously peering into the dark-green waters. "Do you think that dwarf got eaten?" Lump rubbed his face along Kit's thigh to get her attention. When she looked down at him, he shook his head. "Do you know what they are?" she asked him. He gave her a big doggie-smile in response. "Tell me later then. You can't be shifting right now."

CHAPTER TWENTY-ONE

THE PORT AUTHORITY

As they walked along the docks, heading towards the Port Authority offices, Kit got a sick feeling in her stomach. What if, whatever that Makara thing was, ate that poor dwarf she'd pushed into the sea? She shuddered thinking about him dying beneath the surface of the water, some monstrous creature ripping him to pieces.

"Kit, hurry back. There are people... they're trying to take Char!" Angel's voice was frantic.

Before Kit had a chance to say something to Indie, he was already running full-out, his feet banging heavily on the dock-boards as he ran. "Help him," Kit yelled to the boys as she and Lin started running as well. In a heartbeat, Runt and Lump were flying down the dock, passing Indie in mere seconds.

Without breaking stride, Kit pulled her dragon hammer from its sheath. "You've been awfully quiet, Fury. Whatever it is that's been eating you, let it go. We've got work to do." When Kit didn't feel the familiar touch of the dragon, she called on the hammer's power, igniting its blinding light.

By the time Kit reached the end of the dock, she had already caught up to Indie. About one hundred paces away, there were about fifteen people trying to take control of their horses. While Runt and Lump attacked, the three horses were kicking wildly, sending several of their assailants sprawling across the mud-covered ground. Those people still standing had multiple ropes around the necks of the horses, pulling them in various directions, staying clear of the horses' hooves and teeth.

"Release my horses, now!" Kit bellowed, just before she came within striking range. When none of them stopped, she barreled full force into one of the larger men holding onto Angel, slamming the big man onto his back. Kit brought her elbow down into the man's face, with a resounding crunch. Before she had a chance to stand back up, a black streak – Runt, flew past her, attacking a tall slender woman wielding a long, curved sword at Kit's back. There was a blood-curdling scream when Runt closed his jaws on her elbow, his teeth breaking skin and bone, forcing the would-be attacker to drop her weapon.

Kit popped up to her feet, spinning about, searching for her next target. Her heart was pumping hard, but there was a quiet serenity within her, something she would never have thought she'd experience mid-battle. She took a deep, cleansing breath when it became clear to her that every would-be thief had been dealt with. Judging by the way they were all moaning and rolling around in the mud, she was confident there were no fatalities.

"Don't let anybody get up," Kit instructed the boys. "If anyone tries to run, bite off their feet." Lump and Runt immediately started patrolling the fallen, making sure that they all stayed put.

"Let her go, Char," Indie said to his big stallion who had one of his attackers by the hair, holding her up while her feet kicked wildly. With a shake of his head, he tossed the woman onto the ground and then stepped on her chest, pinning her in the mud. Indie walked over to the thief, putting his sword to her throat. "Why were you trying to steal our horses?"

"... can't... breathe," the woman wheezed. "Help me!" Indie looked up at Char and shook his head. The big stallion snorted before removing his hoof from her chest.

"Thank you," the woman cried. "We weren't trying to steal them. We weren't."

Indie remained quiet for a moment, before giving the woman a wicked smile. "My horse says otherwise. He says that you are their leader, and that you told your people to take the horses and hide them in the warehouses." The woman's eyes went wide in disbelief, her gaze shifting between Indie and the angry black stallion glaring down at her.

"They were left unattended," the woman whimpered, acting justified for taking the horses. "As members of the Port Authority, it's within our mandate to remove any unattended items from the dock area."

"You're Port Authority?" Kit asked, suddenly much keener on hearing what this woman had to say. When the woman nodded, Kit took a knee next to her. "So, you must know Rayan Staul."

The woman nodded again, with more enthusiasm this time. "Cap's our boss."

"Good," Kit said as she stood up. "Get your people on their feet and escort us to your boss. Now!"

The woman gingerly stood up, grasping her chest where Char had been standing on her. She called for her people to get up. Some of them did, but many more stayed where they were. After screaming a series of orders at them, several more pulled themselves to their feet, but there were still several who would not, or could not, comply.

"Help those who can't stand," Kit said to Lin. She remembered the potions that Jayne had given her, just before they'd left. "Use some of our healing potions if you have to. They're in my saddlebags."

Kit approached one of the men who was still laying prone. His leg was badly mangled, a crimson pool beneath him was slowly seeping into the wet ground. She listened carefully to his breathing, finding it low and raspy. "Hear me, Titan," she said softly just before her hands started to glow golden. As she placed them on the gaping wound, she felt an intense pain in her own leg. A moment later, her pain passed, and the man's mangled leg was once again whole. When Kit stood, she presented her hand, offering to help him to his feet. He returned the gesture with a scowl.

"You'll pay for this," he growled at Kit, picking himself up off the ground. After gingerly testing his leg under his own weight, he took a step closer to her. "The masters will rip you apart and I'll feast on your remains."

"How's about I let my friends here rip you apart and feast on *your* remains?" The boys came padding up beside Kit, helping to make her point. The man's face went pale at the sight of the two canines, particularly so when he looked at the dire wolf. "Judging by your reaction, perhaps you'll be a bit less... surly with me?" The two boys pulled back their lips, exposing their formidable teeth. Without a word, he pushed past Kit and the boys, and took up a position behind the Port Authority leader.

I'll need to keep an eye on that one. He saw Runt as a wolf.

Kit gave everyone a big, feigned smile when they were all grouped together. "Alright then, let's go see your boss." She motioned to the woman. "Lead the way."

As the group headed towards the Port Authority offices, they walked past a sizeable crowd that had gathered during the altercation. "Nothing more to see here," Kit said. As she scanned the group, she caught sight of a woman with long blonde hair in the crowd, but she disappeared into the throng before she could get a better look at her.

⊷⊶⊷⊶⊷⊶

The office building itself was a squat, wooden structure with what looked to be a tiled roof. The building might have once been a bright, cheery white, but it had been many winters since it had seen a fresh coat of paint. The signage was even more worn, with the words, Port Authority, barely even visible.

Each stair groaned as the group climbed the short flight of decrepit wooden steps. When the man Kit had healed started to climb them, she grabbed him by the elbow. "Stay out here with the horses. If anybody bothers with them, my friends here will rend you limb from limb." The man attempted to pull his arm from Kit's grasp, but she maintained her hold on him. "If you try to leave, well," Kit pointed down at his badly torn trousers, "those old wounds will look like a small scrape compared to what they'll do to you." Again, the man tried to free himself from Kit's grip, and again, he failed. Kit dug her fingers into his flesh, causing him to wince. "Understood?" When the man finally stopped trying to resist her grasp, she let him go and headed up the stairs and into the building, stopping just before she reached the doorway.

"If he tries to run," she said to the boys who were standing on either side of the man, "you are free to eat him." She let her eyes move to Angel. *"Let me know if anything is amiss,"* she said through their bond. *"I have no idea what we're walking into here."*

As Kit stepped through the doorway, the scents of spices, alcohol, and body odor overwhelmed her senses. There was something sour in the air, so strong that she could practically taste it. There were crates everywhere; in some cases, stacked as high as the ceiling. In addition to the people Kit had come in with, there were likely another twenty or thirty people in the expansive room, inspecting the contents of each crate.

Kit followed her group, wending their way through the cargo and desks that covered the dirt floor, until they came to a door with a small sign that read, "No Admittance." The woman, the group's leader, motioned to the door with her head. "You'll find Cap in here." The woman crossed her arms in front of her chest, waiting for Kit to open the door.

"Lead the way," Kit said with a silky, threatening tone.

The woman simply shrugged, opened the door, and stepped inside. As soon as she did, a man bellowed out, "Bango, get out, and close the damned door!" There were muffled screams and sounds of people rushing about inside the room.

Kit pushed past Bango, a strange name if she'd ever heard one, to find an overweight, middle-aged man dressed in nothing but his small clothes. There were a number of barely dressed women in the room with him; most of them bound and gagged. Kit's face turned red with rage. "Get everyone who tried to steal our horses in here. NOW!"

The entire crew came piling into the office, with Indie and Lin at the rear, making sure none of them slipped away. When they were all in, Indie slammed the door shut, using his body to block any chance of escape.

"Bango, what is the meaning of this?" the man screamed out, his skin reddening while his jowls flapped about. "What are these people doing in *my office*?"

Kit ignited the light of her hammer again, causing her golden eyes to flash. "Staul, shut up, sit down, and listen!" Kit growled at him, bits of spittle flying from her mouth.

"Who do you think you are, you stupid little girl?" the man bellowed back at her. He quickly ran his fingers through his thinning salt and pepper hair and puffed out his chest. His lower lip protruded heavily as he attempted to don an air of superiority. "I am Allister Buttsworth, the lord of Cormorant, and I will have you all flayed for this intrusion."

Kit stepped up and kicked the fat man in the groin, causing him to buckle over and topple forward onto his face. He whimpered softly as he lay prone with his abundantly sized buttocks sticking up into the air. "I don't like being lied to," Kit spat at him. "Do it again, and they will be the last words you'll ever speak." The fat man fell over onto his side, maintaining a tight grip on his injured *parts*. He made a few unintelligible noises before he started bawling.

"Who is he?" Kit screamed at Bango. "Tell me true."

"He is who he said." Bango squirmed under Kit's gaze. "He is Allister Buttsworth, but he is not the lord of Cormorant. He's a ruling member of House Hanse, but he doesn't hold a seat of power." When Kit got a questioning look on her face, Bango gave her a smug smile. "You really don't know anything about this city, do you?" The woman strode up to Kit. Whatever fear she had previously shown melted away. "The masters are going to…" Kit's foot abruptly cut off her words when it landed squarely into her chest, slamming the woman into other members of the Port Authority. As she tried to get to her feet, Kit kicked her again, this time in the ribs, using the toe of her leather boots. The woman screeched in pain as she curled up into a small ball, trying to ward off any additional blows.

"The masters are the least of your problems, you foolish woman," Kit threatened, grabbing Bango by her ratty black hair, dragging her to her feet. "I might be new to Cormorant, but I'm a quick study." The woman struggled weakly against Kit's hold, her face contorting in pain as she did. Kit pulled a bone-hilt dagger from a sheath on Bango's thigh, and threw it at Lord Buttsworth, sinking its eight-inch blade into the wooden floor, inches from his thigh. The fat, nearly naked man recoiled from the knife, blubbering uncontrollably.

"They'll kill you. They'll kill me. They'll kill all of us if we disobey," Bango said as she dropped down to her knees. "If we don't follow the lord's orders, the masters simply replace us with someone who will." Kit listened carefully; the truth of the woman's words washed over her. She took a knee, leveling her eyes with Bango's.

"By the time I leave this city, there won't be a *master* left standing, but I'll need your help. If you refuse, I won't hurt you or your family. But I will have to lock you up, to prevent you or your people from warning the masters." Kit stood, offering Bango a hand up.

"I don't see how a little girl, such as yourself, is going to rid this city of the masters, but I will help however I can." Bango walked over to where Lord Buttsworth was cowering and yanked her dirk from the floorboards next to him. He winced at her actions, drawing himself away from the woman. She stuffed the bone-hilt dagger back into the sheath on her thigh. "You're pathetic," she said to the whimpering lord, "and your days are numbered."

"Just like that?" Lin asked. "You're going to help us against the masters just because Mistress Kit said she was going to rid the city of them?" Bango shrugged.

"I've seen everything I needed to see," she said. "The tide is changing, and I believe Mistress Kit will do what she says. If she can rid us of the masters, we will follow her to the ends of the earth. If any of my crew acts against any of you, I will declare them traitors and deal with them accordingly." Bango looked to the members of her team; all of them acknowledging their agreement. Kit felt they were all speaking truthfully, at least those who spoke their agreement aloud. Apparently, they'd rather serve under anyone who wasn't a vampire master.

Sickened by the lord's sniveling behavior, Kit motioned to several of Bango's people. "Take this man, gag him, and lock him up someplace where he won't be found – and get some clothing for these women."

As soon as Bango had finished putting her people into motion, Kit pulled her aside. She growled at the woman, shaking her head. "Why did you bring me in here, to this office? Where is Harbourmaster Staul?"

Chapter Twenty-Two

Slaves, Weapons, and a Plan

Bango's people had already left Lord Buttsworth's office, leaving her alone with Kit and her cohorts. Lin had given the lord's sexual playthings some blankets to cover themselves while Bango's people fetched them some proper clothing. Kit stared at Bango, waiting for an answer to her question.

"I brought you here because I wanted to gauge your reaction," Bango responded, holding Kit's gaze. When the priest didn't respond, she continued. "There have been a couple of young men snooping around here for the past few days, asking questions, and spending a lot of time with members of the Union. I wanted to see for myself who you were."

"The *Union*?" Kit had a vague recollection of the name, but she couldn't remember from where she'd heard of it.

Bango rolled her eyes at Kit. "The *Fair Traders Union*? You've never heard of them?" When Kit shook her head, Bango huffed in frustration. "How can you possibly hope to affect change if you don't know the major players?"

Kit shrugged, smiled, batted her eyes, and patted her hammer all at once, making Bango laugh out loud. "I have Titan at my back and friends by my side. What I lack in knowledge, I make up for in *enthusiasm*."

"You are not the person I was expecting," Bango said as she shut the door to the office. She looked over at the fat lord's sex slaves. Until that moment they had been standing quietly in the corner, wrapped in blankets, covering up their nakedness. Bango gave them a small smile. "Not the person at all."

"You were expecting me?"

Bango's eyes traveled up and down Kit, as though she was trying to take measure of her. "The way your friends spoke of you, I was expecting something... more."

"What friends?" Indie asked, moving in beside Kit. "Nobody knew we were coming."

"That's not exactly true," Lin called out from where the women prisoners were. She had been *examining* them closely while the others were talking. She smirked at Indie when he gave her an incredulous look.

"Tell me of my friends," Kit demanded. "Where are they now?"

"I believe their names are Treedale and Mukale," Bango replied, raising her eyebrows, challenging Kit to deny what she was saying. "A Nomad and a Berrat. They're not much better at this than you are, and you didn't set the bar particularly high."

Kit's heart started racing. Treedale and Mukale were supposed to gather information, not meet with people, and they certainly weren't supposed to talk about her coming to the city. "I asked you where they are."

"I have no idea, not exactly anyway." Bango shrugged, giving one of the female prisoners a questioning look.

The prisoner was a tall, slender woman with long, dirty blonde hair. She dropped her blanket to the ground and walked towards Kit, perfectly comfortable with her partial nudity. When Lin tried to cut her off, she paused, raising her empty hands in a defensive pose. "Last I heard, they were going to try to break into *King Karter's* house. They're looking for the manifests for tonight's shipments."

"And who are you, and who is King Karter?" Kit asked. Her head was starting to swim again. There was simply too much information coming in from too many directions.

"My name is Luna. Until a few days ago, I was Logan Buttsworth's girlfriend. His dad, the fat lump of lard you so skillfully emasculated, is his father." Luna shivered while managing to maintain a surprisingly serene appearance. "Robyrt Karter is the head of House Hanse, and he is the self-proclaimed King of Berrathia."

"Your boyfriend's father was going to..." Kit's face screwed up with revulsion. Whatever terrible things were happening to him at that moment, well, they weren't terrible enough. "Why? What sort of sick, twisted individual is that man? How badly broken does someone need to be to even think about something so horrendous, let alone actually try to carry it out?"

"Logan, and many of the younger House members, want to get out of the slave trade. Since the Split Crows took over Taseko, things have become too reckless, too violent. But the other House members, the older ones in particular, won't give it up. There is too much gold and too much power at stake."

Once again, Kit's mind was drowning in the information. She had no real plan for what she was going to do once she got to Cormorant, other than trying to find the man who had taken Treedale. She suddenly felt like a little girl trying to hold back a flood with nothing more than her bare hands.

"Just stop talking. Everyone, just stop talking. I need some time to think!" Kit was breathing heavily now, dark spots dancing in front of her eyes. When she felt a pair of strong arms gently wrap around her, she turned towards them, into the comfort they were providing. At that very moment, more than anything else, she just wanted to lose herself in the reassurance of Indie's embrace.

"If you want to do something about tonight's shipment, time is a luxury you don't have." There was an unexpected softness to Bango's demeanor, despite the sense of urgency in her words. "The tide is coming in and I expect the ships will set sail in no more than two hours."

"Why would Mukale want to get the ship manifests?" Lin asked, still keeping a close eye on Luna. "They're transporting slaves. What more do we need to know?"

"There are more than just slaves being taken on the ships," Bango responded, sounding a bit exasperated that Kit was still hiding within Indie's embrace. "There are seven ships heading out tonight. We don't know which ships will be carrying slaves, which will be carrying weapons, and where each ship is heading. The manifests will tell us all that, and more." Lin's reaction clearly showed that she was the only one who understood what Bango was getting at, forcing her to continue. "We want to stop the slave ships, especially the ones headed for Faol."

"What kind of weapons are being shipped?" Kit asked, pulling herself from Indie's arms.

"Mostly silvered," Bango replied. "We expect that Faol is planning on starting a war with Lycos, which, as you know, is lousy with lycans; were-creatures of all sorts. They're particularly vulnerable to silvered weapons."

Kit didn't know what she was hoping to hear, but anti-lycan gear wasn't it. But, if Faol was equipping for war, then there should be a large number of weapons and armor in that shipment. Kit's eyes suddenly lit up. "Where would these silvered weapons be stored?"

"All the shipments leaving the harbor are stored in the warehouses by the docks," Bango replied. "But they've likely already been loaded onto the ships."

"Where are the dwarves being held?" Kit continued, her words coming out faster than her brain could keep up. "The ones who were just unloaded. And what about the Berrat people who the Auctioneers are planning to ship out tonight? Where are they being held?"

"The dwarves are likely in warehouse eleven." Bango tapped her finger to her chin as she considered her answer. "It would make the most sense since it is the only one with empty pens, and they're incoming, not outgoing. As for the Berrat, they're in several warehouses. There is likely close to two thousand of them being shipped out tonight."

Whatever indecision or anxiety Kit had felt before, it immediately vanished. A plan, such as it was, began to form in her mind. It wasn't really a plan, but an idea, a thought, a concept. Unable to explain it, she simply started barking orders. "Find the weapons," she ordered Bango. "If they're on the ship, have them offloaded. If they're in the warehouse, hold them. Whatever you do, make sure they're readily accessible. And where are the masters? The two vampires who were on the docks. Where would they be if they're not overseeing operations?"

"The masters are likely in the same warehouse as the dwarves," Bango responded, wondering where Kit was going with this. "If the weapons are already on the ships, there is no way for me to get them off. There would be no reason to order their removal."

Kit's eyes flashed golden at the woman, as righteous fury built up inside of her. "I don't care how you do it, but you're going to do it. If the weapons are not available when I return, well, we'll likely all be passengers on the ships – or food for those sea monsters in the harbor." Kit's head spun to Lin. "Go with her. Make sure everything goes as planned." Kit reached into a pocket and produced a dragon tear, tossing it to Lin. "Tell me where the weapons are once they're secured. Make sure every crate is opened. We won't have time to fuss with them once things start happening."

"What are you planning?" Lin asked as she tucked the dragon tear into her tunic.

"No time to explain, just do it. Okay?"

"Yes, Mistress," Lin replied, giving Kit a sly grin and a grandiose curtsy. "As you command."

"Kit, you need to get out here. Now!" Angel's voice was agitated, but not fearful. *"There is someone trying to sneak up on us, but whoever it is, they're very bad at it."*

Kit was just about to bolt for the door when she spun around to ask where she would find warehouse eleven. Bango barely had a chance to point out the direction of the building when Kit raced past her with Indie close on her heels.

CHAPTER TWENTY-THREE

TO CATCH A SNEAK

Kit came charging out of the port authority offices, her hammer at the ready, her head on a swivel. The horses were all standing together with the boys sitting calmly a few paces from them.

"Who's trying to sneak up on you?" Kit asked Angel through their bond. The small roan motioned with her nose towards the corner of the building. There were a good deal of shrubs and crates and other refuse there, affording, whoever it was, plenty of cover. A panicked look crossed Kit's face.

"Where's the man I left out here with you?" she asked, looking around.

"He tried to run," Angel answered, a hint of wicked joy in her voice. *"The boys caught him before he got very far."* Kit looked over at Runt and Lump. Their muzzles were covered in blood and they both had a look of satisfaction on their faces. Kit shook her head. She wasn't sure if she was upset or proud of them. She motioned towards the corner of the building, where Angel had said the sneak was.

"Don't let whoever's there get away," she said with a mischievous grin. "But just hold them, whoever it is."

Lump and Runt immediately broke towards the corner of the office building. Lump took a path around the side of the shrubs while Runt simply jumped over them. A moment later, there was a screech, followed by a long string of curses. When Kit arrived a few seconds later, the boys had a dwarf pinned against the wall of the building.

"Sweet Gaia, git yer mongrels off me," the dwarf cried. "I'm just doin' what ye asked me ta do."

"I thought you got eaten," Kit said, her eyes wide. She scrubbed the back of her neck and blew out a breath. "After I tossed your kin into the water, there was a huge splash. I thought a Makara got you."

"That was no sea-devil," the dwarf said holding out his hands to the boys, letting them sniff him. "Ya throwed that man right on top of me. I nearly drowned. We dwarves are not strong swimmers. Not much need of paddling around in the water when you're hundreds of feet down in the mines." Both Runt and Lump warmed up to the dwarf, letting him give them a good scratching. "My name's Coldforge."

"You're alive!" Indie exclaimed as he came skidding around the bushes, both swords drawn.

"And you're late," Coldforge grinned. His bright orange beard and mustache hid most of his face, but his smile still managed to show through the unruly mass of facial hair. "My name's Coldforge." The dwarf stuck out his meaty, heavily calloused hand. The pair clasped forearms. The dwarf's grip practically crushed Indie's bones as they completed their greeting.

"Can your kin fight?" Kit asked. "The ones who got taken off the ship. Are they warriors?"

"Girl, we're dwarves. We are natural born miners and natural born fighters. When we're not diggin', we're scrappin'." Coldforge's happy demeanor suddenly changed. "Proper folk give their name when someone offers them their own. As I said, my name is Coldforge."

As though it was a sufficient reason for not answering her question, Kit simply responded. "We're a bit short on time for pleasantries, but since you asked so nicely, my name is Kit, and this man is Indie. The golden retriever's name is Lump, and the dire wolf's is Runt." Kit had completely forgotten that Runt's spell prevented the dwarf from seeing him in his natural state, but the illusion melted away as soon as she said he was a wolf.

"Gaia, protect me!" Coldforge screamed, backing up hard against the building. "Yer a freakin' monster!" Runt whimpered at the dwarf's assertion, his eyes showing deep hurt. The puppy's reaction melted the dwarf's heart. "No 'fence, big fella. You kinda caught me unaware." Coldforge's attention went back to Kit. "Is it some kind of frookin' joke, calling this guy, Runt? He's the biggest wolf I've ever seen."

Apparently, whatever hurt Runt felt at the dwarf's words was immediately forgotten and forgiven. He promptly started washing the man's face, his tail wagging frantically as he did. When he finally pulled back, the dwarf's wild orange beard was now soaking wet, looking even more chaotic than ever.

"Okay, so you can fight," Kit growled, interrupting the festivities. She pulled her dagger from its sheath and offered it to him.

"I'd rather have that mithril hammer, girly, if it's all the same to you. If'n you're not willing to part with it, I'll just use me hands." When the dwarf curled his hands up into fists, they looked more like blocks of granite than flesh and bone. Coldforge looked down at his stone-fists. "Family trait," he said with a grin. "We don't always have access to a fine hammer like yours, or a nice hefty ax."

"Follow me," Kit said as she sprinted off towards the back of the office building. Indie and the boys followed suit, and the four of them quickly left Coldforge behind. When Kit reached the far corner of the building, she looked back to see the dwarf, puffing hard, trying his best to keep up. "Is that as fast as you can run?" she hissed at him. The dwarf was practically gasping for air when he caught up to the rest of the group.

"We dwarves are not runners," he said, still wheezing heavily. "Diggers, fighters, and drinkers we are – but we don't *run*. Maybe I can ride the big feller?" When it became clear that Runt would like nothing more than to carry this man, Coldforge leapt up onto his back. "He's a lot softer than them frookin' firebugs we ride in the mines."

Kit wanted to ask about the firebugs, but there were more pressing matters to attend to. Without a word, she bolted from her spot and raced across the road towards the warehouses behind the office building. The two warehouses in front of her were massive, with large numbers *four* and *five* on them, written in dark red paint. "We're looking for warehouse eleven," Kit whispered to Indie as they ran side by side down the alley between buildings four and five. Coldforge was coming up behind them, whooping and hollering. She groaned to herself. This man had no idea how to sneak. Feeling that there was no hope of arriving at the warehouse *unannounced*, Kit decided to just run full out until she located the building. As soon as she got to the end of the alley, she came to an abrupt stop and signaled to her cohorts to do the same. Directly across the street was building eleven.

There were large double doors at the front of the warehouse; one closed and the other slightly ajar. Eight guards were milling about in front of the entrance, none of whom appeared to be paying any attention to what was going on around them.

"Do you trust me?" Kit asked Coldforge, motioning for him to get down off Runt.

"I suppose," the dwarf replied, the corners of his mustache pushing upwards. "Ye saved me hide, so why wouldn't I trust ye."

"I need you to pretend to be my prisoner," Kit continued; her comment sounding more like a question than a statement. "I need a reason for approaching the building. One that won't set everyone on us all at once."

"You've got the eyes of a goddess, with the heart of a dwarf." Coldforge's whiskers were practically dancing on his face. "Walk me right up to 'em and then we'll crack open some skulls."

Kit chuckled. "I was going to get them to show me where your kin are kept, but your idea works, too."

"Ye don't need to have somebody show ye the way. These boys here got me scent." The dwarf gave Lump a good scratch on his hind end. "I expect they could find me kin in the dark, even if they're a league away."

Indie stifled a laugh. "You do have a *unique aroma*," he said. The dwarf's eyes danced with mischief, clearly taking no offense to Indie's insinuation – outright declaration – that he smelled.

"We don't have time for this," Kit growled. She promptly grabbed Coldforge by the beard and started dragging him towards the guards. The dwarf quickly grasped his hands behind his back, making it look like he was in manacles.

"I caught the one who got away," Kit called out to the guards, spinning her hammer in her hand. They quickly snapped to attention, surprised by the small woman's declaration. The idea that a prisoner had escaped put the guards on edge. It definitely wouldn't go well for them if the masters knew somebody had run off on their watch.

"We didn't know any had escaped," one of the guards said as he led three others towards Kit and her cohorts. "We'll take him from here." The remaining four guards quickly closed the gap as they hustled to catch up to their comrades.

"So that you can take the credit for my catch?" Kit said, pushing her way through the group of guards. "Not going to happen. If anyone's going to get the credit for catching this smelly little man, it's going to be me."

Not liking Kit's attitude, one of the guards grabbed her by the shoulder. "Hold it right there," he sneered, as he tried to spin her around.

"Ye have no manners," Coldforge said as he grabbed the guard's wrist, snapping it in his hand like a twig. "Ye don't lay yer hand on a lady without her permission." Using his other hand, he punched the guard in the ribs, breaking them as easily as he had broken the bones in his wrist. The guard made a weak, wheezing sound before coughing up blood, spraying it across the ground.

The remaining guards were stunned by Coldforge's brutal attack. Before they even had a chance to bring their weapons to bear, Indie ran two of the guards through with his twin longswords. Their eyes bulged as he pushed the blades of his swords into them, up to their hilt. Before the guard in front of her had a chance to process what had just happened, Kit slammed her hammer into her face, sending her sprawling across the ground.

Not wanting any part of this confrontation, the four remaining guards broke for the warehouse. Before Kit could issue an order, the boys took off after the fleeing sentries. Then, without hesitation, Kit joined the boys in their chase.

Lump quickly dropped one of the guards, grabbing her by the ankle, while Runt quickly disabled another, biting him high on his hip, tearing open his leg in the process. Not stopping to finish him off, the dire wolf continued on, clipping another in a similar fashion. The last guard, a woman, had almost made it inside when Runt fell on her. She barely had a chance to call for help before the dire wolf ended her life with a single bite to the back of her neck.

While Runt dragged the woman away from the entrance, Kit finished off the two he had hamstrung, and Indie ended the life of the woman Lump had brought down.

"Yer pretty handy with yer weapons," Coldforge said, breathing heavily after his short sprint. "I haven't had a fight this good in many moons."

"I'm glad you're enjoying yourself," Kit responded dryly. "Let's get inside and find your kin."

Lump's dog-form shimmered slightly before he changed into his human form. "Frookin Helja!" Coldforge practically screamed. "Yer a weredog?"

Lump completely ignored the dwarf. "There are vampires inside. Both Runt and I can smell them." Coldforge's hand unconsciously went to his side, holding the spot where the vampire had plunged his clawed hand inside him.

"Let me and the boys deal with them," Indie insisted, taking up a position between Kit and the entrance to the warehouse. "We're trained to fight them, you're not."

"And I can naturally resist their compulsion," Kit challenged him back. "We go in together, or I go in alone." Kit shook her hammer in front of her face. "Besides, with all of Lin's enchantments, I'm loaded for vampire, and if Fury ever decides to show up, I can roast them before they can try anything." Kit shook her hammer a few more times. "C'mon Fury, whatever it is you're pouting about, let it go!"

"They're coming," Lump interrupted, just before shifting back into dog form.

"What have we here?" one of the two vampires asked as he stepped out from the warehouse, his black cloak flapping behind him. The wind shifted, blowing the creature's putrid odor directly towards Kit. She tried to not react to the stench but doing so was no simple feat.

"I have one of your prisoners," Kit replied smoothly. "These guards tried to take my prize from me."

"And who are you?" the other vampire asked, running his fingers through his heavily oiled hair. "It's not very often that somebody brings us a dire wolf."

Okay, they're enemies. Not that it was much of a surprise, but if they were seeing Runt in wolf form, they clearly planned on doing Kit and her cohorts harm. "The wolf is mine, but I believe this smelly little guy is yours." Kit pushed Coldforge in front of her, causing him to stumble awkwardly.

"I thought I had killed you," the first vampire said, moving slowly towards Kit. "I see why you make such good miners. You're as resilient as you are ugly." As the vampire spoke, his fingers elongated, turning into wicked claws.

The vampire suddenly vanished and in less than a heartbeat later, materialized in front of Kit. His eyes were wide, seemingly full of surprise. He made an odd gurgling noise as he stood motionless before her. His bottom jaw dropped open, exposing the steel within. Thick black blood poured out from his gaping mouth. It was only then that Kit noticed Indie holding a sword in front of her, the blade sticking up under the vampire's chin. As Indie extracted his blade, the vampire dropped to the ground at Kit's feet.

"Bind the girl," the remaining vampire called out, magic dripping from his words. "She will make a fine bride."

Indie put his blades away and grabbed Kit by the arms. His grip was like iron. She tried to break free, but he maintained his hold.

Both Lump and Runt began to snarl at the vampire as he strode towards Kit. They moved in opposite directions, trying to flank the creature. "Down," he commanded. Again, Kit could feel the magic in his words. The boys immediately dropped to the ground, seemingly held by some unseen force.

"Wait until he's closer," Indie whispered, barely moving his lips.

The vampire gave Kit an arrogant grin. "Foolish mortals, thinking you can stand against me, a full-fledged vampire." He slowly ran his tongue across the tips of his fangs. "I can't wait to taste you," he continued as he moved closer, snuffling at the air. "Your blood will be honey-sweet. I can smell its intoxicating aroma already. With each beat of your heart, it calls to me, beckoning me to take you, to make you mine for all eternity."

Kit tilted her head to the side, inviting his bite. With a flick of her head, she threw her long black hair over her shoulder, fully exposing her throat.

"Take me," she whispered, her voice deep and husky, full of desire. The vampire's pace picked up, his strides becoming longer, more purposeful. Kit licked her lips and moaned softly as he neared. The vampire, now standing directly in front of her, ran his long, clawed fingers across her cheek, tilting her head even further to the side.

"I want you…" she sighed as she looked up into his black, lifeless eyes, "to die!"

"What?" His astonishment came to an abrupt halt when Kit's hammer bursts forth in a blinding flash of light. The vampire's confusion turned to agony when the hammer's white-hot brilliance fully engulfed him.

The vampire continued wailing, screeching, writhing, as the dragon hammer's white light continued to engulf him. All the while, Kit continued pushing as much of the hammer's magic into the creature as she could. The smell of burning flesh stung her nose. Just as the wailing started to die off, the vampire's eyes turned a dull gray, as whatever *life* had been in them, dissipated.

The moment Kit released the hammer's magic, the white light engulfing the vampire dimmed. She wrinkled her nose at the smell of charred flesh. She was about to comment on the acrid scent when a pair of hands grasped the vampire's head from behind him. There was a quick tearing, grinding sound, followed by a spray of blood as the hands ripped the vampire's head from his shoulders. The now headless corpse tilted slowly to the side, until it fell to the ground, revealing Pental, holding the disembodied body part.

Chapter Twenty-Four

WEARHOUSE ELEVEN

Pental stood motionless, holding the vampire's head in his hands, its blood dripping onto the ground in front of him.

"Hello, Kitten," he purred, a slow smile spreading across his face. "I didn't expect to find you doing my dirty work."

Surprise, shock, fear? Kit was unsure which emotion was holding her, paralyzing her. She could feel blood, the blood that had splattered across her face when Pental had beheaded the vampire, starting to trickle down her forehead, into her eyes.

"Perhaps I misjudged you," Pental continued. "Perhaps my actions spurred you forward, to stand against the injustices my people are enduring." A smug look of satisfaction crossed the vampire's face before he turned into a cloud of dust and blew away with the wind.

"Why would he kill his own kind?" Indie asked, clearly unnerved. "Why didn't you kill him? He was less than an arm's length from you."

"Frookin' Helja, girl," Coldforge added, wiping some of the vampire's blood from his own face. "You have the most wondrous hammer that I've ever seen."

Kit looked to her friends, all of them appearing as confused as she was. She absentmindedly wiped some more blood from her face. Finally, her resolve kicked in, her mind returning from whatever far-off place it had traveled. "We need to hurry." Not waiting to see who was following, she dashed for the entrance to the warehouse.

As soon as Kit passed into the dimly lit building, the smells of urine, feces, death, and decay made her gag. She covered her mouth and nose with one hand and held her now ignited hammer in her other. The warehouse was huge, the light from Kit's hammer barely penetrating the darkness. Cages, stacked five deep, covered the floors. Most of them appeared to be empty, and those that were not, had decomposing corpses in them. To her right, three Berrat children of no more than ten cycles, crawled towards her, over the dead bodies in their cell. They were so thin, so terribly, heartbreakingly thin. They stared at Kit with vacant expressions that reminded her of Ashkey, the boy she had rescued from the Crimson Ale, only much worse. The children didn't say a word, they simply watched her through hopeless eyes. Kit desperately wanted to turn away, to shield her heart from their devastating depression. Instead, she took in the sight, in its entirety. She let it penetrate into her soul until she could feel a blanket of pure loathing wrap around her heart.

"I'll be back to set you free," she whispered to them. "I promise."

A heavy lump sank into the pit of her stomach as she left the prisoners behind. She walked down the hallway between the crates, heading toward a ruckus coming from deeper within the warehouse. Picking up her pace, she started following the sounds. Lump and Runt bounded past her, quickly leaving Kit behind. A few seconds later, the sounds abruptly died off.

Kit gave chase, running towards the last place she'd seen the boys, just before they'd turned down another hallway. As she turned the corner, vast cages came into view; cages filled with dwarves; Runt and Lump standing in front of them. Many of the captives scurried to the back of their pen, while others moved to the front, shielding them with their mostly nude bodies. Kit couldn't help but notice how powerfully built they were, men and women alike. An enormous padlock secured the door to the first cage. Without giving it much thought, Kit swung her hammer with all her might, intent on shattering the iron lock. There was the familiar burst of blinding white light on impact. The sound of mithril striking metal rang throughout the entire warehouse. When Kit's vision returned to normal, she grimaced at the undamaged padlock, still securely holding the door closed.

"The lock's been ensorcelled," one of the dwarves said from within the cage. "The bars as well."

"Sweet Gaia, git them out of there," Coldforge bellowed, with Indie at his side. With all the hair on their faces, it was hard to get a read on the prisoners' reaction when they saw Coldforge; part surprise, part joy, but mostly relief.

"Hit it again, girl," the dwarf yelled, "or let me do it!"

Kit protectively pulled her hammer away from the outstretched hands of the dwarf.

"T'won't do no good, Coldforge," the dwarven prisoner replied. "Yer gonna need the key. The magic bound to these cages is too strong."

Kit looked back to Indie. "Check the vampires for keys," she said. "We don't have much time before the ships will set sail."

Indie gave Kit a small smile. "Like these?" he asked, tossing her a keyring with several jet-black keys dangling from it.

"I love you." The words fell from Kit's lips before she had a chance to stop them. Her face immediately flushed. "I mean..." Her golden eyes locked onto Indie's. She desperately wanted to retract her words, even if they were true. This wasn't the time or place for such things. A look of hopeful anticipation spread across the young man's face. If Kit took it back, tried to undo her words, it would certainly crush him. "Holy Helja, I wanted to say thank you, but..." Even though she hadn't finished her sentence, Indie's face was already beginning to crumple. "I do love you! It's just, well, I wanted to tell you when we were alone – not in," Kit waved her arms about her head, the light from her hammer casting bizarre shadows as she did. "... all of this."

"Frook, girl," Coldforge slapped Kit on the back with enough force to bounce her off the cage bars. "No better time than the right-now to profess your love. Tomorrow might not come for us."

"I love you, too." Indie took a few steps closer to Kit. "And we can talk about it later, after we get this job finished."

The young man's quiet grace sent goosebumps down Kit's arms; her heart pounded heavily in her chest. More than anything, at that very moment, she wanted to hold him tight and tell him over and over how much she loved him.

Instead, she gave him a coy smile and jammed one of the keys into the lock. She gave the key a twist, but the lock refused to yield.

She frowned heavily as she pulled the key from the lock and tried another, with the same effect. She pulled the key, and tried another, and another, and another. With each attempt, Kit's frown deepened. She started to growl. She was down to her last key. Kit dropped her hammer to the ground, letting it fall on the sawdust-covered, mud floor. She grasped the padlock in her now free hand. As she held the rough-hammered steel, an unexpected coldness crept up her arm.

Slowly, reluctantly, she pushed the final key into the lock. "Titan, hear me," she whispered. "Don't let me fail this day. Don't let me fail these people. Don't let me fail you." Kit closed her eyes and tried turning the key. Her heart dropped when she felt resistance, the key unable to turn. But just when she was about to abandon all hope, the padlock clicked open.

A pair of massively thick, hairy arms suddenly seized Kit from behind.

"I knew I liked you, girl," Coldforge exclaimed, practically jumping from foot to foot, tossing Kit about in the process. "Let's git 'em out of here."

There was a chorus of hoots and hollers as the imprisoned dwarves came pouring out of the cage. Indie quickly took the keys from the padlock, and headed to the other cages, releasing the prisoners from within. When he looked for Kit, he saw her away from the revelries, staring into her glowing hands. As Indie approached, she closed her hands and the light from within went dark.

"What was that?" he asked, standing seductively close to her.

"The dragon tear," she said, still staring down at her clenched hand. "The weapons are still on the ship. Lin and Bango couldn't get them unloaded." A deep rage started to build up inside her. She was close to freeing these slaves, from stopping the ships, but without the weapons, there was no hope.

"Why the long face?" Coldforge asked, stepping between Indie and Kit. "It's time for joy and celebration."

"They couldn't get the weapons off the ship." Indie shook his head, looking defeated.

"So?" Coldforge said, his orange whiskers pulling towards his ears. "Without the vampires to protect them, we can liberate whatever they've got on those ships."

Kit chuckled at the dwarf's enthusiasm. "They've got weapons and armor, and you've got bare fists."

"These beauties are all I need," Coldforge shrugged, "but the others will have steel clubs to fight with." He motioned over his shoulder to where the dwarves were. They were actively disassembling the cages, breaking them down into smaller parts. "When you opened the locks, it broke the magic seal on the cages. Now they're just raw materials, and that's what we work best with."

Kit pulled out her dragon tear, staring intently into it. A moment later, it burst to life, a tiny image of Lin appeared within the swirling blue and white light. "We're coming. All of us. We have some weapons; hopefully enough to take the ships."

"Bango is still arguing with the ship's captain. He's trying to set sail, but the Port Authority is holding them off. I'm not sure how long she can keep this up." Lin's head swiveled back and forth. She cut off the link before she said anything else.

"Let's get moving. Take whatever weapons you have, and move out," Kit bellowed. "We're going to be taking a black ship filled with weapons and armor. If the ship's crew resists, kill them. If they concede, take them prisoner." A murmur broke out amongst the dwarves. There seemed to be some dissension among them. They clearly believed the slavers deserve no quarter, only death.

"Not all do this by choice," Kit called out, silencing the crowd of dwarves. "Many are forced into this, by whatever means the Auctioneers have at their disposal. Those enemies who fight back, kill them. Everyone else is to be left unharmed." Kit's eyes flashed golden as she walked among the dwarves, her righteous zeal emanating from her like a beacon of hope. "We do not kill anybody who doesn't fight back." Many of the dwarves acknowledged her words, while some continued to shake their heads. To those who were resisting her orders, she moved in closer. "We do not kill anybody who doesn't fight back. I will personally end anybody who disobeys my order. If you don't like it, wait here. Otherwise, step in line and follow my lead."

Still, too many of the dwarves were being obstinate, defiantly refusing Kit's commands. Coldforge stepped in beside her. "If you won't follow her command, you'll follow mine," he boomed. "I am your prince, and you'll follow what she tells ya, like I'm tellin' ya myself."

The entire group suddenly took a knee, their eyes cast down upon the ground in front of them. "By Gimlie's beard, we obey," they intoned as a single voice.

Coldforge looked up at Kit, his eyes twinkling at her. "You did frookin' good, girl. But my kin can be a bit thick sometimes, not knowing what side is up unless it comes from their own."

Kit didn't respond. She just shook her head and started heading for the exit, the sound of synchronized footfalls resounding behind her.

Chapter Twenty-Five

The Vole and the Puzzle

When Danny cleared the bottom of the door in Lord Byssus' private chambers his vole nose was assaulted with a myriad of scents, most of them vile. He immediately picked up the smell of the poison that he was using on his daughter, plus what was most likely rotting food. Laying atop the cacophony of vile odors was the lord's horrendous perfume of lavender and musk. Perhaps it was the stench of the room that forced the man to wear such an odoriferous fragrance. Even though the room stunk, it was otherwise spotless and fastidiously tidy. Since there were no visible signs of spoiled leftovers anywhere in the chambers, Danny could only surmise that the putrid food was being placed in hidden, hard to find spots. Maybe it was the Berrat's way of getting back at the lord, even if it was little more than an inconvenience.

What was missing from the room was the lord himself. Danny turned back to the entrance, finding the door barred from the inside. A series of thin windows, closely resembling arrow slits, made up most of the north wall. They were too thin for the fat lord to squeeze through, so he could not have left that way. Kandyce's room had one large window that faced the south. It seemed as though the lord was more interested in keeping anybody from entering his room via covert means. It was a smart move that could keep most people from entering through a window, but it didn't really stop a shapeshifting Berrat who could take the form of a small creature, winged or otherwise.

On the east wall of the room was a huge, poorly constructed hearth capable of holding a roaring fire. Based on the wall of north-facing windows, that fireplace was the only thing that would keep the lord from freezing on a winter's night.

How in Helja did this man rise to power? He doesn't seem intelligent enough to understand even the most basic of strategies necessary for living in the high north.

Danny gave his tiny vole shoulders a shrug as he scampered around the room. He kept his extremely sensitive nose close to the stonework as he tried to pick up the fragrant hints of Lord Byssus' presence. With the overpowering reek of rotted food permeating the chambers, Danny struggled to concentrate on the scents of lavender and musk. The fragrances were strongest at the front of the hearth, but there was one scent trail that ended abruptly at the west wall. Danny backtracked several times, trying to discover if perhaps the lord had simply followed the same path away from the wall, but, to the best of his vole-nose's ability, that wasn't the case. The lord had walked up to this wall and simply disappeared. He ran his nose close to the corner where the wall met the floor. There was a tiny, nearly imperceptible gap here, perhaps for a secret doorway of some sort. Where the rest of the room's construction was questionable at best, if this was a secret door, it was created by someone with master level craftsman skills.

Danny switched back into his Berrat form, giving himself a better view of the full wall.

Titan's snowballs!

There was no sign of any doorway here. The stonework along this wall was as bad as anywhere else. If there were a secret door, it should easily stand out. Danny harrumphed as he tried to puzzle through the problem.

The lord's footsteps ended right here. There's a tiny gap at the base of the wall, but there's no sign of a door. Lord Byssus' footsteps led up to here, but they didn't lead away.

He ran his fingers along all the stones, hoping to find a trigger of some sort. He pressed on the stones that were within an arm's reach of where the steps ended, but they were all solid. In frustration, he banged his head against the wall. That, too, had little effect except to give him a headache.

What would you do, Kit? How would you get past this?

Danny stared blindly at the wall for several more seconds.

You'd likely just bash your way through the wall, that's what you'd do.

The thought made Danny chuckle. He turned around and surveyed the room again. Nothing was amiss. Everything was neat and tidy. Even the hearth was cleaned out.

Who cleans a hearth?

With renewed enthusiasm Danny bolted across the room and stuck his head into the fireplace. He looked up the chimney flue, sure that this was the way the man had exited the room. Whatever hopes he might have had were immediately dashed when he found the thick iron bars that would prevent anybody from entering or leaving through that way.

There were so many footsteps here. I was sure...

The lord hadn't used the fireplace as a means of escape, but it could easily be the location of the trigger to the secret doorway. It was here, somewhere. All he needed to do was find it. A small grin crossed his lips. Everything here was fastidiously tidy, and every bit of metal was highly polished. The only things that stood out were the sconces on either side of the hearth. They were highly polished, but they were also badly scratched.

The lord wore a lot of rings. They could easily have caused the scratches.

Danny walked over to the sconce on the left. He had to stand on his tiptoes to reach it, but thankfully, he was taller than the average Berrat. He grasped it in his hand and pulled down. It gave way easily and tilted away from the wall. Nothing happened.

"Titan's snowballs," he muttered while staring at the far wall. "I was sure it was the key." Danny's head swiveled until he was staring at the other sconce. With a small shake of his head, he walked over to it, wrapped his hand around it, and pulled. It didn't budge. It wiggled slightly, but it didn't pull away from the wall like the other had. He gritted his teeth and tried again, and again, but his efforts were in vain.

But it wiggles. If it wiggles, then maybe...

He tried twisting the sconce, and it moved slightly more, but still to no effect. He tilted his head to the side and considered the problem further. He quickly grabbed it again and twisted in the other direction. It was stiff, but it moved. As it did, there was a loud grinding noise behind him. Relief spread through his body as though a great weight had been lifted from his shoulders. He quickly spun around, expecting to find the secret passage revealed. The smile on his face fell away as he stared back at the unchanged wall. He cursed heavily through gritted teeth and turned back to the sconces.

One spins and one pulls.

He looked back at the first sconce.

One spins and one pulls.

He spun the sconce in front of him again. It turned freely. There was no grinding noise. There was no resistance. There was no resistance on the pull-sconce the first time he tried it. He cocked an eyebrow and walked over to it. He wrapped his fingers around the brass fitting and pulled. It barely budged. He wrapped both hands around it and pulled again. It moved a bit more but not significantly. He tightened his grip and placed one of his feet against the wall to get better leverage and pulled with all his might.

Nothing. No movement at all. It was just – stuck.

Bloody Helja, what is it with you?

He stared back at the sconce on the other side. He had turned it after having caused the grinding noise. He stalked over to it, spun it again, back to where it had been after he turned it the first time. He nodded at it when nothing happened. He walked back to the other side and, with both hands, gave the sconce a tug. It pulled easily, followed by another loud grinding noise. He took a quick peek over his shoulder, fearful that all this effort would lead to yet another failure. A wide grin split his face just as a loud pounding started, coming from the entrance to the chambers.

"Let me in," the lieutenant bellowed from the far side. "Open this door, right now." The man was hitting the door hard enough that the thick beam across the door shook – slightly. Danny chuckled to himself as he skipped across the room to the secret door and the staircase that led down into complete darkness.

He was about to begin his descent when a loud ruckus outside drew his attention. He bolted to the window slits hoping to get a look at what was going on below. They didn't offer much of a view, but what little he could see was a large contingent of soldiers working their way through the huts toward the lord's manor. He had no idea if they were coming for him or if it was the captain returning with his men. Without much of a thought, Danny switched into vole form, clambered up the wall to the window slit and leapt off the edge.

The feeling of the wind whipping through his fur was very pleasant, but it would end terribly if he didn't act fast. He hadn't considered whether or not he could switch from vole to phoenix form without first turning back into a Berrat. Well, it was too late to change his mind. The ground was already coming up fast on him.

The tiny vole spread its legs out to the sides just before it squeaked out, "Burn!"

Danny's vision immediately turned red as the fur covering his tiny body was replaced with fiery feathers. He dipped close to the ground before soaring upwards and around the manor towards its front. As soon as he cleared the corner of the building, the battle came into view. The captain's soldiers were in pitched combat against the lord's personal guard. The quarters were tight, and the lord's guard seemed to have the upper hand. These were well trained warriors accustomed to fighting side-by-side. They worked as a unit, opening and closing gaps in their defenses, luring their enemy into death traps.

The phoenix's battle cry drew the attention of everyone, combatants, and spectators alike. Danny was just starting to go into a dive when he saw the lieutenant come bursting through the entranceway into the throng of guards. With a quick slash, he took down the guard directly in front of the doorway and with a kick, he knocked another off balance, sending her crashing into the guards standing in front of her. Had this man not tried to stomp on him earlier?

Whatever the lieutenant's motives were, he was currently fighting with Captain Bowwind and his soldiers. The phoenix tilted his tail slightly, banking him to the left and directly into the largest batch of guards. He made solid contact with one, bursting into a shower of red sparks when his flames plunged into the woman's heavy, gray-enameled armor. She barely had a chance to scream before she erupted into a molten blob.

Danny swooped up into the sky, banked hard, and unleashed another battle cry. His single attack had broken the spirit of the gold-cloaked guards. Many threw down their weapons and took a knee, while several simply ran. Those who did were quickly cut down by the captain's soldiers. Those who surrendered were spared. In the background, well behind the battle, Lady Kandyce was standing with Sky Eyes, Breayn, and Ryn, in his white bear form. Danny could only guess that they had stayed with the woman to offer her protection should the battle go sideways on them. Between the lieutenant and the captain, the lord's personal guard were under control, so the phoenix headed towards Lady Kandyce. He swooped low, slowed his speed to the point of nearly stalling, switched back to Berrat form and landed, somewhat gracefully, in front of Ryn. The great white bear huffed and threw a thick paw at Danny's head. The huge claws raked the air in front of his face, just shy of his nose.

"I found the entrance to your father's secret hideaway," Danny said to Kandyce, giving Ryn a bright smile as he did. The white bear shimmered, and he returned to his Berrat form.

"Sorry about the paw," Ryn said, even though he didn't look particularly apologetic. "You had a little *smug* on your face that I was trying to wipe off." Danny appreciated his bit of humor and inclined his head slightly.

"Too bad *jealousy* can't be burned away," he retorted, "but if it could, there wouldn't be much left of you."

Ryn's eye twitched slightly.

Chapter Twenty-Six

THE SECRET PASSAGE

Kandyce pushed her way past Ryn and Danny, who were still glaring at each other. The woman had a kerchief in her hand, and she was holding it out to Garret as he approached. Blood spatter covered the man's face and clothing. With a nod, he accepted the gesture and wiped the areas around his mouth and eyes. The woman tried to point out a few more errant bits of gore, but the captain ignored her.

"Is it over?" Sky Eyes asked. "Have the lord's people been dealt with?"

"My people are detaining the last of the lord's personal guard," Garret said, turning to the lieutenant. "It looks like Lieutenant Barclay here is going to need a new surcoat."

Breayn was listening closely to what some passersby were saying. She held up her hand to her cohorts, asking for silence.

It appeared that the Berrat who had witnessed the pitched battle were wandering aimlessly about, looking confused and concerned. From what they were saying, they had no real understanding of what had just transpired. The idea that The Phoenix had come to free them rippled through the population. Many of them believed it was Lady Kandyce's doing, that she was responsible for the attack on the lord's army. One passerby had suggested that she was trying to take over her father's holdings and that The Phoenix was helping her.

"We need to locate Byssus," Danny suggested. "Standing around here is just giving the man more time to escape." Ignoring the 'who put you in charge' look that Ryn was giving him, he adjusted his black-feathered cloak and headed toward the manor. The group made their way past the soldiers and the spectators, into the white stone building, and up to the second floor.

Ryn surveyed the thick wooden door leading into Lord Byssus' chambers. He turned back to Breayn and shook his head. Old Sky Eyes seemed somewhat amused at the Berrat's reaction while Lady Kandyce tapped her foot on the uneven stonework of the landing.

Captain Bowwind, with Lieutenant Barclay at his hip, attempted to open the door only to find it still barred from the inside.

"Maybe you can stand over there," Danny said to the lieutenant, pointing to the far side of the landing. The soldier's expression was flat as he considered the Berrat's request. He slowly took a few steps away from the door, his jaw stiffening as he did. Garret gave them both a questioning look, unsure what this exchange was all about. As Danny's body melted into the form of a vole, the captain's look changed from questioning to accusing. The lieutenant ignored it, staring at the gray-brown rodent as it scurried beneath the small gap below the door. A moment later, the loud scraping noise of wood on metal announced the removal of the heavy wooden bar from the inside of the entrance.

"Unless he had an alternate escape route, Lord Byssus is still within," Danny said as he opened the door.

The room was just as he had left it, with the door to the secret passage still open. While the rest of the group moved towards the passage and its stairway down to the unknown, Sky Eyes examined the room. He lingered for several moments by the man's bed. It was covered by a thick red duvet with gold embroidery and piping. A mountain of down-filled pillows was stacked at its head. At the corners, four thick wooden posts led up to a sheer canopy. The posts were finely carved with a spiral-twist pattern. He frowned at the deep scratches that marred the wood, likely the result of *guests* being secured to the bed with manacles.

"There is no fate fitting for a man of his depravity," the old Berrat said. His voice was thick with emotion, drawing the attention of those standing at the top of the hidden exit.

"A man has but his life to give for his crimes," Garret said with a frown, "but our slimy lord will also be paying with soldiers and gold, enough to crush the Split Crows and free the north."

"My father's wealth and power will fall to me, Captain," Kandyce said, "but perhaps we should find the slimy lord before you start deciding what to do with his holdings." While Garret withered slightly under the lady's words, the lieutenant smirked.

"Why don't you lead the way," Danny said to the lieutenant. "I think I'd prefer to not have you at my back. For now, you can be the vanguard." The lieutenant's smirk never left his face. He simply shouldered his way through the group until he stood at the top of the staircase, looking down into the darkness.

"I don't suppose any of you have a candle," he said without looking back, "it's pitch black down there." Danny's stomach clenched at the comment. The staircase down was incredibly narrow and even though he hadn't started heading into the inky blackness, he could already feel the weight of it pressing in on him.

"I could set you on fire and push you down the stairs," Danny offered, his own voice sounding thin in his ears. Breayn gave him a questioning look, which he ignored. He took a deep breath and centered himself. "Move, lieutenant. Your lord awaits."

The entire group descended the stairs with the lieutenant at the lead and the captain taking up position at the rear. Danny really didn't like the idea of having anyone at his back, fearful that someone might block his escape route should the darkness continue to crush him beyond his limits.

As he descended, he let his fingers trail along the wall. Unlike all the other stonework in the building, this part of the house had been expertly crafted. After only a few steps, what light had spilled into the stairwell from the secret door became useless. The lieutenant's description of pitch blackness was spot on, and it was overwhelming.

Danny hadn't kept track of how many stairs there were before they reached the bottom. Despite it being too dark to see, he could feel the oppressive confinement of the stairs lessen, as though they had just stepped into a much wider corridor. His breathing eased, knowing that he wasn't in such tight confines. He held his hand out in front of himself, finding Lieutenant Barclay within his reach, but he couldn't see him at all. It was like staring into a great void.

"Keep going," Danny said. He really didn't want to go deeper into the darkness, but it was the only way they were going to locate Lord Byssus.

They had taken perhaps twenty steps when the tunnel turned sharply to the left. The deeper they went, the more anxious Danny became. He considered how tall the building was and decided that, at this point, they were well below ground level. The air here was damp and heavy. The smooth stone walls were slick with moisture. The occasional root penetrated the stonework, giving it an almost fuzzy feel. Danny quickly pulled his hand away, fearing that it wasn't roots but instead the web of some insidious spider. He could feel the phoenix calling to be released, to help light the way with its flames.

"It's a dead-end," the lieutenant said from somewhere ahead of him. "We can go no further."

Danny's first reaction, other than to run for the stairs, was to believe that the man was lying, but then he thought back to the complex puzzle he needed to solve just to open the door to the secret passage in the lord's chambers. Maybe there was another step, one that would expose the door that allowed entrance into the lord's hideaway.

As he stood, pondering the situation, the other members of the party walked past him. Each time someone touched him, he panicked, fearful that some loathsome creature was about to make a meal of him.

"What do you mean, a dead-end?" Ryn asked. For whatever reason, Ryn's voice made Danny feel a bit better. after all, if Ryn wasn't afraid of being in a dark, dank tunnel, then why should he be? Why indeed? It wasn't rational, but the feeling was there just the same. His heartbeat was thrumming in his ears. His fear was real, even if it was irrational.

"The path ends at a stone wall," the lieutenant replied. "You're welcome to check for yourself if you don't believe me."

"It's likely another puzzle," Danny offered, "like the one I had to solve to get us this far." Yes, a puzzle. Something to take his mind off the relentless, oppressive blackness.

"Or it's all an elaborate trap," Kandyce said, her voice pitchy. The panic coursing through her was palpable. "We should leave, quickly." The woman practically bowled Danny over as she ran blindly down the hall. Sweet Titan, the woman's fear did nothing but cause his own phobia to come screaming up at him.

"Lady Kandyce," Garret yelled out as he gave chase, slamming solidly into Danny, sending him skidding across the slick tiled floor. As the pair's footsteps receded into the distance, the young Berrat searched for purchase along the wall to help pull himself to his feet. The wall here was free of roots and felt slightly warmer.

"Nobody move," Danny said, just before he transformed into his vole form. As his body finished its transformation, the shapes of the others came into murky view. He couldn't *see* them, but it was as though his sense of smell was so acute that he could make out their forms purely by their scent. If he wasn't so preoccupied by finding the entrance to the lord's lair, he'd have found this fascinating. He quickly scampered to where the floor met the wall, searching for the lord's pungent perfume. The little vole took a deep, calming breath.

My fear is gone. Apparently, the little guy has no phobia of dark, confined spaces.

Even though the close proximity of the others made locating the scent more difficult, Danny was able to pick up the lord's trail. He had definitely stood here, but he could smell that the scent went further, towards where the lieutenant was standing. Keeping close to the edge, to avoid being stepped on, accidentally or otherwise, Danny moved deeper into the tunnel. Even from a distance, he could still smell the lord's lingering presence.

The vole kept to the edge of the floor, following the lord's trail until his snout made contact with the dead end. Both the floor and the walls were covered in the threads of tiny roots that had penetrated the stonework. Using them for purchase, Danny scampered up the wall, sniffing for where Lord Byssus may have placed his hand on a sconce or some other such trigger to open the final door.

The lord's scent was easy to follow, but Danny was unable to find the place he had actually touched the wall. It always seemed to be away from the edge, and yet right next to it. It was at that moment that Danny decided he despised puzzles almost as much as he despised tight, dark spaces.

The little vole stopped mid-stride as he was clutching onto a root that was thicker than most. The lord's scent was very near, but it was not on the wall. He tried to calculate how high from the ground he was by smelling the lieutenant's form. It was then he noticed that the lord's scent started and stopped four times. The lieutenant's body was directly in behind the odd pattern.

It's a ladder.

Once he had figured it out, the answer was obvious. Danny quickly leapt from his perch, landing awkwardly on a wooden rung. The scrabbling of his claws drew the attention of the lieutenant who promptly swatted him to the ground.

"Was that necessary?" Danny asked after switching back into Berrat form. The lieutenant yelped.

"I didn't know that was you," he replied, gulping thickly. "There are all sorts of creepy-crawly things underground."

"Sure," Danny said, using a rung to pull himself off the ground. "You might have mentioned that this tunnel ended with a ladder."

"It does?" the lieutenant replied. If he was lying, he did an excellent job of feigning surprise. "All I felt were wet roots." Danny shook his head in the darkness before he started ascending the ladder. The thought of fresh air and light pushed him. Hand over hand he climbed until his head slammed into something solid. Stars danced in front of his eyes for a moment while his head and neck throbbed from the impact.

"Holy Helja," he ground out. "This ladder goes nowhere."

"It's got to lead somewhere," Ryn replied. "Feel around."

"You feel around," Danny yelled back. If it wasn't so dark, he'd have sworn the room was spinning. He quickly hooked his arm onto the rung, fearful that he was going to tumble from his perch, into the darkness. Everything seemed to lurch as he felt his body fall away from the wall. His mind must have been playing tricks on him because he still had his arm locked around the rung. A deep rumble came from up the hallway. Red and yellow lights danced on the walls, reminiscent of a bonfire, illuminating the corridor that led back to the secret stairway. It was only then that Danny realized that the ladder had pulled away from the wall and he was dangling from it. The entire ladder was the lever to opening the door. He released his grip and dropped roughly to the ground.

The group ran towards the well-lit corridor. As they turned the corner, they found Lady Kandyce and Captain Bowwind not far from the base of the stairs, staring into a brightly lit room.

"Father," Kandyce said from her place in front of the now open doorway. "And Lord Wing, I presume."

"An unforeseen turn of events," Sky Eyes muttered as he led Breayn and Ryn up the tunnel towards the pair, with Danny and the lieutenant a few paces behind them. With her chin held high, Lady Kandyce stepped boldly into the chamber. Captain Bowwind stayed close to the woman, his hand gripping the hilt of his sword. The others followed the pair into the room, leaving Danny and the lieutenant alone in the tunnel.

"After you," Danny said, motioning to the open doorway. The lieutenant shrugged and stepped inside.

Chapter Twenty-Seven

The Lord's Hideaway

Danny followed the lieutenant through the doorway, into Lord Byssus' secret hideaway. The door itself appeared to be constructed of a solid piece of thick granite. Knowing how to use the lever was the only way to get past it. That gnawing sense of dread, from being trapped below the ground gnawed at him again. It was only when his vole spirit reached out to him did the phobia diminish. He didn't know he could communicate, even if it was only emotionally, to the spirits he was hosting. The thought of it warmed him.

The room was massive, at least four times the size of the lord's second floor chamber. There were two hearths with warm fires burning brightly within. The hard tiled floors were covered in thick, dark rugs and upon the wood-paneled walls, richly colored tapestries hung, adding to the room's luxurious feel. Between the hearths, torches burned at regular intervals, providing ample light to highlight the opulent furniture that filled the room. It explained why the lord's upper chamber was fastidiously clean and why there were no ashes within its hearth. Lord Byssus lived down here, snug and warm in his secret location, away from where others may choose to do him harm. The man might have been cruel and heartless, but he wasn't as stupid as Danny thought.

Lord Byssus smiled warmly from an oversized chair upholstered in the same red and gold fabric as the covering on his bed. He was dressed in a fine blue robe with a high collar and puffy sleeves. He had a look of arrogant self-importance, with the slightest hint of a smirk. Danny's eyes only lingered on the lord for a few seconds before they were drawn away to the red-headed Berrat sitting in the chair across from him. He was draped in black feathers from head to toe, save for the black leather boots that stuck out from the bottom of his cloak. A bright, cheerful fire burned in the hearth behind them, casting them both in a warm, ethereal glow.

Four Berrat serving girls, dressed in pink, gauzy fabrics, entered through a door at the rear of the room. They stood motionless, staring at the new arrivals.

"My lord?" one of them asked, her voice was timid and shaky.

"Leave us," Lord Byssus barked, his eyes never leaving Danny and the others. One of the women dropped her silver tray. It clattered on the tile floor, sending its contents skittering across the room. "You filthy bitch, you'll pay for that!" the fat lord screamed, his face turning purple. The Berrat sitting next to him seemed unperturbed by the events.

"You were a hard man to find," Lord Wing purred. "If only I had known that you'd ultimately come to me. Many lives could have been spared."

"Where are my parents?" Danny asked. It was the first thing that popped into his mind when the man spoke of lives lost. A sick, twisted smile flicked at the corner of The Wing's mouth.

"Did you know that we Berrabbithi can subsume the spirits of our kin?" The Wing said, standing calmly from his seat. He glided over to the fire and stood motionless, staring into its flames.

"Heretic," Breayn spat. "We can only bind with animals, and only those that are willing to allow us to host them."

Lord Wing turned towards the woman, regarding her carefully as though having only just noticed her presence. "Hello, Breayn Fox-Dancing," he said, inclining his head. "How nice of you and your cousin to both be here. It would seem that those fool seers were actually worth the gold I paid them. Too bad I only found out they were correct after I executed them. A sad loss really. I'm sure there are more seers whom I could draw on, aren't there, Old Sky Eyes."

"You know my name, and yet we have never met," the elder said, stepping up like a shield before his cohorts.

"I know many things," Lord Wing said. "Your presence here is among the most... inconsequential of matters."

"I would ask you then, Lord Wing. Did your seers warn you that today would be the last day you'd draw breath? That today would be the day that you would be consumed in flame and sent to the Beyond?" The Wing scoffed at the old man's assertions.

"In a land of fire and ice, ice always wins. You can raise a flame and it may warm you for a short length of time, but the cold snuffs it out, never to warm another soul again."

"Your arrogance will be your undoing," Danny said as he strode towards the Crow. Both Kandyce and Garret followed in his wake, while the rest of his cohorts fanned out across the room. He grinned when the familiar ring of steel being drawn from a scabbard reached his ears. "Your end comes now."

Danny could feel the phoenix pleading to be released, desperately wanting to be free to wreak havoc upon the two evil lords.

Patience, my fiery friend.

A smug look of victory crossed the faces of Lord Byssus and The Wing. What did they know that Danny did not? The answer came quickly when a deep, stabbing pain exploded in his back and burst forth from his chest. He looked down to see the end of a crimson-soaked sword emerge from his ribcage. He stared at the blade that had appeared quite unexpectedly.

The small vole spirit within, squeaked out in confusion. He tried to calm the poor thing, but his mind was a jumble, trying to process what was happening. From somewhere behind him, a woman screamed, or was it two? He couldn't tell for sure, it sounded like it was coming from a tunnel, far, far away.

His confusion turned into raw, unbridled rage. He wanted to turn to see the lieutenant's ugly face, but the blood-soaked blade protruding from his chest made that impossible. The rough bottom of a boot struck him low from behind, sending him sprawling onto the floor. He rolled over onto his back and scowled at the grim-faced captain standing over him.

The room was going dark as a deep coldness gripped him. He felt a hand on his face. He couldn't be sure, but it might have been Breayn, leaning over him, yelling at him. The darkness continued to creep into his vision. Perhaps someone had snuffed the fire out in the hearth. Yes, that would have made some sense. That would explain why he was suddenly so cold.

The captain? Why was Garret standing over him, holding a bloodied sword?

None of this made any sense. The captain was an ally. He had introduced him to Sky Eyes. He had protected Lady Kandyce. The faces of those who stared down at him turned into shadows as the light of the room diminished.

I'm sorry I couldn't save your village, Kit. I'm sorry for so many things that I'll never get to say to you.

As darkness enveloped him, Danny could feel the pull of the Great Cycle. A bright light filled with warmth and a sense of well-being beckoned to him. Even though he had much left to do on Orth, the call of the nevermore was just too powerful. It drew him to itself, its bright light and warmth filling his soul with peace and tranquility. As his soul traveled to the light, the warmth grew, slowly building into a raging inferno. The light became blinding as the heat raged, consuming him body and soul. Perhaps this was Titan's punishment for turning on him, for not being true to his vows as an acolyte of the Temple. Just when he thought he could endure no more, he remembered. As he did, his vision returned, everything cast in shades of reds and oranges. The traitorous face of Captain Bowwind was the first to become clear, his mouth agape, his eyes wide.

The man appeared a brilliant red, while the others were all bright yellow, except for Ryn who was orange. He still couldn't understand why Ryn appeared differently. Perhaps the phoenix could differentiate between friend and foe, seeing them as yellow or red. Perhaps Ryn's feelings toward Danny were mixed.

"I will take my place as ruler of this forsaken land," Garret screamed out as he raised his sword, ready to strike at the phoenix. "I will not be denied my prize." The man's eyes were wild, filled with a crazed lust for power.

The phoenix unleashed its war cry, its sound echoing off the walls.

At the captain's back, the lieutenant strode forward, lifted his sword over his head, and brought its blade down on the captain, striking him where the man's neck and shoulder met. Lady Kandyce screeched out in terror as a thick, red splatter sprayed across her face.

When the captain's lifeless body fell to the ground, the phoenix turned to face Lord Byssus and Lord Wing, both of whom appeared to be a deep crimson. A sudden fear ripped through Danny's soul. Lord Byssus' hands were outstretched before him, a swirling blue frost surrounding them. This was the same attack that had left Danny incapacitated. The cold had been so intense that it had pushed the phoenix deep within, making it impossible for Danny to call upon her. But where terror gripped the Berrat, and the tiny vole, the phoenix spirit showed no concern.

The lord's attack will do no harm.

Danny didn't know why that thought popped into his head. It was perhaps foolish, wishful thinking. The pain of the last attack was excruciating. He had never endured anything so devastatingly painful in his entire life.

The lord threw his hands forward, unleashing a whirling ball of ice at him. Danny cringed, waiting for the impending impact of the frosty orb. There was a loud hissing noise as the magical attack struck his flames, filling the area with steam for a very brief moment. Lord Byssus, his expression a mixture of confusion and fury, continued his attacks, repeatedly hurling sphere after sphere of ice at Danny until the man collapsed in a heap on the ground, disappearing beneath the low, thick fog that now filled most of the room.

"You're everything we'd hoped you'd be," Lord Wing said quietly as he regarded Danny. "I was doubtful, but my eyes don't lie to me."

"You will pay for what you've done," Kandyce said. It wasn't clear if she was talking to her father or the Lord Wing, but it didn't really matter.

"He will for certain," The Wing said, kicking Lord Byssus, "but what happens to me has not yet been written."

"Nothing is written," Sky Eyes offered, "but your fate is sealed. How and when your death will come to pass, is the only question remaining."

"The gallows are already prepared," the lieutenant said, moving in beside Sky Eyes.

Danny was going to make sure that they both paid. With a quick flap of his wings, he launched his fiery body at the Crow slaver, once again screeching out his battle cry. Lord Wing had just enough time to give a look of amusement before the firebird burst through his body. Danny banked hard, preparing to make a second pass. When The Wing came into view, he was still standing where he'd been a moment ago, unsinged, and unharmed. The lieutenant leapt over the fallen captain, unleashing a two-handed swing with his sword, looking to separate the Crow's head from his shoulders. The blade passed harmlessly through his body.

"It's an illusion," Breayn screamed out. "Find him, he can't be far."

The thick granite door to the chamber slammed shut, followed by a horrible grating noise. Ryn was the first to reach the exit. He paused a moment as he looked for a handle on the door, finding nothing but smooth, damp stone. His body shimmered for a moment before transforming into a great white bear. Standing on his hind feet, he raked the door repeatedly with his eight-inch claws, barely doing any damage at all. He stepped back a few paces and hurled his bulk at the door, hoping to bash his way through. His body hit with a sickening thud, and he dropped to the ground blocking the way further. A moment later, he was back in his Berrat form laying unconscious on the tiles.

Danny swooped one more time around the room. He considered throwing himself at the door as well, hoping his firebird form would have a better outcome, but changed his mind at the very last second. He swooped around one more time before hurdling towards the hearth. As his body entered into the roaring flames, he turned upward. He was well up the chimney before he remembered the thick metal bars that blocked the flue of the fireplace in Lord Byssus' chambers. Fortunately, this room didn't have the same security feature built into it.

The chimney was narrow, but the firebird had no difficulty navigating within the rough stone confines. He beat his wings again, increasing his speed as he flew skyward. He erupted from the top of the vent, finding himself above a hut, directly beside the Lord's manor. He screeched out a battle cry and circled the large stone building.

All eyes were staring up at the phoenix as he emerged from behind Lord Byssus' stone manor. He released yet another battle cry just before he burst through Kandice's window. He flew through her room, out her door and into the lord's chambers. He was flying much too quickly when he switched back into Berrat form. Rather than try to land on his feet, he allowed his body to tumble, which broke his fall and slowed his speed considerably. He skidded across the rough stone floor before coming to a halt. From the secret passage he could hear the footfalls of Lord Wing ascending the stairs. Danny calmly pulled his bow from his shoulder and nocked an arrow.

CHAPTER TWENTY-EIGHT

THE BLACK SHIPS

The sun was low on the horizon, streaks of oranges and reds cast the buildings in a surreal light. The thumping of the dwarven footfalls sounded more and more like war-drums as they moved towards the harbor at an inexorable pace. When Kit cleared the Port Authority office building, the full sight of the harbor came into view, causing Kit's heart to sink.

Heavily armed and armored soldiers covered the docks and the shores in front of them. There were many hundreds of them. One of the black ships, with long paddles protruding from the hull, was already pushing away from the docks. A small company of soldiers held Lin, Bango, and the rest of the port authority off to the side. Kit caught Lin's eye, her chest tightening when she saw Lin shaking her head, a large swath of blood darkening one side of her face.

"Give the order and me kin will tear them apart," Coldforge rasped. "Many will die, but we will win the day."

This wasn't what Kit had planned, not even close. Her mind was once again racing, trying to process what her eyes were telling her.

Where did all these soldiers come from? How did they know to be here? Are they always here to send off the fleet?

Her hand holding her dragon hammer was shaking uncontrollably.

Sweet Titan, I can't send these people to their deaths, even if they're willing to do so.

All Kit wanted to do was close her eyes and go to sleep. Even though her heart was pumping so hard that she could feel it pounding in her ears, this was all more than she could take in.

A visceral, elemental scream from the far side of the building stole Kit's decision on what to do next. Her mouth fell agape as four massive yetis came barrelling across the yard, running on four legs, covering ground thirty paces at a time. Many of the soldiers broke ranks, routing from their position. Many more fell into formation, readying themselves for what would surely be a devastating encounter, a catastrophic loss of life.

"Titan's snowballs," Kit uttered, still not believing what she was seeing. "They frookin' did it." Her head spun back towards Indie, the boys, Coldforge, and the rows upon rows of barely clothed dwarves. "Those yetis are with us," she screamed, enthusiastically waving everyone forward. "Engage the soldiers, kill those who fight, leave any who don't."

"By Gimlie's beard, we obey," they chanted back, stamping their feet as they did.

"Free the slaves!" Kit cried out as she bolted into the fray.

"Free the slaves," the rest of her cohorts called out behind her.

"*We come,*" Angel said through their bond. Kit looked to her left to see Angel and Char streaking across the yard towards them, Whistler trailing a few lengths behind. Angel barely had to slow, catching Kit as she leapt onto her horse. As Char passed Indie, he grabbed his long black mane and, using the horse's momentum, lifted himself onto his charger's back. Runt and Lump were barking out their own war-cries as they took up positions beside the horses. Angel suddenly burst forward, her hooves igniting the ground as she bared down on the soldiers, none of whom were paying attention to anything other than the rampaging yetis.

"Free the slaves," Kit yelled again as Angel charged into the crowd of soldiers, trampling some, knocking many more to the ground. They fell under the small roan's fiery footfalls like wheat in a hurricane.

Kit blew through the first wave of soldiers and continued on towards those who were holding Lin and Bango. Whatever resolve they had crumbled immediately when they saw Kit baring down on them. "The yetis are with us!" Kit screamed. Realization dawned on Lin as she remembered Kit's interaction with the Berrat at Silverhawk, and the deal she had helped them make with the Gigas hunters.

Kit didn't slow down as she cleared the last of the soldiers. Instead, she headed down the docks, continuing to pick up speed as she did. The black ship was now a good distance from the pier, much farther than Angel had jumped before. Just as they reached the end of the dock, she screamed at her horse.

"Fly!"

Kit's stomach dropped as Angel launched herself from the sea-worn dock. The familiar exhilaration of being airborne ignited Kit's spirit. In the day's failing light, the pair glided silently over the dark, murky sea. As the salt air stung her cheeks and the wind whipped her hair behind her, a sense of wellbeing permeated through every stitch of her soul. The distance between them and the ship closed in a heartbeat. The horse's hooves skidded across the worn deck on impact, jarring Kit from the glorious moment in time.

Not even waiting for Angel to come to a stop, Kit threw herself off the horse's back, towards the man at the ship's helm, his eyes bulging from their sockets at the sight of the crazed woman, waving a glowing hammer above her head.

"Yield!" he screamed, cowering beneath his upraised arms, attempting to shield himself from Kit's wrath. "I yield! I yield!" he screamed again.

"Bring this ship back to dock," Kit yelled as she ran past him towards the scimitar wielding crew that was rushing towards her. There were too many of them, and Kit knew it. She was running to her death, but she didn't care. The vision of the poor children in the cage fueled her rage. The idea that this had happened to so many people pushed her to the brink. Without warning, her hammer, her dragon hammer, ignited in blue flames that quickly ran up the handle and up her arm until they wreathed her entire body in fire.

"Did you miss me?" the familiar voice of Fury called to her. "I knew you'd be fun to be with."

Kit completely disregarded the dragon, even though she was thrilled that he had chosen this very moment to show himself again. As she leapt from the ship's quarterdeck, brandishing her flaming hammer, the crew's interest in combat immediately vanished. They threw their weapons to the ground, like they, too, were on fire.

"Get your arses below deck and get this tub back to port," the man at the helm bellowed. Judging by the way the crew was jumping into action, he was the captain of the vessel. They may have also just wanted to avoid the crazy, hammer-wielding woman.

As the ship slowly began to change course, Kit gathered up the dropped weapons and tossed them into an empty rain barrel strapped near the main mast. With her still flaming hammer in hand, she climbed the stairs toward the captain. He dipped his head to her, "Thank you for not killing me and mine."

"What's your cargo?" Kit barked at him.

"Weapons, armor, and alcohol," he replied quickly. "And several crates of wolf pelts."

"Wolf pelts?" Kit snarled at him. The idea that there were crates of pelts on board brought back the memories of the wolf spirit, it's rage, it's profound grief at the death of its pack.

"When that big ice feller and his giant wolf said to put them on board, we put them on board."

"Ice fellow?"

The captain held his hand over his head, as high as it could reach. "Had to be nearly nine feet if he was an inch. His skin was blue, like ice." The man's eyes lit up as he remembered another detail. "He carried a bone weapon, a trident. Ya, that's what it was, a giant bone trident."

Kit staggered backward, the revelation rocking her to her very core. This man was describing Ymir, Titan's chosen disciple, who, like Fenrir, was a god in his own right. Titan had bestowed tremendous powers upon him so that he might help find someone to free him from his icy vault.

What could Ymir want with slaves? To what end? He's Titan's chosen.

Chapter Twenty-Nine

The Sea Dragons

Once the initial terror of the charging yetis had passed, the soldiers rallied, their training and experience kicking in. Using their long spears, the soldiers managed to hold the giant white creatures at bay, while other soldiers worked to flank them. The dwarves, fighting with nothing more than steel bars and bare muscles, drove the soldiers to the shoreline, dealing and taking heavy losses as they did. They fought with berserkers' rage, but the soldiers' weapons had a reach advantage, allowing them to inflict grievous harm as the stout fighters' closed ranks.

Many of the soldiers had turned coat, following the commands of Bango, creating even more mayhem on the battlefield. It made it impossible to tell friend from foe.

"Char has fallen!" Angel screamed at Kit. *"I can't hear his voice!"*

The ship was turning too slowly. The conflict would be over before Kit was able to join in. *"Can you make the jump?"* Kit asked, her eyes searching the battlefield but to no effect.

"It's too far and I have no room to run," Angel replied, her mind scattered, frantic.

Kit pushed her dragon hammer into it sheath and dove into the dark waters. She wasn't much of a swimmer to begin with, and the thick sea weeds grasping at her arms and legs were not making it any easier for her. The weight of her armor was dragging her down, her efforts to swim were futile. She was sinking into the sea's inky depths and there was little she could do to stop it. A thought came to her. She didn't know if it would work. Father Hoarfrost had told her she could only perform this miracle once a moon. Did the rising of the new moon mark the beginning of a new month? Only one way to find out.

"Titan, hear me! I require your strength!" she called out through her mind. Her body was immediately wracked with a cold so intense that her skin felt as though it was on fire. As when she had called upon Titan's strength in the library, the pain was excruciating, but at the same time, it felt so very, very good. With Titan's power coursing through her, Kit kicked her legs hard, propelling herself through the water towards the shore. The seaweed was nothing more than a minor annoyance as she cut through it with each stroke of her arms and each kick of her legs.

A huge silver-blue creature passed in front of her, bringing Kit's progress to a halt. The vortex created by its wake tossed Kit like a leaf on the wind. Not knowing the creature's intentions, she pulled Fury from his sheath, igniting the hammer's brilliant white light. As the light penetrated the depths, nearly a dozen of these creatures came into view. They were swimming all around her, moving in close before darting away.

They were fearsome looking, with bony heads, huge teeth-filled mouths, and a single spiral horn protruding from the middle of their foreheads. Their beady black eyes gave no indication of intelligence, but there was something about them, something that made Kit think they were a sea-dragon of some sort. As quickly as they had arrived, they sped off into the depths.

Kit quickly pushed her hammer back into its sheath and renewed her swim for shore once again. When it was finally shallow enough for her to stand, waves crashed at her back, knocking her down, tossing her about as they rolled away from the shore. Even though the footing here was uneven, she pumped her legs, driving her knees high, trying to get out of the waist-deep water. As another wave struck her from behind, she threw herself forward, letting the wave carry her closer to shore, closer to the soldiers who were all busy dealing with the army of dwarves in front of them.

"Fury," she called out when she was but a few paces from the shore. "Light them up!" She held her hammer out before her, pointing its mithril head at her enemy. On demand, the hammer ignited into blue flames, bursting out at the soldiers, setting them ablaze.

Kit continued moving forward, into the ranks of the soldiers, the dragon-fire continuing to roast them as she did. The soldiers not incinerated on contact, dove into the water, desperate to extinguish the flames consuming their bodies. Now having to fight on two fronts, the soldiers quickly fell under the relentless attack of the dwarves, driving more and more of the soldiers into the salty seawater.

As the battle raged around her, Kit continued to search for Char. In the distance, Indie and Lin knelt next to the fallen horse. Disregarding the bloody mayhem, she raced through the mass of bodies towards her friends. Char was lying on his side, unmoving. Lin was working feverishly at his flank while Indie held the great stallion's head in his hands.

Kit came crashing down beside Lin, examining the horse's body, looking for any signs of injury. There were multiple lacerations about his chest and neck, but it was the broken shaft of a spear, sticking out low from his torso, that was the fatal wound. "Help him!" Indie cried out, a crazed panic in his voice. "He's dying." Indie's eyes were glassy, his lower lip quivering uncontrollably.

Kit's eyes locked on Lin's as the woman slowly shook her head. Whatever she had tried to do to heal the animal, it had been unsuccessful. Char's chest was barely moving. With each beat of his heart, more and more of his lifeblood was spilling out of him.

"Titan, hear me!" Kit screamed out as she placed her hand on the grievous wound. Tearfully looking back to Lin, her hands once again ignited into their gold healing aura. "When I start," she said to Lin, barely able to get the words out, "pull the spear from his chest."

"Don't!" Fury said to Kit, "You'll die if you try to heal him. It's not Titan who provides your healing power, it's you. That power comes from within you."

"Shut up!" Kit screamed at her hammer. "I can't let him die!"

"You'll both die!" Fury choked back at her, his voice thick with emotion. "You'll both die."

"Now!" Kit yelled at Lin as she placed her hand over the wound. When Lin pulled the shaft, Char bellowed in fear and agony, thrashing under Kit's hands. With Titan's strength coursing through her, she kept the stallion as still as she could while her healing magic burst forth. An intense pain blossomed in her own chest as her golden aura engulfed the stallion. It was so excruciating that she had to fight to maintain consciousness. She was suddenly unable to breathe, blood spurting from her mouth and nose. Gritting her teeth, she pushed more of herself into her healing power, even as tiny flashes of light danced at the edges of her vision.

"Kit, stop!" Fury screamed at her. His voice sounded so far away, barely more than a whisper passing through the gauzy haze obscuring Kit's vision.

"Your life is not yours to give," a voice, quiet and smooth said in Kit's mind, pulling her back from the mists tugging at her soul. *"You truly are a strange creature; unlike any I have ever witnessed in my timeless existence."*

"Tiamat?" Kit called out as her lids popped open to see Indie's tear-filled eyes, looking deeply back into hers.

"You're back!" he whispered, finally exhaling.

"Where's Tiamat?"

"Who's Tiamat?" Lin asked from Indie's side. "You kept calling out the name."

"She saved my life, again." Kit tried to sit up, but her head was spinning so badly that she could barely lift it. "Where's Char?" she cried out, pushing Indie aside as she clambered to her feet, barely able to maintain her balance.

"He's with Angel," Indie said, pointing across the shore to where the two horses were standing, facing each other, their necks intertwined. "She jumped off the black ship and swam to shore."

Kit's eyes looked about, trying to take in everything she was seeing. "The battle's over?" she asked. Soldiers were lined up near the docks, relieved of their weapons. The dwarves stood watch over them, their faces grim. Not far from the moored black ships, there was something of a celebration happening on the docks. Hundreds upon hundreds of Berrat were milling about, hugging and dancing. "How long was I out?"

"After you healed Char, you collapsed," Indie answered.

"You stopped breathing. Your heart stopped beating," Lin added. "I did everything I could to revive you, but nothing worked."

"I died?"

"I don't know," Indie replied, pulling Kit into his arms. "Your skin was cold as ice. Fury even tried to warm you, but..." he squeezed her hard in his arms. "I thought I had lost you."

"You, all of a sudden, started breathing – and you started calling out to somebody named Tiamat." Lin placed her head on Indie's chest so she could get her face closer to Kit's. "Who's Tiamat?"

"A Fate," Kit replied, pulling away from Indie. "A friend, I think." Kit looked up into Indie's eyes. "She saved Indie's life, and now mine. If that's not a friend, I don't know what is."

"And it will probably cost her dearly," a rich deep voice intoned from behind Kit, startling the trio in the process. Kit spun around to find Tyr standing there, in his young, handsome, charming persona. "Hello, Kitten," he smiled at her. "You've been busy."

"Who are you?" Indie challenged, reaching over Kit's shoulder, trying to grab the man who had just appeared out of thin air. When Kit blocked him, Tyr gave Indie an arrogant smirk.

"Indie, you've actually met him before but likely as brother Snowbank. He gave you the blessed bow, the one you used to drive Pental away at Templeton. His real name is Tyr. Tyr, this is Indie – my boyfriend." Both Indie and Tyr inhaled sharply at Kit's declaration. "Tyr and Tiamat are Fates; powerful beings who have reached across the universe for the sole purpose of tormenting us."

"Oh, Kitten," Tyr whined, clutching his hands to his heart. "You wound me, deeply." When Kit scowled at him, he dropped the act. "We did not intend on tormenting anyone, other than Titan and Orth, that is."

"Why will her saving me cost Tiamat?" Kit asked, ignoring Tyr's protestations. "Is this because of your idiotic rules?"

"Idiotic?" The word grated from Tyr's mouth in disbelief. "Life, like games, has rules, and they're meant to be followed. When you break the rules, you pay the price."

"You break them all the time!" Kit scoffed back. "What price have you paid?"

"More than you realize, obviously." There was a pained look in the Fate's eyes, something Kit would never have expected. "I'll do what I can to smooth things over with Mephitis, but Eris is already screaming foul. Would that make things better?" Tyr said with a smile, the hurt look disappearing as quickly as it had come. "More importantly, maybe, is that you are a delight to observe, a joy to behold, and you are gaining more and more affection from my kind every day." And with that final declaration, Tyr disappeared with a pop, leaving behind an almost sweet, musky fragrance as he did. A moment later, a coyote howled in the distance.

CHAPTER THIRTY

THE AFTERMATH

"Kit," Bango interrupted, pulling Kit away from her conversation with Lin and Indie.

"Make sure every prisoner in the warehouses has been set free," Kit said to Lin. "I don't want any of them left in there a second longer than necessary. I promised some children." She found herself struggling to get the words out. "I promised to come back and free them."

Bango turned to Lin, holding up her hand for her to stop.

"No need," she said. "I've already instructed my people to take on the task. The prisoners will be taken care of immediately."

"Thank you," Kit said. She looked exhausted and emotionally drained. She looked at the woman's blood-spattered face and clothing. "You wanted to speak to me?" Bango's jaw tightened, and she nodded briskly.

"We've got a problem with the dwarves."

The last thing Kit wanted to hear was, *we've got a problem*. She was weary down to her bones, every muscle in her body was aching, and even though today was an incredible victory, her heart ached for all the poor souls who were wandering about aimlessly, not knowing what was going to happen to them next.

"What's the problem with the dwarves?" Kit asked, trying her best to sound interested.

"They're wanting to start a funeral pyre for their dead."

"What's wrong with that?" Kit asked, understanding that many cultures honor their dead in different ways.

"If there is a fire by the docks, people will come to investigate. When they do, they'll bring soldiers with them, likely lots of soldiers. It's going to draw unwanted attention." Her eyes were wide as she tried to make sure her point was getting across.

"Oh, right," Kit replied, suddenly understanding the issue. "Another battle won't go well for us. We lost too many people already."

Bango nodded her head slowly. "We lost nearly three score dwarves in the fight, but if it's any consolation, we've picked up at least five times that many soldiers who've decided they'd rather fight with us than against us."

"It's no consolation," Kit scowled. "We shouldn't have had to lose a single dwarf, or Berrat, or any other prisoner for that matter. The soldiers are military personnel, paid for their service, but the prisoners don't belong here. They had homes and families. The slavers ripped them away from everything they loved. They died because they wanted to be free."

"You can't look at it like that," Bango replied, running her fingers through her tangled mass of black hair. "Most of the soldiers here are conscripted; they have no choice but to fight for their lord. Most of the people are against slavery, but they fear for their own lives. To stand against the slavers means either death, or a life of slavery. If any of the soldiers switched sides, it's because they believe in what you're doing. They believe you will save them, free them from their own oppressors."

Kit grunted at the revelation. "That explains why they gave up so quickly, despite the fact they outnumbered us so heavily." She scrubbed her face with her hands, her weariness worsening. "If the soldiers would rather not fight us, then maybe we can use that to our advantage."

"The dwarves are already unloading the weapon shipment," Bango said as she pulled out a scroll. "But they're also unloading the crates of alcohol."

"So?" Kit asked. "I'd say they've earned it."

Bango shook her head. "According to the ship's manifest, it's very rare, very expensive dragon brandy."

"Dragon brandy isn't alcohol," Fury interjected, startling Bango as he hovered beside Kit. "We dragon lords began *brewing* it when we first started recruiting humans to help us escape our bonds." When neither of the women responded, he continued. "The brandy, when imbibed in small quantities, bestows *gifts* to the drinker. The nature of those gifts depends on the dragon that created the brandy. It almost always bestows strength and endurance, but it can also impart heightened magic and even breath weapons."

"Breath weapons?" both Bango and Kit asked.

"Fire, frost, poison," Fury said. "They can blast it out of their mouths, like a dragon. If they drink it in small quantities, over many moons, the gifts become permanent. How much does the manifest say there is?"

Bango reviewed the scroll, performing mental calculations as she did. "It looks like there are nearly seventy cases, so almost eight hundred bottles."

Fury whistled at the number. "Assuming they are standard bottles, that would be enough for tens of thousands of doses."

"What happens if somebody drinks too much of it?" Bango asked, rolling up the scroll.

Fury chuckled lightly. "In theory, it could turn a human into a dragon, but more likely, it will kill them outright."

"Wait," Kit interrupted, spinning Bango around to face her, her eyes wild. "Where did you get the manifest from?"

"Treedale brought it," Bango replied, wondering what the big deal was. "He gave it to me a short while ago."

"Where is he?"

Bango scanned the area for a short while, trying to spot him amongst the crowds of people milling about. "Over there!" she cried out, after finally spotting him. "He's with his friend, and the four yetis." Kit didn't even wait for Bango to finish the sentence. She was already bolting towards her friends, bumping heavily into more people than she would have liked along the way.

Kit pushed her way past the yetis until she was face to face with Mukale and Treedale. Even though both of their faces lit up when they saw her, Kit's face was a confusing mixture of joy and anger. "What did you think you two were doing, breaking into the lord's manor like you did?" She screamed at them. She suddenly cringed at her own words as she realized just how much she sounded like Sister Miyuki when she scolded Kit for her own misbehaviours.

"We're happy to see you, too," Treedale replied playfully, barely able to contain his joy at seeing the young priest.

"You're early," Mukale added, giving Kit an affectionate hug. "You caused quite a stir."

"Sister Standing Bear," one of the yetis said, holding out his massive paw; "Thanks to you, we were able to complete our spirit quests."

"And thanks to you, we won the day," Kit replied, placing her hand in the giant's white paw. She didn't know what to expect before she touched the yeti, but silky soft fur and plush palm-pads wasn't it. "You and your friends were truly incredible." She turned to face the other three. "Had you not shown up, I think this would have turned out very differently."

"Our families have been freed," another of the yetis said, "but many died today. The dwarves were already free, but they fought to rescue the Berrat. They laid down their lives, so that others might live."

Suddenly, a cold chill ran up Kit's spine. She hadn't seen Coldforge since the mayhem began. "Sorry, I have to go. I need to find someone," she said frantically as she began her search for the prince. Without another word, Kit raced towards several dozen dwarves gathered along the shoreline.

"Have you seen Coldforge?" she asked as she burst into the group. The dwarves were solemn, barely reacting to Kit's question. "Have you seen him?" she pressed harder, grabbing one of the dwarves by his massive blood-soaked shoulder, prodding him for an answer.

"We have not seen our prince since the battle started," a woman finally responded, her shoulders slumping heavily. It was only then that Kit saw the many bodies wrapped in linens, laying on the ground. "We have prepared our kin for their return to Orth, but it's too far to return them to their mountain homes for a proper burial. We cannot even build a pyre, to send them to Gaia."

"Prepare the pyre," Kit said, placing her hand on the woman's shoulder. "We will give them a send-off worthy of their bravery and sacrifice."

"Thank you," she replied, bowing lightly to Kit. "You might find Coldforge at the brandy-ship. If he releases it, be sure to put aside a case for us." The dwarf managed to find a smile, even if it was half-hearted. Kit offered Titan's blessings and headed off towards the black ships.

As Kit passed groups of people, mostly Berrat and Nomad, many were in shock, not knowing how to process everything that had just happened to them. Many were angry, looking for a place to unleash their hatred on those who had captured them, but many more were thankful that they would be returning home, to their friends and families.

Are they hungry? Where will they sleep tonight? How can I return them home?

Kit's heart was breaking, witnessing the misery and the suffering firsthand. With each face, her resolve to put an end to the slave trade deepened.

There were hundreds of dwarves on the docks, many dressed in heavy armor, obviously taken from the ship's cargo. They all still seemed to be carrying the same steel bars they had used during the battle. As Kit walked among them, they congratulated her on the victory, but like the other dwarves she had met, their mood was sullen.

Kit exhaled heavily when she caught a glimpse of Coldforge in the distance. She hadn't realized she'd been holding her breath, fearful that her new friend hadn't survived the battle.

"We need to mourn our dead," Coldforge said as he made his way through a throng of dwarves. He shared the same subdued demeanor as his kin. "We lost many this night, and we need to give them a proper send-off."

"I've given your kin orders to prepare the pyre," Kit offered. "But it's going to create a stir when the ceremony begins. When people see the flames, they'll come to see what's happening – and send soldiers, more likely than not."

"My kin are weary, but we will fight again if we must."

"With any luck, it won't come to that," Kit said with a wisp of a smile. "I've got the makings of a plan."

CHAPTER THIRTY-ONE

KING KARTER

It was well into the night when the first flames of the funeral pyres caressed those who had fallen in combat. Dwarf, Nomad, and Berrat bodies were all being honored together for the sacrifices they had made for kin and stranger alike. As the dry driftwood tinder ignited, it spread quickly, engulfing the larger timbers, until each pyre was a raging inferno. The dwarves' voices rose with the flames, starting off low and haunting; slowly building until their song filled the cold night air. They sang of valor and sacrifice, of joy and sorrow, and of family and duty.

Despite the fires' intense heat, Kit shivered, thinking about the lives cut short by her actions.

"You did a good thing," Indie offered as he wrapped his arm around Kit's shoulder. He was mesmerized by the pyres, their flames now reaching nearly one hundred feet into the darkness. "These were meaningful deaths if there are such things. Every person believed in what they were doing; they believed in you." Indie stole a glance down at Kit, only to find her face rigid, full of resolve. "If you had told them they'd die, I believe they would have helped you, anyway; the cause was just, and it was necessary."

"I've seen too much death lately," Kit muttered under her breath, barely loud enough for Indie to hear her. "It seems that everywhere I go, death follows."

"Justice follows," Indie said, pulling Kit towards himself, drawing her chin up to look her in the eyes. "You have brought justice to these people – freedom.

A revolution is starting, and you're the reason; you're the one breathing life into it."

"I don't want to start a revolution," Kit choked out. "I just want the slavery to end. I want people to lead normal lives. I want people to be able to go to sleep at night and not fear their family will be gone when they wake."

"Slavery has become a way of life, and the only way it will end is through change – and change is brought about when people stand against those who would oppress them." Indie managed a small smile. "And that, my love, is a revolution."

Despite the profound sadness all about them, at this moment, Indie was the only thing in Kit's world. Looking into his eyes, everything else melted away.

"Kit, people are coming. Soldiers!" Angel broke into Kit's mind, yanking her from the moment's revelry.

"Soldiers are coming," Kit said to Indie. "Spread the word."

Not more than five minutes later, the first of the soldiers came into view, marching down the main street towards the docks. They were coming at a fast pace, yet still maintaining rank and discipline. A second and a third cohort followed closely behind the first. There were far more soldiers coming than Kit, or any of them, had expected. It appeared that the lords had sent their entire contingent of troops.

"Cease this activity immediately," a soldier, dressed in gold armor and a plumed helm, bellowed as he approached. He barked commands at his men, ordering them to extinguish the fires. As the soldiers approached the pyres, the dwarves threw off their cloaks, exposing their full armor and weaponry. The sight caused the soldiers to halt, their gaze switching between the wall of armed dwarves and their leader. "Kill them all!" the man in gold yelled, his voice full of fervor.

Before the soldiers had a chance to react, there was a sound of steel clashing on steel coming from the alley between the Port Authority offices. All eyes turned as hundreds of Berrat came pouring out, slamming their weapons together in rhythmic harmony. Among their numbers, four yetis emerged, roaring out battle challenges of their own.

From the docks came the sound of heavy footfalls pounding out in unison, drawing everyone's attention, as nearly another hundred port authority guards came forth, with the harbourmaster at their lead.

Finally, from behind the soldiers, a tiny Berrat child called out and several hundred wolves and dire wolves took up position behind her. The sight of the animals made Kit's heart swell.

"There is no need for bloodshed," Kit called out, setting her hammer alight. "I give you a choice," she continued as she strode towards the man in gold armor. "You can join our ranks, or you can leave in peace."

"And what if we choose to fight, little girl?" the man practically spat the words into Kit's face.

"Then you will be fuel for the funeral pyres," Kit replied, shaking her head. "You might be willing to die here, to protect your wealth and power, but your soldiers are not."

The man in gold sneered at Kit. "I am Robyrt Karter, and this is *my* city, and these are *my* soldiers, and they will follow *my* commands."

"I am honored to meet you, Robyrt Karter," Kit said with a slight bow, batting her eyes at him. "And I am Sister Kit Standing Bear, Acknowledged by Titan, Savior of Aarall." Kit gave him a broad smile, "And I am the new leader of House Hanse."

Kit's final declaration made Robyrt laugh. "You?" he asked, stepping up a bit closer to Kit so that he could look down his nose at her. "You plan to unseat... me?" As he said the words, the man's eyes turned black, and his hands ignited in bright red flames. *"I am the head of House Hanse, the King of Cormorant! I am the Deceiver!"* The man's voice reverberated with each word, shaking the surrounding ground.

"Fury, you there?" Kit whispered, her hand resting on the hammer's head. She felt his power pulsing through the mithril, bringing a wicked smile to her face.

Kit pulled Fury from his sheath and lightly tapped it on the self-proclaimed king's breastplate. With each tiny strike, a small bit of light burst forth. "Last chance to leave alive," Kit offered, as she took a big step away from the man.

When he didn't move, Kit chuckled. "You have some interesting magic, but I'm guessing you can't call on dragon fire." The dragon hammer immediately burst forth in blue flame, quickly spreading up Kit's arm, engulfing her entire body in fire. Amid Fury's flames, Kit's eyes glowed brighter and brighter, golden flames licking from the corners of her eyes.

"You will burn in the fires of Helja!" Robyrt screamed as he hurled a fireball into Kit's chest. As the red flames met Kit's burning blue aura, they disintegrated, burning up on contact. The self-proclaimed king's face went slack as he took a few steps away from Kit. "It's not possible," he stammered. "This isn't over," he screamed just before he winked out, shrouded in a cloak of shadows.

Kit stood there, staring at the empty space in front of her for a few moments before the crowds of people all started to cheer wildly. The flames surrounding her body dissipated, leaving her armor smoking, as an acrid scent burned her nose. There were now people clapping her on the back, shaking her hand, generally congratulating her for defeating King Karter, but it was only barely registering with Kit. Something about King Karter felt – off. It wasn't until she felt a warm breath at the side of her neck that she snapped out of the trance she seemed to have fallen into.

"You are amazing," Indie said, practically having to scream in her ear to be heard over the din. Kit smiled back up at the man, the world once again drifting away from her as she did.

Kit felt a yank on her sleeve. "Excuse me," a tiny voice cried out, barely audible over the celebrations. "Excuse me!"

Kit's eyes went wide in shock when she saw the face of a young Berrat girl staring up at her. "Amilta! What are you doing here?" Kit could see the small girl's lips moving, but she couldn't hear anything she was saying. "Can we talk later?" Kit screamed at her. "I can't hear what you're saying." Amilta nodded vigorously and smiled brightly back at her before melting into her wolf form. She let out a small yip before weaving her way through the throng of people.

"Bring me as many commanders as you can," Kit yelled at Indie. "I need to talk with them, in private, away from all this noise," she said, pointing to the Port Authority offices.

Chapter Thirty-Two

Captain Karter

Even from within the office where she encountered Lord Buttsworth, the noise from outside still managed to permeate the room. Kit hadn't heard what had happened to the fat man after the port authority had taken him into custody. She hoped he was sitting in a small cage, bound, and gagged, forced to feel what his prisoners had gone through. Whatever it was that had happened, it was too good for him.

From her place in the room, Kit watched as Coldforge led a group of soldiers into the office, with Indie, Lin, and Bango taking up the rear.

As they came in, Kit motioned to the soldiers, and Bango as well, to take a seat on crates that she had lined up. There weren't enough chairs in the office, so Kit had improvised. Bango gave her a confused look when Kit insisted that she sit with the other soldiers.

Kit walked up to Bango first, her face grim. "What is your true name?" she asked the woman. When Bango replied with a questioning look, Kit scowled at her.

"Bango," she replied, fidgeting under the intensity of Kit's stare.

"That is not your true name. Do not try to deceive me."

Bango recoiled slightly and swallowed hard. "My name is Bandolion Goggler, but everybody calls me Bango." Several of the soldiers sniggered, drawing the immediate ire of Kit.

"Who do you serve? Whose leadership do you follow?"

"Yours, Mistress Kit," Bango replied boldly, jutting her chin out as she did. Kit inclined her head slightly in response to the woman's assertion.

"What is your name and whose leadership do you follow?" Kit asked the man sitting next to Bango.

"I am Captain Tym Windspeak, commander of Lord Gillan's army." His voice was deep and seductive, as though he was a practiced orator. "If you mean to overthrow the ruling house, then I follow you." The man held Kit's eyes, his stare never wavering.

"Thank you," Kit said, inclining her head slightly to him. "And what of you?" She asked the tall, slender man next to him. "What is your name, and who do you follow?"

"I am Captain Logner, commander of Lord Buttsworth's army. I follow you," he declared with absolute conviction.

Kit moved in closer to the man; close enough that she could smell the cheap wine on his breath. "Why are you lying to me?" she asked, as sweetly as she could manage.

"I speak true," he said, pulling his face away from Kit's. "I speak true."

"Who is your second in command?" Kit asked, batting her eyes slowly.

"Lieutenant Maidsson," he replied, a questioning look on his face. "Lieutenant Athur Maidsson."

Kit quickly turned to Bango. "Find this Athur Maidsson and bring him here." With a sly grin, Kit added, "And bring me six of your people; we've got some prisoners to put away."

"Yes, Mistress," Bango replied with a wide grin. "As you command." And with that, Bango headed for the exit while Captain Logner started to protest whatever was about to happen to him.

"I don't like being lied to," Kit commented in an offhanded way. Beads of sweat emerged along the captain's brow. His head started swiveling about, searching for a friendly face or a quick exit.

Kit sighed heavily. "I can't imagine your motivation at this point. Since you continue to stand with the slavers, I can only surmise that your heart is black, black as coal."

"No, you don't understand," the captain stammered, his eyes getting wilder by the second. "I'm being forced to do this. They'll kill my family."

"And yet you continue to lie to me," Kit said, shaking her head. "You are definitely not being forced into doing anything and I don't even think you have a family." Kit motioned to Coldforge, and he quickly grabbed the man's shoulder, causing him to scream out in pain. "Hold him until the Port Authority returns," Kit said. "Try not to break too many bones while we're waiting." Again, the captain screeched out in pain as the dwarf's grip closed a bit tighter on him.

"And you?" Kit asked the short, stout woman sitting next to Captain Logner. "What is your name and who do you follow?"

The stout woman stood from her crate and cleared her throat. "I am Captain Rustnig Karter; my friends call me Rusty." The woman paused a moment, taking a deep cleansing breath. "If you will stand against my father, then I will stand with you."

"Your father is the... man I dealt with outside?" The woman nodded to Kit's question. "And you would stand against him?" Again, the woman nodded. "I need you to speak the words aloud," Kit said, her eyes hard as flint.

"My father was not always the man you saw today. He was once a good man and a great leader." Rusty got a far-off look in her eyes. "That was until we came here, to this accursed city, and he became a slaver. He is not the man I knew. He is no longer my father."

"And what of the people in your command," Kit pressed. "Who will they follow?"

The woman scoffed. "They used to follow me; some may still, but the rest — they now follow you."

When Kit's eyes turned on the remaining soldiers, they all immediately gave their names and professed their allegiance to Kit, without her having to ask. Accepting their statements as fact, and accepting the captains as loyal followers, she immediately began to make plans with them, the first of which was to put Captain Karter in charge of the guard, promoting her to the rank of general. Kit couldn't say why the woman should be put in charge, but something about Captain Karter said that she was the right choice.

The conversations continued for another half hour before Bango returned with Lieutenant Maidsson. Kit was about to speak with him, but General Karter stepped in front of her.

"What is your name, young man?" the general asked him, her tone imposing. When the young man's face went white, the general moved in closer, having to crane her neck upward to look at him. "You will speak when you are spoken to!" she bellowed at him, causing him to flinch further.

"Ma'am?" he hesitated, his eyes moving to Kit, perhaps hoping for some form of intervention or perhaps a suggestion of how he should answer.

"Who are you looking at?" the general bellowed at him again, causing him to take a step away from her. She immediately closed the distance until her ample bosom was pressing against him. "I'm the one speaking to you lieutenant, so I'm the one you should be looking at." When the young man's eyes returned to the general's, she asked him again. "What is your name?"

"Maidsson," he squeaked out, taking another step away from the general. "Lieutenant Athur Maidsson." The man's eyes shifted over to where his captain was, to where the dwarf was squeezing his shoulder, making his captain writhe in agony.

"If you make me tell you to look at me again, lieutenant, I will carve out your eyeballs and shove them down your throat!" The man's attention immediately returned to the general, his eyes now becoming glassy. "Who do you follow?" she bellowed at him, again moving up until she was pressing her body against his. When he made another squeaking noise, she again yelled at him. "I can't hear you, lieutenant!"

The young man set his jaw and swallowed hard. "I follow her," he said, pointing at Kit. "Kill me if you have to, but I follow her."

"Good answer," the general said, patting him on the chest. "A very good answer indeed, Captain Maidsson."

"Are you up to taking over Lord Buttsworth's army?" Kit asked, her tone dramatically gentler than the general's. She looked over at Logner, still squirming in Coldforge's grasp. "You are allowed to decline," she continued. "No harm will come to you or anybody else who does not wish to fight with me – as long as you don't fight against me."

"I am not much of a leader," the newly appointed captain replied. "I don't know if my people will listen to my orders."

"Your orders come from Mistress Kit," Lin said as she stepped up. "They'll listen to them as if they came from the woman herself. You will only need to explain that to them once." When Logner screamed out in pain again, Lin inclined her head towards him. "Nobody will question your orders."

"Your first order of business," Kit said, "is to have this man bound and gagged and caged right next to your old boss." Kit looked towards Bango, "If Harbourmaster Bango's people can show him the way."

"It would be our distinct pleasure," one of the Port Authority responded. "It will give me a chance to give that fat pig another kick when I see him."

As the Port Authority led Captain Maidsson and his captive out of the office, Bango shook her head at Kit. "Cap is still the harbourmaster," she said. "You can't just *remove* him. It's not right. He's a good man, stuck between a rock and people with long, pointy teeth."

"He will be announcing his retirement tomorrow," Kit said. Bango's refusal to take his place, if he was not willing, only served to reaffirm her trust in the woman. "He and his family will be taken care of; they'll be safe." Kit scrubbed her hands across her face and stifled a yawn. "We need to take care of the freed prisoners. Make sure they have a place to sleep and food to eat."

"My father's estate could host them," Rusty offered. "There are not enough beds, of course, but there is enough space for everyone, and the larder has enough food to feed them for the better part of a year."

"My people don't need shelter," a small voice said from the entranceway. "We Berrat are content in the wilds, but I'm sure they would accept the food." Amilta gave Kit a wide grin as she stood in the doorway with Runt and Lump at her side, and seven gray wolves at her heels.

"Whatever works best for your people," Rusty said, bowing deeply to the child. "I trust the wolves you're with are friendly?"

"As long as they are treated with respect," she beamed back at the general. "We care for the land, when the humans do not."

"Okay, okay," Kit said, trying to diffuse the situation before it even started. "General, can you make sure everyone is properly cared for, given what they want, what they need? Maybe explain to everyone they can go home as soon as we figure out how to get them there?"

"Of course, Mistress," she replied with a small bow and a warm smile; a reaction Kit hadn't witnessed in her before.

"Please don't call me that," Kit said as Rusty started heading for the exit. "My name is Kit, or Sister Kit."

"Yes, Mistress Kit," she replied with a bow, before heading outside.

"I need to speak with you about your friend here," Amilta said, motioning to Runt. "He is not as he appears to be, is he?"

"Why would you say that?" Kit asked, her own hackles rising at her question.

"He is of our kind. I can feel it. My pack can feel it. But our eyes, they say otherwise."

"Fenrir placed a spell on him, so that he appears as a golden retriever, instead of a dire wolf." As expected, Kit broke the illusion when she admitted to his true nature, allowing Amilta and her pack to witness his natural form. Amilta gasped at the revelation, immediately dropping her head before the great wolf. Her pack followed suit.

"Lord Amaruq!" Amilta said, her eyes still lowered. "You have returned!"

Chapter Thirty-Three

AMILTA

"Lord Amaruq?" Kit asked, as she moved closer to give Runt's neck a good scratch, her fingers getting lost in his thick, black fur.

"The Prime Alpha, the leader of the north-eastern pack," Amilta replied, still keeping her eyes downcast. "He sent me here, to this city, to find Shade and his master."

"Amilta, stand up," Kit demanded, as she started scratching the neck of Lump, who was jealously vying for her affection. "His name is Runt, not Amaruq." Kit's insistence that Runt was not Amaruq fell on deaf ears. "He's just a puppy, barely six moons old," she said, trying a different tactic. "He looks older than he is because Fenrir changed him into a full-sized adult; so that he could protect me."

"Six moons?" Amilta asked. "But..."

It suddenly dawned on Kit. "The wolf spirit," she said, pondering out loud; "was Amaruq the dire wolf that I killed, the wolf that nearly killed Indie?" Kit looked over at Indie, wondering what he was thinking.

"He's the spitting image of that wolf," he said, surprise spreading across his face, like his eyes had just opened for the first time. "I never noticed before."

"Runt is his son," Kit said, turning back to Amilta. "He was the runt of the litter. After the poachers killed his mother, I cared for the pups. Most of them returned to the wild, but Runt chose to stay with me."

"He has been touched by Fenrir?" Amilta's eyes were wide and full of wonder. "He should take up the mantle of Alpha Prime. Amaruq appointed no other. Fenrir must decide."

"I don't think Runt would willingly leave Kit's side," Indie said, holding out his hand to Amilta. "My name is Indie; these fine ladies are Lin and Bango, and this stout man is Coldforge."

Amilta inclined her head to each of them in greeting. "You have a fine pack, Sister Kit."

The comment made Kit giggle. A sly grin crossed her face as she watched her friends, looking for their reaction to the girl's remark. Judging by their faces, they were all happy to be deemed members of her pack. "Is there something you need from me?" she asked Amilta, as the last of her giggles fell away.

"Maybe," Amilta said as she walked inside the office. She called her own pack inside before shutting the door behind her. "Amaruq sent me here, to Cormorant, to seek out his pack's omega, a dire wolf named Shade." The little girl's face screwed up as she tried to find the words. "Shade, or whoever he serves, was making the wolves of Arnnor sick. When an infected wolf bit another, the infection spread. Once the disease had taken hold, Shade was able to speak into the minds of the sick wolves, driving them to do things, things against their nature."

"The tip of the spear," Kit muttered, thinking back to her conversation with Fenrir. "We need to find who's wielding it."

Amilta stared blankly at Kit as she voiced her thoughts.

"There were poachers," Kit continued as she tried to put the pieces together. "Fenrir said the poachers, the ones I destroyed, were the tip of the spear and I needed to find who was wielding them. I thought they were the ones making the wolves sick."

"That doesn't make sense," Amilta replied. "The people who were killing the wolves; they were only killing the healthy. Why would they make the wolves sick?"

Kit shook her head. "They were using the sick animals as a reason for killing the healthy," she said, as her thoughts started to coalesce. "The sick wolves were attacking farms, their livestock and even people." She looked to Indie, suddenly remembering that the sick wolves had killed his whole family. "People were afraid of them. Nobody would complain about poachers killing off the wolves, even by the thousands."

"Killing the wolves," Amilta said, realizing what the poachers were doing, "prevents Fenrir from gathering information across the lands. We are her eyes, the eyes of Titan."

"Sweet Titan," Kit exclaimed, "is Shade a dire wolf as well?" When Amilta nodded, Kit's eyes went wide in disbelief. "It's Ymir who's behind this. The black ship captain said an ice giant and a huge wolf were overseeing the loading of the crates onto the ships. There were crates of wolf pelts."

"Ymir, the chosen of Titan, the god my family worshipped?" Indie's voice sounded far off to Kit, like he was speaking from a different room. "That's impossible!"

"It's not impossible," Fury said, refuting the young man's claim. "Some of it makes sense, a lot of sense."

"You have a talking war hammer?" Amilta's eyes lit up with excitement. "Can I hold him?"

"No, you cannot hold me," Fury said with a scolding tone, floating out from his sheath. "I'm not just some plaything..." Fury suddenly started to laugh, remembering how he had scolded Kit, telling her he was not some plaything to be left in a corner and forgotten about. "I am pleased to meet you and your pack, Amilta," the tone in Fury's voice changing completely. "You may look, but don't touch." The hammer burst into blue flames, spouting small gouts as he spun in circles, much to the wolf-child's delight.

"Why does it make sense?" Kit interrupted, grabbing Fury by his handle, quickly putting an end to his theatrics.

Fury's flames died out immediately when Kit took hold of him. "We dragons have always been suspicious of Ymir's loyalty to his god. Titan bestowed divinity status upon him, so that Ymir might seek out people strong enough to free him, but Ymir never did. He always looked to be building his own army, an army of people willing to swear fealty to him, and him alone. Just look at the Jotunheim Temple."

"That's not right," Indie screamed, his hands clenched into tight fists, his face turning a deep red. "My father was a faithful servant of Titan, a member of the Jotunheim Temple Guard. He taught me and my sister of Ymir, Fenrir, *and* Titan. He told us of Ymir's task, to seek out those who would free his master."

"I meant no disrespect to you or your father," Fury responded, "but the temple in Jotunheim exclusively prays to Ymir. There isn't a single statue of Titan, not a single one. If your father was faithful to Titan, then he hid it from the Temple. By your own words, you may have well described why Ymir hates Titan. He saw him as his master, not a deity to be worshipped."

Regardless of whether Fury's assertions made sense or not, Indie wasn't having any of it. Without saying a word, he stormed from the office, slamming the door behind him, loosening the doorframe in the process.

"It's late," Kit finally said, breaking the awkward silence. "We all need some rest. We've got a lot of work ahead of us and we can't do it if we're asleep on our feet." She tried to stifle another yawn, but it got away from her. She let out a long groan as her mouth gaped open.

Chapter Thirty-Four

A Wing and a Prayer

Danny, with his arrow nocked and drawn, waited in Lord Byssus' chambers for his quarry to come into view.

With each of The Wing's footfalls, as he climbed the stairs from Lord Byssus' secret chamber, Danny's heartbeat got faster and faster. The Crow's top assassin was only a few steps from death, and he would be the one to deliver it to him. Lord Wing would never harm another, never again. Danny would do this for the Berrat people, for his cousin Breayn, but mostly for his parents. The images from his past burst into his mind's eye.

What if they're not dead? What if he knows where they are? What if he's holding them?

Lord Wing's eyes were wide when he came through the secret doorway. He hadn't expected to find Danny there, let alone holding a nocked arrow, pointed at him.

"You are full of surprises, aren't you?" The Wing stepped into the room, wearing a cocksure look on his face that made Danny's blood boil. "Are you planning on shooting me, or are you just going to wave that arrow around all day?"

When the arrow struck him in the shoulder, pinning him to the stone wall behind, the Crow laughed. It was a horrible, awful laugh that made Danny's skin crawl.

"You should have killed me when you had the chance." The Crow's eyes were wild. This man was insane, and it was pouring off him by the bucket load.

"Where are my parents?" Danny screamed at him. He already had another arrow nocked and drawn.

"Well," the Crow said, with a voice that was much too calm. He stepped forward, pulling the arrow's shaft through his body like it was nothing at all. Danny released the second arrow, hitting him in the other shoulder, pinning him to the wall once again. The Wing hardly flinched. He simply stared down at the new arrow protruding from him.

"That was rude," he said. "You ask me a question and before I can answer..." His words were cut off when another arrow struck him again in the first shoulder, pinning him harder against the wall. The Crow glared at Danny; his lips pressed together so tightly they were turning white.

"You should know, I feel no pain, so your actions are little more than a nuisance, but they are serving to raise my ire." He looked down at the arrows sticking out from both of his shoulders. "If it will make you feel better, I can just stand here."

"You can stand there and answer my questions," Danny said. The phoenix desperately wanted to be released, to end the man's miserable existence, but he managed to keep it at bay.

"Your father is dead," Lord Wing said like he was commenting on the weather. "He was useless to me." Another arrow slammed into the wall, nicking the Crow's ear in the process. Danny's hands were trembling badly while tiny flames licked at the corners of his eyes.

"Liar!" The young Berrat's scream seemed to please The Wing.

"Your mother, on the other hand, was too sweet to destroy. Too important to give to King Faol. Her, I keep close." The Crow tapped on his chest and his eyes widened slightly. "She will be with me for eternity."

"Liar!" Danny screamed again, nocking and releasing another arrow. Like its predecessor, it crashed into the wall just beside the Crow's head, nicking his other ear.

"Danny, run!" the voice that came from The Wing was not his own. It was the voice of a woman. It was the voice of his mother.

"Shut it, bitch," the Crow screamed. "I was going to let him live, let him serve me, serve my master, but now he will die. I will kill him slowly. I will make him suffer."

"Mother?" Danny's voice was barely a whisper. His bow clattered onto the stone floor. He remembered The Wing's words, when he had asked him if he knew that a Berrabbithi could subsume the spirit of their kin. He took a step towards The Wing, a flush creeping up his neck.

"Danny, run! You can't win," the voice of his mother again bursting from The Wing. The man punched himself in the face, repeatedly, perhaps hoping to cause harm to the spirit within. Danny heard the voice. He knew it was his mother's. Nothing in Helja or Orth could make him leave her behind with this lunatic. But if he killed The Wing, what would happen to her? This was the last thought to pass through his mind before his head slammed against the far wall. The Wing had him by the throat and was pounding his body against the side of the hearth.

How? How was he so fast?

Spots were dancing in front of Danny's eyes as darkness crept in at the corners of his vision. He could barely make out the crazed expression on The Wing's face as he drew him back and slammed him against the wall yet again.

"Titan, hear me," Danny whispered out. He called upon his god, begging for him to bestow a battle spell upon him. Unlike his previous attempts to commune with his god, there was no higher power there to listen to his plea. What little grace Titan had given him as an acolyte, he had taken away.

"There is no one to save you, boy," The Wing said as he tossed Danny across the room. His body careened off one of the bed posts, cracking it into two pieces. His face scrubbed across the rough floor before crashing into the wall, just beside the stairway to the secret chambers. The room was spinning heavily. Danny's stomach roiled. He tried to stand but he couldn't get his feet steady under himself. He took one wobbly step towards The Wing before the floor tilted heavily to his left. He lost his footing and tumbled into the secret passageway. His head slammed hard against the wall. His world pitched severely and a moment later, he was careening down the stairs. Pain exploded in his head, shoulder, and back. The light from Lord Byssus' chamber winked on and off as his face bounced off the stairs and up against the walls. After what felt like an eternity, the spinning, tumbling, bone-jarring plummet came to an abrupt halt. Danny was on his back, looking up through a tunnel of darkness with a dim, shaky light at its end. The light wavered slightly and then darkened. A black figure had stepped through the weakly illuminated entrance and stood at the top of the stairs, laughing. The sound made his head feel like it was about to split open.

Danny scrabbled to his feet, using the wall next to him to help keep himself upright. The moist, cool stonework and hairy roots told him he was back down in the secret passage. The Crow's form became a spectral-like silhouette as he descended the stairs. Danny turned and bolted down the hallway, bouncing off the walls several times as he tried to maintain his balance. He held his hands out in front of himself, hoping to not crash, headfirst, into a wall. The echo of his footfalls told him he was nearing the end of the tunnel. He slowed just before his hand hit the wooden rung of the ladder. He quickly scampered up before shifting his weight away from the wall, drawing the ladder like a great lever. The now familiar sound of the secret door opening was music to his ears. The hallway was instantly filled with the warm coruscating glow from the secret chamber.

The Wing stood frozen at the turn in the hallway, a look of uncertainty on his face. The deafening roar of Ryn's great white bear forced the Crow to look away from Danny. His look of uncertainty turned to derision as he turned towards the stairway and the door to Lord Byssus' hideaway. The great bulk of the bear darkened the hallway as it charged forward. The Wing disappeared from Danny's view as he bolted around the corner, towards the great beast bearing down on him. With the phoenix desperately wanting to be freed, Danny gave chase.

The young Berrat rounded the corner just as Ryn spewed forth an ice storm from his gaping maw. Holding his hands out before him, Danny tried to shield himself from the stinging ice pellets that bit into his face. Through the frosty mist, he could barely see Breayn running up along the bear's side. She moved through the blizzard as deftly as a fish through water. A tempest swirled around her as she passed through the frozen mass. She held her hands out before herself and the blizzard intensified.

"Hello, brother," a strange, high-pitched voice echoed from The Wing. "I had wondered where you had gotten to." Breayn ignored the comment and dashed forward, throwing her shoulder into the Crow assassin, knocking him onto his backside. She knew the voice, or more accurately, Boreas, the North Wind, knew the voice. It was that of his brother, Eurus, the East Wind. With Breayn tapping into the air- elemental's powers, his consciousness was dangerously near the surface. She could feel what he was feeling, she knew his thoughts as if they were her own. He was drawing strength from his brother. Breayn had difficulty enough dealing with Boreas on his own. The woman dropped to her knees and clamped her eyes shut tight. With all her being, she tried to press The North Wind down, to prevent him from escaping.

"He holds the East Wind," she screamed out.

Whether Ryn understood the danger she was in or not was unknown, but he hurdled himself at The Wing. Just as he was about to throw his bulk upon the man, a hurricane force wind ripped down the corridor. Ryn's claws dug deeply into the stone allowing him to hold his position. He roared out in frustration as he lowered his face, trying to maintain his grip on the stone.

"Polar fire," Sky Eyes yelled as he emerged from the chamber. Immediately, his body glowed with a pale blue aura, and an exquisitely crafted short bow appeared from nowhere into his left hand. As he drew back the bowstring with his right, an ice-tipped arrow materialized. His hair whipped about him as the gale force winds threatened to hurdle him towards the stairs. The old man ducked low, and the bow disappeared. He hunkered down, using Ryn's body as a windbreak as he ran forward. Danny's head must not yet have cleared. It was the only explanation for how lithe and graceful the old man was as he moved. Sky Eyes clutched hold of Ryn's thick white fur and clambered his way onto the bear's back.

Danny watched, transfixed, as The Wing lay on his back, laughing maniacally, his long red hair whipping around his face, his cloak of feathers flapping and fluttering about his body.

"Warrior Spirit," the old Berrat intoned. "Unto you we have offered the lives of our people. Unto you have our families prayed. It was for this very moment that we paid the price for your protection." The old Berrat's body took on an unearthly white glow. For barely a breath, the gossamer form of a great bear formed around Sky Eyes' body. The ethereal figure coalesced around Ryn, enveloping him in a brilliant silver-blue aura. Filled with the strength of the great spirit, Ryn roared yet again and took several quick steps forward before lunging himself at The Wing. His tooth-filled maw took the Crow by the waist and savagely shook him.

The Wing screamed out as the spirit of Eurus left his body. A whirlwind ripped towards the stairway. "I am free of this retched vessel my brother," it shrieked out. It blew past Ryn, Breayn, and Sky Eyes, cackling as it escaped up the stairway behind them. The Wing coughed up a gout of blood as he beat his fists ineffectually on Ryn's snout while the bear continued to thrash him about.

"Danny, I can return your mother to you," The Wing cried out, his mouth covered in a mass of dark pink foam. He continued trying to free himself from Ryn's jaws. "If I die…"

"Ryn, don't kill him," Breayn yelled, still fighting to keep Boreas from escaping. "We need her!"

Ryn paused. He stared down at his mate kneeling on the wet stone floor of the tunnel. A small, almost pleading sound escaped his mouth just before he released The Wing, dropping him to the floor like a bag of wet grain. The Berrat hit the tiled stone floor with a whump, and a large amount of his lifeblood sprayed out from beneath him. Ryn had mauled him badly. It was unlikely he would survive his grievous wounds.

"Heal me, and I'll return Dyanna's spirit." He rolled over onto his stomach. The Wing's black feathered cape hid most of the wounds, but the spreading pool beneath him told the tale.

"We have no healers," Breayn said as she picked herself up off the ground. "How do we save Dyanna's spirit?"

The Crow laughed, coughing up more blood in the process.

"Don't let her die with him," Danny pleaded. "Let my phoenix try to heal his wounds."

He quickly knelt next to the battered Crow. The thought of using the phoenix to mend his wounds was repulsive, but he would do anything to save his mother. Danny placed his hands on the Berrat's back in a fashion similar to when he had brought Ryn back from the brink. With all his being, he called upon the spirit of the phoenix, he called upon its life-giving flames.

The phoenix did not respond.

Phoenix I need you. I need to save my mother.

Again, the phoenix did not respond. Danny could feel him resisting, refusing to do as he demanded. Danny looked up to see the concerned looks of his cohorts hovering over him.

"Titan, hear me," he pleaded. He so desperately needed the god to listen, to answer his call. But in his heart of hearts, he knew it was futile. Titan had withdrawn his graces, and he had no actual healing skills.

"Titan, hear me," Danny bellowed, craning his head up to the heavens. He pressed his hands harder upon the back of The Wing and called out again. "Titan, hear me."

The god was not listening.

"Give me back my mother," Danny wailed, striking the blood-soaked cloak with his fists. He rolled the Crow over onto his back, exposing the man's cruel grin. "Let me say goodbye to her."

The Wing pulled a dagger from his waist and pressed it to Danny's throat. The blade was razor sharp. A thin stream of blood trickled along its edge.

"She's gone," he cackled. "And you can join her in the Beyond." Before he could draw the blade across Danny's throat, Ryn's bear form lunged forward, took The Wing's head in his terrible jaws, and crushed it like a grape.

Chapter Thirty-Five

One Less Crow

The great white bear dropped the lifeless body of The Wing to the stone floor. Danny stared up at Ryn, a deadly look in his eye. The fool had just murdered his mother.

"Ryn, what have you done?" Breayn said, her voice raspy. "You've sent her to the Beyond before she could say goodbye. Before I could say goodbye."

"I thought..." Ryn said after he transformed into his true form. The Berrat stared down at the lifeless, mutilated Crow.

"You thought what?" Danny asked just before punching the man in the face, sending him sprawling to the ground. "You thought you'd deny me my family?" The phoenix was rising to the surface, ready to set the world ablaze.

"I thought I could capture her soul," Ryn said, not bothering to wipe the blood from his split lip. "I thought that, if Dyanna was there and I killed The Wing, I would capture her spirit."

"Why? Why would you think that?" Breayn said. She had moved to position herself between Danny and her prone mate. "It's never been done."

"He did it," he screamed out. "He captured her soul."

"He was Berrabbithi," she replied. "We only accept the spirit of those willing to join with us."

"My mother would have never willingly allowed him to take her spirit," Danny screamed, pushing Breayn to the side, knocking her hard against the wall.

"She may have," Sky Eyes said, "to save your life. Perhaps she believed she could help sway his twisted mind." Danny glared at the old Berrat. A frown slowly grew across his face, flames flickering in his eyes.

"Never," he screamed. "She would never have allowed it. Never!" Sky Eyes reached out to comfort the young Berrat.

"If she did not do so willingly, then The Wing killed her and subsumed her spirit before she could return to the Beyond."

"She was not fully under his control," Danny said. His body slumped. He sounded defeated. "She returned to speak to me." He pushed his way past the lot of them and trudged towards the staircase. He paused when Breayn spoke.

"What happened?" Breayn asked her mate. "When you ended his life, what did you feel?"

"Nothing," Ryn replied. "I felt no spirit within him. It was as though he was an empty shell."

"That makes no sense," Danny said from his place at the base of the stairs. "My mother was there within him. I spoke with her. She tried to warn me."

"No, it doesn't make any sense at all," Sky Eyes said, his brow creasing heavily.

Lieutenant Barclay stepped out from the hideaway, holding a semi-conscious Lord Byssus by the scruff of the neck. Kandyce was a few steps behind him with the four Berrat serving girls beside her. She gave her stepfather a look of utter disdain. The lieutenant spied the mutilated remains of The Wing.

"I guess it's just one for the gallows then," he said, holding up Lord Byssus by the collar of his fine blue robe.

"The gallows are too kind," Danny said, practically spitting the words out. "He will burn."

"Please, no," Lord Byssus pleaded. He looked down at his ring-encrusted fingers.

"There is no punishment that is too cruel," Kandyce said. Lord Byssus' eyes widened as he caught sight of The Wing's crushed and mutilated head. Again, he glanced down at his hands.

"Please, no. I have information. I can tell you where you can find the others, The Claw, and The Beak." Danny felt his words were no more than a desperate ploy. This man was a monster, willing to say or do just about anything to save his own skin.

"What of my parents?" Danny asked. "Where are they?" Lord Byssus' eyes grew wide and his panic visibly lessened.

"I can take you to them. I know where they are," he replied eagerly. The fat lord's jowls quivered as he nodded vigorously. "They are safe, unharmed."

"I don't believe you," Breayn said. Her gray eyes were a gathering storm, ready to be unleashed on the man.

"I know of your parents as well," Lord Byssus said. He cast his eyes downward, his voice less enthusiastic. "Your father is at Wantage, with The Beak. Your mother is..."

"Where?" Breayn demanded. "Where is my mother?" The blood drained from Lord Byssus' face, turning him pale.

"Her body is at Wantage as well," Lord Byssus replied, swallowing hard. Breayn stumbled backward. She hadn't truly believed that her mother was alive, but hearing of her death, from this wretch, was like having a dagger plunged into her heart. Ryn quickly moved to her side and wrapped his arms around her.

"Who killed her?" Danny asked. He desperately wanted to unleash the phoenix and simply incinerate the man.

"She's not dead," Lord Byssus screeched, holding his hands out in front of himself, trying to ward off Danny's advancing wrath. "She's..."

"She's what?" Breayn asked, the tiniest twinge of hope turning her gray eyes a deep blue.

"She's an empty husk," Lord Byssus said, cringing away as he spoke. "They removed her spirit from her."

"What do you mean, removed her spirit?" Danny asked. "How could somebody do that?"

"Where is my mother's spirit?" Breayn interrupted, pushing away from Ryn. "What do they want with it?"

"It is to be sent to King Faol. At least, that's what I heard." A hint of satisfaction crept across the fat lord's face.

"How could you have heard anything?" Kandyce asked. "You've never left the city. These are just pathetic lies to save your miserable skin." The comment made her stepfather laugh. He could not hold back the patronizing look he gave his stepdaughter. His sniveling behavior had lasted for all of thirty seconds. Danny punched him in the stomach, knocking the air from his lungs. It took Lord Byssus several moments to get his voice back, but his look of condescending superiority never diminished.

"I still have my spiders," he said, clutching his belly. "They cling to the walls. They hide in dark corners. They listen and they report back to me." He turned to Breayn, his look smug and self assured. He had hit their tender spot. He knew it and now she knew he knew it.

"So then," Breayn started, the fury in her eyes once again roiling, "where are Danny's parents?" The fat man just grinned at the question. The smug, self-important look he had made Danny want to rip his face off.

"Where do you think he's hated more?" Ryn asked Kandyce. "Here or in Wantage?" The question caught the entire lot off guard, including Lord Byssus.

"Wantage," Kandyce replied, a quizzical look in her eyes. "But I'm sure that the people of Lilloet would enjoy skinning him alive just as well. Why? What does it matter?"

"Well," Ryn said, his eyes leveled on the Lord who was again staring down at his hands. "I'm thinking we can put him in the stockades. Let the people torment him and abuse him, the way he did them. Whatever he knows, will eventually come out, if only to save his own skin. I think it's what he cares about most." Lord Byssus' smug look of self assurance drained from his face.

"Your mother is in Cormorant and your father is in Wantage," he blurted out. "Danny's parents are gone. I don't know where they are. They were captured long ago, likely sent to King Faol. He wants the Berrabbithi. He wants to learn of their magic, their power over living spirits. Please, just kill me. Don't leave me to the people." Whatever skill as a liar the man had, vanished. His face was getting redder with each heartbeat.

"Why is my mother in Cormorant?" Breayn asked.

"I don't know why," he whined. "I don't know. She was a gift, or something. King Karter wanted her. I swear on my eyes, I don't know why." Danny looked to Breayn. He had never heard of King Karter before. Again, Lord Byssus looked down at the rings on his hand. He twisted one of them, a silver band with a large sapphire stone. That familiar blue aura started to gather around his fingers. Danny punched him in the stomach again.

"What is it with these rings?" he asked. He grabbed at the blue gemstone and his hand immediately became numb from cold. Disregarding the pain, he started wrenching the rings from the man's fingers. Lord Byssus cried out when one of his fingers snapped while Danny ripped a ring from it. After he had removed every bit of jewelry, he stuffed them in his pocket.

"I want to go home," Kandyce said, "and I want to put my father on display for the people until he rots, and the crows have cleaned his bones."

"We can make that happen, Lady Kandyce," the lieutenant said. "With your leave, I will take this poor excuse for a man to the stockades here. Might as well let the people say goodbye before we head east." Danny wasn't sure he liked the idea of Lieutenant Barclay taking Lord Byssus. He wasn't sure where the man's loyalties lied. He wasn't sure if the man had tried to stomp on him while he was in his vole form.

"I don't know that I trust you," Danny said. He strode back to the fallen body of The Wing and placed his foot onto the mutilated man's chest. "If you betray us..." before he finished the words, the Berrat assassin's body burst into flames.

Breayn motioned with her head towards Lord Byssus. "Ryn, maybe you should accompany the lieutenant. We don't know how many of the lord's men are still loyal to him."

"I'm coming, too," Kandyce said, following as her father was being dragged up the stairs. The four Berrat serving girls followed, their eyes never leaving their feet.

Sky Eyes inclined his head to Danny. "And now the prophecy of The Wing's demise is complete." He quietly turned and followed the others up the staircase, leaving Breayn and Danny alone below.

"I think Lieutenant Barclay tried to kill me," Danny whispered just as the last of the footfalls faded off in the distance. "While I was a vole, he tried to stomp on me." Breayn's brow furrowed, and she glanced back up the stairs.

"Are you sure?"

"Sure enough that I can describe the wear patterns on the bottom of his leather boot," Danny replied, his eyebrows raised. It was entirely possible that, from the vole's perspective, everyone looked like they wanted to stomp on him, but in this case, the intent had seemed clear. He supposed that it was possible that the man was simply trying to not step on him.

"It makes no sense," Breayn replied. "I watched him fight the lord's personal guard. He killed the captain right after the man stabbed you." She got a funny look on her face. "I saw the captain run you through. How did it not kill you?"

"I think it did. I think the phoenix inside me wouldn't let the Great Cycle claim me." He really didn't like trying to describe what had transpired. In part because he didn't fully understand what had happened, but mostly because the whole experience was deeply personal. His cousin picked up on his emotional distress and quickly changed the subject.

"We need to go to Cormorant. I need to find my mother."

"But there is so much more we need to do here. I think we've started something, something big. Don't we need to see it through?" She leveled her gaze at him for several seconds, a visceral, primal sound escaped her lips.

"Sometimes I feel bad for your mate. You can be a bit pushy." Danny's infectious grin spread across his face. Breayn's eyes turned from deep blue to a swirling mass of gray, like she was about to unleash a storm upon him. "Yes, that there, that's exactly what I was talking about. That *thing* you're doing right now."

Breayn's gaze never wavered. Danny gave her a quick wink and then made his way up the stairs to the lord's second floor chambers, his body groaning and protesting with every step he took.

There was a loud commotion coming from outside the lord's manor. Danny was utterly exhausted and heavily bruised from his tumble down the stairs but there was no time to rest. He blew out a long breath and stepped out the front door to see what the commotion was all about.

Red-cloaked soldiers clogged the entire area. They were entirely too tall, making it impossible for Danny to see what was happening. Beyond the mass of bodies in front of him, there were loud, angry shouts, but their words were lost in the din. Taking a step back to give himself some room, Danny transformed into the phoenix and launched himself into the bright morning sky. Nobody seemed to notice. Whatever it was that was happening, it had drawn their complete and undivided attention.

It didn't take Danny long to gain enough altitude to see what the disturbance was. Lady Kandyce was leading the way through the throng, pushing back the bystanders like a boat floating through reeds. Directly behind her was Lord Byssus and the lieutenant who was pushing the fat lord along at the tip of his sword. Behind him were Ryn and Sky Eyes, keeping a wary eye on those who got too close to Kandyce. From his lofty vantage point, Danny couldn't see anyone who might have been trying to help Lord Byssus. Any soldiers who were within striking distance of the parade seemed to be cheering the group on.

Up ahead stood the gallows. The raised platform was teaming with Berrat. How they had learned about what was happening was beyond Danny, but the news had obviously traveled quickly through the community. People were filling the streets, flooding towards the village's epicenter. It seemed there wasn't a single soul who didn't know there was a spectacle in the making. A war cry burst forth from the phoenix as Danny swooped lower to get a better look. Many cringed in fear while many more cheered with enthusiastic delight. As he again gained altitude, he unleashed another cry, eliciting even more cheers from the growing crowd. The rush of excitement coursing through him was exhilarating. Knowing that he had been a part of freeing the people of Kit's hometown made his heart swell.

I did it, Kitten. I did it, just like I'd promised.

Danny continued to circle back over to where Lord Byssus was. A skirmish had broken out amongst the soldiers when a small group of red cloaks had made a futile attempt to free their lord. It was short-lived however, as wave after wave of soldiers fell upon those who had remained loyal to their cruel master. Why they would stand against overwhelming odds was beyond reason, but that was the way things went sometimes.

Breayn had joined Ryn and Sky Eyes, taking up the last spot in the procession towards the gallows. As they neared, Danny swooped low hoping to scatter those who were still up on the raised platform. Many leapt down as the firebird flew by. Many more cheered with upstretched hands. Danny changed the angle of his wings, slowing himself quickly. He had hoped to gracefully land on the top of the gallows, like so many birds he had seen landing softly on the limb of a tree. Just before his feet were about to touch down, he switched back to his Berrat self.

He was not a bird.

He had no practice landing, oh so lightly, on a branch.

His foot caught the top bar of the gallows, sending him careening forward, his arms flailing uncontrollably. Those who were near the stage watched with a mixture of horror and amusement as he tumbled awkwardly. Just before his body slammed onto the wooden platform, the young Berrat tucked into a ball, fell heavily onto his shoulder, and sort of, popped up to his feet.

The entire crowd stared at the stage. They all fell silent.

He quickly spread his arms out and smiled at the mob. He shook his head to clear the hair from his face, before bowing dramatically.

Still nothing.

As he raised his head, Lady Kandyce and her entourage came into view. Lord Byssus was behind her, with an indignant look on his face. With a jab of the lieutenant's sword, the fat man stumbled forward. His once majestic clothing was now filthy and torn. The side of his face was covered with a thick layer of mud, or perhaps it was dung. Either way, the sight made Danny smile to himself.

Behind the lieutenant were Sky Eyes, Ryn, and Breayn. Danny's cohorts were no longer wearing their Crow uniforms. He looked down at himself, seeing he was still dressed in a Crow cloak. He quickly ripped it off his body and held it out in front of himself. In a moment, the cloak burst into flames. Those who stood nearby looked at what he was doing with confusion.

"The Split Crows will never again hold any power over you," he declared, his speech full of righteous vigor. With the crowd's silence, his baritone voice carried across the gathered multitude. "Lord Byssus' tyranny is at an end." A murmur spread through the Berrat, but there were no cheers. There were no adulations being heaped upon Danny for his part in the liberation of Lilloet.

Lady Kandyce climbed the stairs to the gallows. Her father and the others followed her onto the platform until they were all gathered, standing next to Danny. The crowd remained mostly silent, transfixed at what was happening before them.

"I will be taking my father and all of my soldiers back to Wantage," Kandyce called out. "We will be gone before the sun sets upon this city. We will never return, except under a banner of friendship."

Still, the crowd remained mostly silent. There were a number of soldiers who banged their mailed fists against their breastplates, a few more even cheered, but the Berrat continued their dubious murmurs. Sky Eyes moved from his place at the back of the group to the front of the platform.

"People of Lilloet," he intoned, his arms outstretched, his face turned towards the heavens. "Gaia has heard your pleas. The great warrior spirit has heard your pleas." At his last statement, the visage of a great white bear appeared at Sky Eyes' back. It stood twice the height of a Gigas. It bellowed out a roar that shook the platform. The soldiers who stood near the stage staggered backwards, trying to ready their weapons. The Berrat screamed and rushed towards the gallows, weaving their way through the soldiers, bowing their heads when they neared. The great warrior spirit roared out again, and the Berrat cheered wildly.

Danny gawked at the visage of the huge bear that stood at Sky Eyes' back. He had little recollection of what he represented to the Berrat people. He only had a vague memory of the stories told to him by his parents. He caught sight of Ryn and Breayn, both of whom had taken a knee, genuflecting to Sky Eyes. He quickly dropped to a knee and followed their lead. When Lady Kandyce did the same, some of the soldiers took a knee, but most put a fist to their chest and bowed their head respectfully.

CHAPTER THIRTY-SIX

THE ABSENT GIANT

It was late afternoon and the bulk of the soldiers had already headed out towards the docks on the North Sea. There were eight heavy warships waiting to ferry the troops to Wantage. The plan was to wait until the army was aboard before they let the ships' captains know there would be a change of plans.

Before all the soldiers had left Lilloet, they had cut Lord Byssus down from the gallows. He had been hung by his wrists for the better part of the day, giving the Berrat citizens of Lilloet a chance to *say goodbye* to their cruel lord. By the time he had been carried off the large wooden platform, he was a mass of dried blood and bruises.

Lord Byssus' occupation of the city had been for less than a cycle, but the damage he had caused could take a generation to repair. While many Berrat celebrated, others seemed unwilling to believe that this was over.

Sky Eyes had promised to stay in Lilloet, to help heal the city and the neighboring villages. Those elders whom Lord Byssus had not executed returned to their homes where they could help their people get back to a sense of normalcy.

"No," Ryn ground out. The man's eyes were so intense that it made Danny flinch.

"I'm going with Danny to Cormorant," Breayn said, ignoring Ryn's objection. "You need to go back to camp to tell Ulip and the others what happened here."

"Taseko is on the way," Ryn objected. "We can all tell Ulip together. Afterwards, I will fly you to Cormorant. While we're there, Ulip can lead the raids on the Crows. He doesn't need me." Danny was about to speak up, but he recoiled after a quick glare from his cousin.

"You know what kind of state Ulip's in. He won't be a good leader right now, at least not until he gets his head straightened out."

"And if I don't fly you, how do you plan on getting there?" Ryn crossed his arms over his chest, his eyebrows raising slightly. "You're losing control of Boreas and now that Eurus knows you're hosting his brother's body, he's going to try to free him."

"I have Boreas under control and Eurus is gone. He lost his form when The Wing took his spirit." Breayn took Ryn's hand in her own and looked deeply into his eyes. "We can ride horses from Taseko to Cormorant. It will take us longer, but I don't think a few extra days will matter. My mother's been gone for a long time." Danny shook his head at the comment.

"I think it's best if you let him fly you there," he offered, drawing a look of surprise from Ryn. "The dog soldiers said ships will be leaving harbor tonight when there is no moon in the sky. If they leave with those silvered weapons on board..."

"We haven't slept in nearly two days," Breayn said. "What possible good could we do? We'll be in no shape to fight."

"I won't need to fight," Danny said with a bit of a grin. "I just need to set those ships on fire. I could do that in my sleep."

"You can't set the ships on fire," Breayn said shaking her head. "They could be loaded with slaves. My mother might be on board."

"Well," Danny said scrubbing his hands over his face, "we can figure it out when we get there. But if we ride there, the ships will be long gone, and your mother might be gone with them." Breayn pinched the bridge of her nose as she considered his words. After several moments, her shoulders slumped.

"I'll think about it. It would be much easier than riding a horse." The resignation in Breayn's voice was obvious but Ryn didn't care. He gave Danny a curt nod in thanks, drawing a scowl from the woman.

"I said I'll think about it. I will decide after we get back to Taseko."

"What of Lieutenant Barclay?" Danny asked, staring across the compound, watching the last of the soldiers loading Lord Byssus onto a wagon. "Do you think we can trust him and Lady Kandyce to be true to their word?"

"Do we have a choice?" Sky Eyes asked as he strolled up. "If Lady Kandyce has been speaking false, then I imagine that she'd have already made a move against you. I believe the lieutenant has already proved his loyalties."

"I doubt Kandyce will do anything to help us though, once she's retaken Wantage," Breayn said, taking Ryn's hand. "I expect her motivations are purely self serving, but I hope I'm wrong. If nothing else, I doubt she'll be the cruel leader her stepfather was."

"Self serving or not," Ryn replied. "When the Split Crows find out she has turned against them, they're going to send everything they have at her."

⟨⟩

The sun was low in the western sky. Heavy cloud cover had moved in, hiding what might have been a glorious sunset on an exceptionally good day. Rather than fly ahead of Ryn and Breayn, Danny chose to stay close and practice his aerobatics, which mostly consisted of swooping past Ryn's great hawk form. Each time he did, he got closer to the couple. Each time he got closer, the look of annoyance on Breayn's face became more and more pronounced.

Danny's antics had helped the time pass quickly. He had climbed high above the clouds as they neared Taseko, hoping that any Split Crows who happened to be looking up wouldn't see the firebird. They continued for a few miles past the city and descended into a clearing in the middle of a dense forest. He switched back into his Berrat form when he was barely a foot off the ground, landing lightly on his toes. Dropping into an open field was so much easier than trying to come to rest on a wooden beam.

The clearing was surrounded by tall Berrathian pines. Their deep green foliage and the trees' heady scent was a welcomed relief to the firebird's monotonous aroma of smoke and flame. But then again, nothing beat the sensation of flight. Having his other senses dulled was an easy price to pay to be able to soar above the world.

Not wasting any time after landing, Breayn headed north towards their settlement.

"Do you expect the dog soldiers to be at the camp?" Ryn asked. "I'm not sure how Ulip will take it if he finds out that they followed him home." Breayn didn't answer as she nimbly skirted between the bows of two large pines.

"I liked them," Danny said. "If their group, whatever they were called, were fighting with us against the slavers..."

"Their group is called Mortem Lupus," Breayn said without looking back. "From what little I've heard about them, they are made up exclusively of lycans, who are particularly deadly when fighting vampires. I think it's why King Faol is making a push to wipe them out."

The group continued in silence for several minutes with Breayn at their lead. She stopped suddenly and crouched down. Both Ryn and Danny had their bows nocked in the time it took to inhale. Breayn held up two fingers and pointed off to the group's right. The two men trained their arrows in the direction she had pointed.

"Hold," she whispered. "They're not Crows."

"How can you tell?" Danny whispered, his eyes straining to catch any movement.

"Come out now," Breayn said, her voice a scolding tone. "Because they're ours."

"Aw," a young Berrat said as he slunk out from beneath the branches of a particularly large pine. "How did you see us?" A second Berrat youth came out a dozen paces away from the first, his head low.

"I didn't see you," Breayn said, her eyes bright. "When I stopped hearing the birds chirping, I knew they had been disturbed. Without their song, I could hear your footfalls."

"Why are you not at the camp?" Ryn asked, stowing away his bow and arrow.

"There have been humans snuffling around," the younger of the boys replied. Danny suddenly recognized them as the two who had served him coffee the morning after his arrival. The other boy stepped closer.

"We've been keeping an eye on them, leading them away if they got too close." Both boys started nodding in unison.

"Where's Ulip?" Breayn asked. "Why did he not deal with them? Did he not return to the camp?" The two boys shook their heads.

"Do you think the dog soldiers...?" Danny asked. He didn't finish the sentence for fear of unnecessarily frightening the boys.

"Unlikely," Ryn said, shaking his head. "What's more likely is that he went home to his clan, or whatever is left of them."

"Tell me of the humans," Breayn said. "How recently have you seen them."

"Yesterday, mid-day," one of the boys replied, looking to his cohort for acknowledgement. "We've been out scouting since sunup. You are the first people we've seen today."

"Return to camp and let the others know I'll be back after sundown," Ryn said. "I will have a good deal of news to share." The two boys nodded and slipped into the trees.

"You need to find Ulip," Breayn said, rubbing her temples lightly. "I don't like that he never returned to camp. I don't like that the dog soldiers got this close. If they had changed into their wolf forms, they'd have likely sniffed us out."

"There is no moon tonight, so they likely can't shift for two more days." The way Ryn said that sounded more like wishful thinking, rather than an assertion of fact. "I believe they are on our side, but their appearance was too timely, too coincidental."

"Do you want to go looking for Ulip?" Danny asked. He looked past the dark green bows surrounding them, up to the darkening sky above.

"No," Breayn said, her lips drawn tight. "Ulip can take care of himself. Right now, we need to get to Cormorant."

"If Ulip's gone home, he might not be coming back," Ryn said. There was a look of expectation on his face.

"Then the camp will be yours to command as you see fit," Breayn said, inclining her head slightly to her mate. "Ulip always said that you were his second. In his absence, you're in charge." Ryn's chest puffed out, ever so slightly, at his mate's words. He gave his body a shake, like a dog trying to rid itself of water, and in a moment a great hawk stood in his place. Breayn clambered up on his back and in a wingbeat, they were airborne. Danny smiled as they rose out from the forest. In a moment, he erupted into flames and launched himself skyward.

CHAPTER THIRTY-SEVEN

REUNION

Despite having drawn the curtains in her room, the mid-morning sun still managed to shine into Kit's eyes, waking her from a troubled sleep. She tried to roll over, only to find that she was pinned under her blanket by a mass of golden fur, snoring loudly beside her. "Good morning, Lump," she said, barely able to open her sleep-filled eyes. "Where's Runt, eh, boy?" The bed suddenly jounced heavily as the great wolf pounced up beside Lump, reacting immediately to the invitation to join Kit. A huge slobbery tongue scraped across her cheek and eyeball, eliciting a joyful laugh. "Thanks, Runt, I'm up."

When Kit finally managed to extricate herself from the knot of blankets, she smiled at the eight wolves lying on the floor beside the bed, all sleeping soundly. She didn't remember Amilta and her pack coming into her room, but Kit was asleep before her head hit her soft, fluffy pillow. She had never slept in a bed that was so comfortable. Apparently, this was how the rich lived, every day of their lives.

It had been too dark when she came into the room last night to see the high-polished furniture, the paintings, and the tapestries that covered the walls. She hadn't noticed the plush, low-back chair in the corner that her friend Indie was sitting in, his face dark, his eyes bloodshot. His unexpected presence startled her slightly.

"My father was not a traitor," he declared boldly, before casting his eyes downward. "He was a good man, and a great father."

Kit's heart broke for him. She had no idea what to say nor how to heal his pain. "Sit with me," she offered, patting the bed beside her. When the brooding man didn't move, she patted the bed again. "Please."

"We have work to do," he replied, storming out of the room, rousing the wolves in the process.

"Indie spent the night?" Lin asked, as she came through the door a second later. "He looks pretty angry. Did you fight?" Cautiously stepping between the pack members sprawled out on the floor, she frowned. "You had a slumber party? Without me?"

"No, nothing like that," Kit said, managing to get past the boys, swinging her feet to the floor. She chuckled to herself, watching, as several wolves yawned and stretched. "He's upset with what Fury said about Ymir. He fears his father was a traitor for worshipping the ice god." Kit grabbed one of her boots, feeling something inside when she slipped her foot into it. Pulling it off again, she looked inside, finding the note Jayne had given her. Not wanting to look at it right away, she quickly tucked it back into her boot after she had slipped it on.

"If what Fury said is true," Amilta interjected, "then Ymir is the traitor. Those who followed him; they were deceived. It doesn't make them traitors."

"I doubt he sees it that way." Kit grabbed her armor that she had thrown into the corner, uncovering Fury.

"When will you learn to treat me with respect?" the dragon hammer asked as soon as Kit uncovered him.

"Sorry," she said, pulling on her armor over the clothes she had slept in. She wrinkled her nose when she smelled herself. Between the horse riding, the swimming, and the fighting, and then laying with wolves, she had a rather unique, almost sour, aroma. "Are you sure about Ymir? Do you really believe he's a traitor to Titan?"

"I'd shrug if I could," Fury replied, "it is only a theory, a theory based on subjective information."

Kit turned her attention back to Lin. "How long have you been awake?"

"For a while," she replied. "The soft beds remind me of home, with my parents. Everything about Lord Karter's manor reminds me of my parents. They're not pleasant memories." Lin shook off her dark thoughts, her face brightening somewhat. "Rusty, I mean, General Karter, has most of the freed prisoners gathered in the back gardens. Many of them left to find their own way home in the darkness, but many more spent the night. Rusty put out enough food to feed them for a week. I'm guessing the servants were up all night preparing for this morning's feast.

"I could eat!" Amilta said brightly. "So could my pack."

"Me, too," Kit said as she slipped Fury into his sheath, her stomach rumbling in agreement. "I need a moment of your time," she said quietly to Lin.

The rest of the group poured out of Kit's room, practically running down the hallway for the staircase leading to the main floor. Kit and Lin followed them far enough to watch them make it down to the foyer below. She laughed out loud as she watched Amilta, her wolves, and the boys scrambling for purchase on the highly polished stone floor as they raced through the house looking for the back gardens.

"What's up?" Lin asked, her eyebrows raised.

Kit reached into her boot and pulled out the parchment she had stowed inside. She still hadn't taken time to read it. She slipped it into Lin's hand and whispered to her, "Give this to Bango. I'm going to need to speak with everybody on this list."

Lin quickly examined the note and gave Kit a quick nod. "You go on ahead," she said. "I want to get some things from my room before I go find Bango." She gave Kit a deep bow and giggled to herself before darting down the hallway.

When Kit started descending the staircase, she found Indie sitting in a lump on the bottom step, leaning against the wall.

"You've got to let it go," she said as she took a seat beside him. "You know your father. You know he was a good man. Don't let doubt soil his memory." She reached over his shoulders to pull his chin towards her and gave him a gentle kiss. "Let's get some food, and then you need to sleep." Indie was about to object, but she shook her head at him. "Saying no is not an option. C'mon, show me how to get to the food. I'm starving."

"Thank you," Indie said with a small, shy smile. "Everybody's headed this way, so I'm guessing this is the path to the food."

Kit wrapped her arms around Indie's elbow, leaning into him as they walked through the manor. She couldn't help but marvel at the sheer magnitude of the wealth required to furnish and maintain such a dwelling. "If this is all from the slave trade, I can see how it could bend the soul of the weak-minded. If we sold all of this, we could buy enough weapons and armor to outfit ten thousand soldiers, at least."

"There is a fortune in here, no doubt," Indie replied, seemingly noticing the opulence for the first time. "Finding buyers might be a problem though. There are not many rich enough to afford all this."

"Food!" Kit exclaimed, releasing Indie's arm, racing out a set of doors leading to the gardens. There were tables and tables of roasted meats, breads, vegetables, and many wondrous things that Kit didn't recognize.

She joined a group of Berrat standing at a table laden with fresh fruits and a variety of cheeses. She smiled warmly at them as she grabbed a handful of snacks before heading to the next table featuring a whole cooked hog, surrounded by roasted vegetables. She pushed the cheese into her mouth before cutting herself a huge slab of meat from the roast's hind end. There were several Berrat at this table as well, with many more gathered around in small groups, all talking excitedly among themselves. Kit addressed them all with a quick nod as she took a large bite from the slab of meat in her grease-covered hands. When she saw that most were using tin plates to eat from, Kit started looking for something to put her own food on.

"Here you go," Indie offered, holding out a fine ceramic plate to her. "Were you looking for this?"

Kit's face turned red as she flopped her chunk of pork onto the dish, spraying its juices in the process. Her cheeks were full of food, but she managed to mumble out a thank you. She pointed down at the pork and nodded her head vigorously.

"It's delicious," she said after she finally swallowed, before scampering off to another table.

After spending what felt like an hour of non-stop eating, Kit took her plate of sweet-cakes and started looking for some place to sit, under a nice tree perhaps. As she wandered about, she finally located a large oak away from the chattering crowds. In the shade of the tree were the boys, Amilta and her pack, and two Berrat women. Runt had his head in the lap of one of them, while Lump laid beside him, his stomach distended from eating too much.

"Titan's peace upon you," Kit offered as she approached. "May I join you?"

"I'd like that very much," one of the Berrat women replied, her face beaming with joy.

"Ananak!" Kit screeched out, dropping her plate of food, grabbing her foster-mother in a deep embrace before the woman could even get to her feet. The pair fell in a pile on the ground, amid the wolves who were quickly gobbling up Kit's fallen snacks. Before Kit even realized it, she was weeping uncontrollably on her mother's shoulder, incomprehensible words coming out between sobs. "Oh, how I've missed you."

Riva pushed the hair from Kit's face, brushing away the tears still falling down her daughter's cheeks. "Oh, little piece of my soul, my little Kitten, I have never left your side, even if you couldn't see me." Riva's eyes were full of tears, full of love. "You needed to be on your own, so you could grow, so you could become the woman you are destined to be. But like during the Rite of the Way, I was there, watching from a distance, waiting to find out what path you would take." Her mother pushed more hair from Kit's face, staring into her golden eyes. "You look more and more like your mother every day." She ran her fingers along the swath of bright red in Kit's hair. "Except for this," she said with a bright smile. "This is different. A gift from your father, perhaps?"

Kit made a small gurgling noise, instead of the words she had intended to say. She quickly pulled Riva to herself, pressing hard against the woman who'd raised her, her mother. Her body started to shake as sobs once again took hold. "I'm so sorry, Ananak," she managed to say. "I'm so sorry I was such a stupid, willful child. If only I had understood what you were doing for me, how much you had done for me."

"Such wisdom from a woman who has only lived through sixteen summers," Riva said with a coy smile. "How much you have grown since you set out on your own, just five short cycles ago. You have matured into a beautiful young woman, who consorts with the gods."

"What?" Kit asked, not that she was denying her association with the gods, but...

"Titan's peace upon you," the other woman offered, distracting Kit from her mother's words.

"Fenrir, you honor me." Kit replied, quickly bowing her head.

"There is no need for formality," she said, in her melodic, sing-song kind of way. "I would like to think we are beyond that." The little god gave Runt's fur a rough, playful rubbing. "Isn't that right, Runt?"

"Why are you here?" Kit blurted out. "I mean, I'm very happy to see you, to see both of you, more than I can ever express..." the words came tumbling out of Kit's mouth, with no idea what it was she was trying to say. "You're not here to take Runt are you, to make him the big leader, or whatever name it was that Amilta called it?"

"To make him Alpha Prime?" Fenrir asked with a bright, cheery laugh. "No, but if he would ever willingly leave your side, he would make a great leader, when he's a bit older." Runt smiled at Kit, his tongue lolling out to the side. "I'm afraid I'm here for much less pleasant reasons."

"When you were young, Riva had a vision," Fenrir began. Kit protectively took her mother's hands in her own when the god said her name. "She foresaw the fall of Ymir, and the rise of a dark power." Fenrir paused a moment, allowing Riva to speak if she chose to. "Your mother's foresight is extraordinarily strong, but not very clear. Her visions leave much room for interpretation. I had thought Ymir's fall would mean his death, but it seems that the vision was his fall from Titan's grace."

"So, it's true? He's behind the poachers and the sickness that spread through the wolves?"

Fenrir shook her head. "Not just that. I believe he's behind the rise of the slavers as well. His attack on the wolves is to keep me from discovering what he is doing."

"How can I fight a god?" Kit asked, squeezing her mother's hands as she did. "Just dealing with the people is already more than I think I can cope with. I can't fight a god."

"It should not have to come to that," Riva offered, giving Kit a sad smile.

"But he may well retaliate for what you've done to him here," Fenrir added. "What happened last night was a major disruption of his plans."

Chapter Thirty-Eight

Ailman Juuls

"Mistress Kit," Rusty said, interrupting what had been many minutes of blissful peace. Kit reluctantly lifted her head from her mother's lap, wishing the time with Riva would never end. "I'm sorry to bother you, Mistress, but I need to speak with you."

"Speak with me?" Kit asked, her brain a bit foggy as she dragged herself back to reality. When she noticed that Rusty had a man, a blonde Western human man by her side, Kit quickly popped to her feet. Behind the pair were four guards in flat-black armor. Before Rusty had a chance to speak, Kit gave the blonde man the once over. At a glance, she determined that he was unremarkable in every possible way, except for the arrogant, demeaning air he had about him while he looked down his nose at her.

"This is Ailman Juuls," Rusty said with a tiny flourish, my *father's* chief advisor. "I found him this morning, trying to enter your room."

"I see," Kit replied.

I recognize that name, but from where?

She knew it was important, but she couldn't quite put her finger on it. Pushing the notion aside, she turned her attention to Ailman. "And why were you trying to get into my room?"

The condescending man straightened his back, making himself stand a bit taller, allowing him to exaggerate his air of superiority. "I am the lord's chief advisor and as such, it's my responsibility to know everything about everyone who enters his home."

Kit looked around the grounds at the throng of people milling about, continuing to enjoy the bounty set out for them. "I don't think the *lord* will be coming back anytime soon," she said with a tiny smirk. "Since I'm assuming the leadership of House Hanse, maybe you should be reporting to me?" Kit maintained her smirk and raised her eyebrows at him for good measure. When the man's expression didn't change at all, Kit's smirk grew to a full grin. "If you are to be *my* chief advisor, what advice would you offer me?"

Ailman's eyes narrowed ever so slightly at the question. "My advice to you? Run. Run away and don't stop running until you're so far away nobody will care that you even exist."

"Do I look afraid?" Kit asked, her expression turning from playful to deadly serious.

"No, Mistress, you don't. But you should be."

"I've dealt with your lord once. If he decides to come back, I can deal with him again."

"You caught him off guard," Ailman said, "something that doesn't happen very often. Next time, he'll be prepared, and you'll be dead."

"And how is it that you know I caught him off guard?" Kit asked. Until this point, she got the feeling that the man was speaking true, even if he wasn't saying much at all.

"Because I saw your encounter with him. I do not fight alongside of King Karter, but as I said, it's my responsibility to know everything."

"Are you still loyal to your lord?" Kit asked, knowing this would be the one question that she wanted a truthful answer to.

"No."

"If your loyalty is not to your lord, who is it with?"

Ailman crossed his arms. He took a few breaths considering his answer. "My loyalties are my business."

Kit's eyes flashed golden. "I think your hanging would make a lovely spectacle. Perhaps a rope around your neck will loosen your tongue?"

The lord's chief advisor stared at Kit for a few seconds. "You have pretty gold eyes," he said with a hint of *something* in his voice. "But I've seen prettier."

Kit's expression immediately went flat. "Rusty?" she asked, while staring at Ailman with her pretty gold eyes. "Do you have a place to *hold* this man?"

Rusty chuckled and pushed the lord's advisor towards the four guards in black. Without a word, they escorted their prisoner back towards the manor.

"Another thing, Mistress," Rusty said. "The people are getting restless."

"The people?" Kit asked, as she continued to watch the guards taking Ailman away. At no point did she pick up a hint of deception in his words, and the feeling that she should remember his name kept gnawing at her.

"The freed prisoners, Mistress. The Berrat, the dwarves, and the Nomads. They want to know what is to happen to them."

"Gather them; all of them," Kit replied, brushing loose dirt and grass from her backside. "Gather all the soldiers and the commanders. I want the people together, so I can address them all at once."

"Where shall we gather, Mistress?"

Kit chuckled at the question. "You know this city better than I do, Rusty. Where do you think we should gather? It needs to be someplace where I can be elevated, so people can hear me." Kit stood on her tiptoes, jouncing a few times. "And where they can see me."

"There is a balcony here at the manor," the general started, trying hard to suppress a grin. "The balcony looks out over the front gardens. Since most of the people are here already..."

"That will be fine," Kit said, looking down at her disheveled self. "How long until you can get everyone together?"

"We can have everyone here in just a few minutes." Rusty paused for a moment. "But if you'd like to freshen up first, we can make it a couple of hours." A look of relief crossed Kit's face, but it turned sour when she looked down at herself, realizing that there was no hope for her clothing.

"Nothing of mine would fit you," Rusty said, immediately understanding Kit's concerns. "But I'm sure we have a wardrobe or two stuffed with clothes that will fit you fine."

"Can you show me where I can get changed?"

"If you can find your way back to your room, I will meet you there. I just need to get things started, so that everybody will be here on time for your address; and I'll find somebody to bring you hot water for a bath." The general didn't bother waiting for a response before heading off.

Kit turned towards her mother, Amilta, and Fenrir. "Will you be staying for a while?" she asked them.

"Amilta and I have some business to attend to," Fenrir replied, gently lifting Runt's head from her lap. "But we won't be far."

"I'm not going anywhere," Riva said, "I'd like to spend some time with you if that's okay."

Kit's eyes immediately welled up. "I would love that," she said. "I've missed you more than you could ever know."

"I might understand that better than you think," Riva replied, taking her daughter's hand in her own.

Kit and her mother bid Fenrir and Amilta farewell before heading up to the room Kit slept in, with Lump and Runt bounding along behind them. The two women walked in silence, taking time to simply enjoy each other's presence. For Kit, the years apart from her mother melted away, everything feeling like it did between them when she was but a child, except she wasn't a child anymore.

They spent some time speaking with several of the freed prisoners, all of them wanting to know what would become of them. In each instance, Kit tried her best to allay their fears, to let them know that everything would be okay, but in her heart, she feared that she was lying to them; saying things that they wanted to hear.

"How times have changed," Riva said to Kit as they entered the manor. "When you were young, the Berrat people shunned you; now, they hang on your every word." She squeezed her daughter's hand. "My visions of your future were filled with conflict and death, and I feared for you. Had I seen what you would do, how you would cope..." Kit's mother stared up at her, her eyes wide. "I'm so proud of you!"

As they climbed the stairs to the second floor, a line of women carrying pails paraded past them, heading into her room. "Your bath is almost ready," an older woman, dressed in a solid black uniform, said to Kit as she exited her room.

"You're very kind," Kit replied, unsure of how to deal with *servants* caring for her.

"Lady Karter told me to provide you with suitable clothing." As much as she tried, the woman was unable to stop herself from wrinkling her nose. "I can have the clothes you're wearing laundered."

"Thank you, but it's not necessary," Kit replied sheepishly, running her hands over the sleeves of her tunic, fluffing the fur of her armor's collar.

"Oh, but it is, sweetness," Riva replied, letting Kit know that she did in fact smell. "I'll go with this nice lady to pick out some clothes for you. Strip out of what you've got there and leave it where someone can find it." Riva patted her hand, a grin spreading across her face. "They may need to burn some of it."

While Riva and the woman left to find her some clothes, Kit headed into her room, the boys following her in. Much to her surprise, somebody had cleaned and tidied her quarters. Kit's bed was made, and her knapsack was laid neatly on top of it.

"Your bath is ready, Mistress," a woman said as she entered the room from a side door. "Would you like me to help you undress?"

Kit's face turned bright red. "No, thank you. I can manage on my own."

"It's no trouble, Mistress," she replied, seemingly intent on providing this service to Kit. "I will have your clothes laundered, while you soak." As Kit continued to shake her head, the woman pouted slightly. "Please, Mistress, let me do this for you. What you did for me, the house staff, well, for everyone; it means more than you'll ever know." As she spoke, the woman started to unbuckle Kit's armor. Feeling the honesty of her words, Kit relented, letting the woman help prepare her for her bath.

"Please, call me Kit. What is your name?"

The question seemed to catch the woman off guard. "No guest has ever asked me that," she declared. "Not in the seven cycles that I've been here. Not once." The woman bowed deeply. "My name is Ellynora."

As Kit followed Ellynora into the adjoining room, she was greeted by a large tub, filled with steaming, hot water. Beside it was a table with jars of soaps and oils, the likes of which Kit had never seen before. She gave the woman a questioning look, unsure of what to do with the contents of the jars.

"These are cleansing salts," Ellynora said, pointing to the tallest jar on the table. "Once you're in the water, take a handful and use it to scrub your skin. This jar contains plant extracts that will cleanse your hair, and make it smell wonderful." The woman got a bit of a nervous look on her face. "But I'm afraid it can't help with the mass of tangles you've got there."

Despite standing nude before a woman that she had never met before, this was the first time that Kit felt embarrassed. "I've got an enchanted comb in my knapsack," she said. "It can take the knots out."

"You get yourself in the tub," Ellynora said with a warm smile. "I'll fetch your magic comb."

Kit shivered slightly, standing alone and naked on the polished stone floor. The bath was still steaming heavily, filling the cold room with a light fog. She gingerly put her hand into the water, fearful that it would burn her. Despite the fact that it looked to be near boiling, the heat was comfortable, soothing. Suddenly filled with a desperate desire to dunk herself under the water, Kit jumped into the bath, causing the contents to slosh heavily, spilling a good amount across the floor.

"I'll bring some towels for that," Ellynora said, clucking her tongue when she saw the watery mess. "I'll return shortly. And, so you know, your dogs have made a mess of your bed. They're both stretched out, sleeping soundly. I tried to get them off, but they made it clear they weren't moving."

Kit shrugged, then smiled, her eyes somewhat apologetic. She didn't really know how else to reply. The boys had always slept with her, even when she hadn't invited them to. After a few more clucks, Ellynora exited, leaving Kit to her bath.

Following the woman's instructions, Kit grabbed a big handful of salts and started scrubbing her arm. At first, they felt like tiny shards of glass, cutting into her skin, but a moment later, they transformed into a fragrant paste. The sensation of rubbing it into her skin was heavenly. She quickly continued grabbing handful after handful of the salts, scrubbing every inch of her body from head to toe, each handful relaxing her muscles and soothing her spirit.

After having used nearly the entire jar of cleansing salts, Kit started on her hair, dunking her fingers into the jar of plant extracts. The contents reminded her of the holy oils used at the Temple, except the delicate scent of these emollients did not assault the senses. Holding her oil-soaked fingers in front of her nose, she inhaled deeply, reveling in the scents of forest and wild blossoms. With a huge smile, she started working the oil into her hair, her fingers continuously becoming entrapped in the mass of tangles.

"Maybe we should use your magic comb first," Ellynora suggested as she walked in with a huge stack of fluffy sky-blue towels in her arms. She placed the towels on a chair in the corner before throwing a good number of them onto the floor, letting them soak up the flood Kit had created.

Once the towels had soaked up most of the water, the woman took Kit's comb and began running it through her hair; each stroke miraculously removing the tangles while distributing the oils throughout. "I don't know where you got this comb from," Ellynora said with awe, "but it might be one of the most marvelous things I've ever seen."

"It was a gift from a friend," Kit said, thinking back to when Lin had enchanted the comb for her.

Several minutes passed in silence as Ellynora continued to comb the knots from Kit's hair, adding more cleansing oils as she did. "Can I ask you something?"

"Sure," Kit said, as her mind aimlessly drifted amid the heavenly aromas.

"Why are you here?"

"What?" Kit asked, sloshing about in the tub a bit, surprised by the question.

"It's just that, you're not from here, so why are you helping us?"

"I'm a priest of Titan, and I will seek out injustice wherever it may be."

"But why here? Why come to Cormorant? Surely there is injustice that needs to be dealt with wherever you are from."

Kit shrugged, sloshing the water some more. "I expect Titan has led me here, on my journey to free him. But truth is, sometimes I feel like I'm chasing a storm, one that is forever building, but always out of reach."

"Child, you are the storm." Ellynora put herself in front of Kit. "And you will cleanse the lands with ice and fire." The woman closed her eyes and took a deep breath. "From the ashes, a sword will rise. From the wilds, a child will seek the passive, a mighty roar unleash. From the heavens, a star will fall, to lay waste to the wicked and break the circle."

"Where is that from?" Kit asked, suddenly feeling uncomfortable.

"My father used to sing that to me, when I was a child still living in Lycos. Many of our beliefs, tidings we know to be true, are told in song." Ellynora laughed warmly at her remembrances. "Even if they are hard to listen to. They don't have much of a melody."

"The people are gathered," Riva said, entering the bathroom. "Are you ready to dress?"

"She just needs to rinse her hair," Ellynora said with a wide grin, just before shoving Kit's head and body underwater.

THE ADDRESS

After refusing to put on any of the pretty things that Riva had returned with, Kit finally settled on a simple white tunic, tight-fitting black leather breeches and a red surcoat. They would have been better suited on a boy, but they were much more practical and comfortable than the other offerings.

Rusty led Kit to an enormous set of double doors. She opened them with a grand flair, inviting Kit to lead the way. "This is my father's *receiving room*," she said, sounding almost apologetic. "A place he reserved for his honored guests."

The room was huge. There were several large, highly polished tables, each one surrounded by sixteen, exquisitely crafted, upholstered chairs. She shook her head at the sheer opulence. Past the tables, there were likely twenty plush, overstuffed chairs and half that many similarly fashioned couches.

"How many honored guests does your father have?" Kit asked, feeling somewhat *underdressed* as she walked around a bit.

"What are you planning on telling them?" Indie asked, his eyes running up and down Kit's form. "You look beautiful, in case you didn't know." Kit's fear of being underdressed melted away with Indie's compliment. He couldn't know, but it was exactly what she needed to hear at that very moment.

"I have no idea," Kit replied, batting her eyes. "And I smell really good, too."

"If you two are finished?" Rusty said, drumming her fingers on her thigh.

"Wait," Lin shouted as she came running in. "I've got something for you." She was holding out a small chain with a tiny pearl dangling from a silver clasp. "I put a small enchantment on it," she said with a grin. "So that the people can hear you better." Kit shook her head, not understanding what her friend was getting at. "Put it on," she insisted, shoving it at her. "It will help project your voice, so everyone will hear you."

"Oh," Kit said, taking the delicate necklace from her friend. "Thank you."

"You won't even need to shout," Lin added, offering to help tie the clasp behind Kit's neck. "Just speak normally; it will do the rest."

"Okay," Kit said, taking a deep breath to help calm the nervousness she could feel rising up, making her knees wobbly.

Rusty pulled back a set of heavy drapes, revealing two enormous stained-glass doors. The sunshine passing through the windows set the room alight with blues and greens, making the already opulent room look otherworldly. When she pulled open the doors, the sounds of the people outside came crashing into the room. "It looks like the entire city is out there," Rusty said with a low whistle.

Kit's knees were now even weaker. When she peeked out the doors, she looked out at the thousands of people gathered in front of the manor. "Titan's snowballs," she exclaimed when she saw the crowd, causing them to all roar with laughter. Lin pointed to the necklace, her lips in a tight smile. The realization that every person outside heard her words made Kit blush. Now, terrified she might say something else – inappropriate, Kit strode out onto the balcony, receiving a cacophony of cheers, hoots, and hand clapping as she did.

"Titan's blessings upon you," Kit started, deciding her traditional form of blessing was the right course of action. There didn't seem to be many Titan worshipers here, based on the rumblings coming from the throng beneath her. Kit's legs became so wobbly that she had to grasp the balcony railing to steady herself.

When the crowd finally went silent, and Kit had taken control of her fears, she took a deep breath and began.

"Last night, we came together; friends, family, and strangers alike, to stop the black ships from leaving port." Even though every single person present already knew this, they erupted in cheers nonetheless. Kit paused, giving them time to rejoice before she continued.

"Many of the soldiers here, who used to do the bidding of House Hanse, turned their swords on their oppressors, helping to ensure our victory." Again, the crowd cheered at her words, with the loudest, most jubilant cheering coming from the many hundreds of soldiers present.

"You are all wondering what will happen next." This time, as Kit finished her sentence, the crowd went deathly quiet, not wanting to miss what she might say. "I'm not sure what to tell you," she continued, trying to formulate a plan on the spot. "I am not a great speaker, somebody who can find just the right words to make you all feel good, but I am honest, and I will always speak truthfully to you." Kit waited another moment, letting her words sink in while she looked out at the tens of thousands of people present.

"All who want to go home, will. I cannot undo what has been done, but I will try to find a way to heal the wounds you have all suffered. Those of you who were ripped from your homes, if you wish to return, I will make sure it happens. Those soldiers who were forced into service, you are free to go home as well, to live your life as you see fit. Those of you who live here, fearful of what the ruling body may do if you oppose them, can start your lives anew, knowing that the tyrants have been removed and will be replaced with people who will run the city in the service of the community who lives here." When Kit stopped to take a breath, the crowd again erupted in celebrations, carrying on for several minutes before dying off.

"Every word I spoke was the truth, but it was not the whole story, the whole truth." Kit gripped the wooden rail of the balcony a bit tighter, as she leaned out over the edge. "The slavers, the Auctioneers, the Scarlet Tide; they will not give up their holdings easily. By now, the word of what transpired here has likely already met their ears. They are likely preparing to retaliate, to take back what they have lost." A murmur, the hopes and fears of everyone, spread through the crowd like a wildfire burning through dried grasses.

"We dwarves will stay and fight by your side." The unmistakable voice of Coldforge, carried over the throng. His words were immediately followed by the yetis' deafening roar, along with yips and howls of wolves that appeared from a wooded area to the far left of the gardens. The offers to fight began small, with individual voices calling out from the sea of people. With each declaration, two more joined in, their voices building like a tidal wave until the people were chanting as one, surging body.

"We fight for freedom. We fight for justice. We fight for the people."

Kit motioned to the others, asking them to join her on the balcony. When General Karter stepped forward, the chanting immediately died off, replaced by murmurs of distrust.

"I know that you trust me," Kit said, trying to put the people's concerns to rest. "If you didn't trust me, you wouldn't be gathered here today; you wouldn't be offering to fight by my side." The crowd immediately went silent. "I have put Rustnig Karter, Rusty, in charge of the city's army, your army. Like you, she lived in fear of her father. Like you, she was helpless to act. Like you, she wants to make life better for everyone. I know her heart to be true, and if you trust me, then you can trust that she will act in your best interest."

When it looked like the people were willing to accept Rusty as their army's commander, Kit continued. "I don't know what will happen over the next moon, but I repeat, anyone who wants to leave may do so with my blessing. To everyone who wants to stay, I thank you for your support."

As Kit removed her necklace, the crowd started chanting again. "We fight for freedom. We fight for justice. We fight for the people."

When they were all back inside, and Rusty had closed the doors and drawn the curtains, Kit plopped herself, cross-legged, on the floor. After tucking away her voice-amplifying necklace, she looked at the others in the room with her. "So, how do we make it happen?"

Chapter Forty

RAYAN STAUL

"Where did you get the necklace from?" Kit asked before jamming a large heel of bread into her mouth. The group had been discussing strategies for many hours when Kit's rumbling stomach had made it impossible for the conversation to continue.

"Coldforge," Lin replied, licking bacon grease from her fingers. "His dwarves set up a forge in the cellar, and the Hobgoblins created the most elaborate alchemy apparatus I've ever seen. I got the pearl from the offloaded cargo. There were all sorts of jewelry. Many of the stones and metals used to craft the pieces make powerful reagents."

"What do they want with a forge?" Kit asked, knowing it was a stupid question before the words finished leaving her lips.

"They're using the steel from the cages to make weapons, hammers, axes, shields, and something they call crossbows." Lin's eyes were lighting up with excitement as she talked of the dwarves' workmanship. "Those crossbows, they shoot stubby little arrows that can pierce through plate armor, like its nothing more than vellum." Lin suddenly screwed up her face like she'd just sucked on a lemon. "The hobgoblins helped me with the enchantment on the necklace. I think I learned more about enchanting from them in an hour than I have learned in my entire life."

"That must be why they were brought here; to make enchanted weapons," Indie suggested, as he fed the boys strips of meat from a large, barely cooked roast.

Lin's eyes were continuously turning back to the room's entranceway. "I'm guessing Rusty won't be joining us for lunch?"

"I don't think she's coming back," Indie responded, tossing some more meat to the boys. "She's trying to figure out living arrangements for the people who want to stay. She also mentioned establishing barracks for the soldiers; a common location for them to all live together."

"The woman's a marvel," Lin said, with a hint of a sigh, making Kit roll her eyes.

The steady sound of boots, clomping along the stone floors, announced the arrival of people well before they made it to the room's entrance. Lin's eyes immediately brightened as she tucked her hair behind her ears. Her face crumpled when Bango came in with a heavy-set man, perhaps in his early forties.

"Harbourmaster Staul," Kit said, jumping to her feet, offering the man Titan's blessing. "Thank you for coming to speak with us."

"Thank you for asking nicely," he replied, laughing at his own joke. "Please call me Rayan. May I?" he asked, pointing to the spread of food. "Haven't eaten for a while." He began patting his ample belly, laughing some more at his special brand of humor. With a boyish grin, he waddled over to the table, grabbed a plate, and heaped food on it. "Bango says you have a *proposition* for me."

Kit quickly grabbed a small scroll from the food-laden table. "I want Bango to take over as harbourmaster." The fat man paused, just as he was about to pop a large hunk of cheese into his mouth, his face going pale. When Kit realized her words scared the Helja out of him, she started stammering. "No, no. No. It's not like that. I have something. Something to offer you if you'll let her take your place." Kit jammed the scroll into the poor man's face, causing him to stumble as he retreated from the perceived attack. "Please, read this."

The harbourmaster let the hunk of cheese fall from his lips, onto the floor. Lump, who was already sitting beside the man carrying the large plate of food, snatched up the morsel before it had a chance to bounce a second time. Staul blinked a few times and placed his heaping plate on the table. He snatched another bit of food and swallowed it quickly before accepting the scroll. The man's ears were turning bright red, obviously fearful of what the scroll might contain. A smile wide enough to split his face replaced the terrified look as the harbourmaster made his way through the document.

"Seriously?" he asked, his eyes wide in disbelief. "I get this, for stepping *away* from my job?"

"Is it enough?" Kit asked, hoping desperately for a positive response to her question.

"Girl, after what you did for this city, I should tell you." The man paused long enough to find another hunk of cheese on his plate and stuffed it into his mouth. "I'd have done what you're asking for free. Truth be told, I thought you thought I was one of them slavers, because, well, I have been helping them." He swallowed the cheese down, shaking his head as his face turned beet red. "Not that I was helping them. I mean I was, but if I didn't, they'd have killed me and my family and everyone else I care about."

"Relax," Kit said, trying to calm the poor man down. "I know you're a good man, stuck in a hard spot." The harbourmaster stuffed another piece of food into his mouth, his face still a horrible shade of purple. "You are not required to help us, even if you accept the gift that I'm offering you. But I'd be grateful if you could make sure that Bango understands every aspect of the port's operations, above and below deck, if you get my meaning."

"Oh, you want the *ledger* then," Rayan replied, the color of his face returning to normal, mostly. He grabbed another bite of food and popped it into his mouth. "It has every transaction, every single deal, shipment, manifest... everything."

"Where is it?" Kit asked, leaning in closer, waiting for the man to stop pushing more food into his mouth. She suddenly wondered if that's what she looked like when she was enjoying a meal. It made her cringe.

Staul swallowed his mouthful of food as his hand reached out for more. He stopped abruptly when Kit started growling at him. "I don't have it," he declared, as though the four words explained everything completely. When Kit's growling got louder, the fat man began stammering again. "King Karter has it; or had it. He never let it leave his grasp. He never let anybody look at it. If he didn't take it when he left, it means it's likely somewhere here, inside the manor."

"We need General Karter," Kit mused, loud enough for everyone to hear. "She is the most likely person to tell us where to look." Kit turned her head slowly until she was facing Lin. She cocked an eyebrow at her. "Would it be safe for me to assume that you'd like to go look for her?" Lin gave her a small grin before she bolted from the room, giving everyone a good chuckle.

When the mirth finally fell from Kit's face, she returned to questioning the harbourmaster. "I'm also assuming you'll give her the keys to all the buildings?"

"Oh, yes," he said, pulling an enormous ring of keys from his waist. He tossed the set to Bango. "I'm glad to be rid of that weight."

The words sounded like a double entendre to Kit, but she let it go. "Besides giving her the keys and explaining the ledger, I'm assuming there is much more you can teach Bango."

"Oh, yes," the fat man muffled out after pushing some sweetbreads into his face. Several painful seconds passed as he tried to quickly chew and swallow the food. "Yes, indeed. For example, do you have the manifests for the ships you took control of?" Bango nodded and pulled a thick scroll from the satchel at her waist. "See here," Staul said, pointing to the outermost column in the manifest. "These codes, they say where the shipment is going, and this column next to it has the codes for where it came from."

"They're just symbols," Bango said, staring over the man's shoulder. "What do they mean?"

"They're codes that identify the city the item came from or where it is going to." He pointed to the code on the third line. "See this line here, where it says *Miners*?" He waited a moment as Kit and Indie both moved in closer to see what he was showing Bango. "This first code, is Goldstone, that's a city in the dwarven mountains of Miran Knott." The fat man whistled thinking about it. "It's gotta be the dwarves. They brought them a long way, an exceedingly long way, indeed. But that's not important right now. This symbol beside it, that's here, Cormorant. It says they were coming from Goldstone and going to Cormorant."

"What's this here?" Kit asked, pointing to a line in the middle of the page. "It says *Livestock and Recompense*. There was no livestock on the ships."

"Slaves and payment," Staul sighed. "Blood slaves most likely. I don't know what the payment would be for, but the master ledger would have the details. See here," he said, pointing to the first symbol. "This says they come from Cormorant, but it's likely they were taken from a village in the barony, and not the city itself. But this is curious," he said, pointing to the destination symbols. "It's got two destinations, which means that the cargo will change hands at the first city before being transported to the final destination."

"What are the cities?" Indie asked.

"The first one is Templeton and the second one..." Kit cut off the fat man's words before he could finish.

"Templeton?" Kit asked. "The town in Aarall?"

"Yes, I expect so," Staul replied. "From there, they are to be shipped to Two Peaks."

"That's impossible," Indie exclaimed, snatching the manifest from the man's hands, as though holding it himself would change what the document stated. "Lord Aster, the man who rules the town, would never... he just wouldn't. I saw him, he loves his people."

"Well," the harbourmaster said, as he took the scrolls back from Indie. "If the second destination is Two Peaks, then I'd say it was bound for Templeton in Aarall."

"Blood slaves being delivered to the king's city?" Kit suddenly realized that she was clenching her fists so tightly that her fingernails were digging into her palms. "Has the sickness spread to the heart of our kingdom?"

"Who is to receive the shipment in Two Peaks?" Indie asked. "Where does it say that on the manifest?"

"It doesn't," Staul responded, shaking his head. "The answer will be in the ledger," he continued, reaching for another bite of food. "But the ship's captain would also know. He'd need to ensure the cargo was delivered into the correct hands."

"Get him," Kit growled at Bango. "Bring him here. Now."

Chapter Forty-One

Muul and the Mysty

"I'm not saying a word!" the ship's captain screamed at Kit when she asked him who was to receive the shipment. Bango had introduced him as Captain Muul, of the black ship *Mysty*. Assuming he may have been acting against his own moral compass, that he was forced to captain the slave-ship, Kit began her questioning in a kind, gentle fashion. But it quickly became obvious that this man's heart was as black as the hull of his ship, and that he enjoyed his job, transporting lesser beings like cattle for the spawn of Faol, the vampire king.

"You'd rather die here and now, than have a chance to live? To have a chance to right the wrongs you've committed?" Kit pulled her hammer back, threatening to deliver immediate justice. The Temple had taught her how to humanely interrogate a prisoner, to extract information from them, all in the name of justice. Unfortunately for Captain Muul, Kit was now playing by a different set of rules.

"I don't like being ignored," Kit growled. The boys each took a position at Kit's side, baring their teeth, adding to the threat. "Fury, how's about we turn up the heat." Kit looked at the hammer in her hand, waiting for it to burst into flames. "Fury? You there?"

Muul chuckled, despite the ongoing threats of a dire wolf and a very intense looking golden retriever. "You's crazy, girl," he laughed louder. "Talkin' to a hammer?"

"Yup," Kit replied, with her favorite sweet girly smile, batting her eyelashes. "I am a bit crazy." Kit punctuated the sentence by kicking the man in his nether regions, causing him to bellow in agony before dropping to his knees.

"Pick him up!" she screamed at Indie and Bango who were both standing next to the captain. "Pick. Him. Up!" she repeated, this time, with a low, steady voice. As soon as the captain was on his feet, Kit kicked him again, this time with enough force that the impact lifted the man several inches into the air. The captain's eyes went blank before he dropped back down to the ground, making pathetic whimpering noises as he slowly rolled around on the floor, desperately grasping his groin.

"Pick him up," Kit repeated, keeping her voice deep and steady. The man barely even resisted as Indie and Bango dragged him to his feet. He weakly tried to turn his hips, to protect himself from another of Kit's attacks. "I can do this all day," she said with a bright cheery voice, shifting her own hips like she was about to unleash another attack.

"Stop," Muul whimpered, tucking his knee up a bit higher, still trying to protect himself. "I was instructed to deliver the cargo to Lord Aster; everything, all the cargo was to be delivered to him."

"Who was he to deliver it to?" Kit asked, her nose now close enough to the captain's that she could feel his ragged breaths on her face.

"I don't know," he replied, trying to twist away from Kit, weakly fighting against the grip of his captors. "I swear on my child's eyes, I don't know."

"Hang him," Kit said as she walked away, giving her dragon hammer a bit of a shake. "Make it public. I want everyone to know what his crime was, and that it cost him his life. Leave him for three days. Let the crows have their fill, then give him to the sea."

"Kit!" Indie shouted out as she left the room. "We need to talk."

"Where are you, Fury?" Kit whispered to her hammer, shaking it again but to no effect.

"Kit." Indie took the priest by the hand when he caught up to her. "We need to find out who in Two Peaks is to receive the shipment. We already know there is corruption in Silverhawk, but if it goes all the way to the king, there is no way we can fight this."

"If we can't find the ledger," Kit said, the gold in her eyes glowing with rage, "then I will get the information from Lord Aster, even if I have to kick him all the way to the kingdom's capital city."

"Kit, stop!" Indie pulled her around, forcing her to face him. "Think about this. Arnnor shares a border with Faol, but the vampire king has never attacked. He's never made any overt threats to Arnnor, not ever. Why do you think that is? Why would he bypass the kingdom right next to him and raid Berrathia instead? Why are the Scarlet Tide working out of Silverhawk?"

"I don't know," Kit replied, shaking her head. "But I'll get the answers from Aster, and then I'll decide what to do next."

Indie led her to a red velvet bench in the hallway. Once they'd both taken a seat, he continued. "I doubt he'll know, especially if the shipment is going to the king himself. I expect whoever it is he'll deliver it to will be expendable, someone who will be removed once the shipment goes to its final destination."

"That makes sense," Kit said as she buried her face into the palms of her hands. The task felt hopeless, much too big for one girl to overcome on her own. She took a deep breath and straightened herself. "How did you come up with that?"

"Just from watching what's been happening," he replied with a shrug. "Everybody at the top has been insulated from any of the dirty operations. Look at Silverhawk, the Crimson Ale. It's run by vampire wannabees with the Auctioneers providing the muscle. They always talk of the masters, but they only show up occasionally, if at all. And the vampires we faced here, in the warehouse. They were weak. They had to have been newly sired."

"They were weak?"

"For a vampire, yah, they were weak. The one who was trying to use compulsion on us; he had almost no magic behind his commands. It took no effort at all for me and the boys to withstand it."

"You can withstand compulsion? How?"

Indie's face went dark at the question. "The vampire training," he replied, staring down at his hands. "It was a big part of what we had to learn."

"How? How could you practice the skill?" Kit's jaw dropped open. "You fought vampires as a part of your training? How? Where?"

"Captain Harding, your father, created a training facility below the Watch's dungeons. He has prisoners; vampire prisoners." Indie's hands began to shake. He grasped them tightly together, trying to stop the tremors.

Kit placed her hands over his, trying to help calm him. Unbeckoned, her hands began to glow a soft pale gold. "I love you." Her eyes searched out his, the glow intensified when he finally made eye contact with her. "Whatever it was that my father put you through, I have to believe he did it for the right reasons."

"They were starved," Indie replied, tearing his gaze away from Kit's. "Weakened to the point where they could barely function, forcing them to act instinctively." Indie's fingers caressed the skin on Kit's hand, aimlessly drawing patterns as he continued. "The boys and I were brought to a room that one was caged in. We sat outside his cell, just out of his reach, in pitch blackness. We could feel his mind reaching out to ours, calling us closer, begging us to feed him. Once..." Indie shuddered, "I tried to let him bite me, to let him feed from me." Tears were now falling down the man's face as he recollected his encounter. "As soon as I got near, the room filled with a blinding bright light, driving the vampire to the back of his cell, away from the bars. Whatever hold he had on me instantly vanished. A moment later, the light disappeared, and we were left alone in the oppressive darkness again."

"You don't have to tell me," Kit said, wrapping her hands around Indie's again.

"No, it's important that you understand what our training gave us, what it did to us." Indie took a deep breath and shuddered before beginning again. "After I failed, after I gave in to the vampire's compulsion, I felt a hand on my shoulder. I nearly jumped out of my skin. It was Lump. He had changed into his human form. He asked me if I could *feel* the compulsion, feel the way its tendrils wrapped around my mind, the way it worked against my defenses. He told me that when I felt that, to grab onto a memory, something that would anchor me.

I immediately thought of you. You are my anchor, it's you who grounds me, keeps my mind from slipping away. We sat together; me, Lump and Runt for hours. We sat in front of the vampire while he tried to penetrate our minds, to bend them to his will, to coerce us into letting him feed on us." Indie gave Kit a weak smile. "He couldn't get a hold on me. Not even a little bit. Not with my memory of you, my love for you, keeping his foul magic at bay."

Kit's chest was heaving deeply, her throat going dry. "Is that how I was able to withstand Pental's compulsion?" Kit asked weakly, trying to control her burning desire to wrap her arms around the man sitting beside her, the man who just professed a love so deep that it can withstand the magic of a vampire's compulsion. "I want you. I want to give myself to you. Now."

Before Indie had a chance to respond, the sound of footfalls spoiled the moment.

CHAPTER FORTY-TWO

THE ANTECHAMBER

"Kit, I found Rusty," Lin exclaimed, her eyes bright and full of excitement. "She says she knows where her father keeps the ledger." When she noticed the flushed look on Kit's face, Lin gave her a coy smile, a blush of her own spreading across her cheeks. "Bad timing?"

"Where is it?" Kit asked, the glow from her hands finally dying off.

"It's likely in an antechamber off my father's office," Rusty replied, suppressing her own grin when she saw the uncomfortable look on Indie's face, his hands folded on his lap. "The door to his office is next to where Indie's sitting." Rusty breezed past them, opening a pair of massive, polished black-oak doors. Indie remained seated, seemingly in no hurry to stand up. "Come in when you're ready," Lin said to Indie with a wink. "We'll be inside."

As Kit and Lin followed Rusty into her father's office, the general walked to a bookshelf on the back wall. "One time, when I was much younger, I was playing in here and I accidentally found the trigger to a secret door." She ran her hand along the edge of the bookshelf, feeling for the switch; a change in the wood's texture that would tell her how to open the door. "When I was in his antechamber, my father found me. He was furious. I thought he was going to whip the hide right off my backside." Her brow furrowed as she continued to search, unable to find the way in. "I was right here when I opened it," she said, an apologetic look in her eyes. "I swear!"

"Can I try?" Lin asked. As Rusty moved away from the bookshelf, Lin took her place. She muttered some words as she ran her hands over the shelves, tiny wisps of orange smoke trailing her fingers as she did. As she continued, the smoke swirled, changing from orange to green, just before the wisps disappeared into a crack between two of the bookcases. As her hand followed the smoke, her eyes lit up. "Found it!" she declared enthusiastically, just as she depressed a small lever causing the shelf to nudge slightly inwards. Giving Rusty a big grin, she pushed on the bookcase causing it to fully swing inwards, revealing a dark room illuminated only by the light of the office.

Kit pulled out her dragon hammer and scowled at it before igniting its bright white light which filled the entire room.

"It's pretty much as I remembered it," Rusty declared as she stepped inside, her eyes searching every nook and cranny in the room. "Now we just need to find the ledger."

"How'd you do that?" Indie whispered to Lin. "I didn't know you knew magic."

Lin pursed her lips and eyed Indie up and down. "Nice to see that *things* have returned to normal with you. Life is full of all sorts of surprises."

"You didn't answer my question," Indie replied. He was not sharing Lin's playfulness.

"No, lover boy, I didn't," she responded to him with a wink. "We ladies need our secrets. It's what keeps us interesting." And with that, she blew Indie a small kiss before heading into the antechamber to join the others. She laughed brightly when she heard Indie mumbling behind her.

"Can you do what you did to find the door?" Kit asked Lin as she came in. "You know, to find the ledger."

Lin shook her head as she inspected three golden canisters on the mantle of the fireplace. "That spell only works on finding a passage. If the ledger is magical, I could probably detect it though."

"How would you know if it's not magical?" Rusty asked. "There's no harm in trying to detect magic items, is there?"

"I'd need a gemstone, a pearl, something like that to perform the spell," Lin said as she took one of the canisters from the shelf, running her fingers over the embossed runes covering it. There was an unexpected coldness to the metal. Just holding it caused a deep chill in her hand. "These are interesting," she thought out loud. "They look like soul vessels." Since nobody seemed to be paying any attention to her, Lin grabbed a leather satchel sitting on one of the chairs and stuffed the canisters into it.

"Will this do?" Rusty asked, pulling a small earing from her right earlobe. "It's pretty small, but it's a diamond."

"Thank you," Lin said, taking the tiny earring from the woman. She pulled out her obsidian dagger and used its needle-sharp point to pop the gemstone from its setting. Pinching it between her thumb and forefinger, she held it up to the light from Kit's hammer. "It's pink!" she said, expecting everyone to understand. When she saw that nobody appreciated the meaning, she pushed her lips into a thin, flat line, and shook her head. "Don't any of you read? Pink diamonds are not from around here. As far as I know, the only place where they exist is on the southern continent, in the mountains that surround Rendheart." She groaned loudly when she saw the blank stares coming back at her. "Rendheart? The capital city of Ungael? The realm of the spider god?"

"Arachnielle?" Kit asked, hoping her question didn't make her look stupid.

"So, there's more to you than beauty and smoking hot eyes." Lin said, grinning widely at her friend. "Yes, Arachnielle, the spider god. These come from the forested mountains that surround her capital city, Rendheart." Lin walked over to the massive, black onyx desk, carefully placing the tiny gem on it. "It seems a bit of a waste to destroy such a pretty, illegal gem." Her eyes went to Rusty. "Are you sure you're okay with me using it?" When Rusty nodded, Lin shrugged. "Okay then, let's make some magic." She held her hand out to Kit. "May I borrow your hammer, for just a moment?"

"Since Fury doesn't seem to be around to object, and I did promise that I'd give it back to you if you ever asked for it..." Kit presented the weapon, inclining her head slightly as she did.

"I'll give it right back," Lin said, studying the tiny crystal. "I just need to..." Lin finished the sentence as she rapped the hammer lightly on the diamond. When she pulled the hammerhead away, she frowned deeply at the still intact gem. "A bit harder then," she said as she brought the hammer down on it, using considerably more force this time. "You little piece of…" her words trailed off as she shook her head, the gem still untarnished. Lin took another swing at the gem, striking it with enough force to create a massive dent in the black stone desk. When she pulled the hammer away, the tiny gem was still whole, except now it was deeply embedded in the stone desktop. "Helja," she exclaimed as she tried to pull the gem from the table, breaking a nail as she did.

"At least now we know why they're so expensive," Rusty laughed as she inspected Lin's hand, grimacing at her mutilated fingertip. "We should bind that, before you lose your whole nail."

"May I?" Kit said holding her hand out to Lin, a small grin tugging at the corner of her lips. "If I'm not interrupting your tender moment."

"Thank you," Lin said, sticking her tongue out at her. "Would you mind?" Lin asked, displaying her mangled fingertip to the young priest. Kit smiled sweetly before calling upon her healing power, quickly fixing Lin's wound. With a deep blush spreading up her neck, Lin pulled her hand back. She drew her dagger and popped the tiny jewel from the stone desktop.

Kit held out her hand to Lin. "Can I borrow your knife? And my hammer? Maybe it will shatter with a more *delicate* touch?"

"You, delicate?" Lin laughed as she handed the weapons to Kit. Her face was still a bit flushed. "You fight with a war hammer. That doesn't scream *delicate* to me."

"If you're finished, maybe you can put the diamond on the desk, somewhere you didn't dent the Helja out of it?" Kit raised her eyebrows, challenging Lin to find more cutting words. Instead, Lin rolled her eyes and placed the tiny crystal on the desk, away from the ruin she had caused.

Kit placed the tip of the dagger on the diamond, trying to not let it scoot out when she applied some pressure. As soon as it felt steady, she rapped lightly on the dagger's pommel, her hammer releasing a bright flash of light on contact. When Kit's vision cleared, she smiled down at the tiny pile of shards and powder on the desk. "Delicate touch," she smiled at Lin, handing her dagger back.

"Thank you," Lin said, just before scooping up the now shattered diamond. After moving to the center of the office, Lin started her spell, holding the diamond shards in the palm of her left hand while weaving intricate patterns with the fingers of her right. As she did, tiny tendrils bloomed from the shards, starting off pink, shifting to white as they stretched out in all directions. Tiny beads of sweat formed on the spell-caster's brow as she spoke strange words. The patterns traced by her fingers increased in speed and complexity, drawing more and more tendrils from the dust.

The group watched in awe as the magic finger-like wisps dipped and wove about the room, searching for any magic within. Many of the tendrils sought out Kit, her hammer, and the tiny pearl necklace she had stowed in her pocket. They licked up and down her form, seeking their targets, any magic she could be holding onto. Seemingly annoyed by their intrusive behavior, Kit swatted at the probing wisps, as though she could scare the magic away from herself. Finally, the tendrils dissipated, dispersing into nothingness.

"Kit, you're glowing," Indie said, his mouth agape.

"So is this drawer, and that satchel," Rusty said, moving to the glowing desk drawer.

"The glow will last a few minutes," Lin offered as she used her sleeve to mop the sweat from her face. "Anything magical, or in direct contact with something magical, will glow. The brighter the glow, the stronger the magic."

"I guess our mistress is extremely magical," Rusty said, feigning shielding her eyes. "You're lit up like a harvest bonfire."

Kit held up her hammer and smiled. "Lin put enough enchantments on this to last a lifetime," she said, intentionally not mentioning that the weapon contained a piece of Fury.

"What's going on with that satchel?" Indie asked. "It's glowing nearly as much as Kit is."

"I put some cannisters in it," Lin said, rushing over to grab the bag from its resting place. When she pulled one of the golden cylinders out, it was shining so brightly that it was nearly impossible to look at. "Whatever this is, it holds powerful magic."

"Can you put it away?" Rusty asked, turning away from the dazzling illumination. "I'm sure it's extremely important, but we need to see what's in the magicked drawer. I'm hoping it's the ledger." When Lin stuffed the cannister back into the satchel, the room's light returned to normal.

"Give it a go," Indie said to Rusty, pointing towards the drawer. "Let's see what's inside."

"Wait!" Lin yelled, stopping the general before she touched the drawer. "It might be glowing because of what's inside, but it might also be glowing because it's magically trapped. If it is, touching the drawer can set it off."

"How can we tell if it's trapped?" Kit asked, giving the drawer her absolute best frown.

"There are spells to detect traps and even disable them," Lin said, kneeling down in front of the drawer, hoping to discover its secrets just by staring at it. "But I don't know any of them. But I have them in my library, back in my cell in Aarall."

"What happens when the trap is sprung?" Indie asked, kneeling down beside Lin.

"Depends on the trap," Lin said, waggling her eyebrows at the man. "Men set traps to bring women to their chamber. Women set traps to capture a husband, or a wife. Maniacs like King Karter, would likely set traps to kill anybody who tried to get at his ledger."

"Is that your plan?" Kit asked, stroking the hair on the back of Indie's head. "To trap me in your bed chambers?"

"Is the trap spent, after somebody sets it off?" Rusty asked, shaking her head at Kit, not appreciating her playful banter.

"I think so," Lin said. "Traps aren't really something I've done a lot of research on, so I don't know how they might work."

"I don't think it's a trap then," Indie suggested, staring at the drawer's small keyhole. "Even if it killed the person trying to break into the desk, the next person to try would get in and the ledger would be gone."

"Oh my," Lin said, elbowing Indie in the ribs. "Handsome and smart. No wonder Kit is smitten with you."

"What is it with you?" Rusty said exhaling loudly, pushing both Indie and Lin out of the way, knocking Lin over in the process. She grabbed the drawer's handle and tugged. Nothing happened. "It's locked, not trapped. Okay, now can we figure a way to get past the lock?"

Lin laughed, picking herself up from the ground. "It's either glowing because it has the ledger inside, or because the lock is ensorcelled. It's not dangerous, but we still can't get past it, not without the key, at any rate."

"I wonder?" Indie asked as he crawled under the piece of furniture. "Sometimes they are open underneath," he said, his legs sticking out from beneath the desk. "I might be able to reach in through the back," he ground out, straining as he contorted himself into position. "Nope. The drawers are fully encased. There's no gap at the back of the desk."

"I'll be right back," Kit said as she bolted from the room, only to return a minute later with Lump and Runt by her side. "Time to put aside delicate and unleash brute force." She gave the dire wolf a scratch under the chin. "Ready to turn this desk into an ice-block?" she asked, waving her arms to get everyone else out of the way.

When her cohorts were a good distance away from the desk, Kit closed her eyes. "Titan, hear me," she intoned, icicles forming on her hands, up the shaft of the hammer to its mithril head. Pointing the hammer, she unleashed a stream of frost at the desk. From beside her, Runt opened his mouth, spewing a similar cone of frozen air at the piece of furniture. In seconds, ice encased the entire desk. "Thank you," she said, patting the wolf's thick black fur. "I need you to stand back with everyone else now."

"What are you doing?" Rusty asked, managing to furrow her brow and bulge her eyes simultaneously.

Without responding, Kit stepped up to the desk and with a two-handed, overhead swing, brought the hammer down onto the block of ice, unleashing a blinding flash of light and a ka-boom that knocked Kit off her feet. When she opened her eyes, a mist filled the room. It was so thick that she could barely see her hand in front of her face.

"Everyone okay?" she asked, waving her hands about, trying to dispel the fog. Several groans and whimpers let Kit know that her people were still alive, but she had no idea if they'd been injured.

"I'd say that qualifies as *indelicate*," Lin moaned from what sounded like the far side of the office; both Indie and Rusty reacting with weak laughs.

"Lump? Runt? You guys okay?" Kit called out. A warm furry body rubbed against her thigh, while an enormous slobbery tongue scraped up her face. As the vapor started to thin, the devastation became visible. The room was in utter shambles, and the desk was in so many pieces that it would be impossible to tell if it was ever anything more than a pile of black rubble.

From somewhere within the pile, a faint glow peered out, like a tiny beacon, sucking the hope from Kit's chest. Deciding it was a good place to start digging, she pulled back hunks of stone and wood, pushing them aside, exposing more and more of the ominous glow. Bending over, she extracted the mangled remains of the drawer's lock, its magic still intact, even though it was no longer attached to anything. "I'd say your father got his gold's worth when he paid somebody to magically lock the drawer."

Rusty, sporting a few nicks and cuts on her face, neck, and hands, moved in beside Kit, rummaging through the debris. "That was incredibly foolish," she admonished Kit, pulling a thick, red leather-bound book from the wreckage. "But surprisingly effective."

Chapter Forty-Three

The Fair Traders Union

"What do you mean its encoded?" Kit asked, trying to get a look at the ledger. Rusty turned away from her as she did, shielding the book with her body. "Where are you going?" Kit yelled when Rusty walked away, heading for the antechamber's exit.

Flipping through the pages of the ledger, Rusty strolled from the office, out into the hallway, and into the receiving room, with Kit and the rest of her cohorts following behind her.

"Can you read this?" she asked the harbourmaster. He had plunked himself in a large chair. The remains of several plates of food were strewn around him. Disregarding the man's gluttonous mess, she pushed the book under his nose, pointing to the mass of glyphs and scribbles covering the page.

"No," he replied flatly, wiping a bit of food from his mouth and chin. "Whatever that boom was, it made me drop my meal."

"What do you mean, no?" Rusty asked, pushing the book at him again. "Are these not the same symbols as were on the manifest?"

"No," the fat man repeated. "They're not the same. I don't know what they mean, well..." he paused for a moment, running his fingers over the scribbles. "They kind of, sort of, look like Berrat writing, but not."

"Will you let me see it? Please?" Kit pushed in beside Rusty, holding her hands out for the ledger.

"Here," Rusty said with a sneer, shoving the book at her. "Have a look."

"What is your problem?" Kit asked, taking the book from the foul tempered woman. "You've been angry with me ever since we entered your father's office."

"Because it's *my* father's office. It's *my* father's antechamber, and it *was my* father's desk. Because you're a guest in *my* house and you march around like it's yours to do with as you please."

"That makes no sense," Kit responded, practically screaming at the woman. "We're here searching for a secret ledger, trying to free slaves, trying to stop all the horrendous things your father's been doing – and you're angry because I broke his desk?" When Lin moved in close beside Kit, Rusty's face went dark, her eyes moving from Kit to Lin and back to Kit again.

"You're jealous of Kit?" Lin squeaked out, unable to hide her growing smile. Quickly moving beside Rusty, she took the woman's hand in her own. "Is that it? You think I'm interested in Kit?" When she saw the woman's face redden, Lin kissed her hand. "Oh sweetness, Kit's an amazing woman, but she's hopelessly, helplessly in love with that towering hunk of a man. I've been making cow-eyes at you all day, but you never – am I right? You're jealous?"

"Can you read it?" Rusty asked Kit, trying to move the conversation in a different direction. Lin moved, squeezing herself between Kit and Rusty, putting her face directly in front of the general's, locking her eyes on the woman, demanding a response. "A little," Rusty finally said with a sheepish tone. "Okay? I said it. Can we get on with the problem at hand?"

"Much better," Lin said, giving her a quick kiss on the lips.

"No," Kit said. "I can't read it, but Rayan is right, it is Berrathian based."

"I thought you could speak all forms of Berrat," Indie said, running his fingers along the edge of the book's cover, "from your time in the library."

"I can understand every language in the north," Kit said, still staring intently at the page. "This is Berrabbithi, a language that died out many, many years ago."

"How do you know the language? Why can't you speak it?" Indie asked.

"Father Hoarfrost gave me a box," Kit started. "This was before I went into the library. The box was filled with writings, drawings, and bones." Kit suddenly realized that she hadn't seen that box in ages, not since after her birthday; after Danny left for Taseko. "Danny can read it," she blurted out. "Something in the box, one of the bones, burrowed its way under his skin. It gave him the power to translate the words." Seeing that everyone was giving Kit a look that she may be losing her mind, she waved off her ramblings. "We need to go to Taseko, to bring this ledger to him."

"I think that's going to have to wait," Bango said from the doorway. She came marching into the room with several young nobles following in her wake. They were all dressed in fine clothes, and they all shared the same look of entitlement, except for one.

"I think before you head off," Bango said, "you should speak with the younger members of House Hanse." She passed Kit the slip of parchment containing the names of those friendly to Aurora's Guard. "I couldn't bring them all here," she whispered. "One of them is in a holding cell here at the manor."

"What is the meaning of this?" one of the men just brought in challenged, straightening his bright blue surcoat. "I am Ator Gillan, son of Lord Usip Gillan, and I demand to know why I've been dragged here against my will."

"We are to pay for our fathers' sins," said the only one of those brought in who didn't look to be *above* everyone else.

"And you are?" Kit asked.

"Logan Buttsworth, Mistress," he replied bowing his head deeply enough to be respectful, but not so deeply as to appear obsequious.

"Your father is Allister Buttsworth," Kit said with a pained look on her face. "I've met your girlfriend, Luna." Logan immediately started wringing his hands. "Don't worry," Kit said, feeling the man's anxiety. "She is well."

She turned her attention to the two young women who had remained silent up to this point. "And you are?"

One of the girls jutted out her chin and tossed her long blond hair over her shoulder. "I am Cilya Ashtown, daughter of Lord Mervin Ashtown, the most powerful merchant in the north. When he returns, he will have you flayed."

"And I am Ashlay Ashtown," said the girl standing beside her, jutting out her chin, tossing her long blonde hair over her shoulder, mimicking her twin sister perfectly. "And after our father finishes flaying you, he'll cut you into tiny pieces and feed you to the chickens." When her sister groaned, Ashlay pouted slightly. "I meant to say, he'll feed your pieces to our dragon."

Cilya buried her face in her hands.

"Your father has a dragon?" Kit asked, trying hard not to smile.

"Of course, he does," Ashlay replied, jutting her chin out even further.

"No, he doesn't," Cilya ground back.

Kit's face went slack. Ashlay was telling the truth and Cilya was lying. Clearly, Cilya did not want everyone to know that their father, in some way, had a dragon. Kit knew that the dragons were all bound to their mountain ranges, but somehow, this merchant had a connection to one of them. Not wanting to give away anything more than was necessary, Kit chuckled.

"I'm so scared," she said, her chuckles turning into a full-on laugh. "He's going to feed me to an imaginary dragon." Cilya's shoulders slumped slightly while Ashlay's face turned a brilliant shade of red. Before anybody had a chance to speak further, Kit held up her hand and walked to the far side of the room, keeping her back to the others. She opened the note that Jayne had given her, to see what information it might contain. "Titan's snowballs," she muttered to herself.

Kit,

Under no circumstances let this note fall into anybody else's hands. The information contained here is for your eyes only. If somebody were to make their associations public, it could put our entire plan in jeopardy.

Fair Traders Union

- Cilya Ashtown

- Ator Gillan

- Logan Buttsworth

Aurora's Guard

- Ashlay Ashtown, Cilya's twin sister

- Bandolion Goggler

- Ailman Juuls

Ailman Juuls, that's the name that Kit knew she had heard before but couldn't remember, the man she had locked up. Well, she thought to herself, at least nobody will think we're friends. Suddenly, Kit got a pain in her stomach. She had given this note to Lin, and she had a *propensity* for selling information if it suited her purposes.

Why don't you read things before stowing them away? Kit admonished herself. She suddenly remembered the note that Danny had given her, the note she'd stowed away and had never bothered to read.

"Kit?" Indie whispered over her shoulder. "Are you okay?" She nodded, continuing to maintain focus on the note. "Kit? You've been standing over here by yourself for a while now. What do you want to do with these people?"

Kit spun around, brushing past Indie as she returned to the group. She pointed to Cilya, Ator, and Logan. "You three, stay here. The rest of you, out!"

"Mistress?" Rusty asked. "You want all of *us* to leave, too?"

"Yes," Kit said, glaring at her for having to repeat her order. "And I want you to bring Ailman Juuls here to see me. Now."

"Yes, Mistress," Rusty said, inclining her head in acknowledgement. With a quick clap of her hands, the woman bellowed, "You heard her, everybody out. Now."

As Rusty was shepherding the occupants out, Staul started grabbing handfuls of food as he passed the buffet table, giving Kit a smile and a wink as he did.

"You, too, lover boy," Rusty called out when she saw Indie lagging behind. "Our mistress said, everybody but this lot. That means you, too." When Kit gave him a tight-lipped grin, Indie shook his head and followed the rest of the crew out of the room.

"Okay," Kit said, once they were alone and Rusty had closed the door. "Tell me about the Fair Trader's Union and your role with them." Kit waited for a moment, giving them all a chance to think about their answers. When it was clear that nobody was going to step forward, she plopped herself into one of the overstuffed chairs. She swore under her breath as she pulled the remains of a half-eaten sweetbread from beneath her.

"Don't sit here," she said, moving to a different chair, wiping the remains of the food off the tails of her surcoat.

Kit pushed herself into the back of the new chair, causing her feet to lift off the ground. She eyed the other seats that were nearby, motioning for the others to sit, but nobody moved.

"Do you really think I am your enemy?" she asked, as her feet bobbed in the air. "I just freed all the slaves who were about to be shipped out, and many more who were bound for places unknown. Surely you can't believe it was all a ruse just to expose you."

"Where's Luna?" Logan asked, taking the seat nearest to Kit. "Please, tell me."

"Your father is evil," Kit said, wondering if she should tell the man sitting next to her what his father had been doing. "He had Luna and several other women... in a compromising state of undress when I found them in his office." It looked to Kit like Logan was about to vomit. "Luna was untouched, unharmed," she continued, suddenly wishing she hadn't shared this information with him. "She spoke very highly of you," she added, hoping it might allay some of the man's fears. "When I saw her last, she was being cared for by Bango and her people."

"Why are you here?" Cilya demanded, still refusing to take a seat.

"My name is Sister Kit Standing Bear, acknowledged priest of Titan. I stand for justice, and I am here to right the wrongs the Auctioneers and the Scarlet Tide are bringing upon the peoples of Arnnor and Berrathia. But I'm just one person and I can't do it alone."

"And you think we're going to help you?" Cilya asked. She had somehow managed to stick her nose even higher into the air as she posed the question. If she was in fact born with a silver spoon in her mouth, Kit had a burning desire to ram it down her throat.

"I will help you," Logan said. "We need to stop what's been happening."

"So will I," Ator added, taking a seat on the other side of Kit. "My family is deeply entrenched in the Auctioneers, but if you can help fix that, I'm yours to command."

"Why would you tell her that?" Cilya screeched out. "We are sworn to never reveal our association with the Union."

"We didn't tell her we belonged to the Union," Logan said, shaking his head. "We just said we'd help her."

"Well, she'd have figured it out quickly enough on her own." Cilya walked away in a huff, flipping her long hair over her shoulder.

"Did any of you meet with my friends, Treedale and Mukale?"

"Yes," Cilya said, her voice now filled with resignation. "They were trying to find out about the last shipment of slaves. They seemed interested in finding a particular man. Treedale said the man had kidnapped him."

"Were you able to help him?" Kit asked.

"Yes," Ator replied. "We knew exactly who they were looking for."

"I believe the man met with an untimely demise," Cilya said with a wry smile as she returned to the group, taking a seat on a small sofa across from Kit.

"Untimely," Logan laughed. "I'd say that's one way to describe it. We helped them capture the man. We figured that if everything Treedale said was true, that he needed to *deal* with the man personally." Logan shook his head. "I don't think anybody expected *that* to happen."

"What happened?" Kit asked, getting annoyed that they were dragging out the story much more than they needed to.

"Well," Ator started, chuckling a bit. "You've got to know, this man they were looking for, he was a terrible, horrible, awful man."

"Was?"

Ator nodded. "Well, after we helped them catch him, they bound his feet and hands and carried him out to the docks. The Berrat boy, he turned himself into a horse, grabbed the man by his feet and dangled him over the water."

Logan jumped in, taking over the tale. "Treedale started asking him questions, trying to find out who he was and who he worked for. Every time he asked a question, the man only laughed at him. Each time the man laughed; the horse dunked him in the sea. Each time the horse dunked him, he held him under water a little bit longer."

"They drowned him?"

"Nope," Cilya laughed. "A makara bit him in two. He nearly dragged Mukale into the water with him."

"Titan's snowballs!"

"I know," Ator laughed, feigning disgust. "It was amazing."

Once Kit got beyond the thought of a sea monster chewing up the slaver, she pressed the trio for information on the Fair Traders Union. It was a difficult conversation to follow, with each of the three interrupting and talking over the others. Apparently, they had been dying to share what they knew with someone, anyone really, so long as they were willing to listen.

"Okay," Kit said, once the chatter had died down. "Let me see if I've got this straight." She took a deep breath and gathered her thoughts. "The Auctioneers are slavers, made up mostly of Western and Southern humans."

"There are Eastern humans in the Auctioneers as well," Cilya piped up.

"And Eastern humans as well," Kit said with a growl, causing Cilya to clamp her hand over her mouth. "And the Auctioneers sell these slaves all over the world."

With her hand still clamped over her mouth, Cilya nodded.

"King Faol is buying up most of the northern slaves to use them to feed his vampire population. But they are also selling them to Arachnielle followers on the southern continent." Ator was about to interrupt, but Kit gave him the same glare. "The Fair Traders Union is raiding the slaver ships, freeing prisoners when it can, selling arms and armor to anybody willing to take up the fight against the slavers."

Ator nodded.

"And the Scarlet Tide are here to oversee the incoming shipments of slaves," Kit said finally, thinking that she had made a decent summary of what the three had been telling her.

Cilya unclamped her hand from over her mouth and blurted out, "We also work with the Mortem Lupus." She immediately clamped her hand back over her mouth, while Ator and Logan gasped.

"Who are the Mortem Lupus?"

"They're pirates," Logan said, shaking his head at Cilya. "Lycanthrope pirates. They are mostly werewolves, but there are a number of other types among their ranks."

"Do you mean shapeshifters, like the Berrat?"

"No, not like the Berrat," Logan continued. "It's a long story but the people of Lycos have been jealous of their northern neighbors, well, forever. They wanted to be able to shift like the Berrat. They even brought Berrat back as mates, hoping that they'd gain their powers."

"But they never did," Cilya jumped in. "Instead, they got their magic all twisted up. They created monsters."

"Monsters?"

"They can't control their shifting," Ator added. "They are somehow tied to the moon. When the moon is full, they are at their most powerful. When the moon is new, like it is now, they are at their weakest."

"That's why the Auctioneers only move prisoners on the nights of the new moon," Logan said, finally joining into the conversation. "It's why they are moving the silvered weapons. They're sending them to Ravenlord to equip the sailors there. The silvered weapons are extremely effective against the lycans."

Kit's head was beginning to swim again. There was too much information, and she couldn't keep up with it. She breathed a sigh of relief when Rusty barged in with Ailman Juuls at her side.

"Thank you," Kit said to the three members of the Union. "We'll talk more later."

Logan, Cilya, and Ator began arguing amongst themselves as they headed for the door, making Kit wonder how they ever got anything done.

Chapter Forty-Four

Aurora's Guard

"General, can you bring Bango and Ashlay back in please?" Kit offered one of the overstuffed chairs to Ailman, warning him away from the food-encrusted seat that the gluttonous ex-harbourmaster had been sitting in.

While Rusty was out gathering the other two, Kit quietly addressed the chief advisor. "You work for my mother," she said as a statement, not as a question. The man flinched slightly at her assertion. "You said I have pretty gold eyes, but that you've seen prettier. I believe you were referring to my mother, Aurora." The man replied with a stone-like expression.

"Fine," Kit said with a heavy sigh. "We'll wait for Bango to come in and confirm my suspicions."

"You play a dangerous game, girl."

"In case you haven't noticed, we live in a dangerous world," Kit replied, hovering over him, trying to appear menacing. "Do you deny that you work for my mother?"

"I will neither confirm nor deny anything," he replied with a smug look on his face. "If you are who you say you are, you can tell if I'm lying."

"I can. You can either confirm my suspicions or we can wait for Bango to do it for you."

"I will not break my oath."

When Rusty entered the room with Bango and Ashlay in tow, Ailman crossed his arms and looked away.

"Thank you, general," Kit said. "I'll call you when I need you."

"Yes, Mistress," Rusty replied. She quickly exited the room, closing the door behind her.

Even though both Bango and Ashlay could see Ailman, neither of them acknowledged his presence. When Kit took her seat beside the man, they followed suit, sitting nearby. Ashlay began fidgeting in her seat, unsure of what to do with her hands.

"Which of you has not met my mother?" Kit asked. When nobody replied, and after waiting a few minutes, the young priest tried again. "Bango, you have sworn fealty to me. I am asking you a simple question and yet you sit there, tight-lipped."

"She's not allowed to answer you," Ashlay said. A moment later, her eyes went wide, and she immediately clamped her hands over her mouth.

"Bango?" Kit prompted.

"Mistress Kit, I will follow you to the ends of Orth. I will die for you, but I will not break my oath."

"Fine," Kit screamed at them. "Keep your oath and when people start to die because I don't know what you know – then it's on you." Kit stormed across the room, grabbing what looked like a statue of Ymir. Giving the figurine her absolute best frown, she crushed it in her fist and watched as the bits slowly fell between her fingers.

"They cannot break their oath to me," said a voice from one of the room's many windows. Kit turned to see a woman in a black cloak sitting on the windowsill, her long blonde hair pouring out of the upturned hood like a platinum waterfall.

"You," Kit said, stumbling a few steps backwards.

"Me," she said, pulling back her hood. The woman's skin was pale, almost golden in color, or maybe it was merely the reflection of her solid gold eyes. "I've waited a long time to meet you," she said with a sad smile. "I cannot stay. Not yet. It's not time for us to be together." The woman slipped down from the windowsill and glided across the room to the trio, touching each one lightly on their forehead. The eyes of each of them turn milky white on contact. "You may speak freely with my daughter. Whatever order she gives, you will follow as though it came from me personally."

As the woman headed back towards the window, Kit cut her off.

"Are you my mother?"

"You are my child, but I am not your mother," she replied, her voice wavering as she did. "Riva is your mother. It was through her love and guidance that you became the person you are." The woman smiled warmly. "I chose well."

"Why did you leave me?" Kit asked, unable to control her emotions as tears flowed down her cheeks. "Why didn't you love me?"

"Oh, my sweet angel," the woman said, taking Kit's hands in her own. "I could not bring you with me, even though leaving you behind nearly killed me. I suppose that was my humanity."

"Your what?" Kit choked out. "I don't understand."

"You will." The woman glided past Kit, over to the double doors leading out to the balcony. As she opened them, a cold wind burst into the room, blowing the drapes inward. Looking out the window, Kit's birthmother sighed heavily. "A storm is coming," she said, staring out the open doors. When she turned back to Kit, her golden eyes were full of tears. "I am sorry for what you will endure today. I only wish I could stop it for you."

"Stop what?" Kit asked rushing to the balcony as her mother climbed onto the railing. Before she could take hold of her, the woman dropped to the gardens below. When Kit looked over the edge, her mother was gone. In the distance, across the front garden, Kit saw people running and screaming, fighting against a wave of soldiers heading towards the building.

"Kit!" Indie screamed as he came crashing through the doorway. "You need to get downstairs. Now!"

Kit drew her battle hammer from its sheath. "You'd better be there when I need you," she scolded her weapon as she raced out the doors into the hallway.

"We're all downstairs, waiting for you," Indie said as he took the lead, racing towards the staircase.

"What's happening?"

"The masters," Indie replied, taking the steps to the main floor four at a time. "They have hostages."

As Kit came down the stairs, Rusty, Lin, and the three members of the Fair Traders Union met her. They looked frantic, panicked. "Where are the boys?" she screamed out. When nobody responded, Kit got a sick feeling in her stomach. Without hesitation, she blew past her cohorts and continued on towards the manor's front door. Kit had no idea where she was going, or what she was running into, but she followed in the direction her soldiers were moving.

"You've got to save us," one Berrat woman screamed as she latched onto Kit's arm. "They'll kill us all!"

Kit practically threw the woman to the ground trying to shake her off. A part of her felt badly for how she had just treated the Berrat, but she had no time for pleasantries.

The cries and wails continued as Kit worked her way through the crowd, barely able to move forward through the throng. Many more were grabbing onto her, begging her for help, and each time, the young priest tossed them to the side as she continued to press forward.

As Kit finally passed the last of the escaping population, she tripped over the dead bodies of fallen soldiers, each one having had their throat ripped open.

"Move!" Kit screamed at the wall of soldiers in front of her. When nobody obeyed her command, Kit tried pressing her way through the mass of bodies, but her progress was too slow; there was too much commotion; the yells and screams were drowning out her voice before it even left her mouth.

The pendant!

As quickly as she could, Kit reached into her pocket and pulled out the tiny pearl pendant. "Titan, hear me," she muttered as she slipped it over her head. The head of her hammer immediately began to crackle with energy as she once again started pressing against the wall of soldiers.

"Move!" she bellowed. The pendant immediately magnified her voice, creating a shockwave that knocked everyone aside, clearing a path all the way to the source of the disturbance, the center of the fear that had gripped the people, her people.

Kit's chest went tight when they came into sight. There were three pale-skinned men, dressed in long black cloaks standing on the waist-high ledge of a large garden pool. Emblazoned on their chests was the same symbol Kit and Lin had tattooed on their neck in Silverhawk; two crescent opposing moons, bisected by a dagger. Each of them held a prisoner in their hands, a Berrat boy, a Berrat woman, and a young Nomad man.

She was about to run headlong into the fray when a strong hand grasped her shoulder, stopping her in her tracks. She spun around, ready to unleash her hammer. She paused when she realized it was Indie, his face a picture of fear.

"Don't," he pleaded. "I can feel their minds, their magic, from here. They're the real thing. You can't beat them."

"No!" A scream from behind Kit drew her attention away from Indie. Lin had her swords drawn as she raced past Kit. It's only then that Kit saw what she was doing. The prisoners the vampires were holding were Mukale, Treedale, and her mother, Riva.

Pulling away from Indie's grasp, Kit followed Lin as she raced toward certain death in order to save her brother.

"Kneel!" the vampire holding Kit's mother commanded. There was an eerie calmness to him. Despite several hundred soldiers waiting to kill him, and two crazed women rushing at him, he appeared utterly disinterested, as though the people were nothing more than insignificant nobodies.

Lin practically fell on her face at the vampire's command as she attempted to halt her forward momentum. She crashed heavily to the ground before picking herself up and taking a knee. Kit slid down beside her, making sure she was uninjured, taking a knee beside her. A moment later, Indie followed suit, kneeling on the far side of Kit.

"Excellent," the vampire laughed. "Bow before your masters like the good little sheep that you are."

When Kit looked back up at the vampire, she witnessed the look of resignation on her mother's face. A fire began to build inside her, a fire so intensely hot that it made her feel like she was about to erupt. Gripping the handle of her hammer tighter, she stood and began walking slowly towards her mother.

"Kneel!" the vampire said, raising his voice, causing it to become shrill. Kit could feel the vampire's magic washing over her, but it had no effect.

"Let my mother go," Kit snarled. "If you harm her..."

"This day is my purpose," Riva cried out. "Today, my child, I will ignite your soul!"

As Kit continued to close the distance at her unhurried pace, the vampire raised his clawed hand over his shoulder. The other two vampires followed suit.

"Kneel or they die," the vampire screeched. "You will stop."

The fire building up inside Kit was now so intense that she was having trouble maintaining focus. She felt like there was something inside her, clawing at her chest, just begging to be set free.

"I love you, Kit," Riva said, closing her eyes, awaiting her inevitable death.

"We can't save them all," Indie said over her shoulder. "I'll save Treedale, you save your *mother*."

"No living soul shall die this day," Kit growled. The deep visceral sound of her voice boomed from her chest, magnified by the magic of her pendant. The familiar blue flames of Fury began to lick about the head and handle of her hammer, intermixing with the flashes of the crackling energy supplied by her prayers to Titan. When deep red flames joined into the mix, bursting forth from her hammer, from her hands and from her eyes, Kit started to chortle.

With deadly intent, the vampires brought down their clawed hands, committed to slashing open the throats of their captives. With inhuman speed, Kit flashed next to the vampire holding her mother, catching his hand before it could complete its mission. On either side of her, Kit heard the shrill cries of the other vampires, shrieks of terror and of agony.

"You would dare to harm my family, my friends, those people I love?" Kit's voice boomed forth, her tiny pendant continuing to amplify her speech. "I suppose I should thank you, showing up here today, for everybody to witness." The vampire gave a strangled whimper. "These people trust me, believe in me, knowing that I will deliver them from the likes of you and your foul sire."

The bright red flames surrounding Kit's hands began to spread to the forearm of the vampire, causing him to writhe in agony. "This cannot be," he groaned, as his eyes widened. "You, cannot be."

"And yet, I am," Kit said, giving the vampire a wicked smile. "And now... you die." With Kit's words, her fire quickly spread up the vampire's arms just before he entirely burst into flames, his mouth opened and closed soundlessly as the raging inferno enveloped him, charring his skin and liquifying his eyes. In moments, the vampire's skin started to crack. His burnt skin dissolved into ash and blew away in the growing north wind.

Kit spun around, looking to kill the other two vampires, finding them both on the ground, Lump and Runt rending them to pieces, a pack of gray wolves assisting in the kills. Kit's head spun back towards Mukale and Treedale. Outside of a stunned look on their faces, they both appeared to be physically unharmed.

"Frookin' Helja!" a familiar voice called out drawing her attention away from the boys. Standing beside Indie, with several dozen dwarves behind him, was Coldforge, sharing the same dumbfounded look as Kit's boyfriend.

Suddenly remembering her mother, Kit turned back to see her still standing in the same place, sharing the same expression as Indie and Coldforge. Everybody was staring. Bright flashes of light danced before Kit's eyes, swirling and twirling, just before blackness engulfed her.

Chapter Forty-Five

An Unlikely Outcome

Kit opened her eyes to a great black void. In the infinite distance, tiny pinpoints of light sparkled and spun, creating minuscule kaleidoscopes of color as they did. She shook her hammer, igniting its bright white light.

She was sitting on a large rock, in a glade by a small pool, on a tiny island floating in the vastness of space. She had been here before. It was familiar, yet foreign.

"That was unexpected," said the unremarkable old man, sitting cross-legged in the emerald-green grass. He was plucking lightly on the strings of his lute-like instrument. Each pluck of a string produced a small burst of color that floated and danced merrily about him before dissipating into the void.

"Anu?"

"I have seen many futures for you, little angel, but that was not one of them."

"What do you mean?" Kit asked, slipping down off the rock.

"I hope you don't mean to strike me with that," Anu said, pointing to her hammer. "I am not well versed in polite conversation, but I can only guess that holding a weapon over someone is, well, not very polite."

Kit looked down at her hammer and grinned. "Sorry, I'm just using it to light the area."

"Oh, of course," Anu said as a circle of lit torches suddenly appeared around them. "I forget that you still have limited vision."

Kit extinguished the light of her hammer and sheathed it. "Why am I here?"

"Because you bring me joy, little angel."

"Am I some sort of pet to you?" Kit growled. The idea that Anu dragged her to this place, without her consent, irritated her beyond rational thought.

"My pet?" the old man asked, his eyes sparkling brightly. "Not in any of this universe's infinite number of possibilities are you ever my pet, or anybody else's for that matter."

"She has disrupted the balance," said a hissing voice from behind Kit. "Your prophecies are in jeopardy." Kit turned to see the strange, yet beautiful visage of Mephitis behind her, the woman's water-snake-covered head tilted in a questioning way. As she ran her rat-like fingers across her alligator-skin arms, she practically cooed.

"The prophecies were never meant to be final," Anu said, patting the ground beside him, inviting Mephitis to sit. "But they did represent the most likely outcome for the world you disrupted."

"That was never our intent," Mephitis said as she took a seat beside Anu, her long rat-like tail curling around her like a security blanket. "We just wanted to be free of them."

"And how do you think that's working out for you?" Anu asked, with a small grin, his eyes alight with curiosity. "You never expected the likes of her, now did you?"

"I don't like being talked about," Kit said, folding her arms across her chest. "Especially if I'm standing right in front of you."

"No," Mephitis laughed, "we certainly did not."

"She is a puzzle," Anu replied; "practically an impossibility."

"Stop it," Kit screamed at them, her fists balled at her sides, red flames beginning to spill out between her fingers.

"You need to control that," Anu said, still smiling sweetly at her. "It will lead you where you do not wish to go."

"Control what?" Kit asked, the fire dying out as quickly as it started.

"Your daemon within," Mephitis said, as she morphed into a terrible creature with skin of molten rock and obsidian wings and matching inky-black eyes. "Your dark celestial self."

"My what?"

"A gift from your father," Anu said. "An improbable possibility has come to pass. He passed on a piece of himself that was buried so deeply, nobody even knew it existed."

"A piece of my father?"

"Isn't she a joy?" Anu asked, falling onto his back, rolling around in the grass. "You should tell her what she is."

"I cannot," Mephitis answered, morphing back into her *normal* self, wringing her long rat tail in her long rat fingers.

"Your kin did well, choosing you to be arbiter," Anu said, finally stopping his dog-like antics. "She has enough clues to figure it out for herself."

"And if she is too thick to figure it out on her own, she can always ask her canine friend."

"You're breaking your own rules, Mephitis," Anu said, his eyes practically swirling in his head. "She doesn't know what he learned in the library."

"Do you mean, Lump?"

"Oh, now I've done it," Mephitis said with a surprisingly soft, delicate laugh. "It will probably be the end of me."

"What?" Kit asked, her brow furrowed.

"She shared information that she was not supposed to," Anu said in a sing-song sort of way. "This was not in any of the possibilities I had foreseen either."

Mephitis disappeared with a slight popping sound, leaving a thick green swirling mist behind her.

"She will probably face the power of the four, dissolution being the penalty for her crime." Anu stood, holding his hands out to Kit. "She will probably take the place of your mother."

"What do you mean by that?" Kit asked, taking Anu's hands in hers.

"Your mother was meant to perish today," Anu said in a matter-of-fact tone. "From the prophecy. She was one of the eight destined to die."

"I broke the prophecy?"

"Maybe," Anu said with a devilish grin. "Or maybe you've created a new prophecy, something I never foresaw."

"I don't understand," Kit said, gripping the old man's hands tightly, begging him for more details.

"You're not supposed to understand, nobody really does." He sighed deeply. "As I said, prophecies are likely outcomes, based upon the path of the universe. As the path unfolds, the likelihood of any one future becomes more and more clear. That is until somebody remarkable comes along. Somebody with the ability to change the future."

"And that's me?" Kit squeaked out.

"Only time will tell," the old man said with a bright, cheery laugh. "Bring forth the future."

Bright flashes of light danced before Kit's eyes, swirling and twirling, just before blackness once again engulfed her.

The Awakening

"Nice hair," a voice said, echoing through the blackness.

"Back up, let her be," said another voice, a deeper voice.

"Kit, my love, come back to us," said a third voice, in a soft nurturing tone. Kit's eyes fluttered open to see her mother, Riva, staring down at her. "There you are," she said softly, gently brushing a stray strand of red hair from her cheek.

"Ananak?"

"Hush, my love. Take a moment," Riva said again. "You gave us all quite a start."

"What happened?" Kit asked, trying to lift her head off her mother's lap.

"Ye fried yourself a vampire, is what," Coldforge said, looking over Riva's shoulder. "Ye pups took down the other two. The look of surprise on their faces..." The dwarf's words trailed off as he started to laugh, delighting in the deaths of the bloodsuckers.

Kit suddenly sat bolt upright, causing her head to swim for a moment. "Ananak, you're okay!" she screamed out, wrapping her arms around her mother's neck, squeezing it so tightly the woman could barely breathe. "I thought you were going to die."

"So did I," Riva said when Kit finally released her. "I was supposed to die today."

"What?" Kit asked, as her mouth dropped open.

"It doesn't matter," Riva said with a crooked smile. "I'm happy my vision turned out, differently."

"Where is everyone?" Kit looked around haphazardly, barely able to focus on her surroundings. She was on the ground in the front garden. There were hundreds of soldiers and thousands of people here only a moment ago. She blinked a few times, trying to chase her confusion away.

"Hello, my love," Indie said, taking a knee beside Kit. "You really have to stop scaring us like that."

"What did I do?"

Indie chuckled. "You don't remember?" When Kit shook her head, he took her chin in his hand. "You only saved the day." His eyes were wide, and his voice was full of awe. "One second, you were beside me; the next, you transformed into... something new. You moved so fast. I never saw you leave my side. A moment later, you were setting a vampire ablaze."

"You turned him to ash," Lin said, sharing the same awe-struck voice as Indie.

"You ignited your true self," Riva said. "Just not the one we were expecting."

"What do you mean?" Kit's world was starting to spin again. She remembered nothing of what had happened to her, at least she didn't think she remembered.

"Hush now," Riva said as she stood up, helping Kit to stand as well. "Your mother will explain it to you soon."

"But you're my mother," Kit cried out, again clutching the tiny Berrat woman as her emotions came flooding out. "You've always been my mother, my true mother." Kit's words quickly became incomprehensible as her tears turned to sobs.

"Would you prefer I told you?" Riva choked out, suddenly overwhelmed by her own emotions. Kit made a grunting noise that Riva could only assume was a yes. "Let's get you inside then. You're going to want to sit down."

With their arms still wrapped around each other, Kit and Riva headed back into the manor with Indie, Lin, and Coldforge. It was only after they'd entered the building that Kit realized Runt and Lump weren't with them. "Where are the boys?" she called out, her head swiveling about as she scanned the area.

"It's okay, Kit," Indie said, trying to calm her worries. "They're with Amilta and Fenrir."

"Fenrir's here, too?" Kit asked with a sniff. Her hand suddenly went to her throat. "Where's my necklace?"

"It's right here," Indie said, pointing to a small pocket on her surcoat. "You were sort of moaning when you were unconscious. Everyone could hear, so I slipped it off you." Kit closed her eyes for a moment, trying to remember her dreams but they were difficult to hold on to.

"How long was I out?" she asked. It seemed a lot had happened since she had encountered the vampires.

"Much too long," Riva said, avoiding answering the question directly.

"Mistress Kit," Rusty said as she came marching towards the group, a half dozen soldiers at her back. "I'd like to set up a second barracks."

"I didn't know you had set up a first barracks," Kit replied, wiping her runny nose with the back of her hand.

Rusty grimaced when she saw the long strand of mucus stretched between Kit's hand and her nose. She quickly pulled a handkerchief out from a side pocket on her surcoat. After handing it to Kit she pointed in the general direction of her nose. "You've got a little, something, smeared across your face."

Kit blushed slightly as she cleaned the errant... stuff... from her nose and cheek.

Rusty pointed to another spot on her chin that she had missed. "I used one of the main warehouses to set up a barracks for your soldiers. I wanted them to be together, sleep together, eat together, train together. But, after today's *display*, the barracks I set up are too small."

"Display?" Kit asked. Her tears had stopped but her eyes were still wide and glassy.

"Well, after what you did to the vampire, well, a good majority of the rescued slaves wanted to enlist in your army."

"My army?"

"Yes, your army." Rusty was chuckling at the young priest's look of confusion. "I may be organizing them, but they fight for you. They are *all* fighting for you." Kit turned to Indie, giving him something of a sheepish grin.

"I have an army."

Rusty cleared her throat. "If it pleases you, Mistress Kit, I'd like to set up a second barracks for the newest recruits. There isn't a real soldier among them. I'd like to house them separately, so they, too, can eat, sleep and train together. Their training will be different, and I don't want them to be discouraged seeing the veteran soldiers going through their daily routines."

Kit gave her general a broad smile. "Whatever you think is best, Rusty." Just as the general was about to leave, Kit stopped her. "What about the other freed prisoners? Have arrangements been made to get them back to their homes?"

"They *are* home, Mistress," Rusty said with a smile. "Those who didn't enlist in your army have chosen to live in the city, under your protection. I have arranged for housing for those who wish to live within the city walls. A location has been set up in a forested area just outside the city for those Berrat who wish to live in a village of their own making. I've already gotten supplies organized to help them do that."

"Thank you," Kit said, walking over to her general, giving her a deep hug. "Thank you, for everything."

"The pleasure is mine, Mistress." And with that, Rusty and her small contingent of guards headed off.

"I have an army," Kit said with a nervous laugh as she turned back to her mother and friends. "Is anybody else hungry? I'm starving."

CHAPTER FORTY-SEVEN

ANGEL AND DAEMON

Copious amounts of food covered one of the tables in the lord's receiving room, what Kit was now referring to as her *War Room*. It seemed like an odd location for Kit and her allies to gather, but the room quickly became her de facto meeting place. She somehow understood now why Rusty's father liked the room so much. Even though it was ridiculously large, it still somehow managed to feel cozy, intimate even.

"Are we going to talk about what happened to you?" Indie asked, interrupting Kit before she could take another bite from the mound of bacon on her plate.

"What do you mean?" she asked as she folded a long strip of the heavily salted meat into her mouth.

"You killed a vampire with your bare hands. You turned into a giant ball of fire. You're..." Indie started waving his hands up and down, pointing to *everything* about Kit.

Kit looked down at her hand that had already grabbed a few more strips of bacon. "You mean because my skin's pale?"

"Your skin is pale, your hair is all red, and your eyes..." Indie paused, wondering how to best describe his love's new, solid-gold eyes.

"What about them?" Kit said, batting her eyelashes at him.

"They're different." Indie took Kit's chin in his hands as he gazed at her. "It's like looking into a pool of molten gold."

"Do you like them?" Kit asked, slowly stretching upwards until her nose was nearly touching Indie's.

"They're mesmerizing."

"Do they make you want to kiss me?" Kit moved a bit closer until her lips were barely brushing his. Indie's chest started heaving, his breaths now coming in quick, ragged gasps.

"I'll bet her lips taste like bacon," Lin said, her face only a few inches from the pair. Indie curled his hands into fists, glared at Lin, and stormed out of the room.

"Why do you do that?" Kit shook her head and walked back to her seat with the others.

"Do what?" Lin asked, throwing her arms up in the air. "Maybe if you two would stop making lovey-dovey eyes in public, and get *busy* in private, I wouldn't be around to interrupt." Lin gave Kit a wicked, playful grin.

"You're evil," Kit said, throwing an apple from Coldforge's plate at her.

"Bad to the bone," Lin laughed, skipping across the room before leaping onto one of the overstuffed couches. "So, do you still want to head to Taseko to find Danny? I'll bet your pompous friend is already neck-deep in troubles." Kit moved to the chair next to Lin, flopping into it like she was too weary to stand.

"We need to find out what's in the ledger," Kit said as she picked at an errant thread on her chair. "But we've got a long list of things we need to take care of here," she added with a heavy sigh, letting herself sink back into the overstuffed piece of furniture. "I just wish either Father Hoarfrost or my dad were here to tell me what to do."

"Can I make a suggestion?" Rusty asked, with an entourage of people following her into the room. At the smell of bacon, Runt and Lump broke past the woman and sniffed the food on the table, waiting for someone, anyone really, to offer some to them. When nobody did, they both snatched up as much as they could carry before heading to a quiet corner to enjoy their treats.

"I suggest we eat this food before our furry friends finish it off," Coldforge declared, taking a bite from one of the many apples on his plate. "We don't get much of these below the mountains." Juice from the apple was dribbling down his lips into his unruly orange beard.

"What's your suggestion?" Kit asked, not even bothering to look at her general. "Does it involve me sleeping for several days? I feel like..." Kit's words were cut off by an unexpected yawn.

"Yes, and no," Rusty replied, pushing Coldforge out of the way so she could sit beside her. "I think you need to stay here for a while and help me get your followers all moving in the same direction. Your actions today won their hearts, but people forget quickly. Without you here to spur them on, they'll likely lose focus and want to go home."

"If they want to go home," Kit said with a shrug, "why not let them?"

"Because you need them as badly as they need you," Bango answered, pulling a chair in closer. "What you did today will cause a ripple effect across the kingdom. If you can't produce a unified front, all will be lost."

"How can you know that?" Kit asked, suddenly feeling an overwhelming urge to close her eyes and sleep until the moon was full.

"Let's just say that I got it from a good authority," Bango said with a small wink.

"Oh, right," Kit replied with a knowing grin. "Did this good authority have anything else to say?"

"Only that you've caused a stir in Silverhawk. The raids you launched against the slavers have caught the attention of the Scarlet Tide."

"That matches my information as well," the young warrior version of Fenrir said as she joined the group. Amilta, in her Berrat form, was standing timidly behind her.

"Fenrir," Kit said, jumping to her feet, trying to bow quickly, and failing miserably.

"Please, Sister Kit, I've told you before, you don't need to do that." The wolf-god's response made Amilta giggle wildly.

"Please, take my seat," Kit insisted, despite the tiny god's resistance. Fenrir shook her head and reluctantly took a seat in the large chair. Amilta crawled up beside her, flopping her legs across Fenrir's lap.

"Are my friends in Silverhawk safe?" Kit asked, deciding at the last second to not use anyone's name.

"So far," Fenrir replied as she tried to get the fidgeting Berrat girl beside her to settle down. "Reinforcements have been deployed, just in case."

"Why is the Scarlet Tide so interested in Silverhawk?" Kit asked, her head starting to swim again.

"We think King Faol is finally about to make his play against Arnnor," Bango said.

"Not anymore," Cilya interjected, with her twin sister, Ashlay, nodding in agreement. "The shipment of silvered weapons was a key component. Without them, they are at a significant disadvantage if the Union gets involved."

"How's the Fair Traders Union going to stop an invasion from Faol into Arnnor?" Bango asked. "If Faol attacks, they're going to do it by land, not by sea."

"Because the bulk of Faol's army is in Ravenlord right now," Logan Buttsworth butted in. "They were planning on using the silvered weapons to wipe us out before they made landfall in Arnnor."

"Is there any chance we could mount an attack against them in Ravenlord?" Kit asked. "We've got seven black ships at our disposal. We could sail our army in on them and hit them before they know what's happening."

"You're cleverer than you give yourself credit for," Rusty laughed. "I had the same thoughts." When Rusty felt Lin jabbing her in the ribs, she corrected herself. "*We* had the same thoughts. Okay, it was actually Lin's idea, but I approved it."

"Our *friends* can likely offer some help, as well," Bango offered.

Kit sighed heavily at the woman's remark. "We're working together, Bango. If we can't trust them to say who you work for, then this whole *thing* will die here, and us along with it." Bango made a strangled sort of noise. "Bango, Ashlay, and Ailman Juuls all work for my mother. They're all members of Aurora's Guard. My mother has sworn to defeat Faol and remove the vampire scourge from the land. Since the vampires rely on the Auctioneers to deliver them blood slaves, we're already hurting them by disrupting their trade."

There was a stunned silence that immediately filled the room.

"Frookin' Helja," Coldforge said. "Your mother is Aurora Windsong, the celestial god?"

"The what?" Kit asked, barely able to get the words out.

"Your mother is part celestial," Fenrir said with a small grin. "Which makes you part celestial as well. I'm just not sure where the red hair comes from."

"I'm part angel?" Kit asked as a shiver crawled up her spine.

"Part angel, part something else, too," Riva said. "Something dark."

"Ananak?" Spots danced in front of Kit's eyes. "What do you mean, something dark?"

"It's unheard of," Riva declared, "but you may be part dark celestial – a daemon."

"I knew I liked ye girl," Coldforge burst out, clapping his hands for joy. "Me pointy eared cousins, those frookin' elves, call us dark elves. Ain't nuthin' dark about us. We just don't like flittin' about in the trees with them. We'd rather mine, drink and scrap."

"I'm an angel and a daemon?"

"I knew you were going to be fun," Fury declared, floating up from Kit's side.

"You picked a fine time to show yourself," Kit said as she snatched the hammer from the air. "Where have you been? Where were you when I needed you?"

"I've been busy," Fury said with as much sarcasm as he could muster. "But I've always been by your side when you truly needed me."

"Where have you been?" Kit growled, the bone shaft of her hammer beginning to smoke beneath her hand.

"If you're trying to hurt me," Fury laughed, "you're going to need to bring something other than fire. But, if you must know, I've been talking with Tyr. Apparently, Lin has managed to secure another piece of me."

"I what?" Lin asked, shaking her head, denying any knowledge of what Fury was talking about.

"Those gold cannisters," Fury declared. "They're soul vessels. You might be surprised to hear who you've got stored in the other two containers."

"Hold on," Kit said, motioning with her hands for everyone to stop. "What's a soul container?"

"It's powerful magic," Lin said, "powerful, dark magic. Supposedly, a necromancer – a death mage, can pull the soul out of a person and cram it into a container. The soulless person becomes an empty husk. Another disembodied soul can then possess the empty husk. It's also possible, apparently, that a necromancer of sufficient skill could transfer their own soul into the husk."

"My cane, your hammer, is a soul container," Fury said. "If I could get the piece of me in that golden cannister, I might be able to merge the two pieces of me together in this hammer."

"What would that do to the hammer?" Kit asked.

"Hard to say," Fury replied. "I suppose it depends on which piece of me is in that canister."

"Okay," Kit said, remembering Fury's initial statement. "Who's in the other two containers?"

"Get me out of the cannister and into this hammer," Fury said in his arrogant sort of way. "You do that, and I'll tell you who's in the other two."

"Really?" Kit asked, "You're actually going to hold that information ransom?"

"It's not very often I get any leverage," Fury said. "I have been helping you now for nearly a moon. Is it too much to ask that I get some help in return?"

"Fine," Kit said, throwing up her hands in frustration. "I'm going to bed. We can figure out how to deal with this tomorrow." She was already at the door by the time she'd finished the sentence.

CHAPTER FORTY-EIGHT

DANNY'S MESSAGE

Kit walked down the hall and slipped into her room. The silence, the peace of being alone, was glorious. She threw herself onto the soft bed and gathered pillows around her, like she was building a small set of walls to protect herself.

She suddenly jumped up from her bed and grabbed her knapsack. She looked fondly at the battered piece of equipment. She had been dragging it around for what seemed like forever. She dug into one of the side pockets and pulled out a small scroll. After rolling it around in her fingers for a while, she broke its tiny wax seal.

Danny, what did you say to me? Why couldn't you say it to me in person?

She unfurled the parchment and started reading.

Kit, my love,

I know in my heart you'll understand why I have to leave, why I can't ask you to come with me. As I sit here, alone in my room, I find myself thinking of you, like I do on most nights, wanting desperately to hold you in my arms. Ah, but alas, that is not in my future. Indie is your future and mine lies somewhere else, with someone else.

You have been, and will always be, my best friend. You're the only person I can share the real me with. I don't need to be anyone but myself when I'm with you, and that is a gift beyond reckoning.

So, tonight, I will leave for Taseko. I have to find my parents. I need to know they're safe. I need to start a new life.

I know we will meet again, and when we do, my heart will sing with joy. Until that time, set the world on fire and take no prisoners. You are destined for greatness. I've known it since the first time I met you.

Your friend forever,

Danny

Kit took a deep breath when she finally finished. She didn't know what would be in his letter, but somehow, this wasn't what she had expected it to be. Just as she slipped the scroll back into her knapsack, there was a light rap on her door.

"Yes?" she asked as she tossed the satchel onto the floor.

"May I come in?" asked the voice on the other side of her door.

"Yes."

Indie walked inside, looking more than a bit ashamed of his earlier behavior. "Can we talk?" he asked, stepping into the room after standing in the doorway for several seconds, not saying or doing anything.

"No."

Indie's face crumpled.

"Come in and shut the door," Kit said. She waited until the look of confusion on the man's face finally subsided.

"Lock it," Kit said as she rearranged the pillows on her bed, tearing down the wall she had built around herself.

Chapter Forty-Nine

Fire Drake Clan

Ulip was sweating heavily when he arrived at the foothills to Spur's domain. His people may have had a symbiotic relationship with the red dragon and his fire drakes but returning to his mountain home without an offering in hand, well, it just wasn't wise. He had run for a full day without rest, spurred on by a growing need to return to his roots. His desire to bring an end to the Split Crows had taken him away from the laws of his people and the beliefs he held so dearly. When he found his village empty, not a living soul present, desperation welled up in his chest. That feeling turned to despair, which had pushed him to travel to this place.

He raised his hands to the heavens and bellowed out. "Spur, mighty lord of the mountain, I am Ulip of the Fire Drake Clan, and I would seek your council." He waited for several minutes but there was no reaction. His chest was now heaving heavily. Not from the exertion of his long run, but at the indignation of not receiving a reply, of any sort, from the red dragon. His thick brow that already mostly covered his eyes, lowered further. He thought of drawing his blade but decided against it. Instead, he put his head down and started running towards the mountain's summit. Crossing into the dragon's domain without invitation would likely be a death sentence, but at this point, he didn't believe he had anything to lose.

The foothills were rugged with nary a path to follow as he climbed. As the ascent became more and more difficult, Ulip changed direction, heading towards the mountain's southern face. The way up the mountain was far steeper on the southern side, but the foothills were fully forested and would likely offer a more direct path. The barren side of the mountain was all uneven rock and boulders. He began to wonder if Spur hadn't caused a rockslide here for the sole purpose of making it difficult to navigate.

The Gigas continued to pick his way through bolder and crag until he reached the forest's edge. He took one more look up the mountainside to see if the dragon had yet reacted to his calls. He huffed at the silent peak and broke into a run, crossing into the heavy pines. The thick scent brought back the memories of his camp and the people he'd left behind, the people he'd been leading, who'd trusted him, who'd followed him. He shook his head and continued along, turning his direction such that he was climbing up the slope.

Despite the height of the pines that shot skyward, the sun came through easily, warming the surrounding air. He was now perspiring heavily, his nearly black skin glistening as he wove through the great trees. A shadow that slipped behind one of the smaller trees up ahead forced the big man to slow. There wasn't a vast array of predators that lived in the northern mountains, but those that did were deadly. Assuming this particular predator was a shadow cat, Ulip drew his blade and blew out a long, slow breath.

He lowered himself into a crouch and took a few tentative steps forward. His eyes were locked onto the tree the shadow had slipped behind, searching for any sign of movement.

"You were not invited, Ulip. To step on a dragon's mountain uninvited can only lead to your ruin." The voice of the Tahr came from behind the Gigas. The shadow he was searching for was likely another. He slipped his great sword back into its sheath.

"The desperate deeds of a desperate man," Ulip replied, holding his open hands out from his sides. Four more Tahr stepped out from the surrounding trees. He had only seen one, but there were many tracking him. He had only heard of their skills as spies. Now he understood why they were so effective.

"What desperation would drive one such as yourself to suicide?" one of the Tahr asked. She was smaller than her male counterparts with small white spiral horns. The four males took a respectful step back, lowering their heads slightly.

"I am Ulip of the Fire Drake Clan. I seek an audience with Spur." The Gigas stood taller, crossing his arms over his bulky chest.

"You seek an audience with the great dragon, but you bring no offering."

"I am the offering," Ulip said, taking a menacing step forward. The female Tahr held her ground, her small pink nose twitching.

"And what will you be seeking of the great dragon after he eats you?"

"I suppose if he's going to eat me, I won't be needing one of his drakes to bear me." He took a knee before the tiny Tahr. "My clan has served Spur for many generations. If that means nothing to him and he feels the need to gnash my bones between his teeth, then we have wasted our lives thinking he is more than he is."

"And in return for your servitude, he allowed you to hunt, and roam unfettered within his domain. It gave your clan access to flora and fauna that could not be found in any other place in the entire region. It gave you access to his magic and his wisdom." The Gigas' face darkened at the Tahr's words.

"We served him so that one day he might be free of his mountain prison. We served him so that when he was free, he would set our world back to rights, to the time before *they* arrived. Was our help not enough for him. Is he so greedy that he would want more of us?"

The little Tahr's face went slack at the Gigas' words. A moment later, she and the other four Tahr vanished into the forest.

Ulip watched and waited. The forest was silent, save for the breeze that rustled the pine needles that covered the ground. A shadow passed overhead, drawing the Gigas' gaze skyward. There was nothing but blue sky above with one wispy cloud that hung lazily in the vast blue.

The thunderous sound of snapping tree trunks shattered the moment of silence. The drumming of footfalls and more trees being sundered was becoming a deafening roar. The forest continued to shake until the first of three fire drakes came bursting through the pines. They bellowed out their challenges, their heads low to the ground, their long serpentine necks poised like snakes ready to strike.

"Hail, soldiers of flame," Ulip intoned, walking fearlessly toward the trio. A blast of fire blew over his head, warning him to come no closer. The sky turned dark as night a moment before the ground shook as though an earthquake threatened to rip it open. A low rumbling growl turned into a bone-chilling screech. A hurricane force wind nearly tossed the giant into the open maws of the drakes that stood before him.

"You would dare to come to my home and insult me?" Spur roared. "If you were not clan-chief, I would incinerate you now, you insignificant piece of flesh." The declaration that Ulip was clan-chief ripped at his heart. He turned to face the red dragon who was a mere hundred paces away from him. At this distance he could easily smell his brimstone breath. The heat from his body alone was nearly enough to set the trees ablaze.

"Being the last surviving member of my village does not make me chief," Ulip said, taking a fearless step towards the dragon's eight-foot teeth.

"You are not the last of your clan," the dragon said, "and you are the oldest, which makes you chief."

"Others survived the raid?" Ulip asked, his heart beating faster. "How many? Where are they?"

"There are only two," the dragon said, his voice much less threatening. "You were the only member that survived the raid. The other two had already left long before." Ulip's shoulders slumped at the news that all had perished. He had no memory of anybody leaving prior to the raid that destroyed his village, except for... a look of pleading crossed his face, his deep-set black eyes glistening.

"The merchant and my sister live?" The giant fell to his knees.

"No," the red dragon said, lowering his head respectfully. "Frode has passed to the Beyond."

"My sister?"

"She lives and thrives in Arnnor."

The Gigas' breath caught in his throat. "Amara lives?"

"She does," the red dragon said. A cold, calculating look appeared in his reptilian eyes. "And I will allow my children to bear you there, if you would but complete a simple task."

THE STORY CONTINUES...

The story continues with *Daemon of Titan*, the next novel in the Priest of Titan series on Amazon.

Afterword

Thank you for reading my novel. Reviews are critical to the success of every indie author. I would ask that you leave a review on Amazon, GoodReads, and Book-Bub. If you have any thoughts or comments that you'd like to share directly with me, I would love to hear from you. You can email me at paul@paulmouchet.ca.

Do you want more stories? You find links to all my novels on my website. You can also sign up for my newsletter, Marvelous Mondays, which I send out every other week. They're full of fun pics, snippets of what's going on in my life, and book news.

Also, if you'd like to discuss my stories with me and other fans, in a safe, friendly environment, please connect with me on my Facebook group ~ Paul Mouchet's Reader's Group.

You'll find the link to all my social media accounts on my website. I look forward to chatting with you.

Happy Reading!